No

Quarter

No
Quarter

A Novel

Book 1 of The Tildon Chronicles

JOHN
JANTUNEN

ECW PRESS

Copyright © John Jantunen, 2018

Published by ECW Press
665 Gerrard Street East
Toronto, Ontario, Canada, M4M 1Y2
416-694-3348 / info@ecwpress.com

Cover design: Michel Vrana
Cover image: © graffoto8 / iStockPhoto
Author photo: Jeremy Luke Hill

This is a work of fiction. Names, characters, places, and incidents either are the product of the author's imagination or are used fictitiously, and any resemblance to actual persons, living or dead, business establishments, events, or locales is entirely coincidental.

Library and Archives Canada
Cataloguing in Publication

Jantunen, John, 1971-, author
No quarter / John Jantunen.

(The Tildon chronicles ; book 1)
Issued in print and electronic formats.
ISBN 978-1-77041-205-7 (softcover).--
ISBN 978-1-77305-212-0 (PDF).--
ISBN 978-1-77090-964-9 (epub)

I. Title.

PS8619.A6783N67 2018   C813'.6   C2018-902506-9
C2018-902507-7

The publication of *No Quarter* has been generously supported by the Canada Council for the Arts which last year invested $153 million to bring the arts to Canadians throughout the country, and by the Government of Canada. *Nous remercions le Conseil des arts du Canada de son soutien. L'an dernier, le Conseil a investi 153 millions de dollars pour mettre de l'art dans la vie des Canadiennes et des Canadiens de tout le pays. Ce livre est financé en partie par le gouvernement du Canada.* We also acknowledge the Ontario Arts Council (OAC), an agency of the Government of Ontario, and the contribution of the Government of Ontario through the Ontario Book Publishing Tax Credit and the Ontario Media Development Corporation.

PRINTED AND BOUND IN CANADA

PRINTING: WEBCOM   5   4   3   2   1

MIX
Paper from
responsible sources
FSC® C004071

For Tanja

If the soul is left in darkness, sins will be committed.
The guilty one is not he who commits the sin,
but he who caused the darkness.

—

Victor Hugo

I

He heard the first siren just after midnight.

A sharp declaration rearing through the window at his back, like an exclamation point on Nina Simone's desperate plea from the stereo that she was feelin' good. He was sitting on Rain's couch and she was straddled on top, her hips thrusting with the precision of a see-saw and her breasts flouncing a doughy-white within the open flaps of her kimono wrap. She was thirty-nine, fifteen years older than his own twenty-four, and wore every one of those in the lines fraying from the corners of her eyes, both pressed shut not so much in the throes of passion as meditative. He was rolling her nipples between his thumbs and forefingers and she was moaning a staccato burst—"Oh! Oh! Oh!"—which Deacon took to mean she was about to come.

He was on the verge himself and to hold out a moment longer he concentrated on the undulating wail rising from the road running along the base of the granite bluff cresting not more than a hop and a skip from Rain's back door. Her house was two stories of crumbling brick sided with press-wood slats, their sky-blue dulled and peeling, curls of paint clung to the spiderwebs spun beneath the eaves, its windows barricaded by thick curtains and dark, a neon sign in the mud room's window advertising Fortune Teller IN/OUT the only thing to say that anyone lived there at all. Not much, really, to recommend it except the widow's watch on its roof. It afforded as pretty a picture of the quaint little tourist town across the river as Deacon had yet to find and as he struggled to deter his own impulse towards climax he imagined himself standing at the wrought-iron fence enclosing the perch, watching the ambulance swoop onto the silver brace bridge below and wondering whose day had just turned foul.

The siren was then diffusing over the open space created by the river basin at the foot of the falls. For a moment it sounded hollow, remote, before it rose again, echoing against the walls of the red-brick canyon created by the string of storefronts along Main Street.

Rain was imploring, "Harder," and that snapped him back.

He pinched her nipples with renewed vigour and she gasped. He eased the pressure for one breath—her body clenching against his—and then squeezed again, this time holding and waiting for the gush, all thoughts of the siren banished as it washed over his pubis, the suction of her insides then pulling at him, making Deacon come too.

With a groan, Rain collapsed over top of him, propping her forearms on the back of the couch. One of her breasts hung limp across his cheek, as soft and flabby as a three-day-old balloon, its owner groaning every time he throbbed. In the distance, he heard the faint blast of an air horn: the pumper truck giving fair warning as it exited the fire station on Dominion, one block up from Main. It was shortly followed by the ladder and tanker trucks doing the same, and then he could hear two cruisers screaming down Entrance Drive, the main artery pumping traffic into town from the 11, a four-lane highway so packed with tourists between the May Two-Four and Labour Day weekends it had inspired the Chamber of Commerce to erect a sign on its shoulder proclaiming, Tildon, Your Gateway to Summer.

The police sirens reached crescendo as they came to the clock tower presiding over the intersection where Entrance dead-ended at Main, the cars taking a hard right and their furor fading as they chased the others northward.

Deacon finally went still and Rain let out a satisfied, "Mmm."

She leaned down, kissed him on the top of the head, and then pulled herself up and off. Cupping her hand over her bush to keep anything from leaking out, she grabbed a tea towel from the green steamer trunk she used in place of a coffee table, tossed it over Deacon's lap, and hurried towards the stairs rising to the second floor.

While he cleaned himself off, he could hear another siren growing louder from the east: a third cruiser, the celerity of its approach telling him whoever was at the wheel must have been snoozing behind a desk when the call came in and was now playing a game of catch-up. Discarding the towel on the trunk, he told himself he ought to go have a look-see at what all the fuss was about, as much because it would give him an excuse to make a quick exit as because it was his job, as the *Chronicle*'s only full-time reporter, to take an interest in such things. He'd not yet stayed the night but, of late, his resolve had been slipping. It was only a matter of time before he'd awake in Rain's bed with the sun squinting his eyes. The smell of bacon would draw him down to the kitchen where he'd find her smoking restlessly over the stove, tending to his breakfast. Then, he'd be powerless but to sit at the table and pick up a fork.

And who knew where that future might have led?

3

He was tired, though, and a little drunk and even more stoned. With thoughts of bed teasing him through the haze, he thought about how nice falling into his own would feel. He could hear water running from the bathroom at the top of the stairs: Rain showering, which she always did after they fucked—her way, he reckoned, of keeping him from running off for at least a few minutes anyway.

Deacon played along by reaching for the tumbler on the trunk. It was half-filled with liquid the colour of rye, though it was mostly Coke and melted ice by then. He drank what was left in one gulp. Between his legs, his wilted manhood parted the flaps of his navy blue dress shirt. He tried to summon the verve to scrounge for his pants, but all of a sudden he was too tired to do anything but rest his head on the back of the couch, close his eyes, and drift off to the languid sway of the song whispering to him from the stereo of dragonflies out in the sun and butterflies all having fun (you know what I mean).

He was startled awake a short while later by Rain asking, "Who was that?"

Dinah Washington had since replaced Miss Simone and her angry demand of "Is You Is or Is You Ain't My Baby" lent its urgency to Rain's stride as she walked past, towelling off her hair. She'd gone grey in her twenties, and a couple of years ago she'd started dying it a murky blonde. When that didn't peel back the years, she cut it into a boyish bob. Last week, she cut it even shorter. She hadn't dyed it since and the blonde spikes, with their grey roots, had come to resemble a porcupine's quills.

"What?" Deacon asked, blinking against his drowse.

"On the phone."

"What do you mean?"

"Your phone was ringing."

"It wasn't."

"You sure?"

"Pretty sure. Since I keep it on vibrate."

"I could have sworn I heard your phone ringing."

She scanned the room, then padded over to where Deacon's green corduroy jacket lay draped over her Reading Chair, the "reading" she meant having little to do with books though there were three—*The Complete Astrologer*, *Signs for Trying Times*, and *A Medium's Guide to the Good Life*—artfully arranged on top of a gypsy cloth beside an unlit candle, squat and pink, sitting on a tea cup's saucer. As she foraged through the coat's pockets, Deacon took up his boxer briefs from the couch cushion beside him. He'd got one foot into those when she was turning back, holding up his phone.

"There's twenty-four unanswered messages," she said.

"You don't say."

"The last was from Dylan."

"What time?"

"Twelve thirty-three."

"What time's it now?"

"Twelve thirty-six."

"How in the hell—"

Cutting himself off short because he knew there was no point in trying to get an answer out of Rain that did anything but make his head ache. He rooted about the floor for his jeans and had just snagged a leg when Dylan's voice rang out.

"—ey, Deke," he was saying through his cell phone speaker. "There's been some trouble at that rest stop off the 118, just past the rock cut west of Meeford Bay. You know the one I'm talking about. I'm going to be here all night. If you're heading this way, I sure could use a coffee." There was a pause, and when Dylan spoke again his voice had quieted, almost to a whisper. "Someone's been killed. Looks like—" Then there was an angry voice yelling in the background, too loud to be anyone but Sergeant Marchand.

"Oh shit," Dylan said. "I gotta go. See you if I do. Bye."

"Sounds serious," Rain said.

"Three cruisers," Deacon answered, pulling on his pants.

"That is serious."

She was smiling in her wry way, and it seemed a bitter rebuke against him thinking it was excuse enough to make another one of his quick exits. Lowering his eyes, he busied himself by foraging through his pants' pockets, a ploy that lasted until he'd found a stick of the gum he seeded his clothes with for such an emergency. When he looked back up, Rain was walking towards him and biting her lip, like maybe she'd read his mind and was now trying to think of something to assure him that it was alright.

He popped the gum in his mouth and she handed him his phone. As he slipped it into his breast pocket, she leaned close as if to kiss him goodbye. But it was his collar she was bound for. It had become tucked into his shirt.

"You okay to drive?" she asked, pulling it out and smoothing it with the flat of her hand.

"I'm fine."

"We could take my car."

"I'm good."

Patting his breast, she trailed her fingers down his chest. The gesture had a scripted feel to it, like a mother, in some old movie, sending her son off to war, afraid she'd never see him again.

"You best be off then," she said.

2

M eeford Bay was a fifteen-minute drive west along the 118, its two lanes leading Deacon's Jeep Cherokee past lakes ringed with pine trees and pockets of swampland overgrown with cattails, ridges of granite looming over both, and nothing in between but hydro poles and the odd flicker of a porch light atop a lintel. Signs flashing by at intervals warned of deer and moose crossings and if the other signs reading Max 80 km/h weren't enough to keep his speed within the legal limit those were at least enough to keep it under one hundred.

His thoughts, as he drove, drifted on a collision course towards the word Dylan hadn't said, and he played a half-hearted game of fill-in-the-blanks to keep himself from thinking about what was really on his mind: how in the hell had Rain known his phone had rung? When his efforts proved futile, he muttered, "Tricks of the trade," like she was some sort of magician schooled in the finer arts of distraction.

Sleight of hand, that's all it was.

She heard the sirens just like you and slipped your phone from your jacket while you were cleaning yourself off with the towel, knowing that if it was something likely to make the news, Dylan would call to give you the heads-up. Waiting in the bathroom until the phone rang then coming out, the phone secreted in the pocket of her bathrobe, asking all coy, "Who was that?" on her way to slipping it back into your jacket, you playing along like some rube just off the farm.

Seemed outlandish, but then this was Rain Meadows he was talking about. Just another petty skirmish in the endless war she was waging against all reason.

The Welcome to Meeford Bay sign flashed by in the Jeep's headlights.

He propped the take-out coffee—black—he'd bought for himself at the twenty-four-hour Tim's drive-thru between his legs and fumbled a smoke from the pack in the cupholder beside Dylan's double-double. The Cherokee was drifting right as the flame touched tobacco and the jolt of its tires slipping off the asphalt startled the lighter from his hand as he fought to regain control. For a moment, it felt like he was going to end up in the ditch, but then he was back on the road, breathing hard and cursing himself for getting behind the wheel after smoking two joints—one on the walk over to Rain's and the other before they'd fucked, washing the latter down with a glass of rye splashed with Coke and ice.

And here he was going to meet a cop.

You should just turn around, he told himself. *It's not like Dylan's expecting you. You could tell him you were asleep.*

So, go on then, do it.

But keeping the unbroken yellow line ahead of him from blurring into two and recurring thoughts of the word Dylan hadn't spoken kept his foot heavy on the gas.

It had been three years since Larry Bidwell, an unemployed

electrician, had kicked in the front door of the house he'd shared with his wife until she'd thrown him out, citing a history of abuse in the restraining order she'd later filed against him. At the time, Candice Bidwell had told her sister it had felt like the start of a whole new life, but a sheet of paper hadn't done a damn thing to stop Larry from returning two weeks later, just before midnight. She was watching television in her living room at the time. Larry had gut-shot her as she rose from the couch and then had taken a sharp right down the hallway leading towards the bedrooms. Candice's wound would prove fatal but not until she was in the trauma room at the South Mesaquakee Memorial Hospital so, as she bled out on her living room floor, she was alive to hear the next three shots—one for each of her two daughters, the third giving her every indication that Larry had then turned the gun on himself.

Dylan had called Deacon that night too. Deacon had been passed out in front of the TV and hadn't got the message until late the next morning. It was almost noon by the time he'd arrived at the scene to find a dozen reporters crowding the police tape strung over the Bidwell's driveway. All of them were from provincial and national news outlets, and Deacon had felt about as comfortable wandering amongst them as a rat would on a snake farm. That was the only time anyone had been murdered in Tildon since he'd started working at the *Chronicle*. It'd be two days before he'd be able to get news of this one into print—if that's what it was—but at least he'd have it up on their website before any of the other papers caught wind—a minor victory at best. But then, as a reporter for a small-town weekly, he'd long since conceded that any sort of victory was better than what he could hope to expect on even the best of days.

He passed Butter & Egg Road, the half kilometre of crumbling asphalt that led to the dozen or so cottages grouped around the Meeford Bay Golf & Country Club. Beyond that, the highway tilted into a canyon blasted out of a chunk of Canadian Shield the locals called Huckleberry Hill. On the other side of the rock cut, red and blue LEDs flared against a haze of smoke settled over the treetops surrounding a figure eight carved into the forest on the eastern shore of the Moose River.

Used to be there was a chip wagon planted where the lines of the figure eight crossed and a dozen or so picnic tables scattered along the loops. But Big Chief's Hot Dogs & Fresh Cut Fries closed years ago, and all that was left was the figure eight and a Commercial Lot For Lease sign nailed to one of the Jack pines framing the driveway. A police car was parked lengthwise between them and Dylan was standing at its trunk holding an orange neon traffic baton. Deacon eased his foot off the gas, gliding down the hill, taking care to activate his right turn signal and maintain his distance from the ditch as he pulled onto the shoulder lest a miscue might dispose Constable Cleary to asking a few questions he didn't really want to know the answers to. When the Jeep had come to a complete stop, he butt his cigarette in the already overflowing ashtray, then foraged his lighter from the floor before fishing a fresh stick of gum out of the pack in the glovebox.

He sat there chewing for a few moments, summoning the nerve to open the door. When he finally had, Dylan was talking through the window of a white BMW coupe stopped in the left-hand lane.

"Just some kids setting fire to an abandoned van," he said, as Deacon stepped onto the road. "Nothing to worry yourself about. You have a good night, now."

The BMW drove off and a honk alerted Dylan to the pumper truck pulling up to the cruiser that blocked the rest stop's entrance. He waved to it on his way over to his car, slipping into the driver's seat and backing it up onto the shoulder. The stench of burning oil hung heavy in the air. It tickled the back of Deacon's throat as he watched the pumper truck pass by, and then the ladder and the tanker too.

"Well, ain't you a sight?" Dylan said and Deacon turned, watching the other hustling towards him. "That coffee mine?"

Deacon held it out.

"You're a saint."

Dylan took it up and peeled back its tab with his teeth while Deacon tried not to pass more than a glance at the checkerboard of seared flesh covering the left side of his jaw and most of his cheek. The scar was a memento from the year and a half he'd spent in Afghanistan manning a Bushmaster cannon on top of a LAV III and he was real coy about how he'd got it. The one time Deacon had asked, Dylan had said that someone had bumped into him while he was shaving, though if that was the truth, he'd have had to have been shaving with a waffle iron.

The ambulance was turning onto the highway and Deacon idled his time watching its taillights receding up the incline leading into the rock cut.

"Looks like I missed all the fun," Deacon said when the ambulance disappeared around the bend.

"How's that?"

"Everyone's leaving."

"Chain of custody. It's a police matter now."

Dylan gulped half the coffee in one go, giving Deacon just enough time to fish his pad and pen out of his pocket. Dylan was wiping his mouth with the back of his hand when Deacon looked back up. There was a gleam in Dylan's eye too keen to mean anything but trouble.

"Hope I didn't catch you in the middle of something," he said.

"Just a good night's sleep."

"You weren't with Rain when I called?"

"Rain? Meadows?"

"You know any other?"

"I wasn't with her. Why would you even say that? She's old enough to be my mother."

"You said it, not me."

"I was sleeping when you called."

"Sleeping, huh?"

"I was."

"So it wasn't you I saw slipping in through her back door a couple hours ago?"

"No."

"And it wasn't you the last two nights neither."

"I don't know what you're talking about."

"Sure looked like you in the pictures I took."

Fronting Deacon his best shit-eating grin, he reached into his pocket and pulled out his phone.

"You were following me."

"We call it patrol," Dylan countered as he thumbed through the onscreen photo gallery.

Deacon had known Dylan since he was twelve and had come to live with George and Adele Cleary—Dylan's grandparents on his father's side. Deacon's parents and younger brother had been killed when his father, driving too fast, had swerved to miss a moose and hit a tree instead. George was a friend of the family, and he'd arranged to adopt Deacon to keep him out of foster care, neither of his parents having had any family willing, or able, to take him in. Dylan was six years his senior and already on his way to the Royal Canadian Regiment, his sights set on the infantry. When he returned from overseas, he enrolled in the police academy in Aylmer and that had led him back to Tildon about the same time Deacon had replaced George as the *Chronicle*'s only full-time reporter. They'd had plenty of time to get to know each other since, both on and off the job. Over the past few years, Dylan had come to treat Deacon like the younger brother he'd never had which, from Deacon's point of view, couldn't have been much different than he'd have treated a new recruit about to go into combat for the first time, needling him without end and otherwise taking every opportunity to remind him how much of a mistake it was for such a scrawny little thing to have enlisted in the first place.

He knew anything he might say would only egg him on and kept his mouth shut, occupying himself by searching his pockets for his smokes.

While he lit one, he watched three of Dylan's fellow officers playing what appeared to be a game of bocce with stones they'd scavenged from the figure eight's gravel. One of them, the bulge at his midsection telling him it was Sergeant Marchand, was lobbing a rock. Deacon saw it hit the ground and spin off into the underbrush, Marchand stomping after it, shaking his head and muttering "*Merde*," which was the only French Deacon had ever heard him speak.

Beyond them, the headlights of a sedan pried through the trees. It shone over the burnt husk of a minivan, parked in the far corner of the figure eight's right-side loop, and glinted off a bald crown he knew belonged to Dr. Albert Ross, the county coroner.

Him and George were old fishing buddies, and Deacon had spent many a lazy afternoon sitting by their side while the two old men fished for muskie in the swampy shallows where the south branch of the Mesaquakee River flowed into the lake of the same name. It was there that Deacon had learned that Dr. Ross was the inspiration for Hubert Cairn, a character in *The Sons of Adam*, the sixth of what George called his Fictions. And like his counterpart, Dr. Cairn had a rather morbid hobby: he collected pictures of dead bodies.

In the book, set in the late seventies, Cairn was a member of Club Mortis, a loosely affiliated network of doctors and police officers, firemen and soldiers, who traded photos of the grisly deceased they'd encountered while on the job. Living in a quaint little tourist town where a kinder, gentler death held more sway than in so many other parts of the world, Dr. Cairn didn't have much to offer his fellow enthusiasts except the odd snap of a bloated corpse hauled out of the lake or the crumpled remains pulled out of a car crash. That was until the titular group of bikers-cum-doomsday cultists had gone on a murderous rampage that made Charles Manson's seem like child's play in comparison.

As the death toll mounted, so too did Dr. Cairn's renown amongst his peers. In the second to last chapter, he'd expressed his concerns regarding his exploitation of the unfolding drama for personal gain to a big-city news reporter, whose own celebrity was predicated on cataloguing the evil that men do. The reporter confided that he too often dealt with a similar crisis of conscience.

> It's hard, he said, when the worse things get, the better
> they seem for me. Gnaws on a man's soul, if you believe
> in that sort of thing.
> Dr. Cairn admitted he did, though not in the biblical
> sense, and that he felt the same way.
> The only advice I can offer, the reporter continued,
> is to get yourself a hobby, something to look forward to,
> so that at the end of the day you can leave all the other
> shit behind.

Advice that was not much use for Dr. Cairn since it was his hobby that had got him into the mess in the first place. Nevertheless, it was of great use to Deacon, providing him with a clue, albeit a cursory one, regarding the dual, and often conflicting, natures of his adoptive father. One was the kind-hearted owner and editor-in-chief of the *Chronicle* and the other an author of twelve novels in which the depraved acts of violence contained within their, often, apocalyptic narratives were only slightly less disturbing than the deviance of their characters' sexual appetites. The first time Deacon read them he wasn't able to sleep for days, fearing what a man who wrote such things—and was then lying in a bed not twenty feet from his own—might have in store for a twelve-year-old boy for whom nobody else seemed to have any use.

While time had eased the worry that George might have something diabolical planned for him, it hadn't done much to reconcile the mystery surrounding George, The Man, and George, The Writer. An answer to that always seemed to be fleeing forever beyond his grasp. But now, staring out at the van and seeing a bright flash—Dr. Ross taking another photo for his collection—it seemed to be on the tip of his tongue. Something about trying to find a way to make sense out of all the bad, but that didn't quite capture it. There was more to it than that. It was like—

Then Dylan was nudging him with his elbow and the thought slipped away.

"Here's one I took through the window," he said, holding up his phone. "Looks like a porcupine's crawled up between your legs."

Averting his eyes from the photo onscreen, Deacon scanned back towards the van. Dr. Ross was at its driver's side door, talking into his cell, probably recording a few notes. It was something Deacon rarely did, preferring a pad and a pen for the simple reason that you couldn't tap a pen against a screen while you were trying to think of something intelligent to say. Or, rather, you could, but it didn't make nearly as satisfying a *thwack* as his was doing now as he turned back to Dylan.

Dylan must have figured the joke had played itself out and was pocketing his phone.

"They didn't take the body," Deacon said, stating the obvious about as close to genuine intelligence as he could muster at one in the morning, his mind a fog of kush and Canadian Club. "The ambulance, I mean."

"They would have, but it's hard to tell where the seat ends and the body begins. Forensics is sending a couple of techs down with a truck. They'll take the whole mess back to the lab in Toronto. The OPP'll sort it out there."

"You said in your message that it looked like—"

"Murder?"

"Yeah."

"Have to wait until the autopsy gets back to know for sure. But dousing yourself with gasoline and setting yourself on fire'd be a fuck of a way to kill yourself."

Deacon went back to tapping at his pad, cycling his thoughts through a dozen similar scenes he'd witnessed in movies, trying to think of what to say next.

"Someone covering their tracks?" he finally offered.

"I'd say."

"Any witnesses?"

"There had to be at least one, but I doubt he's too likely to come forward."

"Who called it in?"

"Someone driving by, saw the flames."

"You got a name?"

"And a statement. He left about ten minutes ago."

"No, I mean for the body."

"Oh. No, not yet."

"You run the plates?"

"Golly," Dylan said, assuming a hillbilly twang, "what a great idee. Now why ain't we a-tink-a dat."

"I take it you did then."

"Name withheld pending notification of the next of kin, you know the drill."

Thwack. Thwack.

"Can you at least tell me if it was registered to a local address?"

Dylan scratched at his scar like he was picking at a scab.

"It was registered to a property on Brackenburg," he finally said, adding as Deacon wrote the name down in his pad, "but you didn't hear that from me."

Brackenburg was a dirt road not a ten-minute drive west along the 118. It had a sign at its entrance warning, Road Not Maintained In The Winter, Use At Own Risk and mainly served to provide access to the cottages lining the northeastern shore of Lake Rousseau. Deacon underlined what he'd written for no other reason than it gave him a few moments before he'd feel inclined to speak again.

Then:

"So it was a tourist?"

"You say so," Dylan answered as a cheer arose from the officers playing bocce.

The two constables were slapping their sergeant on the back and Marchand was doing a fist pump. "That's how you do it!" he exclaimed, and then the game was broken up by Dr. Ross's Cadillac driving over their stones on his way towards the exit.

Deacon tracked past it, letting his eyes settle again on the van. All he could make out in the smoky dark was a blotch of darker still. He thought about what it must have looked like a short while ago—a ball of fire—and then he tried to think if there was anyone he knew who lived on Brackenburg Road. There was someone, he was sure of it. He tapped his pen against his pad. When that didn't do the trick he took a drag off his cigarette, but that didn't help much either.

He dropped the butt at his feet, stubbing it with the toe of his sneaker. When he looked back up, Dr. Ross's car had stopped at the end of the driveway and the coroner was leaning out the driver's side window. He was skinny and pale with deep-set eyes underscored by sacks of dark flesh and always reminded Deacon of a ghoul or a grave robber in one of the Sherlock Holmes mysteries George used to give to him to read. He was saying something through the open window, too low for Deacon to hear.

"It's a helluva mess alright," Dylan replied to whatever it was Dr. Ross had said.

"It's a terrible thing really."

A car was approaching on the highway. Within its glow, Deacon could see Ross shaking his head even as the faint trace of a smile pulled at the corners of his mouth. When the vehicle had passed, he could hear the click of the doctor's tongue against his teeth.

"But then you know what George'd say . . ."

Knowing exactly what George would say, Deacon wheeled around and pointed his feet in the direction of his Jeep. The gravel crunching underfoot blotted out Dr. Ross's voice but was powerless against the tenor of Dylan's response.

"It's looking to be a long one this year then," he said, the upturn in his voice making it seem as if nothing could have pleased him more.

There'd been a time when Deacon's own father would have answered George with the same, and Deacon would have snickered right along with him. But now, imagining Dr. Ross slipping the photo he'd just taken of someone's charred remains into an album alongside the one he'd taken of his family those years ago, it didn't really seem all that funny anymore.

RENÉ

I t had been a shit day so far.

Being a workday, he'd set his alarm for seven, but he'd awoken just after five. The window over his bed beckoned no light and he could hear the buzz of a fly caught behind its screen. That's what must have woken him up. He had lain there, listening to it batter against the glass, telling himself he ought to get up and kill it or else he'd never fall back asleep, all the while knowing that it didn't matter anyway. He was awake now and he might just as well get up as lay there watching the clock's slow shuffle, growing angrier by the second listening to that damn fly—though it wasn't really the fly he was mad at, it was his sister Jean.

Four years ago, he'd been convicted of aggravated assault, and while he was serving his time, Jean had adopted his three-year-old son, Tawyne. After René'd got out, nine months ago, she'd agreed to let him see Tawyne for two hours on the first and third Saturdays of every month. His seventh birthday was on June twenty-first and that fell on a Sunday this year, the day after his regularly scheduled visit. It was a sign that had spoken to René of something beyond mere providence and he'd got it in his mind that he should do something special to mark the occasion. He'd called Jean up the Friday before and asked if maybe he could have Tawyne overnight.

"I was thinking," he'd said, "of taking him up to Gramps's old fishing shack."

It was an hour's walk due north along a trail the old man had blazed himself through the woods extending almost to his back door, built on the shore of a lake too small to bear mention on any map, but which his grandfather called Koué. He had the whole trip planned out. They'd swim and fish off the dock, cook what they'd caught over an open fire for dinner, grill up pancakes for breakfast, and spend Sunday morning out in his grandfather's canoe, casting into the shallows on the far side of the lake where the biggest fish were prone to linger. After he'd made his pitch to Jean, he saw that it all hung on three seconds of dead air, which was about the time it took for her to speak.

"I don't think he's ready for an overnight just yet," she said, and if René could have reached through the phone he'd have strangled her.

He heard the amplified rasp of Jean taking a deep breath and when she exhaled she said, "How about this? You can have him for four hours on Saturday. I'll drop him off at eleven. That way you can have lunch together."

René answered her through gritted teeth: "But I wanted to see him on his birthday."

"We've made plans. We're taking him to Wonderland. He's been looking forward to it for weeks. We've already bought the tickets."

"I see."

"So you'll take him for the four hours on Saturday?"

"Fine."

"See you then."

The phone clicked and it took about all of René's will not to heave it through the closest window. Now, as the conversation replayed itself in an endless loop to the batter of the fly hammering against the window, he felt the rage surging again, seeing her fat fucking face smiling on the other end of the phone, as if she couldn't have been happier with the way things had turned out.

He took a deep breath and held it in for the count of five—what the counsellor at his anger management classes had taught him to do when he felt his mood going into a tailspin.

"Take a deep breath," he'd told the circle of inmates, "and count to five, remind yourself what's at stake, what you stand to lose by coming out guns a-blazing."

For René, it was seeing his son. The judge had handed him five, but his lawyer said he'd be out in three, "if he stayed out of trouble," shooting him a nervous look as he said it, like it'd be a miracle if he didn't serve his full term. Between that look and the counsellor's advice he'd managed to keep his temper in check, though he hadn't exactly stayed out of trouble, counting down from five when the shit did go down and telling himself that in three years Tawyne would be seven and in five he'd be almost ten. It seemed a lifetime between the two and he'd hedged his bets by having Trout, the range's resident tattoo artist, ink a picture of a wolf on each of his hands. He already had the two howling up his neck, which he'd got when he'd turned eighteen and wanted to mark the occasion. While those wolves spoke to him of his clan's past, full of honour and glory, the ones on his hands spoke to him only of his own. Each was running full tilt towards his forearm, their lips curled back into a vicious snarl, the bush of their tails stretched behind and their tips dipping into the crux between his thumb and forefinger. When he clenched his fists it looked like he'd got those wolves by the tail, which was exactly what he'd told Trout he was after.

Laying there now, clutching those mean old wolves by the tail, he counted down from five and then did it again. By the third time, he'd calmed some. He swung his feet over the edge of the bed, sitting up and reaching for the pack of Dunhills on the ledge beside the clock. It was empty. He crumpled it up and threw it against the wall then stood. He walked into the kitchen and took a fresh pack from the carton in the cupboard over the stove. By the time he was exhaling his first drag, the seed of a new plan was already germinating.

You've been meaning to take him up to High Falls anyway, he told himself, High Falls being the best swimming hole around.

Maybe they'd pick up some KFC—Tawyne's favourite—and an ice cream cake from Dairy Queen. He'd bought him a fishing rod from The Bait Shop in town and had already wrapped that up with the pocket knife René's grandfather had given him on his eleventh birthday. He could arrange to borrow Roy's canoe, and after Tawyne opened his presents they could take a paddle downriver so he could try out his new rod. When they got back to the falls they'd climb onto the jumping ledge. The only way to get there was up the side of a rock face, some fifty feet steep.

"Are you really going to jump from there?" Tawyne might say once they'd reached the summit.

"Just watch me."

"But there's a tree in the way."

It was an old pine—a white, René thought—anchored to the cliff ten feet above the water, its tip rising three feet past the highest ledge, meaning you had to take a run if you had any hope of clearing it. And there was no better feeling than clearing that old pine: the world suddenly became a yawning chasm swallowing you whole.

Tawyne wouldn't jump from there, not that first time.

Hell, you were fifteen the first time you jumped.

But there were plenty of other ledges to jump from. The shortest was five feet. He could start from there, work his way up.

By the end of day, he'd be jumping from twenty, you can bank on that.

After finishing at the cliff, they'd swim back across to the falls. Just off from where the main stream gushed into the river there was a little basin hollowed out in the rock. Overflow collected in it, forming a natural whirlpool. They'd sit in there, soaking leisurely amongst the froth until their time was up.

The cigarette was down to the nub by the time he'd imagined that, though he couldn't remember taking more than two puffs. He butt it in the ashtray on the kitchen's fold-out table and took out another cigarette, reducing that to ash while replaying his plans for Tawyne's birthday.

It was shaping up to be one helluva day.

T hat feeling lasted about as long as it took him to take a shower.

The trailer's water heater had gone the month before. He'd been showering in his grandfather's house ever since. He usually only did that after work, but it was already twenty-one degrees according to the weather network app that had come with his phone—its forecast calling for a high of thirty-two with scattered clouds—and he figured a little cold water might do him a world of good. Still, the first blast hit him like an ice storm. The shower barely had enough room for him to stand in, much less get out from under its spray. Wasn't anything to do but clench his teeth and suffer through it. He lathered himself up and rinsed, then turned the water off and reached for the towel that hung on the rack over the toilet.

He walked out of the bathroom naked, as he was often inclined to do, sometimes going so far as to stand in the kitchen and drink his morning coffee before getting dressed, letting the fresh air get at the drips his towel had missed. He bought his grandfather Maxwell House Dark Roast by the kilo, and every few days René filled a Mason jar from the can he kept in his fridge, making his morning fix with the percolator he heated on the trailer's propane stove. It barely filled his travel mug beyond half, but the coffee was boiling hot and strong and didn't suffer much when he topped it off with milk. That morning there were only sprinkles left in the bottom of the jar.

There'd be a pot on in the house, he told himself as he walked to the kitchen table.

He fished a cigarette from the pack and picked up his lighter, flicking the dial, the flame crackling against the tobacco and him studying it.

A fire, he thought. *You can't light a fire at High Falls.*

It was half the reason he'd wanted to take Tawyne up to his grandfather's fishing shack in the first place.

Simmering the bass or pickerel they'd have caught in a little butter, bubbling in a fry pan heated over the open flames, roasting marshmallows, listening to the soft wood crackle and pop and watching embers cast aloft, dancing amidst the night sky's sparkle, him and his son all alone together, might as well be the last two people on earth.

Them laughing.

The thought had barely passed when his bare foot was lashing out, striking the plastic garbage can beside the table. It shot across the room and hit the couch at the trailer's far end. The lid popped off on impact, a geyser spray releasing from within— old coffee grinds peppering the back window all the way to the ceiling, the rattle of rib bones from last night's dinner hitting the glass, a sour cream container splattering its remains over the back of the couch, the garbage can toppling, spewing wadded up paper towels stained with barbecue sauce and an old fly strip clung fast to a milk bag, a pickle jar spilling its juice as it spun, skittering, across the floor, the mess making him madder still.

He closed his eyes and took a deep breath, holding it in for the count of five.

But counting down from five and grabbing those wolves by the tail hardly put a stutter in the rage coursing through him now. His eyes flashed open, scanning about the trailer, looking for something else to smash. Ever since the spring had set in, his grandfather had taken to picking the wild flowers that grew along the fringe of his backyard and arranging them in the vase on the trailer's kitchen table, replenishing those when the old ones had wilted. This day it was tiger lilies, set against the back-drop of a fern.

He was just reaching for the vase when three sharp knocks sounded at the door, enough to stay his hand. And then his grandfather's voice, asking, "Everything alright in there?"

René was breathing hard, impossibly so, his chest heaving, tendrils of spit fuming at his lips. Another knock then, the rap of a knuckle that wasn't sure if it really wanted an answer.

"René?"

No more than a whisper, his grandfather's head pressed to the door, listening for signs of a violence yet to come, so that when René jerked it open, the old man startled back. He was car-rying a wrench as big as his forearm. His hand tightened against its tempered steel as if he was expecting René to have at him, but only for an instant, then it relaxed again. If he noticed his grandson was naked, he made no sign.

"You alright?" the old man asked.

René nodded, though the grit to his teeth told a different story.

A vehicle was passing by on the 118. It was a black SUV—a Navigator—pulling an Airstream behind. The latter was thirty-five feet long if it was an inch, the gleam of its aluminum making the old trailer home his grandfather had salvaged from Bailey's Auto Wreck, and in which René had lived ever since he'd got out of jail, seem no better than a cardboard box.

René watched it until it was out of sight and let his eyes wander back to the old man. He was biting his lip, studying the younger with the same look he used to have when he was wrestling with the crossword on the back page of the local paper, so intent on the puzzle that it seemed to René like he must have thought the very secret of the world was hidden within. When René was in his teens, the delivery person would give out a honk to tell his grandfather the paper was there, and he'd drop everything he was so eager to check the answers for last week's crossword and to get a start on the next.

But that had been years ago.

Though he still got the paper every Wednesday, the delivery person no longer honked and the crossword on its back page remained blank. It had always been a mystery to René what could have been so important about a damned crossword to inspire such devotion and, more so, what had changed in the meanwhile. Seeing that look again on the old man's face—staring at him as if trying to work out a deeper meaning to the violent clatter he'd heard a moment ago and the sudden appearance of his grandson at the door, naked and looking like he was about to tear his head off—struck René suddenly shy. His hand meandered towards his groin as if he meant to cover himself but reconsidered, his fingers idling their time, scratching at the hair that grew in a channel from his pubis to his belly button.

"What's up?" René asked.

"You got a moment before you leave?"

"Roy'll be here any minute," René lied, knowing that his boss wouldn't arrive to pick him up until eight, and here it was not even seven.

"I thought—"

"What'd you need?"

"An extra set of hands. Won't be more'n two ticks on a dog."

"You mind if I get dressed first?"

The old man levelled the cockeyed grin at him that sometimes made René think he was a tad simple.

"Well, I sure wish you would."

An hour later, René heard a honk from the driveway.
He was standing under a Ford Tempo up on the hoist in his grandfather's garage, holding a muffler in place while the old man ratcheted the bolts back into its bracket.

"That'll be Roy," he said.

"Go on, then," his grandfather urged, his tone about the same as if René had been a teenager begging off to go hang out with his friends.

"Won't kill him to wait another few seconds," René said.

"I got three in. It'll hold."

René eased his grip, waiting to make sure his grandfather was right. The muffler sagged a quarter inch but held and René turned towards the door.

"Try not to work too hard," the old man called after him, which was what he always said in place of goodbye.

When he came out, Roy was angling his Silverado towards the road. He caught sight of René and waved and René held up his hands, showing off a filth of rust and grease.

"Let me get washed up," he called as he hurried towards the trailer.

He doused his hands with the No Name detergent beside the sink and scrubbed them with a Brillo pad, rinsing the grime off both together. He took his lunch box from the fridge where he'd put it the night before, and habit had him reaching for the travel mug on the counter, stopping short, remembering there hadn't been any coffee that morning. He left it where it was and snatched the pack of smokes off the table along with his lighter, casting a long last look at the garbage strewn over the couch and the floor on his way out.

The Silverado was parked at the end of the driveway when he came onto the porch. The pickup's left blinker was flashing, like Roy was thinking about maybe leaving him behind.

René set off at a jog.

Roy was thumbing at his Galaxy S7 when he reached the passenger seat. He was wearing what he always did when the temperature hadn't dipped below zero: a plain blue T-shirt, torn at the collar and spackled with white paint, and a pair of jeans worn through at the knees. He must have been looking for a song because the moment René shut the door the opening of Mötley Crüe's "Helter Skelter" blared out of the stereo and he cast René a playful grin as he turned onto the 118, knowing his disdain for '80s hair-metal bands.

The truck picked up speed, and by the time Vince Neil was screaming about riding a slide in an endless loop, René was nodding off.

He was snapped back to it by Roy shouting above the wailing guitars, "You look tired!"

René rubbed at his eyes and leaned forward, casting a furtive glance at the empty cup holder where his coffee would normally be.

"Damn fly kept me up half the night," he shouted back.

"A fly? Why didn't you just get up and swat it?"

"You think I didn't try?"

"It disappeared whenever you got up?"

"Every damned time."

Roy was shaking his head and grinning again.

"They's tricky alright."

3

"So you remember him?"

Grover Parks, the *Chronicle*'s managing editor, was standing in the doorway of Deacon's office. He was wearing his usual white button-down shirt and grey slacks but had forgone his standard V-neck sweater and tie in deference to the air conditioner being on the fritz (the "cooling specialist" he'd called in had told him it wasn't worth the cost to repair, and Grover hadn't yet reconciled himself to the task of writing a cheque for a new one, going on two weeks now). His sleeves were rolled up to his elbows and he'd even left his top button undone, the day already creeping towards thirty degrees and the office beginning to feel like a slow cooker set to high. Curls of white prodded from within the cleft below his neck, the same as the ones lathered on his chin, their ivory sprouting, it seemed, in stark defiance against the ebony of his skin.

"Hard to forget a man like Ronald Crane," Deacon answered.

Ronald Crane was the CEO of Crane Enterprises, a property

development firm out of Toronto. Three months previous he'd bought the Meeford Bay Resort, and his assistant had called the *Chronicle* to enquire about some local ad copy for the newly rechristened Rustling Pines Mature Living Community. The way Bill Churly, the paper's sales rep, had told it, he'd asked her what she was thinking, and she'd answered, "Nothing too extravagant. Construction's still two years away. A quarter page maybe. Just a teaser." Bill told her that was certainly doable, then spent the next fifteen minutes explaining to her why that'd be a mistake. By the end of the call she'd agreed to the deluxe package: four full-page colour ads to run prior to each of the summer holiday weekends to capitalize on what Bill rather euphemistically called the *Chronicle*'s "peak circulation." As a bonus he threw in, at no extra charge, a profile to be written by one of the paper's "journalistic professionals," and a couple of weeks later Deacon drove up to Meeford Bay to talk with Mr. Crane and to take a few snapshots.

Deacon had pulled into the resort's parking lot and parked behind a black Escalade. By the time he had opened the Jeep's door, Mr. Crane was stepping from the SUV's rear passenger door, speaking in a rapid gibberish Deacon guessed was maybe Russian or Ukrainian. The cherub pudge to his cheeks defied his age, in his midfifties Deacon guessed, so that it almost looked like a baby's face had been glued over top of his own. He had a thin stubble of bleach-blond hair over which was propped a pair of aviator sunglasses and was wearing a brightly coloured Hawaiian shirt, cargo shorts, and open-toed sandals, for all intents and purposes the living embodiment of summer, which was maybe a bit of a stretch, it then being the middle of March. He choreographed the end of his call to coincide with the moment he was reaching his hand out to Deacon, saying, *"Do pobačennya,"* into the phone, and tossing it blindly up and over his head, his assistant scuttling to get beneath it. She was a pretty twenty-something brunette, wearing a bright red open-bloused tux, the tails of which reminded Deacon of one worn by a Ringling Bros. lion tamer in an old movie he'd seen on late-night TV. All she needed was a top hat and whip to complete the costume, but Deacon didn't have time to ponder that—the moment she'd snatched the phone out of the air Mr. Crane was giving his hand a double pump.

While they shook, he smiled at Deacon with enough teeth to rival a used-car salesman at the end of a lean month, and he forsook the standard greeting to ask Deacon if he was hungry.

"I'm okay," Deacon answered.

"You sure? We picked up some sandwiches at—" his assistant filling in the name—"The Hungry Bear"—without even a stutter to say he'd misplaced it.

"Salami this thick." He held his thumb and forefinger three inches apart. "And fresh baked bread, just like my grandma used to make. Best goddamn sandwich I ever ate. You sure you don't want one?"

"I'm fine."

"Diane, fetch him a sandwich."

Then, before Deacon could protest again, he'd grabbed his arm and hastened him towards the water, all abuzz about the twelve tonnes of sand that was, at this very moment, on its way from St. Vincent or St. Martin, he couldn't remember which; an island somewhere in the Caribbean anyway.

"It's the whitest sand you ever saw," he opined, and his plan was to use it to rejuvenate the algae-encrusted beach confronting Deacon now.

Diane appeared with his sandwich, but Deacon hadn't more than peeled back its wax paper to see that it was roast beef before Mr. Crane grabbed his arm again and led him on a whirlwind tour of the grounds, seeing in the falling down log cabins and the dank black water of its lagoon his own personal paradise. He carried his extra weight more like helium than lard and moved with the frenetic pace of a squirrel hiding nuts so that it was all Deacon could do to keep up with his stride. He talked about as fast as he walked, and by the time they were circling back towards the driveway, Deacon's hand was cramped from the nine pages he'd filled in his notebook using the cryptic shorthand he'd learned from Grover.

When they reached Deacon's Jeep, Mr. Crane shook his hand again and asked, "You get what you need?"

Deacon replied that he had, and without further ado Mr. Crane spun around towards the Escalade, snatched the cell phone out of his assistant's outstretched hand, and said, "*Dobryj den*," as he brought it to his mouth. As Diane closed the car door behind Crane, she turned towards Deacon, offering him a sprightly wink and smile, the glint in her eyes so bright that it seemed to have burnt itself into his retinas.

And it was the possibility of seeing her again that was on Deacon's mind when he asked Grover, "Why?"

"They're saying he's the man found burnt up in that van last night."

That had Deacon sitting bolt upright.

"What?"

"No official confirmation but the van was registered in his name."

"Where'd you hear that?"

"*Globe and Mail* broke the story five minutes ago." And then before Deacon had a chance to reply, Grover was ducking back into the hall, calling over his shoulder, "Scooped again, eh, Deke? Don't you worry, you'll get 'em next time!"

Three clicks later Deacon was staring at a headline reading,

"Police Say T.O. Real Estate Mogul Ronald Crane Victim of Foul Play."

The contents of the column informed him that Crane's throat had been slashed prior to his van being set on fire and that given his prominence—his $3.68 billion net worth made him the twelfth richest man in the country—the RCMP would be handling the case. It further went on to say that at the time of his demise he was being investigated by the same for possible links to organized crime related to a kickback scheme dating to the late 1990s, the inference being that his "suspected" murder and his "cooperation" might in some way be related. Information that, albeit intriguing, was useless to a small-town reporter who, in his own article on the matter, had included a quote from "a source within the Tildon Police Services" indicating that "foul play was suspected," only to read, when the *Chronicle* came out, that "police are refusing to speculate on the cause of the fire while the investigation is ongoing."

It wasn't the first time Grover had softened his copy. It was something he was especially prone to doing between the May Two-Four and Labour Day weekends in the belief that the cottagers who made up, at last count, seventeen percent of the *Chronicle*'s subscribers during the summer months were looking for a break from the kind of "if it bleeds, it leads" nonsense they were inundated with in the big city papers. Whether that was true or not, Deacon had his doubts, but he'd learned that his doubts were worth about as much as a snowflake in December next to Grover's own opinions on the matter.

The first, and last, time he'd contested one of Grover's editorial prerogatives had been when he was eighteen. He'd written a story about two pit bulls that had mauled a three-year-old boy while he was playing in a sandbox in his backyard. The pit bulls in question were owned by the boy's neighbour and were released one afternoon when the Tildon Police Services raided their master's house on a tip—later confirmed—that it was being used as a meth lab. The dogs had escaped when the arresting officers had kicked in the back door and, finding the boy playing happily in his backyard they proceeded to, in Dylan's words, "tear his little face off."

After Deacon had submitted the article, detailing the events much as described, he'd been shocked to find that the only allusion to the bust or the meth lab was that "two police officers executing a routine warrant in the area had heard the boy's screams and intervened in the attack." When he'd protested to Grover, accusing him in his youthful zeal of "butchering his article," Grover had marched him outside and pointed to the newspaper's honour box stationed on the sidewalk in front of the office.

"What's that say?" Grover had asked and, rather meekly, Deacon recited the words Grover himself had stencilled along the box's top edge: "How about some good news for a change?"

"And what kind of person in their right mind would think that finding out their neighbours were operating a meth lab is good news?"

There'd probably be a few meth heads who'd be plenty happy to hear about it was the answer that had sprung to Deacon's mind. But then, of course, meth heads don't generally read the paper. He held his tongue and had been doing so ever since. He knew that Grover would have absolutely no interest in any revelations pertaining to Ronald Crane's involvement with organized crime, just as he was certain that George most certainly would, deriving as he did no end of morbid delight in any tragedy afflicting the country's rich and famous.

Adele, George's wife of fifty-six years and a second mom to Deacon for the past twelve, had died just before Easter. George had hardly left his property since. Grover and Deacon, so far as they knew, had become his only contact with the outside world, Grover visiting him three or four times a week to play back-gammon or cribbage in the evening and Deacon dropping by whenever the mood struck.

It was a Wednesday, the day the paper came out, and Deacon had nothing on his slate but sweating over the emails he'd relegated to a folder named, Next Week?

There's no time like the present, he told himself, shutting his laptop and locking his office door behind him on the way out.

4

Ten minutes later he was walking up Baker, the street George lived on. It was more like a driveway shared between its only two residences, though both also had a driveway of their own—the Clearys' fashioned out of interlocked brick and the Quimbys' across from it out of gravel, most of which was strewn over their front yard from a winter's worth of snow shovelling.

There were two cars parked side by side in front of George's garage, one a grey Mercedes that belonged to George's son, Edward, and the other a sporty purple Audi that his daughter Louise drove.

Deacon had been on the outs with both ever since he'd taken George's side when they'd tried to get Adele moved into a nursing home after she'd barely survived a bout of pneumonia. She'd been diagnosed with Parkinson's several years earlier but seemed to be doing okay. Then one night she wandered from the house in the middle of the season's first blizzard, wearing only her slippers and a nightdress. She'd been found by a snowplow driver, banging on the front door of the pharmacy on Main. When he asked what she was doing, she'd told him that her son was sick and she needed to get some penicillin. She had a prescription, she said, and became increasingly flustered when she couldn't find it, nor any pockets, in the folds of her gown.

It had taken the snowplow driver a devil of a time to convince her that it didn't matter if she found it or not, the pharmacy was closed, and that she'd better get in his truck or she'd freeze to death. Finally she'd relented, and he took her to the South Mesaquakee Memorial Hospital, which was all of a two-minute drive away.

The pneumonia had kept her there for three weeks before Deacon heard tell of it. He'd graduated from high school that spring. George had insisted he further his education and he'd obliged him by enrolling in the journalism program at Ryerson University in Toronto. He spent a single semester living in a dorm, wishing he was anywhere but there, and when he came home for Christmas he was told Adele was in the hospital. She was due to be released the next day and against the advice of her doctor and his children, George refused to put her in a home, telling them that he'd continue caring for her himself. There'd been a fight, Louise leading the attack in the hospital's parking lot while Edward helped Adele into the passenger seat of George's pickup truck and Deacon stowed her wheelchair in the truck's bed. Louise had accused George of being selfish and refusing to see beyond his own stubborn pride and do what was right for once, her vitriol well beyond what one might reason- ably expect from someone discussing palliative care arrange- ments for her mother.

When George had closed the passenger door and was cir- cling his truck on the way to the driver's seat, Louise grabbed him by the arm, her anger seething as she said, "She almost died! You're too old to look after her. You can barely look after yourself."

It wasn't the first time Deacon had cause to think that the Clearys weren't exactly the perfect family he'd thought they were when he first moved in with George and Adele. He'd heard other rumblings too, most often during the holidays, which were the only times they were ever all together. Deacon had always kept his thoughts to himself, but bearing witness to Louise's open scorn for the man who'd taken him in and treated him like a son when nobody else would had stirred something in him that could not be silenced.

"We'll manage," Deacon had called over, and Louise cast him such a look of spite that it could have frozen fire. When she looked back at George, he shrugged as if the matter was out of his hands.

Edward had treated Deacon with mild disdain ever since; Louise, on the other hand, had treated him with open scorn. Seeing their cars parked side by side in the driveway, he told himself that maybe it would be best if he came back later. Even from the edge of the street, he could hear Louise's voice raised in shrill sanction from the backyard, elevated to a volume that suggested George had fired another housekeeper without her permission. Thinking how it wasn't right for them to be ganging up on him again, Deacon willed his legs forward, looping towards the redbrick path leading past the front door, letting that steer him around the house and into the backyard.

It was almost as big as a football field, its grounds resplendent with cherry and bird berry trees, flower gardens ringed with river-washed stones, and on its western expanse a quarter acre of tilled soil where they grew their vegetables. But ever since Adele had died, weeds had overtaken her gardens and George had stopped mowing the lawn so that it now resembled an old homestead grown wild with its owner's passing, a semblance made ever more so by the small red-brick barn set at the edge of the ravine that bordered their property.

Louise's voice was coming from the direction of the garden and it was punctuated by a series of sharp barks—George's golden retriever, Trixie, providing her own response to the attack on her master. Coming to the cherry tree in the middle of the lawn, Deacon caught sight of George standing in what had once been his prized tomato patch but was now overgrown with raspberry brambles. He had a clutch of weeds in his hand. He was swatting it about, spraying soil loosened from their roots in carefully articulated showers at Louise and Edward.

"I left it to him," he said, "and that's final. You can fight it out with my lawyer after I'm gone, if you want. But it won't do you any good, I'll tell you that."

It seemed to Deacon George must have been talking about him.

Maybe, he mused, *he'd changed his will again,* something he'd done a few times since Deacon had come to live with him and Adele. It had never failed to cause a row, and Deacon had made his opinions on the matter clear. He'd have rather been left with nothing if it meant Edward and Louise would leave their father in peace, a sentiment at stark odds with the secret thrill he felt seeing Louise so flustered now.

Viewed from the back, it was obvious that she'd gained some weight since Deacon had last seen her. She'd been as pretty and slight as her mother in her younger days and the added bulk didn't so much make her look fat as it did wide, like she'd become a reflection of Adele stretched out of proportion in some funhouse mirror. Edward too had borne a strong resemblance to his father when he was young, though looking at the two of them now, they couldn't have appeared more different—George, the wild fray of his beard paired by an old dress shirt and grey slacks with a rip at the knee so that he looked like a chartered accountant who'd spent the last five years stuck on a deserted island; Edward, who was in fact a chartered accountant, clean-shaven and sombre, dressed as if he was meeting his richest client for lunch.

"Be reasonable," Louise urged and that made Deacon smile.

She sounded exactly like her mother had when scolding George for some misdeed, most likely to have about the same effect. Then George was looking his way. There was a plead in his eye, and Deacon gave him a sympathetic wave as he turned and walked on a straight line towards the barn's front door. It had once guarded a herd of sheep and a clutch of chickens at a time when no one thought twice about keeping farm animals in town. After George had bought the house in the early 1970s, he'd refashioned the barn into his private den—a place to read and to write and to generally escape the hubbub of having two young children ever under foot. He'd covered all four walls with shelves and filled those with books. And when he had, he'd taken to stacking new acquisitions on the floor and every other available space, leaving only a narrow path down the middle.

Directly across from the door hung a picture frame. Behind the glass, a sheet of white paper upon which was handwritten in black marker: "Fiction is a bridge to the truth that journalism can't touch." And below that, "Bill." Deacon had long since come to recognize the childlike scrawl as George's own and the "Bill" in question as being the familiar derivation of one of George's favourite authors. Upon entering the barn, Deacon's gaze would invariably seek out the words, coming across them almost by accident, as if the solution to the mystery regarding the dual and conflicting natures of George The Writer and George The Man would reveal itself if only he caught it unawares. And when it never did, he'd tap the glass with his index finger, like he was doing now, as if to give the elusive secret fair warning that he was closing in.

The smell of mildewed paper, which had always defined the barn's character, was diminished by the musk of stale cigarette smoke. It seemed to him as odd, never having seen George himself take so much as a puff, and it immediately drew his attention to George's old Remington Rand typewriter. It was the same machine on which he'd written all twelve of his Fictions, the last published when Deacon was barely out of diapers, and ever since had sat collecting dust on the expansive oak wood desk in the far left-hand side of the barn.

Why he'd quit writing was a matter of some debate.

Grover was Deacon's main source of information on all things Cleary, and after the fourth time Deacon had read through George's collected works—he was fifteen and even then inclined to drop by the *Chronicle* every day after school—he'd asked Grover why George had stopped writing books. Grover had cocked his head to the side and stroked at the curls of his beard. It was what he always did whenever he was pressed to speak on a matter of some grave import, taking a moment not so much to gather his thoughts as to appraise the person in front of him, as if it was they themselves who were determining what he might want to say.

"It's a mystery to me too," he'd finally said. "I guess you'll just have to ask him yourself."

Deacon had been reluctant to do that, for reasons he couldn't readily define. Instead he'd asked Adele one day at the kitchen table while he was helping her prepare a new crossword, which, in the years before she'd succumbed to Parkinson's, had been her one contribution to the *Chronicle*.

"He didn't have the heart for it anymore," she'd answered.

His books had never sold more than a few hundred copies, and Deacon had taken what Adele had said to mean that George had grown tired of seeing the bulk of them end up as remainders, shipped back from stores, if they even made it that far, their front covers torn off and the rest relegated to an ignominious end in some landfill.

But the truth was she'd meant it literally.

"When he turned fifty-five," she continued, "he got angina. Doctor Morrell told him he'd be lucky to live to see sixty if he kept smoking the way he did. Two or three packs a day. And sometimes when he'd run out of those, hand-rolleds from the Mason jar of Drum he kept on his desk. A disgusting habit."

She'd pursed her lips, as if the memory conjured within it the stink of tobacco on his breath and in his clothes, the yellow tint to his fingers and the streaks of tar staining the white of his beard.

"So he quit?" Deacon asked.

"He did, and writing too. Said there wasn't much joy in one without the other. He still wrote for the paper, of course, but never another of his Fictions. And if you ask me . . ."

A bitter note had crept into her voice and she shook her head as if she couldn't quite bring herself to utter what she'd meant to say next. They'd never spoken of it again.

It would be eight years before Deacon would have cause to broach the subject once more, this time with Dylan. They were in his backyard, ten beers into the twelve of Keith's stowed in the cooler between them as they often were by midnight on a Friday when neither had anything better to do than recline in lawn chairs, snapping bottle caps between their thumbs and forefingers, watching the crowns spin off into the dark, listening for the rap of them against the fence to tell them their aim had been true.

Deacon had just come back from the bathroom where he'd found, tucked amongst a dozen or so *Outdoor Canada* magazines in the rack beside the toilet, a trade paperback copy of *My Brother's Keeper*. It was George's third novel and he couldn't have been more surprised seeing it there, as much because he'd never known Dylan to be much of a reader as because it was the only one of George's books that he needed to complete his own collection. (His attempts to find it on eBay had borne no fruit, though he'd found the rest, along with three of his books in German translation.)

When he'd got back to the yard he'd asked Dylan where he'd got it, and Dylan had answered:

"It's George's. Only copy, as far as I know, that's left. Unless Grover has one."

"What do you mean?"

"He only printed up five. Story I heard is, they burnt up the rest."

"What? I—I mean, who?"

"Dad and Aunt Louise."

It seemed doubly strange hearing him say that since the book had been dedicated *For My Children, E. & L.*

"Why in the hell would they do that?" Deacon asked after he'd overcome his shock.

"That's what I was trying to figure out when I took it off his shelf."

"And did you?"

"Haven't made it past page ten."

"Too bad. It's a helluva book."

"Well, I was never much of a reader."

Deacon's gaze settled again on the book in his lap. Its cover was warped from being jammed in the magazine rack and its pages stained with innumerable drips from Dylan reaching out of the shower to grab a towel. He hadn't read it in years and the moment he set eyes on the image on its front—a photograph of train tracks disappearing into a snow-bound wilderness—he was powerless but to crack its spine.

Through his inebriation, the words on page one blurred and the letters set to dancing drunkenly towards the margins on the first page. His head got to spinning right along with them and after a moment he shut it again.

"It's a shame," he said, smoothing the cover to distract himself from a sudden wave of nausea.

"What's that?" Dylan asked.

"That he stopped writing."

"You say so. But then you never had to live with him when he did."

"What do you mean?"

Dylan had then fixed Deacon with the same stare that Adele had almost a decade before, and Deacon was certain that he wouldn't say another word. But after reaching down for another beer and popping its cap, he said, "He was right mean when he was writing."

That made Deacon flinch, same as if he'd been stung.

"Where'd you hear that?" he asked.

"My dad. The stories he told. Made him out to be a fucking monster."

"When he was writing?"

"And most of the time in between too. Got so bad that Grams threatened to leave if he even thought about writing another book."

"So he stopped writing, just like that?"

"For a couple or few years anyway. Then he started on another. She packed a bag the same morning. Stayed with her sister, she was gone for six months. I guess time enough for him to finish whatever he was working on."

"Was it *The Stray*?"

"If that was his last."

"It was."

"Then it must have been."

Deacon thought on that for a moment.

"So how'd he get her to come back?" he finally asked.

"Your guess is as good as mine," Dylan answered. "All I know is she did and except for the paper, he never wrote another word."

Now, as Deacon wound through the stacks of books precariously balanced on either side of the narrow path leading towards the desk, the dusty light filtering through the window washed over the typewriter and a small blue bowl, the same kind that Deacon had once used for cereal. It was full to the brim with cigarette butts and beside the makeshift ashtray there were two stacks of paper, which hardly came as a surprise given what Adele had told him. The one on the left was maybe four hundred pages deep. The page on top read **Chapter 10** and below that Deacon could see that half the lines were crossed out with crude slashes, George's ragged scrawl filling the spaces between and spilling over into the margins, his handwriting becoming ever smaller as they drained towards the bottom of the page— obviously a rough draft. The one beside it was composed of only a hundred or so pages, upside down, what must have been George's rewrite. It was towards this that Deacon was immediately drawn. There was the faint imprint of characters stencilled on the back of the top sheet and he ran the pad of his index finger over their mottled bumps as a blind man would while reading Braille. At the end of the line, he paused and looked back at the rough draft.

It must have taken him over a year to write all that.

A thought accompanied by an empty feeling hollowing out his gut, seeing in the twin stacks not so much evidence of

George's industry but of his own neglect. How else to explain how George could have managed such a thing and him none the wiser? Casting his thoughts then back over the past year.

Whole weeks passing by without you stopping in on George, hardly better than Edward or Louise.

Thinking then of the few times he had. Most often knocking at the front door and hearing his answer in a sharp bark from the backyard. Dixie would be wagging her tail in the barn's open doorway when Deacon rounded the house and before he'd made it halfway across the lawn, George would be nudging her aside and locking the door behind him.

"Just catching up on some reading," he'd offer by way of a greeting, and once right after his wife had died, "Adele sure was right about the rats taking over in there. It's about time I cleaned things up."

Both of which Deacon was now certain were lies. He was working on a new book, must have been. The thought that George had never seen fit to confide that in him had the hollow in his gut feel like it was filling up with cement.

A sharp *yip* startled him from his sudden malaise and spun him towards the door.

Trixie was standing in the threshold, wagging her tail, and a flicker of movement on his periphery turned Deacon towards the window. George was ambling past. And though he hadn't really done anything wrong, it felt like he had and he set off in a mad flurry between the stacks. He intercepted George just outside the door. Deacon locked it behind him and when he turned around George was wearing a bemused grin as if he was keenly aware of why the young man seemed so flustered and was deriving endless delight, knowing he was the cause.

"What you got there?" he asked, as Deacon returned the barn door's key to its place beneath a rock on the windowsill.

"Huh?"

"The book in your hand."

He'd grabbed it from one of the piles on his way past, to use as a cover, and now held it up for George to see. He squinted, trying to read what it was.

"That's a good one," he finally said, and Deacon reached out and plucked the sprig from a raspberry bush that clung to the old man's beard.

"So what was all that about?" Deacon asked, flicking the barbed stem into the yard where it was immediately swallowed up by the sea of dandelions drowning the lawn.

"Huh?"

"Edward and Louise."

"Oh," George said. "It was nothing."

"Didn't look like nothing."

"Too old to put over my damn knee is all that was."

George forced a smile and swatted the clutch of weeds he still had in his hand, warding off the deer fly circling his head. Then, tossing the clump after the raspberry sprig, he wheeled around and started back towards his garden.

"Helluva thing about Ronald Crane," he said, glancing back at Deacon trailing after.

"You heard about that?"

"Dylan stopped by on his way home."

"And he told you it was Ronald Crane killed last night?"

"He did."

Deacon threw up his hands.

"Am I always the last person to hear about everything around here?"

"What, he didn't tell you?"

"Name withheld pending notification of next of kin is all I could get out of him."

"You should have given him a beer. Dylan'll tell you anything once he gets a beer in his hand."

"I'll have to remember that."

They'd reached the edge of the garden, and George stood surveying its tangle. After a moment, he shook his head as if thinking he might as well give it up as a lost cause.

"It's a helluva thing, alright," he finally said. "Ronald Crane dying like that."

The way George scrunched his lips told Deacon that it was plainly gnawing at him, though why that'd be, he hadn't a clue.

"They're saying it was mob related," Deacon said.

That seemed to catch George by surprise, and his head snapped on a sharp pivot towards Deacon.

"Who said that?"

"The *Globe*. Said he was involved in some sort of kickback scheme."

George sucked on his teeth, which he often did when trying to sort something out.

"I guess they'd know better than me," he finally said. Then, "You knew him, that right?"

"Not really. I just met him the once."

"How was that again?"

Deacon told him, and when he was done George shook his head again and bit his lip.

"Long way from being chauffeured around in an Escalade," he said, "to driving some piece of shit Caravan."

"Struck me as odd too."

"He had a cottage up on Brackenburg, I understand."

"He's been coming up here since he was a kid. Best times of his life, or so he said. It's why he bought up Meeford Bay, so when he gets old—"

"But why do you think he was driving the Caravan?"

51

Deacon shrugged. "Your guess is as good as mine."

George scratched at his beard and looked skywards, as if maybe the answer was somewhere up there.

"It's going to be a hot one today," he said after a moment.

"Looks it."

The sun had come out into a cloudless sky. George squinted against its glare and his shoulders sagged as if he couldn't quite bear its weight. He'd always seemed to have the life force of two men half his age, but all of a sudden he looked old and tired and barely seemed to have the strength to stand.

You can fight it out with my lawyer after I'm gone.

It hadn't been five minutes since he'd said that, and as George turned back towards him the memory had Deacon searching the old man's eyes. Their twinkle was undiminished by the passage of time and they gave Deacon some encouragement that he'd be around for a few years yet.

"Grover get around to fixing the air conditioning?" George asked.

"He's working on it."

"You'd think there was a rattlesnake inside the drawer where he keeps his chequebook—"

"—he's so afraid to open it."

The two men exchanged a knowing smile and it seemed like the older was thinking of putting his hand on the younger's shoulder, to offer him a small comfort. But then George's gaze was wandering back to the garden, settling on the patch of overgrown weeds and raspberry brambles with a bitter sort of resignation.

"I best get back to it then."

5

On his return trip to the office, Deacon picked up a sandwich at Mesaquakee Bean, the coffee shop a few doors down from the *Chronicle*. He ate as he sifted through the emails in his Next Week? folder, all the while trying to forget about the two sheaves of paper he'd seen on the desk. And when that didn't work, he told himself, *If he wanted you to know what he was working on, he'd have told you,* that doing nothing at all to lift the weight in his belly.

You ought to just ask him.

Nodding to himself like it was as simple as that and telling himself that the least he could do was feel him out.

Maybe he'd drop by again when he'd finished work.

By four thirty he'd reduced the twenty-odd files in the Next Week? folder to five and called that a day. He stuck his head in the office across the hall from his on the way out and found Grover talking on the phone. Deacon waved him goodbye and Grover cupped his hand over the receiver.

"You heading up to Rainbow Ridge already?" he asked.

Rainbow Ridge was a retirement villa off the 118, just south of town. In the 1960s, it had been a family ski lodge and the poles that had once supported the T-bar still dotted the slope behind it, even though it was about as much a mountain as it was a mole-hill. Then in 1984, sensing a shift in demographics, the owners had converted it to a nursing home. In 1998, they'd sold it to a health-care conglomerate that had added fifty rooms, a billiard lounge, a swimming pool, and the ballroom where, Deacon now remembered, Bus and Edina Harcourt were celebrating their wedding anniversary. In a city paper, they would have called it a human interest story—a puff piece—and it'd have to have been a pretty slow week for it to get more than a few inches in the life-style section. But at the *Chronicle*, it's what passed for hard news and it was an easy bet that, unless something dire happened over the next few days, "Tildon's Oldest Couple Celebrates Their 70th" would be the headline gracing next week's front page.

"Oh shoot," Deacon said.

Grover was glaring at him with a pointed stare.

"You forgot."

"No. I, uh— What time's it start again?"

"Five thirty."

"Perfect."

Normally, Deacon would have handled such an assignment himself, but he'd been looking for an excuse to arrange a little alone time with Suzie Chalmers, their summer intern. It had been less than a month since Darlene Quint, the *Chronicle*'s office manager, had introduced Deacon to her niece, a second-year journalism student at McGill who was looking for some practical experience to give her a leg-up on the competition. She was petite and had milk-white skin, a perfect china doll's face bracketed by the sharp corners of her blouse and a needle point of hair artfully arranged on either cheek. The way she lowered her head when she looked straight at him made his heart skip a beat, and ever since they met he'd been fighting a losing battle trying to convince himself that it would be best if they maintained a purely professional relationship.

He found her at her desk where she was supposed to be managing the paper's social media accounts and instead was texting on her private phone, which was how she spent most of her days. He told her about the party, asking if she'd like to accompany him, and when she balked, he added that it would be the perfect opportunity to cut her teeth, "journalistically speaking." After some delicate pleading, she finally relented on the conditions that he'd ask Grover to let her write that week's editorial, something she'd been after him to do for some time, and also that they take her car. Deacon had agreed and she'd skipped off from work a few minutes early so she had time to get ready.

It was six thirty before she picked him up in front of the office in her late-model Mazda 3. She'd switched the white blouse and black skirt she'd worn at work for a light summer dress in a floral design and Deacon couldn't have imagined an hour and a half better spent. The thought had just crested his mind that maybe he should have changed too when, reaching for the car's door, he caught sight of a mustard splatter on the already ragged cuff of the corduroy jacket, two sizes too large, he'd copped from George's closet when he was eighteen (and had worn almost every day since), that and the flop of long black hair undone over his unnaturally ruddy cheeks often giving Grover cause to remark that he looked like a teenager playing at being an old man. Slipping into the passenger seat, he strapped himself in and set his hands in his lap, concealing the offending stain, though he needn't really have bothered. Suzie hadn't passed so much as a glance his way.

"You know where we're going?" he asked as Suzie turned onto the road.

She frowned at him by way of an answer and it would take him a couple of minutes before he'd summoned the nerve to speak again. She'd just turned onto the 118 and they were descending into what had once been a flood plain and, until the 1990s, also the best farmland in the county, its vale now filled with two grocery stores, a Canadian Tire, a Dollarama, a Best Western, and a half-dozen fast-food outlets.

"So how do you like Montreal?" he asked as she accelerated towards the strip mall.

Until that moment he thought he'd done a pretty good job of concealing his interest, keeping his glances in her direction fleeting, taking the utmost care not to inhale too deeply when she walked past—her scent slightly citric and altogether rapturous—and doing his best not to stiffen on the odd occasion that she placed her hand on his arm when she asked him for a favour (usually to tell Grover that she was leaving early that afternoon or might be in late the next morning).

He now saw that his efforts had been in vain and, more so, that Suzie appeared genuinely repulsed by the idea of something happening between them outside of work.

Witness how her hands clenched the wheel and how she snuck him a sideways glance to see if he might be inclined to press the point.

When the eager sheen to his gaze suggested he would, she asked, "Have you been?"

"No," he answered. "I always wanted to though." Then after a moment of awkward silence: "I've heard good things."

She made a face that Deacon suspected wouldn't have been much different if he'd asked her what her thoughts were on, say, double anal, and that was enough to keep his lips sealed until they were pulling into the retirement home's parking lot.

The front doors led them into the original ski chalet's A-frame and a sign in the lobby directed them down the hall to the Stella Gardner Memorial Ballroom. Just about everyone in town over the age of sixty, it seemed, had shown up to pay their respects. The hall was a bubbling mass of well-wishers thronged around the happy couple sitting on two rocking chairs fashioned into makeshift thrones and set on a plywood riser in the middle of the room. The Harcourts' daughter-in-law owned a Ukrainian catering company and she'd laid out a lavish buffet—eight kinds of something labelled *varenyky*, though they looked just like perogies, cabbage rolls called *holubtsi*, three steaming pots of *borscht*, and a variety of pastries for dessert.

Deacon joined the end of the line, as good a vantage as any to watch Suzie circulate amongst the well-wishers, taking pictures and soliciting quotes from the happy couple. After a while she looked like she might actually be enjoying herself, and Deacon set to the task of loading his plate with a little of everything. By the time he'd reached the end of the table, an elderly vet in his dress uniform was playing a lethargic version of "Moon River" on an accordion, and a crowd had gathered around Bus and Edina slow dancing, cheek to cheek.

Leaning against the wall, Deacon bided his time between bites, searching amongst the grey hairs for Suzie's chestnut. He still hadn't located it as he was wiping the last of the grease from his plate with a dinner roll, and he made a wager with himself that her car would be gone when he got out to the parking lot. But when he came through the front doors it was still where she'd left it. He turned back into the lobby and spotted her in the lounge beyond the front desk. There were two rainbow-striped vinyl couches arranged at angles in front of an electric fireplace and Suzie was sitting in the nearest beside a young man. He was leaning towards her with his hand on her shoulder and whispering something into her ear. Whatever he was saying must have been exactly what she wanted to hear because she was nodding her head vigorously.

Deacon had only been staring at them for a few seconds but it felt like a lifetime unravelling before him. The way the young man's tan khakis and yellow polo shirt seemed to fit him like a second skin, the chiselled grace to his jawline, the widow's peak of hair swept back from his face, his Romanesque nose, his sky-blue eyes, his everything telling Deacon that he'd have about as much luck with Suzie as he would have teaching a bear to thread a needle.

How long he stared at the two of them, he couldn't say. Maybe a minute, maybe an hour. However long it was, he was snapped out of it by a hand bumping against his. When he turned, he was startled to see Rain standing there.

"Hey, Deke."

She was smiling when she said it, though that quickly gave way to a furrowed brow, seeing Deacon's expression contorting into something akin to genuine alarm.

"Rain," he said, doing his best to cover his apprehension, "what are you doing here?"

"These things are a gold mine."

He didn't have to ponder what she meant for longer than it took for a fan of cards to appear in her hand. Each one had on it a crystal ball and he'd barely had time to read her name spelled out in smoky letters within before Rain said, "Isn't that Suzie Chalmers over there?"

It came as a shock, hearing her say that name. He'd never

58

mentioned Suzie, and he glanced towards the lounge as if it was also a surprise to him that she'd be there too.

"You here together?"

"No. I mean, yes. I mean—it's just business, you know."

Rain was smiling at him in her wry way and it was plain she didn't believe him.

"I'll leave you to it, then," she said.

The fan of cards retracted, disappearing into her hand with the deft precision of a magician's trick, her fingers balling to a fist and Rain bringing that to her lips, blowing into the space between her thumb and forefinger and then flaring her hand out in a sweeping motion with such flourish that Deacon halfways expected a dove to come flying out. She then spun with a twirl of her skirt and as she started off down the hall, Deacon noticed one of her business cards, lying face up on the floor where she'd just stood.

He felt a sudden pang in his chest. She must have seen him gazing longingly at Suzie and had left the card behind as a subtle rebuke. Maybe she'd even seen Suzie pick him up at the *Chronicle* and had followed them. A woman scorned like in some old movie, except that didn't sound like Rain at all. Most of the time it seemed like it was *she* who was doing *him* the favour and would be just as happy if he did go off and find someone closer to his own age.

It was a thought he'd had plenty of times before, most often on the walks to Rain's house. As a balm against the sinking feeling he always felt then and that he could feel creeping up on him now, he bent down and picked up the card. He slipped it into his breast pocket and turned back to the lounge.

Suzie was looking his way. Instead of the grimace he might have expected, she was smiling wide and waving. Deacon smiled back, catching his hand before it could produce an awkward wave of its own. He then started forward, his legs settling into a gait that conveyed the idle contempt of a father summoned from his easy chair by his daughter's newest beau ringing the doorbell.

"Are you ready to go?" Suzie asked him, meeting him halfway.

"Any time you are."

The young man touched her gently on the elbow.

"I have to say my goodbyes," he said. "I'll only be a moment."

She watched him walking down the hall, Deacon watching her, waiting for her to breathe. When she finally exhaled, her lips parted just enough that the air whistled between her teeth and Deacon distracted himself by reaching into his jacket pocket, not looking for anything in particular but finding a loose stick of gum nevertheless.

"He's Bus and Edina's great-grandson," Suzie said as he unwrapped the gum and popped it in his mouth.

"That right?"

"He's doing his PhD at Oxford. In economics. He's a Rhodes Scholar."

"You don't say."

"He's staying up at his parents' cottage on Lake Joseph for the summer while he writes his dissertation," she continued. "I said I'd give him a ride home. That okay?"

"It's your car."

6

O n the return trip, Deacon did his best to block out their
conversation, its fervour buoyant enough to make him feel
like he was drowning. The young man, whom Deacon had since
learned was named Rance—Rance!—had started things off by
asking her how she liked Montreal.

"It's the best," Suzie said. "Have you been?"

"No. I've always wanted to."

"It's amaaaaazing."

Deacon couldn't help but recall the terseness of her reply
when he had said the same and he eyed the door handle, wondering if she'd even bother to stop if he wrenched it open and
flung himself out.

You should have just stayed at the Villa, he told himself. *Got a ride
home with Rain.*

A thought that didn't do a damn thing for him now except
make him feel like he was on the verge of being swallowed into
the back seat.

"You'll have to come and visit," Suzie continued. "I'm living in this great house right in the middle of the Plateau. It has seven rooms, and just two of us. *C'est magnifique!*"

"Sounds it."

"It used to be *une bordel.* That's a brothel."

"Really?"

"It's been in François' family for years."

"Who's François?"

"My roommate." She slapped his arm gently with the back of her hand, chiding him for the jealous tenor to his voice before continuing. "He told me that, back in the 1930s, Errol Flynn used to visit it whenever he was in town."

"Errol Flynn?"

"You know, the silent film star. He was the first Zorro."

"Oh, *that* Errol Flynn."

"He was a real lecher too. He liked girls. The younger the better. He married a fourteen-year-old when he was, like, sixty. He died in Vancouver and, get this, the doctor who pronounced him dead stole his penis."

"He did what?"

"François told me he cut it off when no one was looking."

"Why would he do that?"

"It was worth a fortune."

"His penis?"

"Yeah."

"But how— I mean, how would they have known it was his? A buyer, I mean."

"I asked François the same thing. He said it was covered with warts. You know, like, genital warts. It was famous."

"Lucky for the doctor."

"Totally. And he used to fuck in my bedroom!"

"Maybe that's where he got them."

"I know. Can you imagine?"

"Crazy."

"That's what I love about Montreal. There's so much history there."

They were just then cresting the hill leading towards Main. Suzie signalled left and turned away from town.

"Do you mind walking from here?" she said into the rear-view mirror as she pulled over to the side of the road.

Forcing as genuine a smile as he could, Deacon scooched over in the seat so that at least he wouldn't be exiting into traffic. When he'd made the sidewalk he paused a moment before closing the door.

"You'll have the story to me first thing?" he said, leaning back in.

"Will do, boss."

Deacon couldn't think of anything to say other than, "Perfect."

Closing the door and stepping back onto the sidewalk, he lit a cigarette and took a long slow drag, watching the car driving off into the almost setting sun.

H is apartment over the *Chronicle* was only a ten-minute walk.

He'd made it about halfway there when he remembered he'd meant to drop in on George. He backtracked to Anne Street and followed that to Hiram. He took a left and thirty seconds later he turned left again onto Baker.

George didn't answer the door. After ringing the bell three times, Deacon opened it with his key and stuck his head in. It was dark except for a faint glow from down the hall, which he knew was coming from the light above the kitchen stove. Stepping to the adjacent door, he opened it and checked the garage. George's pickup truck was still there and he was just thinking that he must have taken Trixie out for a walk when the dog bumped her nose against his leg.

"Where is he, girl?" he asked as he bent, scratching the golden retriever behind her ears.

Trixie licked his face and Deacon stood again, turning and walking back through the front door, the dog trailing dutifully behind. He followed the red-brick path into the backyard.

There was a light on in the barn's front window and as Deacon came to end of the walkway he could hear a rapid *clackety-clack*, a sound that immediately called to mind a train hurtling down its track. But he knew right off it wasn't that, it was something else; something he thought he'd never live to hear, which was George hammering away at his old Remington Rand.

Coming towards the barn as if on the sly, Deacon skirted the door, open a crack, and peered through the window, seeing through its dusted glass George sitting at his desk. And just like that the weight he'd been carrying around in his belly all day was lifted by the surge of glee he felt watching the old man bent over the typewriter, his fingers a blur they were pounding so hard at the keys.

George was writing again.

TAYLOR

He'd found the Diplomat Hotel by way of a Google search he'd made two weeks previous. He'd entered "toronto bar fight" and hadn't had to look beyond the first hit to know he'd found the place he was looking for.

"Bar Fight In City's Eastside Sends Two To Hospital" is what it had read.

One click later, he was watching a clip from a local news broadcast, a petite, vaguely Persian-looking woman in a low-cut blouse filling in the particulars while standing in front of a row of Harleys parked at the curb.

"The details are still sketchy," she said, "but this is what we do know."

She went on to report that at approximately 12:30 a.m., police were called to the Diplomat after witnesses reported seeing a man beating another man about the head and back with what appeared to be a broken pool cue. Another man had then stabbed the assailant in the neck with a knife before fleeing the scene on a motorbike. Answering a question about a possible motive, the officer in charge of the investigation told the reporter that it would appear the fight had been the result of an internal conflict within the Flaming Eagles Motorcycle Club, a biker gang known to frequent the establishment. He then went on to ask that anyone who had any information etcetera etcetera, but by then Taylor wasn't really listening anymore.

The mention of a pool cue had planted the seed of an idea in his head, and it was well germinated by the time the reporter was talking to a woman identified as a local resident whose face had been blurred to protect her identity (something that Taylor had found funny in that she must have been pushing four hundred pounds, at least half of which appeared to be oozing out from the elastic band of a phosphorescent lime-green tube top).

"Those *bleepin' bleeps* are fighting ever' damn night," she screamed into the camera. "Only time the cops ever sho' up is when one of 'em ends up bleeding in the street."

To prove her point, the camera cut to a pool of blood draining over the side of the curb before returning to the woman, the sight of her lumbering away, making Taylor laugh, thinking that if they'd really wanted to do her a favour they'd have blurred out the outline of her ass, which had immediately put him in mind of two jumbo-sized beach balls half-filled with Jell-O.

"It ain't right," she was screaming, her hands flailing at the air. "It just ain't right."

"You tell 'em, girl," Taylor had quipped as he keyed in "diplomat hotel toronto."

That had given him an address at the corner of Sherbourne and Queen Street East in the heart of Moss Park, the poorest of Toronto's eastside neighbourhoods, and over the next two weeks he'd driven by it a half-dozen times without finding what he was after. Then, finally, two Sundays later, he'd seen a pair of Harleys parked outside the hotel and that had told him that at least a couple of the Flaming Eagles had returned home to roost.

He drove down a side street and parked beside what passed for a park in that corner of the city but really wasn't much more than a vacant lot comprised of a quarter acre of grass stretched between two walnut trees, the requisite junkie slouched on a concrete bench between them. He called Trevor Lourdes, an aspiring filmmaker whom Taylor's sister had met at York University where she was studying theatre arts, the same as their mother had even though both of them had their sights set on the silver screen. Trevor arrived twenty minutes later in his BMW Hybrid along with his assistant Darren. They were an odd pair, Trevor short and stocky, and cognizant enough of the fact that his buzz cut and oddly oversized forearms made him resemble a young Popeye that he'd had a cartoonish anchor tattooed on his arm; Darren, tall and gangly with a hooked nose and a slick of jet-black hair, himself doing a fair imitation of Olive Oyl.

"You bring it?" Taylor asked Trevor after he'd parked behind his Lexus LX 570 and was exiting the driver's side door.

"That's a check," Trevor said, reaching into his breast pocket and pulling out a button-hole camera mounted on the end of a retractable arm. "I've got an app that lets me control it from my phone."

"What about the mic?"

"Double check."

"What are you waiting for then?"

While Darren taped the mic to Taylor's chest, Trevor took a few of what he called establishing shots with the handy cam he'd brought along as a backup. After he got what he needed, the three of them cut through the park on a diagonal which deposited them onto the sidewalk just shy of the Diplomat's front door.

There were two more Harleys parked at the curb, and Taylor took that as a good sign as he heard the crippling volume of ZZ Top's "Sharp Dressed Man" blaring through the grey steel door at the bottom of five cement steps leading down to the bar's entrance.

Its ceiling wasn't more than a foot above his head and that lent the room the impression that it was slowly sinking into the ground, a feeling reinforced by the four square columns spaced at intervals, their plaster wearing deep seams from floor to ceiling and chunks of it broken away altogether revealing the checkerboard outline of bricks beneath. To the right of the door there was a plywood stage, holes the size of boot heels dotting its warp. The only sign that they'd ever actually had a band playing there was a broken drumstick sitting on the window ledge behind it, crusted over with dust so that it looked like a mouldy cat turd.

A cloud of smoke hung in the room, though there had been a law forbidding smoking in public spaces on the books for some years. Through the haze, Taylor immediately spotted three so-called Flaming Eagles seated at a table in the middle of what would have been the dance floor. Another, smaller than the others and wearing a metal brace clamped over the jeans on his left knee, was hobbling around a pool table in the alcove to the door's left, using his cue as a cane under the watchful repose of an even slighter man dressed the part of a shark—his black leather vest matching the fedora pulled down over a pair of acid flash sunglasses, the hat's band ornamented with a couple or three folded twenty dollar bills.

The only other occupants were the bartender and a man leaning against the far wall with his prodigious arms folded over his chest. He bore a striking resemblance to Gimli the dwarf, though he was six feet tall and wore a black T-shirt that read, *Security*. Taylor would learn his name several seconds later, after catching a look at the woman behind the bar. She appeared to be in her mid-thirties but had the body of a preadolescent boy—all bones and angles—and her face was adorned with enough metal to provide a fair accompaniment to "Jingle Bells." She too was wearing a black T-shirt, though hers was sleeveless and decaled with a headshot of Gimli the Bouncer above the words, *You Got A Problem, Talk To Mike.*

Neither of them looked up when the door closed behind Darren, the muffled thud of it lost to a guitar solo. None of the Flaming Eagles paid them any mind either. Only The Shark marked their entrance by clamping a fresh toothpick between his teeth and flicking at it with his index finger, a sure sign that he knew a bunch of marks when he saw them, which had as much to do with the hundred-dollar haircuts the three young men sported to go with their tan khakis and plaid shirts as it did with the long rectangular case that Taylor was carrying in his right hand. It held the Balabushka replica pool cue his father had bought at auction along with a certificate authenticating it had been the one owned by Eddie Felson in *The Color of Money.* It was his father's favourite film and had inspired in Bryson Wane an enduring passion for the game. In turn, he'd passed this on to his son and they'd spent many an evening re-enacting the ageless rivalry between the generations on a three-and-a-half-by-seven-foot stretch of felt-wrapped slate in their games room, about a million miles removed from the sleazy pool halls where "Fast" Eddie plied his trade though, it seemed, no more than a few feet, figuratively speaking, from the Diplomat's bar.

If anyone in the room knew what his father had paid for the cue it would have been a safe bet Taylor wouldn't have made it more than four steps into the room before someone took more than a cursory interest. The case, though, wasn't much to look at, and while Taylor and his friends weren't exactly the bar's regular clientele, their kind had been known to wander in now and again, looking for a little action beyond what they could find at their country clubs and whatever cocktail lounge was in vogue that season. As such, they'd been able to breeze right up to the counter without attracting any undue attention. Taylor took the lead by yelling for a pitcher of Pabst Blue Ribbon above the music while Darren and Trevor did their best to blend into the background.

While the woman filled his order, Taylor set the case on a barstool, unlocked the clasp, and took out the cue. He screwed its two parts into one as he surveyed the action on the pool table.

They were playing nine ball and it was clear that The Cripple wasn't much of a match for The Shark. He missed what should have been a gimmee on the six in the far corner and Taylor watched the other clear the table. The stakes, two twenties, were secured under a plastic ashtray on the ledge that ran along the alcove's far wall. By the time The Shark was folding them into the fedora's black band, Darren had relocated the pitcher and two of the glasses to the table in the rear corner where he and Trevor had settled in to watch the show.

The ZZ Top song had ended and the ominous tolling of a bell preceded the opening bars of track one on AC/DC's *Back in Black*.

It had been almost four hundred years since John Donne had penned his famous warning, and while it's unlikely that he could ever have imagined his poem would resonate so thoroughly in a scuzzy little biker bar in a city that hadn't been more than a few bundles of sticks overlooking a cornfield when he was putting feather to parchment, there was no doubt that he would have been suitably impressed by the reach of, if not his exact words, then at least the sentiments they expressed. For in that moment, there wasn't a soul in the bar who wasn't thinking that those bells were indeed tolling for Taylor, sipping from his beer as he made his way towards the pool table. Just another cocky rich kid taking a break from exams and overdue papers, come down to test his mettle amongst the great unwashed, thinking his daddy's money would make him immune to their stain, not yet cognizant of the fact that he was done for from the moment he came in, mistaking their reserve for apathy when it was something else entirely: antipathy if not outright hate. For what he was, all that he stood for, and everything in his pockets besides. The cue an added bonus, for even if they didn't know its real value, they knew it was worth something; fifty bucks, maybe, at Squire's Pawn Shop just down the block—n to the power of the unknown times that if they happened to probe beneath the case's padding and found where Bryson had stashed its gold-fringed certificate of authenticity.

Boy you're in for a time of it. Order another pitcher for your friends, you'll see.

Such, anyway, were the thoughts churning through at least Taylor's mind and that he hoped were also worming their way into the head of the largest of the Flaming Eagles. Hoping the way he looked, the way he walked, and the arrogance radiating off of him as if it was his birthright would be enough to serve as cause for his anticipated effect. His only real knowledge of these things, mind you, being movies he'd watched in which it didn't take more than a glance to incite riot in a specimen such as the one doing his best to ignore the cocky young buck just now placing a twenty on the pool table, not saying a word as he looked to The Shark for a nod. He found instead an upward thrust of his chin, the gesture and the drift to his eyes motioning towards The Cripple.

Taylor shrugged.

If that's the way you want to play it, so be it.

He busied himself with a cube of chalk, letting The Cripple rack the balls even though that task should have been passed to him since there was no doubt in his mind that The Cripple'd be the one breaking.

And so it was.

Lining up the cue ball, The Cripple threw a quick glance over his shoulder to see if Taylor was looking. Finding him otherwise distracted by the young woman just now coming out of the bathroom, he leant forward and poked the diamond of racked balls with the tip of his cue, so as to confer a slight advantage. The clatter of balls breaking wasn't enough to break Taylor's fixation on The Girl and chuckling to himself as the four and the six found opposite corners, The Cripple looked back over at the young man. The smile parting the biker's lips suggested he knew right then how the night was going to play and also that he'd been on the receiving end of that shit stick often enough to call it justice, as if the universe had nothing better to do than drop some pretty little rich kid into his world solely to provide him with a little payback for a lifetime of poverty, misfortune, and pain.

Such was the impression the smirk on his face gave Taylor when he watched the scene for the first time, later that night. Then, he couldn't help but think that had The Cripple known then that Taylor's thoughts were in perfect symmetry with his own, it might have robbed The Cripple of the obvious satisfaction he felt as he made the shot and moved into position to bank the seven in off the two. The quicker he finished up with the preliminaries, the sooner the main event could begin, the same thought, in fact, that had been on Taylor's mind from the moment he saw The Girl step through the door in the back marked, Chicks.

She was a skinny little thing with a greasy drape of murky blonde curls teasing at what appeared to be two walnuts set on end within the stretch of a skin-tight orange tank top, and though she didn't look much older than sixteen, she walked with the practised swing of a seasoned pro on the way to her next trick. She'd noticed Taylor right away too. She must have also seen an opportunity in the way he was looking at *her* because as she sat on the largest biker's lap she nuzzled her nose into his neck, using that as a ploy so she could sneak a peek at Taylor to see if he was still gazing after her. When she found he was— smiling at her and even having the audacity to wink—she took her old man's ear in her mouth, suckling at its lobe and running her tongue into its canal while her hand wriggled its way past his over-ripe gut, weeding through his short and curlies until it came to the stump of his manhood, no doubt already inflating by the time her press-on nails were raking against its shaft. Every thrust against his leg and toss of her hair meant not so much to make Taylor jealous as it was to prime the man sitting below her so he'd be good and ready when the time came to teach that arrogant little prick a lesson he'd not soon forget.

Taylor played along with her game by feigning a blush then turned back to the table in time to see the five ball graze the side pocket. It came to a rest not more than an inch away, making his first shot one he could have made blindfolded. Three shots brought him to the nine and when he'd sunk that, The Cripple was already reaching into his back pocket for the wallet chained to one of his belt loops.

Taylor left his winnings where they were and chalked his cue, knowing that he didn't need to look at The Girl again to know that she was still looking at him. The Cripple racked the balls tight but Taylor got a good break nevertheless, sinking the four and making the table into a constellation of perfectly spaced stars. If he'd have been playing his A-game he could have cleared the table shooting from behind his back, but he was saving that for The Shark. He intentionally missed a bank shot for the six, making sure to leave the cue ball wedged between the eight and the far rail where The Cripple would have had to channel Stephen Hawking to work out the physics of even grazing the seven. But The Cripple got more spin than Taylor thought possible without bumping the eight. The white curved into a drastic arc and made solid contact with the seven. For a moment it looked like it had a real chance at the near corner, The Cripple wincing and shaking his head as it caught the bumper and spun out.

It wouldn't have put much of a dent in Taylor's plan had it gone in, and it wouldn't really have mattered either if The Cripple had taken the game because of it. Still, it might have given Taylor pause to think that maybe things weren't as cut and dried as he'd imagined. And a little pause, he knew, might be all that it would take for this night to spin off its rails. So he took careful aim with his next two shots and by the time he was circling towards the cue ball to take a straight shot at the nine, The Cripple had all but conceded and was walking back towards his buddies.

The Girl had since reclined into the big man's lap and was spooning fingernails full of white powder into his nose and hers at intervals. The Cripple leant close to his shoulder and whispered a few words. The big man nodded, then turned his head ever so slightly to get a sense of what he'd been talking about, seeing maybe the start of something developing at the table. Taylor was shaking his head and scowling over at The Shark, who replied by shrugging and chewing idly on his toothpick.

"Hell's Bells" faded into obscurity and in the quiet that followed his voice rose in angry declaration.

"I get to break because it's my fucking table," The Shark said, and Taylor threw up his arms in a huff as he turned towards his beer stowed at the corner edge of the bar. It was all for show, this display of mock injustice, for on his periphery he'd just caught sight of The Girl snatching up the empty pitcher from the Eagles' table on her way to getting a refill.

At the other end of the bar, the keeper was fiddling with her phone at the stereo. The time she spent thumbing at its touchpad suggested she was looking for a perfect match to the mood set by the last song and also that she was a little unsure of how things might proceed. Taylor had a pretty good idea though and as he took a sip from his beer, he threw a quick nod over at the table in the rear. Trevor nodded back and Taylor returned his attention to The Girl. She was leaning over the bar and tilting the pitcher under the taps, not more than two feet away from where Taylor was wiping his mouth with the back of his hand.

Being that close to her, it was obvious to Taylor that she hadn't had a bath in going on a week, something he was able to glean by way of the odour souring the air at a distance of three paces—equal parts cat piss and Jack Daniel's if he had to wager a guess—and by the dribble of long-dried blood leaked from a pimple on her left shoulder picked into an open sore. As she waited for the pitcher to fill, Taylor watched her with something akin to genuine interest. She responded by throwing a few glances in his direction, fleeting enough to be called skittish had they not also been accompanied by a look of gleeful malevolence glaring out of her dime-sized pupils.

"You playin' or not?" The Shark called out from behind. He was leaning over his cue about to break, something he seemed reticent to do without an audience to bear witness to his particular form of genius.

Taylor held up one finger as he tilted his glass to his lips, draining the liquid in three easy gulps and letting his gaze linger on the cleavage squeezing from The Girl's top just long enough to make sure she noticed.

When he finally looked up again she was smiling at him through yellow teeth.

"Lester catches you looking at me like that, it'll mean your ass," she said, scraping at the corner of her mouth with one of her cartoonishly long fingernails, each of them painted fire engine red.

"Who's Lester?" Taylor asked, as if he didn't already know.

She jerked her head and Taylor followed the motion back to her table. Lester was glaring at him as a mama bear might at a hunter who'd just set his sight on her cub. As The Girl pushed herself off the bar she made a sound like a hiccup, which could just as well have been a laugh. Taylor watched the wiggle to her step all the way back to the table. She hadn't made it halfway before Lester was on his feet and Taylor tempered his delight by unscrewing his cue. He fit it back in its case and snapped the clasp shut. When he turned back, Lester wasn't more than two strides away, his hands wrecking balls and his eyes reduced to narrowed slits.

But that would have to wait.

A Louisville Slugger had just materialized between them, and Mike the bouncer was wedging the butt end of it under Lester's chin, stopping him short.

The buttonhole camera wasn't good for much beyond discretion, and so, nine days later, when Taylor was sitting in the back seat of his Lexus, watching the scene unfold on the iPad in his lap, the figures onscreen were reduced to shadows playing against the smoky light. But the microphone taped to Taylor's chest had no problem picking up the bouncer's voice, loud and clear.

"Goddamnit, Lester," he says, "take it outside."

It'd never failed to send a chill up his spine, and as the screen faded to black Taylor could still feel the hairs hackling over the back of his neck, his breath held in anxious anticipation of what was to come next.

Taylor watched it through to the end. He was just about to click play so he could watch it all over again when he heard Davis mutter something, sounded like "shit," from the driver's seat.

He looked up from the screen and dislodged the Beats from his right ear, peering between the seats at the hulking black man behind the wheel as if he was going to ask him what was wrong. But they hadn't spoken a word on the two-hour drive from Toronto, and Taylor had no intention of breaking the silence now.

A moment later, the faint strains of a siren arose from behind and he leaned forward just far enough to see the speedometer's digital readout. It was just dropping below 110, a far cry from the 140 he was doing before they'd turned off the 11 just south of Tildon, letting the two-lane 118 lead them in a circuitous route towards Hidden Cove Road where Taylor's family had, his father liked to brag, their own little piece of paradise. Still, thirty clicks over the limit was plenty to get the attention of one of the local Roscoes, which was what his dad called the members of Tildon's police force. The reference was lost on his son but not on his mother who, when he was a kid, Taylor would hear scoff from the passenger seat whenever her husband complained about being pulled over yet again, most often for speeding on this very stretch of road.

"They're just doing their job," his mother would chide. "If you don't like getting pulled over, maybe you should slow down."

But getting Bryson Wane to listen to reason was about as easy as it would have been to drive the family's Volvo through the proverbial needle's eye. For most of the year, the station wagon collected dust in the six-car garage beside their palatial residence in The Windfield's, an exclusive neighbourhood in Toronto's York Mills. When Taylor was young, his dad always made a point of driving it up to the cottage himself the first weekend of summer, giving his driver, and his wife's, the week off, the same as his own father had when he was a boy. Over the years, he'd been stopped so many times that the Roscoes, to a one, had come to know him by name and greeted him with wide smiles as he rolled down his window.

"Well, hello, Mr. Wane," they'd say, "so nice to see you again," making their meaning clear by way of a quip about the police station needing a computer upgrade or a new snowmobile for their fleet, before thanking him for his generosity as they handed him his ticket.

The cruiser was coming up fast behind now, its reds and blues flashing over the evergreens creating an unbroken wall on either side of the road. Davis's hands were gripped hard on the wheel and the muscle running in a thick cord up the side of his neck gave a sudden twitch so it was clear to Taylor that his run-ins with the law had been of an entirely different sort.

And on the heels of that thought, another: the look of surprise on the face of whatever Roscoe it was who pulled them over, seeing that it wasn't Young Master Wane driving the Lexus LX 570 so plainly registered in his name. His confusion given over to alarm as the officer tilted his flashlight towards the rear seats, its glare scouring over the bulge as big as a McIntosh apple cut in half swelling over Taylor's left eye, and that giving the officer every reason to suspect foul play.

"There a problem here, Mr. Wane?" he'd ask, the only thing to express the apprehension he felt at the sight of the hulking black man driving and the rich prick's son, bruised and bloody, in the back seat being the way his hand ever so casually reached to unclip the strap securing his sidearm.

Taylor answering, "No problem, officer," even as he nodded, the pretence of fear widening his eyes, his own hand reaching for the door latch beside him. He'd yell, "He's got a gun!" and throw himself backwards and out of the cab so as to be well clear of the volley of shots sure to follow.

It'd serve that son of a bitch right, Taylor thought as the SUV pulled onto the shoulder, and thus he was sorely disappointed when, a moment later, the cruiser raced past, its siren and lights almost immediately swallowed up by a bend on the road ahead.

Davis breathed a sigh of relief and with nothing to look forward to but a return to the stilted silence creating separate worlds of the front and back seats, Taylor slipped the headphone back onto his ear, returning his attention to the screen.

I n the three weeks since it had been shot, he'd replayed the video more than a dozen times which was barely a drizzle amidst the ocean of viewers who'd watched it after it had been posted to affluenza.com. The website had been Trevor Lourdes's idea. Trevor's father, an entertainment lawyer, had bought him his first camera for his thirteenth birthday and during his teenage years Trevor had accumulated the thirty-odd hours of footage that comprised the fledgling dot-com's archive, tagging along after his older brother, Nick, and his friends, all of whom spent their idle hours testing the bounce of the safety net provided by their parents' considerable fortunes.

It was one of Nick's friends, a Vito Babič, who'd provided Trevor with the inspiration for affluenza.com. Six months previous, he'd swiped the keys to The Toybox—his father's luxury car dealership—in retaliation for having been banned from the lot by his dad two days earlier when, drunk and coked-up, he'd crashed his Aston Martin into a Ferrari Testarossa heading out of the parking lot for a test drive. His dad had changed the security code for the retractable door in the rear of the display room in the interim, leaving young Vito no apparent choice but to drive The Toybox's most expensive car, a McLaren 650s Spider, through the front window. The ensuing police chase was captured on film by Chuck Milner, the owner of the Flyby Helicopter Academy. That evening, he was conducting one of his popular "Eye in the Sky Traffic Watch" classes and thus had the good fortune to be flying over the 401 at the moment Vito was re-enacting a few of his favourite scenes from *The Fast and the Furious*, a half-dozen police cars in hot pursuit.

The chase had ended at a section of the highway that had been reduced to one lane during resurfacing. Vito hadn't seen the preceding warning signs, or simply hadn't cared. When the cement barriers protecting the road crew had finally come into view, so said the police report, at a rate of 51.389 metres per second, he had approximately three quarters of a second to swerve into the only available lane as a last-ditch effort to avoid what anyone watching must have assumed would be a fiery end to his midnight joyride. Vito had somehow managed this feat with inches to spare, though even his (now) well-documented skills behind the wheel hadn't been enough to prevent the Spider from fishtailing out of control, its rear shortly thereafter impacting at 165 kilometres per hour with the back of an airport shuttle van transporting the members of the First Baptist Church of Toronto's choir to Pearson International for the red-eye to O'Hare where they were scheduled to perform at a sister church in the Windy City. There were no injuries from *that* crash besides a few bumps and bruises and a concussion sustained by Jasper Delaine, a plumber who sang baritone. The same couldn't be said about what happened after the McLaren was catapulted into the air. Its trajectory reached a height of four metres, plenty for it to clear the cement barricade on its way to barrel-rolling some one hundred and ten metres through the construction site and crashing to an abrupt halt against the back of an asphalt spreader.

That Vito walked away with only first-degree burns over his left arm, shoulder, and leg from where the hot asphalt had flowed through the smashed driver's side window would later form his father's prime selling point for the entire McLaren line. The families of the three workmen he'd bowled over on his way to earning himself six months' worth of skin grafts wouldn't be able to count themselves so lucky. All were killed on contact and so it was left to their wives to provide victims' impact statements on the occasion of Vito's sentencing. And while the Right Honourable Mathias Crawley himself was seen to dab at his eye with the cuff of his gown more than once at the sight of these widows weeping brazenly upon the stand, he then went on to say that he had no choice but to agree with the defence since it was eminently clear to him that Vito's parents—"owing to their wealth and the corresponding lack of regard for anyone else that it had instilled in them"—had failed to provide any sort of moral guidance to their teenage son and thus he could hardly be held culpable for his actions.

Two weeks after Judge Crawley had suspended Vito's sentence, Nick, for old times' sake, had provided Trevor with ten minutes' worth of footage from The Toybox's security cam. It had opened with Vito standing on the hood of a Porsche 911 GTS Cabriolet and using its front seat as a urinal. He had a sledgehammer propped on his shoulder and he put it to good use during the next eight and a half minutes. His rampage through the showroom was replayed several times during Vito's trial, first by the prosecution to prove their point and then by the defence to prove an entirely different one. Trevor too, saw great potential in Vito's burst of filial acrimony and within a month of becoming affluenza.com's inaugural post, it would rack up a shade over 350,000 hits, along with amassing 12,000 followers, thus providing a suitably attentive audience for Taylor's video, shot several weeks later.

In the first week alone, it had accumulated over 250,000 views, and Trevor had had high hopes that it would be his first post to breach a million. When it had bottomed out at just under 800,000 he'd asked Taylor if he wouldn't mind providing some commentary in hopes of pushing it over the edge. Taylor had originally dismissed the idea, the video having been made for an audience of one and not millions anyway. Faced with the prospect of a two-hour drive into exile, he'd conceded that it would at least give him something to do besides stewing in the back seat. But every time he started it again, he'd become swept up in the drama of the thing and thus far hadn't managed more than a few words of introduction.

So it is that, clicking play now, his voice rings out over the establishing shot Trevor had taken of the Diplomat Hotel.

"I'd found the Diplomat Hotel by way of a Google search I made two weeks previous," it says. "I put in Toronto plus bar plus fight and didn't have to look any further than the first hit before I knew that I'd found the place I was looking for."

It was all he'd managed and as the scene cuts from a shot of his Google search results to the Persian-looking reporter doing her spiel in front of the row of motorcycles, he tried to think of what he might say when the footage caught up with him walking down the cement steps leading into the bar.

He'd broached the subject with Trevor, last Thursday, when he'd gone down to the pool to do his laps. He'd found him and Darren lounging in deck chairs and drinking mint juleps though it wasn't yet ten. Trevor had suggested something that explained why he was there.

"I think it's pretty obvious," Taylor countered. "I'm there to get in a fight."

"But *why* do you want to get in a fight?"

Answering that question would mean compressing ten years of his life into a few short lines, a task that seemed well beyond his own meagre proclivity with words. Mentioning as much to Trevor, Trevor sparked up a joint of what he called his "Inspiration Kush" (not to be confused with his "First Draft Bud" or his "Polish Blend"). Trevor had barely taken a toke before his eyes had suddenly widened, the spark of an idea flaring to life.

"We could film a flashback sequence," he said.

"A flashback sequence?"

"Yeah. You know, to when you were a kid and you beat the shit out of your cousin."

"How do you know about that?"

"Sandy."

"She told you?"

"How your cousin—what was his name?"

"Justin."

"How Justin made you eat dog shit that one time and your dad hired a ninja to teach you how to kick his ass? Shit, it's her favourite 'Lifestyles of the Rich and Fucked-Up' story. I must've heard her tell it a dozen times."

"Master Lo wasn't a ninja." It was all Taylor could think to say.

"But he played one in that movie—"

"*Two Minutes to Midnight,*" Darren piped in.

"A true classic of the genre."

And though it most surely wasn't, they both nodded in deference to Taylor's mother, *Two Minutes to Midnight* being, as it was, her last role upon the silver screen.

Trevor then took another hit of inspiration and it seemed to do the trick.

"We'd need a couple of kids," he said, passing the joint to Darren.

"For the flashback?"

"Yeah."

"I got a nephew. Calvin. He's only nine but he's big. We could use him to play Justin."

"Calvin have any friends?"

"I'd expect."

"We could get one of them to play Taylor."

"Yeah, yeah, yeah."

Turning back to Taylor, Trevor held his hands boxed in front of him to simulate a viewfinder.

"Picture this," he said. "We open on a close-up of a young Taylor's face. Eyes wide, nostrils flaring, mouth parted in a bestial roar. Fists flying in slow motion. Cut to Justin's face. Fear in his eyes as the blows rain down upon him. Freeze-frame as a spatter of blood sprays from his nose. Then cue narration: 'I was ten years old the first time I went looking for a fight.'"

"Hell ya." This from Darren. Then after another toke: "But we'd need to explain why he was beating the shit out of him though, wouldn't we?"

"We could film another a flashback."

"A flashback within a flashback?"

"Tarantino does it all the time."

"Fuckin' right he does."

Trevor had pulled out his pad and they'd set to storyboarding the schematics of the thing. By the time Taylor had finished his laps, Trevor had dispensed with the notebook and Darren was hunched over a MacBook, typing as they bantered dialogue back and forth.

"Such a fucking pussy," Trevor said apparently playing Justin. "Just like your dad."

"My dad's not a fucking pussy," Darren countered as Taylor. "No, scratch 'fucking.' Taylor was a prissy little kid, right. He wouldn't have said fucking."

"So: 'He's not a pussy.'"

"Yeah."

"Hell he ain't! When he was a kid my dad said even the girls used to beat on him."

"That's good."

"He's a fucking pussy alright."

"Well, at least he isn't a bum."

"You calling my dad a bum?"

"And a drunk too. Everyone knows."

"Then Justin sucker-punches Taylor in the gut?"

"Yeah."

"Do we cut to a shot of Justin picking up a piece of dog shit from the yard?"

"No, I think we stay with Taylor, curled up on the lawn. Justin sits on top of him and squeezes his nose shut between his thumb and forefinger. Taylor's mouth opens wide, gasping for air, and that's when we see Justin holding a dried-up turd in his other hand."

And while it didn't exactly happen that way, it was close enough that seeing Trevor and Darren taking such obvious delight in his torment had Taylor snatching up the laptop on his way past, flinging it on a high arc into the deep end of the pool.

He heard a splash that he figured must have been Trevor diving in after it because it was Darren's voice that followed him into the house.

"So I guess that means no flashback then?"

While Taylor hadn't responded, he was thinking the same thing making his way up the stairs towards the kitchen as he did now watching himself descend to the Diplomat's basement door.

It's fine just the way it is.

As the dinge of the cement stairway opened into the smoky haze of the bar, he could feel the Lexus slanting steeply downwards. Glancing up, he saw through the window the shadowed outline of what he knew were thirty-foot walls of pink granite rising on either side of the vehicle.

When he was young, it seemed to him that summer had never really begun until they'd reached the rock cut. It ran for half a kilometre, and the whole time they were passing through the canyon blasted out of a hump of Canadian Shield, Taylor would be kneeling in the back seat, pressing his nose against the window's glass, staring up at the pine trees perched at precarious angles atop the bluff and tracing over the cracks in the stone, all of them leaking water and growing deeper every year so that it seemed to him it was only a matter of time before the whole thing would come crashing down.

His mother would cast him reproachful glances from the passenger seat, telling him to sit back down and put his belt on, but the tone of her voice wouldn't become insistent until the rock walls had begun to taper as they sloped towards the lake. Only then she'd say, "I mean it," and Taylor would slump back into his seat, though he wouldn't yet put his belt back on. Instead he'd lean forward, craning to look through the windshield where the canyon's terminus would seem like a doorway opening onto a summer wonderland: the road curving as it dipped towards the bay, the azure of its waters glimmering as it lapped against the expanse of sand that curved along the shore. On the near side of the beach, the two dozen or so log cabins comprising the Meeford Bay Resort were scattered about the wooded glade that ran between the shore and the highway. At its far edge, there was a channel leading into a lagoon harbouring a fleet of sail boats, their bright orange and red triangles catering to the wind as those in use angled for the open waters of Lake Mesaquakee. And beyond them, the motor boats carving deep grooves far out on the lake would tease thoughts of the Wanes' thirty-five-foot Baja Outlaw and how his father would spend hours at its wheel dragging him behind on an inner tube, Taylor never so happy as he was when he was laying on his back, watching the clouds scroll by, the heat of the sun tempered by the cool spray of water spattering against his bronzing skin.

But as the headlights sparkled off the quartz running in veins through the granite, the canyon now seemed to him more like the walls of a prison than a doorway, a feeling heightened by the dark and the fact that he'd been relegated to the back seat of his own vehicle.

That it was one of his childhood heroes driving only added insult to injury. Throughout his career with the then-burgeoning UFC, he'd been known as The Reaper, in deference to his fighting name, Grimm, though, earlier that afternoon, he'd been introduced by Bryson Wane as Davis Grimes, both father and son knowing full well that an introduction was hardly necessary. Taylor had seen every one of his dozen fights as a heavyweight, three of them live on pay-per-view and the last at the Bell Centre in Montreal where his father had wrangled two ringside tickets for the UFC's first event north of the border. So he'd been on hand to see The Reaper lose his final bout, one that would have put him in line for a chance at the heavyweight title if a submission hold hadn't broken his right arm in the second round, forever ending his career in the octagon.

Earlier that afternoon, he'd been dumbstruck when his father had led him into the glassed-in dome off their kitchen that housed their Olympic-sized swimming pool and he'd seen *that* man standing beside their Jacuzzi wearing nothing but a pair of black fighting trunks and glaring at him with the same stone face he'd greeted each one of his opponents.

"Well aren't you going to say hello?" his father had finally asked, nothing in the way he smiled at his son as he nudged him forward with the tips of his fingers to indicate that the man standing at the far end of the pool wasn't anything but an early present for his son's birthday, being as it was, less than a week away.

"Go on, then."

Taylor didn't need to be told twice. He'd set off at a jog towards Davis, whose head was now lowered, bent to the task of fitting a pair of sparring gloves over his hands. At the time, the gesture hadn't meant more to Taylor than the red bow his mother had tied around the hood of the Mustang GT they'd bought him for his sweet sixteen. And that thought coming into his head at that exact moment added a little skip to his step. The Reaper being here, hired by his father nonetheless, signified to him that all those years trying to wear his father down had finally paid off, the same way the brochures he left scattered around the house when he was fifteen had netted him his dream car. It was only later when he was sitting on his bed after Dr. Coates, the Wane family's physician, had given him a thorough going over to make sure nothing was broken that he'd understood he'd been mistaken about that and maybe a lot of other things too.

He'd heard his phone *ka-ching*, the ring tone he'd given his father's number ever since the day he'd complained that his kids treated him more like an ATM than a father.

Here's something else for you to post online, the text had read.

It had been accompanied by a video from the security camera standing guard over the pool and its first few frames clearly revealed his father nodding his head at Davis Grimes the moment after he'd prodded his son forward. Davis seemed to take it as a sign that the reason he'd been hired was fast approaching and towards that end he'd begun putting on his gloves. To Taylor, that subtle lilt to his father's chin would come to mean something else entirely. It was the moment, he saw, that signified the end of his dream of fighting in the UFC. His father was telling him, in no uncertain terms, that the time had come to put away such a childish notion, and since

Taylor had proven he wasn't man enough to do it himself then it was left to him to show his son the error of his ways.

But that realization was yet to come.

In the two seconds that it took him to traverse the space between himself and The Reaper, Taylor had never been happier. When he reached Davis, he put out his hand and said, "Mr. Grimm, it's so nice to meet you. I'm a big fan, really, a huge fan." His back was to his father so he wouldn't see him nod again until he'd watched the footage an hour later, his father as stone-faced as the man before him suddenly striking out with a left jab, catching Taylor square in the jaw. The force, and more so the surprise, knocked him off his feet, the shock in his eyes plainly visible upon replay as he stared up in static befuddlement at the giant towering above.

The camera wasn't equipped with sound, so it was left to his memory to recall what his father had said then.

"Well, what are you waiting for?" he'd chided. "Defend yourself."

Dutifully, Taylor pushed himself back to his feet, firming his resolve, not so much against the next blow but because he was still trying to give his father the benefit of the doubt, still trying to believe that he'd tracked down one of his childhood heroes to provide him with a few tips rather than as a means of teaching him a different lesson entirely, that realization still as hidden as the kindly doctor who was then secreted somewhere in the wings, waiting to act out his role in a rich man's play, the same way Davis Grimes was waiting on Taylor beside the pool, his arms lowered and his hands relaxed as if he needn't worry about defending himself from the barely-a-man standing before him.

The fight, if that's what it could be called, lasted less than a minute. The Reaper got on top of him and his "ground and pound" left Taylor feeling like he'd been stonewashed and his face mottled into a ghastly mask. Seeing it now reflected back at him in the window, his hands balled into fists as if he meant to pound at the seat, screaming, "It's not fucking fair!"—an act of paltry outrage that wouldn't accomplish anything except, perhaps, providing The Reaper a small measure of satisfaction. That was the last thing Taylor was inclined to do just then, and he took a long slow breath, same as he would have the moment the referee dropped his hands signalling the match was to begin, the expression in the window's reflection assuming the blank stare that he always carried within him onto the mat. It was a look he'd cultivated over the hours he'd spent skipping rope in front of the mirror in the Wane family's personal gym, meant to impress upon his opponent that he really didn't care one way or the other how the match might unfold, a notion immediately confounded by the deft precision of his movements and the ferocity of his attack once the fight had begun.

Outside the window, the rock wall tapered. A thin fringe of pine trees rose in its stead, and beyond he could see red and blue lights flaring against a backdrop of smoke. The SUV slowed as it approached the police cruiser parked on the side of the road, blocking the entrance to a picnic park nestled on the banks of what a small green sign on the shoulder ahead informed him was the Moose River. There were two more cruisers parked on the near side of a figure eight that looped through the stand of pines and cedars. Beyond the screen of trees, he could make out three fire trucks, their headlights and hoses all trained on a vehicle of some sort parked in the far left-hand corner and billowing black smoke. Maybe a minivan.

Nothing worthy of his attention, and he turned back to the iPad, immediately finding a succour in the familiarity of the scene unfolding before him onscreen.

B y the time the vehicle was turning left onto Hidden Cove Road, he'd watched it through to the end again.

The Tylenol 3s Dr. Coates had given him had long worn off and the veins running along his temples were pounding with a heartbeat of their own. He closed the flip cover over the iPad and stowed it in its carrying case and had just zipped that when the SUV turned left again. Habit had him craning to look between the seats just as the headlights glittered over the Wane family's crest: two gold-embossed rams locked in mortal combat and welded to the wrought-iron fence that barred entry to their summer hideaway. A guard who Taylor had never seen before stuck his head out of the gatehouse and waved at The Reaper. A moment later, the gate slid open. As the SUV drove through, Taylor caught a glimpse of the guard picking up the phone, no doubt to call his boss to tell him that "The Package" had arrived.

The dim yellow glow from the rows of Victorian-era gas street lamps his grandfather had imported from Italy led the car on a winding trail amongst the property's ten acres of lightly mani-cured forest. Between the trees he could just make out splashes of colour from the vehicles staggered along the circular drive. Metallic red that must have been Trevor's BMW, the lime green of his sister's Prius, and a spectrum of other hues conspiring to shatter any hope he had for a few days alone to lick his wounds and to think about what he might do next. He could hear the urgent throb of a bass line as the driveway looped away from the lake and he turned from the house and gazed forlorn at the boathouse just then passing by. He'd made the apartment above it into his own little warren ever since he was twelve, and now, he knew, it would come to serve as his own private cell.

The vehicle was then angling on a direct line for the cot-tage's thirty-foot cathedral archway, the top half of which was a stained-glass depiction of their crest set against the jagged peak of a snow-topped mountain. Below it, two rams made of granite reared up on either side of a twenty-thousand-dollar set of double doors made of Bocote wood imported from northern Mexico and aged to look medieval. When he was a kid he used to swing from their horns while he was waiting on his mom to drive him to his golf and tennis lessons, and he could see that someone was now using them to similar effect.

His sister's latest boyfriend—an actor named Marty or Max, he couldn't remember which—was standing bent over at the edge of the marble steps leading to the front door, his arm draped around the horn rising from the ram on the right, swaying back and forth though it was hardly in the service of play. He was puking into his mother's azaleas, using the horn to keep himself upright and not doing a very good job of that either. Sandra was bent over behind him, rubbing his back and offering him gentle words of comfort.

As the SUV pulled up to the house, she looked up, startled, into the headlights' bright, her alarm shortly given way to a smile radiating from her lips, seeing that it was only her brother's vehicle. She was the spitting image of their mother in her prime, who had then drawn an easy comparison to a young Kim Novak. The resemblance was made more so in that she was wearing the Chanel that Celia (then) Birch had worn the one time she'd been invited to the Oscars. It was a simple midnight-black affair with a neckline that plunged almost to her navel, the pair of matching stilettos that had once walked the red carpet making Sandra's every step seem like a high-wire balancing act as she tottered down the stairs towards the driveway.

Taylor took his time getting out, keeping his back to her on the pretence of fishing for his duffel bag over the back seats.

"Bro," she yelled, stretching the word like an elastic band about to snap, so that Taylor knew she was likely to be about as drunk as her boyfriend. "Weren't you supposed to be leaving for Florida today? That *Fight Club* thingy."

"There's been a change of plans."

He'd just got a hold of one of the duffel's straps but hadn't yet summoned the nerve to turn around.

"Won't Monica be surprised."

Hearing the name "Monica" was like a gong going off in his already battered head. He tempered his alarm by stowing the iPad case in the duffel and then searching about the side compartment, making sure he'd remembered his toothbrush (which he already knew he had).

"I thought she was in rehab."

"She got out last week."

"So what's she doing here? She hates the outdoors."

"She's on a health kick. That's what she says anyway, but I think she's just using that as an excuse to kill me with tennis. Four hours yesterday and then she's bang, bang, banging at my door at seven o'clock this morning for round two. But I'm trying to be supportive."

"That doesn't sound like you."

"I'm her friend. And that's what friends do."

"Do friends also try to run you over with their car?"

"That's the old Monica. She's changed. You'll see."

"I'd rather not."

"Well, she's dying to see you again. You're practically all she's talked about since she got here. I can only imagine how she's going to try to kill you."

Taylor cast her a smirk to show her what he thought of that. Sandra was grinning when he'd turned his head, but her mirth quickly turned to alarm, seeing the bulge over his left eye.

"Jesus, what happened to your face?"

"I forgot the golden rule."

"What's that again?"

"Don't fuck with Dad."

Her brow scrunched like she was trying to figure out what he meant.

"The video," she finally said. "The fucking video. The video, fuck."

And then she was spinning like a wobbly top back to the open door, puffing her chest out like she'd been taught in acting school when the scene called for her to project.

"Trevor!" she screamed. "Get the fuck out here! See what you've done to my brother!"

There was no reply from the house beyond a slight uptick in the music's beat and she stormed off up the stairs, hollering through a drunken slur, "Trevor! TREVOR!" Her voice lost to the song's drone as she disappeared into the house.

Fetching the bag from the seat, Taylor slung the duffel over his shoulder. When he turned back, Marty or Max was standing in front of him, adjusting his tie, trying to make a good impression, this being the first time he'd meet his new girlfriend's older brother. All that he managed to achieve though was to smear the vomit running in dribbles down its silky sheen and curdle some of it over his hand. He didn't seem to notice as he then held out his hand to Taylor.

His mouth opened but all he managed to utter was, "I'm—" before his chest gave a sudden buck.

Ten years on the mat had taught Taylor to expect the unexpected, and he was already dodging backwards when the geyser erupted from Max or Marty's mouth—a thin gruel the colour of orange Kool-Aid. He avoided the main thrust but was unprepared for the reach of its splatter, now washing over his sneakers.

Taylor's hands balled into fists and he was on the point of knocking the stupid right out of that boy when he felt the sharp sanction of a steel grip clenching his arm. When he glanced backwards, The Reaper was scowling at him. It was the way he'd confronted each of his twelve opponents while they'd touched gloves and he'd peered down at all but the last of them sprawled out on the mat with the same. It had been a devastating blow to Taylor, watching that final match ringside with his dad, seeing one of his heroes not five feet away, his face pressed into the octagon's mesh, his eyes looking like they were about to pop, his opponent on top of him, doing his best to rip his arm clean off.

And even though the memory now spoke to him not of The Reaper's failure but of his own, recalling it provided a small measure of satisfaction. It wasn't much, given the way his day had turned on him, but enough anyway that he was able to contort his features into the approximation of a boyish grin as he shrugged from the other's grasp.

Marty or Max was gaping at him as Taylor turned his feet in the direction of the boathouse. There was a span of spittle from his chin to his tie and his top lip was trembling, like he was about to cry.

"I—" he was saying.

But Taylor was already pushing past, forcing his legs into the idle gait of a boy with only a carefree summer ahead even as he muttered under his breath, "Could this day possibly get any fucking worse."

7

The night after he discovered George was writing again, Deacon returned to the barn just after dark.

He'd fallen asleep the night before, sitting against the barn's wall, immersed in the thunderous *clackety-clack* that seemed to be striking the very bricks shouldering his back. He'd awoken into darkness sometime after one by the first drops of a spring shower that would see him soaked by the time he got home. Because of that and because it had been years since he'd read any of George's Fictions, he thought he'd bring along a copy of *The Stray* to keep him awake.

Though it was George's last book, all five times Deacon had read through his corpus he'd started with it and didn't see any reason to change his ways now. With the clock on his bed stand reading 9:00, he slipped it from the bookshelf beside his bed. Looking down at its cover, the sight of a man carrying a woman out of a pool beneath a waterfall inspired in him the same flurry of anticipation and dread it had the first time he'd done so.

He'd been nine and even then he knew George to be the author of twelve novels, and also the editor-in-chief of the *Chronicle*, though he mostly thought of him as the old man who would drop by three or four times a year to go hunting with his father.

The Riises lived in a log house Deacon's dad had built on the fifty acres he'd bought with his inheritance when he'd arrived from Denmark, some twenty years previous. Their driveway was a stone's throw from where Falconbridge Road dead-ended at the marsh that swallowed half their property as if the loggers who, well over a century ago, had slaved to carve its ten kilometres out of the muskeg had finally given it up as a lost cause, seeing no end to the swamp's reach. Being so far from town, they rarely had any visitors, so George's arrival was greeted with great jubilation. He always had presents for Deacon and his younger brother, Abel—airplanes made out of balsam wood and whirligigs that spun into the air when you pulled a string, and once a wooden bow and a quiver full of arrows he said he'd made for his own son when he was young—and while their father went to fetch his rifles, Deacon and Abel would rush out to greet him, eager to find out what he'd brought for them this time.

He'd once been a tall man, over six foot four. Age had stooped him at the shoulders so that it had been years since he stood to his full height. To the boys, though, he seemed almost a giant, their own father barely five foot eight, he'd joke, on a windy day, and their mother shorter than him by a head. When they crowded around George, he'd hold whatever he'd brought above their grasping fingers, making them jump for it, their black lab, Trigger, barking and jumping along with them.

And after he finally relented, lowering it to within their reach, he'd say, "Go on, now, wake your father. It's too nice a day to be sleeping it all away."

"He ain't asleep," Deacon would protest.

"He isn't? Then where the hell is he?"

"He's fetching the rifles."

"Well, he's sure taking his sweet Mary time about it."

He'd then turn to the house and catch sight of the boys' mother, Rose, standing at the porch's rail, using her hand to shield her eyes against the bright and maybe also against the unease she felt seeing the larceny in the old man's gaze. She was thirty-two when she'd had Deacon but even then it would have been hard not to mistake her for a woman well into the change of life; her face, as it was, a record of the hard times she'd endured before she met Bergin Riis—one of her top front teeth missing, a mangled lip bearing testament to its abrupt removal, one scar amongst a checkerboard's worth bearing the ragged stitch marks of a bathroom patch job, her nose broken and askew. Hardly anyone's idea of a beauty queen, but still George would do a fair impression of a slide whistle on his way to saying, "On second thought, why don't you just go on and let him sleep."

He'd then make a great show of spitting in both palms. Using the sputum to slick back the thick wash of salt and pepper hair from his forehead, he'd bend to his reflection in the window of his black 1970 Ford Ranger XLT and run his fingers through the tangles of his long white beard though it was unlikely anything short of a pair of scissors could tame its wild.

"But I told you he weren't," Deacon would say. "Look, he's coming down the stairs now."

At that George would press his nose to the window, seeing through its twin that Bergin was just then stepping into the yard, carrying his ancient Lee-Enfield in one hand and his even older Martini in the other.

"Drat," he'd curse, mussing up his hair again and frizzing his beard so that when he popped his head back up over the truck's rooftop he'd look half-crazed.

"There you are," he'd say as Bergin approached. "Your boy said you were asleep."

"Too nice a day to be in bed."

"That's what I told him."

Deacon's father would set the Enfield on the hood of George's truck along with a box of shells, and George would shake his head and scowl, "How come you never let me use the Martini?"

"I told you a hundred times," Bergin would reply, "I'll sell it to you and then you can use it any time you want."

"Now what in the hell would I want with an old piece of shit like that?"

George would be grinning when he said it, and Bergin would be grinning back as he held out his hand.

"Good to see you, George," he'd say, shaking, and George would let his eyes wander back to Rose.

"Good to see one of you anyway."

In all the years he'd been dropping by, the routine had changed so little that when Deacon reflected upon them, his visits seemed to all blend into one. The only time there'd be any deviation beyond the negligible was when he visited in June or early July. Then, while he loaded the shells into the Enfield, he'd say, "So'd you hear . . ." filling in the dots by relating some dismal end met by one of the cottagers who, every year, flocked north seeking a refuge from the city.

When George was done, Deacon would look up at his father and comment, "It's like they ain't born with any sense south of the forty-five, eh, Pa?"

It was a line he'd copped from Bergin—the forty-five being the forty-fifth parallel, which the locals used to demarcate themselves from the city folk in the south. Hearing his son say it, so loud and proud, would bring a smile to his father's lips.

"You got that right," he'd answer. "They ain't yet invented a telescope big enough to see an end to *their* folly."

"It's a terrible thing, really," George would then say, shaking his head, his own mournful expression a sharp contrast to the others' amuse.

George had been on hand plenty of times when the members of the Tildon Police Services hauled another body out of the water, so maybe he was thinking about that or could have been the looks on the faces of the victim's family who'd be waiting on shore, praying for some good news. Whatever was on his mind, the dark clouding his features would shortly depart and he'd look up. There'd be a trace of a smile pulling at the corners of his lips and he'd click his tongue against his teeth as he said, "But, then, you know what they say: summer hasn't really begun until the first tourist's died," as if their sacrifice had been in the service of some greater good.

Deacon's father would respond that it was looking to be a long summer then, or a short one, depending on the date, and George would say, "You're right about that."

Turning to Trigger, Bergin would whistle and the dog would bound ahead, racing for the path that led between the barn and the woodshed. Trigger'd stop just short of the old John Deere tractor Bergin had bought for five hundred dollars and ever since had sat where the previous owner had parked it after the money had changed hands, useless for anything but the nesting grounds for a pair of starlings that returned every spring and as a plaything for his two sons. The dog would bark and his master would hurry to catch up but George would linger a moment. He'd bend to Deacon and whisper into his ear, "There's something for your mother in the front seat. Be a good lad, mind she gets it."

"Come on, then," Bergin would yell impatiently over his shoulder as he passed the tractor, "the day's a-wastin'!"

George would ruffle his hand through Deacon's hair and then stand, setting his navy blue Tilley hat on his head and tipping the brim of it towards Rose as he traversed the yard. In the truck's passenger seat there'd be a bouquet of flowers and a gift-wrapped box of liquorice allsorts, which Rose had often said were her favourite. Deacon would snatch them up, and running towards the house, he'd cast barely a glimpse at George and his father disappearing behind the barn, eager as he was to share in his mother's bounty.

After he'd turned nine, more often than not, he'd eat the handful of candy she'd given him peering up at the top row of the bookshelf in their living room, which is where his father kept all twelve of George's novels. The lower shelves were occupied by duplicate sets of the complete works of Jack London, one in English and the other in Danish, a dozen books by Farley Mowat, an alphabetized row of miscellany covering topics ranging from astronomy to zoology, and twenty-six *Farmer's Almanacs* spanning the years between 1971 to 1997, though Deacon had only ever seen his father read George's Fictions.

Neither Deacon nor Abel had ever seen the inside of a classroom, their mother telling them that after what the government schools had done to her people it wasn't likely that she herself could possibly do any worse. Sitting at the kitchen table, she'd taught them their numbers and letters, and by the time he was six Deacon could read well enough that he'd lie on the bearskin rug in front of the fireplace with one of Jack London's adventures or Farley Mowat's histories propped open against the grizzly's head. By the time he was nine, he'd read all of those, and a few of the others besides. One evening when he went to choose another book, he'd peered up at the top row, thinking maybe he'd like to try one of George's for a change. They were too high for him to reach and it hadn't taken him longer than the walk to the kitchen to fetch a chair before he'd found out that it wasn't an accident they'd been placed beyond his and Abel's prying eyes.

His mother was washing the dishes and hearing the scrape of the chair against the linoleum she'd turned and asked him what he was doing. He told her and she responded by marching across the kitchen, snatching up the chair, and telling him, "You'll do no such thing!"

Baffled by her reaction, Deacon returned to the living room. His father was staring up at a point in the far corner of the room, which he was often inclined to do when he'd finished a page and needed a moment to ruminate on it before turning to the next.

"Pa?" Deacon asked.

His father turned towards him, squinting over the rims of his reading glasses as if he was trying to divine where the voice might have come from though his son was standing not five feet away, plain as day. Taking off his glasses and setting them in the crease of the book to keep his place, he asked, "What's on your mind, son?"

Deacon told him that he'd wanted to read one of Mr. Cleary's books but when he'd gone to get a chair from the kitchen so that he could reach the top shelf, Ma'd told him he'd do no such thing.

"And she was plenty riled up about it too."

"That's because George's Fictions aren't for kids," his father told him.

"How's that?"

"They just aren't."

"But why?"

"They're chock-full of violence for one."

"There's plenty of violence in Jack London's books too."

"It's a different kind of violence."

"What do you mean?"

"It just is. And there's other things besides."

"Like what?"

Deacon's father cocked his ear to the kitchen to make sure he could still hear the clatter of dishes in the sink. When he could, he leaned forward and whispered, "Sex."

"Ah hell," Deacon said, shaking his head. "I already know all about sex."

"You do, do you?"

"I've seen the animals mating plenty of times, now haven't I?"

"Well, that's hardly the same thing."

"And I heard you and Ma doing it plenty of times too, when I was upstairs in bed. At least once a week ever since I can remember. Sometimes twice."

His father blanched and Deacon grinned back at him, thinking that he had him there.

It took his father only a moment to recover, during which time he distracted himself by rooting around in the crevice beside the chair's cushion until he'd found the ace of spades playing card he used as a bookmark. He replaced his glasses with that and closed the book, settling his hand on its cover as if trying to draw a measure of resolve from within.

"That's different," he finally said.

"How?"

"Me and your ma love each other."

"And the people in George's books don't?"

"Some of them do. There's no shortage of love in George's books, that's for sure. It's just—"

Shaking his head and looking at his son, trying to find a way out of this conversation and seeing in his son's steely glare that he'd have to answer him sometime, figuring it might as well be now.

"It's just," he continued, "there's other kinds of sex aside from the loving kind."

"And what kind's that?"

"The kind that kids shouldn't be reading about."

"So when can I read them then?"

"I don't know. Maybe when you're fifteen."

"But that's six years away!"

"Then it will give you something to look forward to."

"What about *The Stray*?"

"What about it?"

"It's about you and Ma, right?"

"Parts of it are."

"So why can't I read that one."

"Because of the parts that aren't."

Deacon thought about that and then after a moment asked, "Well, what's to keep me from reading it when you're not around?"

"I guess nothing, except if your ma catches you reading *The Stray*, she's like to take all of George's Fictions into the backyard and burn 'em."

"She wouldn't."

"You don't believe me? Go ahead and try."

His father had then reopened his book, signalling that was the final word on the matter. Deacon returned to the shelf and scanned the titles within reach, finally choosing *White Fang*, which he'd read twice before but was a personal favourite.

Still, the very next time he found himself alone in the house— his mother in the garden and his father fixing the fence where one of their cows had snapped off a pole—he fetched the chair from the kitchen table again. Standing on it, he'd pulled *The Stray* from its place and then, climbing back down, he walked to the window overlooking their backyard. His mother and Abel were crouched amongst the cucumbers pulling weeds and he couldn't see his father, the broken fence post as it was down towards the road. He'd likely come back by way of the driveway, and Deacon could see that fine so, keeping a lookout on his periphery, he scanned the book's cover.

The drape of the waterfall was painted a dozen shades of blues and greens all smudged together. At its base there was a pool of water, and rising from within it there was a man whose face was also a blur, so Deacon couldn't tell if it was his father or not. He was carrying a woman towards the shore. Her face was likewise obscured, but the leather dress she wore and the flowers in her jet-black hair made it plain that she was an Indian, so it wasn't hard for him to imagine that she was indeed his mother. She lay limp in the man's outstretched arms and appeared to be dead. Seeing her like that, and knowing it was his ma, choked the air right out of his throat.

He stared at it long enough for his breath to return and then he flipped the book over. In the bottom right-hand corner there was a photograph of a young man with black short-cropped hair, sitting at a desk in front of a typewriter. He was looking over his shoulder with the droop of a half-smoked cigarette in his mouth and wearing a surprised look on his face as if whoever had taken the picture had snuck up behind him. He was clean-shaven, couldn't have been older than twenty-five, and hardly looked like the old man Deacon had come to know, though the caption beneath left little doubt that he was. *George Cleary lives in Tildon, ON,* was all it said and after reading that Deacon read through the paragraph above.

It told him that the book was set in the 1850s and was about a homesteader whose son had been killed by a pack of stray dogs. He'd followed them into the northern wilds to seek his revenge, only to run afoul of two Chippewa brothers hunting a Hudson's Bay trapper who'd kidnapped their sister. He read over the paragraph twice, thinking that the sister in question must have been his ma, since she was Chippewa too, and the homesteader his pa, who indeed had killed a pack of dogs after they'd attacked none other than Deacon himself.

He had been only two years old, too young to remember what had happened, but his father had told him the story so many times that it had become as clear in Deacon's mind as any dream. Bergin was chopping the winter's wood in the shed when he'd heard Buddy barking and growling, Buddy being the German shepherd–cross he'd owned before Trigger.

"He was as friendly a dog as you were ever likely to meet," Deacon's father would relate, "and from the way he was carryin' on, I knew it was more than just someone coming up the drive. My first thought was maybe it was a bear, because the last time I'd heard Buddy actin' like that was on account of a black bear that had wandered into the yard. Buddy had soon taught it the error of its ways. He'd treed it in that big old oak out behind the barn and we had to keep Buddy inside for the rest of the day before it got the nerve to come back down. So I wasn't too concerned when I came out of the shed, and that's when I saw it wasn't a bear at all, it was that son-of-a-bitch Pike's dogs."

Warren Pike was the old man who lived alone in a brick two-storey about a half a click down the road. He was their closest neighbour and a son of a bitch because it was he who'd sold Deacon's father the tractor. When Bergin had driven down to his house to find out why he hadn't been able to get it started, thinking maybe there was a trick, Mr. Pike had smiled and said, "Ain't no trick. It's just a piece of shit is all."

Deacon's father had protested, reminding him that he'd promised the tractor'd outlive him and probably his kids too, whereby Mr. Pike had replied that if he had a problem he'd best take it up with his Complaints Department. The old man then motioned with his chin at a spot just over Bergin's shoulder. When he'd turned around to see what he meant, he found all three of Pike's Rottweilers standing in a loose formation behind. The lead one bared its teeth and growled, and if the hackles Bergin saw running down its spine left any doubt that it meant business, that son-of-a-bitch Pike did not.

"You best be departing my property," he'd said. "And you'll want to be quick about it too."

After that, whenever he'd driven by Pike's house, Bergin would curse, "Son-of-a-bitch-may-he-rot-in-hell!" under his breath, often adding, for good measure, "He'll get his due one day, and I hope I'm there to see it." So when he'd come out of the woodshed, all those years later, and seen the three dogs grouped in a semicircle around Buddy, who was guarding the tractor upon the seat of which sat Bergin's son, it had seemed to him that the day of reckoning had finally arrived.

"I wasn't more than two steps into the yard when the three of them attacked. Buddy was a big dog and fierce when he had to be. He'd got one of them Rotties by the throat and had it on its back and then the others were on him and the last sound I ever heard poor old Buddy make was a startled yelp as they tore into him. You were on your feet screaming, 'Buddy!' You were always a fearless child and for a moment I thought you meant to jump to his rescue. I hollered, 'Stay there, Deke!' and you looked up at me with such terror that it unearthed something I'd have sworn wasn't in me. Rage and something else I don't have the words to explain, maybe nobody does. Maybe it's a feeling that predates the advent of words themselves; a part of us buried so deep that we were more animal than man when we last had any use for it and which had suddenly become the sum total of who I was, seeing them dogs ripping apart Buddy, knowing that it'd only be a heartbeat before they'd be doing the same to you."

At that point in the telling he'd pause a moment. There'd be a glint in his eyes that could have been tears thinking of what might have been or just as likely the vestiges of that feeling creeping up on him once again. Whatever it was, he'd savour it for a moment. When he went to speak, his voice would crack and he'd have to clear his throat before starting again.

"It's thirteen strides at a hard run from the shed's door to the tractor. I'd have made the distance in under two seconds but when I think about it now, time seemed to have slowed to a trickle so that it feels like it might just as well've been a lifetime. One of the dogs was waiting on me when I finally got there, standing between me and the others, growling and baring its teeth. I still had the splitting axe in my hand, the same one that's hanging in the shed. You know I call it my splitting axe but really it's more of a maul. I'd just sharpened its edge not fifteen minutes previous, and when I swung it two-handed onto that dog it split its skull right down the middle, burying the blade up to its nub in the ground. I wrenched it loose and swung at another dog, catching it lengthwise across the back and crushing its spine. It let out a most wretched shriek and then the last jerked towards me.

"The speed at which it moved caught me off guard and I just managed to get the axe handle between me and its teeth. I stumbled and then I was on my back, the axe wrenched loose from my grip, my hands grasping at the dog's ears, the only thing I could get a hold of to keep it from getting at my throat. My hands were slipping and I felt then just like I imagine a man facing a firing squad would have as the countdown came to one.

"I could see you," looking then to Deacon, and if he was within reach, setting his hand on his head as if he was thinking that at that moment in the telling he'd have liked to have done the same, one last time. "You had a look on your face of such utter despair that I could see in it my own demise, you watching as I was torn apart, knowing that such a thing would like to have followed you to the end of your days, and what kind of a father was I if I let that happen? So I did the only thing I could to give the inevitable a moment's reprieve. I let go of one of those ears and jammed my arm into that dog's mouth. I felt its teeth clamp down and had it been in there for more than a split second that dog would have chomped my arm clean off. But the moment I felt the sharp piercing my skin, I heard a shot ring out.

"The dog stiffened and there was the hot splatter of blood on my cheeks. I rolled it offa me and looked up at you again. The despair was gone from your face and in its place a look I'd seen only once before. It was that first time you'd stood on your own, pulling yourself up by the seat of a kitchen chair and letting go. Standing there wobbling like you had ball bearings for knees, your face alight with pride and wonder like you couldn't have imagined such a thing was even possible. You were looking over at the house like that and when I followed your gaze to the porch, your ma was standing on the top step holding my Enfield, a wisp of smoke curling from the muzzle, the stock of it pressed to her shoulder, her eyes still sighting along the barrel, such hate in them that I hope I never live long enough to witness it again."

The first time he'd told Deacon the story he'd added, "You may not know this, but your ma's as crack a shot as any man I've ever met." Thereafter, it'd be Deacon who'd ask, his face bearing a facsimile of the look he'd worn that day, "Ma's as crack a shot as any man you've ever met, ain't that right, Pa?" And his father would answer, "And it's a damn good thing too, or I'd be one-armed to this day, if'n I was lucky that is. She shot that dog square between the eyes, and it died so quick, I tell you, it'd have taken a tube and a half of super glue to soften the snarl curled over its teeth.

"I'd just got to my feet and was pondering on that, and what might have been, when your ma strode past and grabbed you in her arms, casting me a most reproachful glare as she turned back towards the house.

"I knew what was on her mind, and I guess I couldn't blame her for being angry. She was thinking about all those times I'd called Pike 'a son-of-a-bitch-may-he-rot-in-hell' whenever we drove by his house, how she'd shush me and say, 'You curse a man, it's liable to come back on you twofold.'

"I now saw the truth of what she'd spoke, though I was a fair turn from sending Pike my blessings just yet.

"While I loaded the bodies of his dogs into the back of the Jeep, I was still cursing his name, and while I drove the half click to his house I'd got to cursing his mother and his father, cursing his kids and his grandkids too. And I had every intention of doing the same to his face once I got there.

"When I pulled to a stop at the end of his driveway, I could see him sitting in the rocking chair he had on his porch. He hadn't made a move and so I figured he was asleep. I slammed the door hard on my way out but that still wasn't enough to rouse him. I hadn't gone more than a few steps when I could see flies buzzing around his head. If they weren't enough to tell me he was dead, the smell comin' offa him when I come up onto the porch most certainly was.

"I stood there staring down at him, thinking of your ma's warning. I tell you I'd never felt like such a low creature as I did then, thinking of what my spite had nearly cost me, as if Pike's malignant spirit had impregnated his dogs so as to enact his revenge for having cursed his name all those times. I hadn't smoked a cigarette in two years—the last one being on the morning you were born—but I had a powerful urge to have one then. I could see Pike's pouch of tobacco poking out of his pocket. I took it out and rolled myself one. After I smoked it,

I thought about rolling another, but I guess I knew where that might've led so instead I went inside and called the police."

And that would have been the end of the story had it not been for George.

That same afternoon, he'd paid his first visit, introducing himself only as a reporter for *The Tildon Chronicle.* Bergin told him what had happened, filling in some of the details he'd left out while giving his statement to the police—about that son-of-a-bitch Pike and how he'd sold him the tractor, how he'd cursed his name even though Rose had warned him not to, and how his first thought upon finding the old man dead had been that his spirit had possessed the dogs to seek his revenge. The first cop who'd showed up told him Pike had likely been dead for almost a week, meaning the dogs were probably just half-starved, and so, he'd told George, he'd come to see that what had really happened was just the universe giving him a tap on the shoulder to remind him as to the error of his ways.

All the while he spoke, George was taking notes, and after he was done he asked Bergin about the Enfield. While Bergin had gone to fetch it, Rose appeared on the porch, carrying Deacon asleep on her shoulder, and George had gone up to her to enquire about the part she'd played in the story. She was shy around strangers and responded to his questions by lowering her eyes and twirling her fingers through her hair, a habit she'd keep for as long she knew him. Bergin came out with the Enfield, and George commented it was the same rifle his father had owned, then went on to say that he hadn't shot one, oh, since he was a boy. Maybe he was baiting Bergin or maybe he was just stating a fact. Either way, Bergin asked if he'd like to shoot one now.

"I wouldn't say no," George answered, which, in later years, Deacon would learn was how he always said yes.

After that he'd show up three or four times a year, always

unannounced. Bergin and him rarely ever shot anything beyond the breeze, and during the hours they spent tromping through the woods, or crouching within a blind, Bergin told George things that he'd never told a living soul: about his father ("As mean an old bastard as you're likely ever to meet"); about how after he'd died, Bergin took his inheritance and fled Denmark; about building his house; and about how he'd met Rose. And though George didn't take notes as he had when Bergin had told him about that son-of-a-bitch Pike and his dogs, he must have kept a clear record of them in his head because, some three years after they'd met, George gave him a copy of *The Stray* and he'd find more than a few of his divulgences recounted within its pages.

Until then, Bergin hadn't been much of a reader. His efforts since he'd come to Tildon rarely strayed beyond the books he kept on the shelf he'd made out of a spruce tree he'd felled at the back of their pasture, the spaces in between filled out with his prized collection of bird skulls. He'd bought the complete works of Jack London at the Owl Pen, the used bookstore on Main. He'd taught himself to read English by following along in the Danish translations he'd read as a kid, the adventures therein luring him to the new world, his possessions when he arrived confined to $24,000, the clothes on his back, and a gunny sack filled with the books he'd nicked from the library on his way out of town.

The Farley Mowats he'd bought on the advice of the Owl Pen's owner, who'd said he was unlikely to find a better guide to his new home than him. And while he'd enjoyed those, they didn't hold a candle to the amazement he felt upon reading *The Stray*. The next time George dropped by, he asked him if he'd written anything else. George said he had and Bergin said he'd sure like to read them too. The following morning a box was sitting on his front porch. Inside it were George's other eleven books. They must have spoken to something deep inside because as soon as he'd finished the lot by rereading *The Stray*, Bergin had gone back and started reading them over again.

All of which Bergin had told his son a dozen times, leaving out only one small detail: what was written on the dedication page of the book Deacon now held in his hand. So it came as a surprise when, opening it up, he found typeset there: *For Bergin & Rose*. And beneath that in a crude scrawl barely more refined than Deacon's own: *Thanks for giving an old man new hope.*

Seeing his parents' names thus inscribed had increased his anticipation and he quickly flipped forward to page one. He'd only just managed to read the opening line—*Asger was in his shed chopping the winter wood when he heard his dog growling from the yard*—before he caught a flicker of movement out of the corner of his eye. Looking up, he saw his mother walking back from the garden, carrying a basketful of lettuce, and Abel clutching a cucumber to his chest and hurrying to catch up behind.

Closing the book, he ran back to the shelf, climbed onto the chair and stuck the book into the gap made by its absence. He'd just returned the chair to its place at the kitchen table when his mother came in. If she'd noticed anything odd about how her son was obviously flustered, his cheeks flushed red and his chest heaving, she made no sign as she carried the basket to the sink to wash the dirt off the greens they'd be eating for dinner.

Ever after, when George visited, Deacon would stand staring up at *The Stray* nestled in the far-right corner of the bookshelf's top row, eating his share of liquorice allsorts and thinking how it'd be a shame if his mother burnt it up in the yard before he had a chance to find out what happened next.

8

When he'd finally come to read beyond *The Stray*'s opening line, Deacon was six months shy of his thirteenth birthday, though it was hardly a cause for celebration.

It had been a mild winter that year. The snow was gone by the first week of March and by the time he'd finished his morning lesson on the Tuesday of the same, the thermometer on their porch was already creeping towards twenty. He got it in mind that it would be a good day to go down to the creek that drained out of the swamp towards the rear of their property.

The swamp was likely to be full with the thaw, and if he was lucky he'd catch a bass, which were known to favour the shelter of the cattails, though, just last year, he'd seen one trying to swim upstream not five feet from the swollen creek's shore. *Maybe it had been frozen in a block of ice*, he'd thought, knowing that happened to some fish, though he wasn't exactly sure that it happened to bass. When the thaw had come, he imagined that the block of ice had been swept into the creek. When the fish had finally melted free, it was miles downstream, swimming against the current and trying to get back home, not moving an inch the whole time Deacon had stood there watching it. He'd cursed himself for not bringing his fishing rod, or better yet his pocket knife, so he could have made a spear. He had run back to get them, but when he'd returned the fish was gone. He'd made the spear anyway and had kept it in his room ever since, thinking he might still find some use for it.

So it was with a great sense of anticipation that he'd come out of the house just after ten with his rod, his spear, his knife, and a plastic grocery bag he'd scrounged from his mother's collection under the kitchen sink in which to carry the fish back. Trigger had got the cancer in his hinds last fall and Bergin had had to put him down two weeks previous. His mat was still beside the wicker rocking chair on the porch and habit had him bending low as if the dog was still alive and he meant to give him a touch on his way past.

And that's when his mother called to him through the kitchen window.

"If you're going down to the creek," she said, "why don't you take Abel with you?"

Deacon hadn't been too keen on the idea. Half the reason he went down to the creek was to get away from his brother, and he'd called back to her, "But you said Abel ain't allowed to go down to the creek without you or Pa."

"You're twelve aren't you?"

"Yeah."

"Then I expect you're plenty old enough to make sure he don't drown himself."

When Abel came out of the house, holding the bow George had given them and the one arrow he hadn't lost, Deacon was waiting at the foot of the path leading past their barn. He turned, ignoring Abel's shouts of, "Wait for me!" and followed the trail on a direct line through the pasture towards the patch of forest where their Holsteins would seek refuge from the summer heat. The ground rose on a steady incline once you breached the treeline. The creek was on the other side of the hill studded with the thirty-five or so sugar maples that they tapped every year for syrup. The pails still hung from their spiles and when he'd reached the nearest, Deacon lifted its lid, peering down at the half inch of clear liquid within.

He was just dipping his cupped hand into it, drawing it back and slurping the sap from his palm when Abel finally caught up, out of breath from running after him in rubber boots. He punched Deacon hard on the arm to tell him what he thought of being left behind and cursed, "Cockfucker," something he'd heard their father holler just last week when one of their cows had stepped on his foot while he was milking it.

"I told you to wait for me," he spat at Deacon.

"And I told you to hurry."

"Ma made me wear my rubbers. You know I can't run when I'm wearing my rubbers."

"And how's that my fault?" Deacon said, turning and starting up the slope, thinking that maybe it wouldn't be such a bad thing if Abel drowned himself in the creek after all.

"Wait," Abel yelled after him. "I want to drink some sap too."

"Drink all the sap you want. I'll be down at the creek."

He heard Abel muttering "cockfucker" again and that was followed by the squelch of his boots as he hurried to catch up.

"What'd you bring that bow for anyhow?" Deacon asked when his brother had come astride.

"I'm going to shoot me a fish."

"I'd like to see that."

"Well, you're gonna."

"You're just going to lose that arrow."

"No I ain't."

"If you shoot it into the creek, you sure as hell are, and I ain't going to make you any more. I made you six last year and you lost all of them except the one. I ain't makin' you any more arrows if you lose that one too."

"I won't. I brought some kite string to tie around the end. That way I can reel the fish in after I shoot it."

"It'll just come loose."

"I'll tie it tight. Double knot it."

"You can't tie knots for shit."

"But you can."

"I ain't tying no knot on the end of an arrow, I'll tell you that."

"Well, then can you make me a spear?"

"You're nine ain't ya?"

"You know I am."

"Then I expect you're old enough to make your own spear."

"I'm gonna hafta use your knife."

"You ain't using my knife."

"But Ma took mine, you know that."

"It's cause you almost cut your damn finger off."

"Well, how am I going to make a spear without a knife?"

"I guess you're just going to have to use your teeth."

"My teeth? I can't use my teeth. How am I going to use my teeth? That's just stupid."

They'd come to the top of the rise. There was a boulder there, half again taller than Deacon and furred green with moss. He ran his hand along its carpet until he came to the down slope on its far side.

"Come on, let me use your knife," Abel was pleading as Deacon let gravity carry him towards the creek.

He hadn't made it more than three steps when something

flit up past his face. Then right after that another flit and then another. The sound of their buzz grew into a roar and Deacon gaped down at his feet, seeing a funnel almost like a tornado rising out of a hole in the ground.

"Bees!" Abel screamed, swatting at the haze engulfing them even as Deacon dropped his fishing rod and spear and wheeled around, grabbing his brother by the hand and dragging him at a hard run back down the hill towards home.

Sharp stabs pinged over the back of his neck and Abel was wailing, "It hurts! They're stinging me. It hurts!"

Deacon felt him stumble and clutched his hand tighter, keeping him on his feet and dragging him towards the slats of light straining through the hedge of cedars at the edge of the forest. Needle points raced in electric shocks up his arms and the back of his neck. He'd been stung a half a dozen times when they'd reached the field. Abel was sobbing inconsolably, his words now lost to the tyranny of his pain. The swarm had relented but there were still two or three hornets chasing after them as they charged along the path leading around the barn, Deacon swatting frantically at their winged pursuers, his brother lagging behind him with the pull of an anchor, wheezing and gasping, then buckling over as they came into sight of the house. Deacon felt another sting on his arm and slapped at it, feeling the crunch of the insect's body against his skin as he looked to his brother, hunched over, his head between his knees, his face a plague of fire-red bumps. He'd lost one of his boots and there was a hornet crawling over the ruffle of his hair but those were the least of Deacon's worry. Abel couldn't catch his breath. He was gulping at the air like a drowning man and peering up at his brother with a crazed fear in his gape.

"Ma! Pa!" Deacon screamed, turning back towards the house.

He saw his mother's head pop up from their garden. She'd

been tilling the soil with a hoe and was holding it like a weapon as if the tenor of her son's anguish had called to mind the memory of the dogs that had attacked him all those years ago.

"It's Abel!"

Deacon felt another sting just above his elbow and the pain of it sent a shudder of rage through him. He swatted at it but the hornet was gone and he hollered after it, "Leave me alone, goddamnit! Leave me alone!" His voice breaking so that it came out just short of a whimper.

Abel was on the ground when he turned back to him, his knees bunched at his chest. A violent spasm coursed through his body and spittle foamed at his lips, his neck swollen almost even with his chin, its skin a deep red, shading to purple.

"It's okay, Ma's coming," Deacon said, bending and taking his brother's hand and Abel staring up at him, panic-struck. Then their mother was there beside them, kneeling at her son, fear warping her face into a hideous mask.

"He was stung," Deacon said, though it was clear for all to see.

Rose was already standing by then, drawing her son into her arms and turning back towards the house, screaming, "Bergin! Bergin!"

Deacon watched after her, his skin on fire and his legs turned to wood, refusing to move until he saw his father coming around the side of the barn, watching as his mother heaved Abel into his arms. Only when his father had turned towards the Cherokee parked at the end of the drive did Deacon find the will to chase after them. His legs picked up speed with every step so that when he'd come to the tractor his feet hardly seemed to be touching the ground.

His mother was already in the Jeep's passenger seat and his father was setting Abel in her lap. He was limp and he sagged between her arms like a long-dead thing. Deacon felt like he was going to be sick but pushed himself harder still, seeing his father circling to the driver's seat, opening the door, and throwing himself in. The Jeep's engine caught on the first try, which in itself seemed like a miracle since it hardly ever started without two or three twists of the key.

The wheels spewed gravel as his father threw it into reverse, his head craned backwards as he spun the wheel, oblivious to Deacon hurrying after. His mother was likewise occupied, gaping in terror at the crumpled form in her lap—her son dying, it seemed, right before her eyes. Only when Deacon slammed his hands on the hood as his father was shifting into gear did she look up, tears streaking down her cheeks, aghast, as if she'd mistaken Deacon for a ghost.

"Get in then, goddamnit!" his father yelled.

Deacon'd barely made the back seat before his father hit the gas, spinning the steering wheel, and racing up the driveway. The door wrenched loose from Deacon's grip, flapping open. He lunged out for it, grabbing hold of its handle just as his father swerved onto the road, the force of the hairpin turn slamming the door shut and sending Deacon sprawling over the seat. His head knocked against the far window's crank and the shock of it momentarily numbed his agony. All of a sudden it felt like he was encased in ice, like he'd imagined the fish he'd seen last year had been. The world was but a pale reflection through its screen. Nothing could touch him and the pain was but a memory. A fleeting moment of relief before the world came hurtling back in the pinpricks seething over his skin. He could taste blood in his mouth. He'd bit his tongue and that added to his agony. He'd ended up on the floor and was wedged between the front seat and the back, listening with dread rapt to the spiralling confusion in his father's voice.

"It doesn't make any goddamn sense," he was saying. "He's

been stung by bees plenty of times. It doesn't make any god-damn sense."

Deacon thinking, *it weren't bees, it was hornets*, as if that might have made a difference, and more so that Abel had never been stung by either.

It's me who's been stung plenty of times.

Four times to be exact, and after every one he'd sworn he couldn't imagine something that could have hurt more than that. But here he was, as if his body had become a hurt factory, pumping out pain in overlapping shifts as the Jeep battered over the pothole-strewn road, bouncing him like those Mexican jumping beans his mother had put in their stockings last Christmas, Deacon and Abel laughing as they did flips on the kitchen table.

"You think there's really worms inside, like Pa said?" Abel had asked him at the time.

"Only one way to find out."

They'd cracked one open with a hammer and sure enough there was an itty-bitty worm under the shell, though really it was a larvae, their father'd explained.

"It'll hatch into some sort of insect," he told them.

He didn't know which, and Abel had said they could check on it at the library the next time they were in town, though by then they'd forgotten all about it.

From the front seat he heard his mother screaming, "He's not breathing!" and the thought pounded in his head that Abel can't die, not without finding out what kind of bug it was—*he can't, he can't, he can't*. An inconsequential thought measured against everything else he'd stand to lose, but there it was looping through Deacon's mind as if by holding onto it, his brother would have to be alright.

Then his mother was screaming again.

"Watch out!"

Deacon didn't have but a moment to ponder on what she'd meant before there was a sound like a train wreck and he felt what seemed like the entire weight of the world pressing down upon him.

9

Later, when he was asked what he remembered about the crash, Deacon would reply that he didn't really remember anything but waking up in the hospital. And really, he'd add, he didn't remember much about the two weeks he'd spent there except the steady beep of his heart monitor and the smiling face of a pretty, young nurse who changed his dressings three times a day.

Dr. Morrell, the Cleary's family physician, was the first person who'd asked him the question. It had been a year almost to the day after the Jeep, the police report conjectured, had swerved to miss a moose and ran headlong into a spruce tree, the force of the impact catapulting Bergin halfways through the windshield as one of the tree's branches impaled Abel through the head and Rose through the breast, the branch itself piercing their seat and grazing Deacon's forehead.

Deacon had come into Dr. Morrell's office for the last of his monthly checkups. Before then Dr. Morrell had only made enquiries of a physical nature, if his headaches were getting better, for example, and whether the pins in his arm were causing him any discomfort. It was only on their final visit together, while he was shining his penlight into Deacon's eyes, that he'd asked about the crash, broaching the subject in a casual tone as if the matter was of no great import. Deacon had been alone in the back of the Jeep for the long side of twenty-four hours before he'd been found. He knew it was those unaccounted for hours that Dr. Morrell was most interested in and also that he had absolutely nothing whatsoever to say about them. Still, he squinted and looked up at a corner of the room as if he was ruminating deeply upon it.

Dr. Morrell waited patiently until it had seemed Deacon might never answer and then prodded him by saying, "It's okay, take your time." Only then had Deacon replied. When he had finished speaking, Dr. Morrell nodded, telling him that that was to be expected, though the tone of his voice made Deacon suspect he was just saying it to humour him, that he didn't really believe he couldn't remember anything but was unwilling to push him further.

The second person who asked him about the crash was Rain Meadows.

The year she'd graduated from high school, her parents had both succumbed to lung cancer, six months apart, and after her father's funeral she'd learned their house had been remortgaged to within a nickel of its worth. Her inheritance hadn't amounted to much more than it and a rusted-out Plymouth Reliant, and her only choice had been between leaving it to the bank or taking over the payments herself. She'd chosen the latter and for the past twenty-odd years had been fighting a losing battle against its descent into ruin.

The house was heated by an old oil furnace, and the cost of keeping it liveable during the colder months had driven her to spending winters cottage-sitting for the Bickers, a wealthy family from Pittsburgh who wanted to keep their chalet warm and dusted on the odd chance they weren't flying south over the Christmas holidays. In the intervening months, she plied her mother's trade, making thirty bucks an hour reading Tarot and listening to a clientele of mostly elderly widows pine after their dearly departed, offering in return her assurances that they were waiting with open arms for them on the other side. But that barely provided her with enough to buy groceries and she'd supplemented this meagre income by taking any number of odd jobs that came her way, most of which amounted to pauper's wages cleaning houses for Tildon's professional class.

She'd once provided this service for the Clearys. Adele had fired her after only a couple of weeks, and though Deacon wasn't privy to the details, he figured George must have been to blame because he'd paid her to write the *Chronicle*'s horoscope ever since.

Deacon was seventeen when George asked him to use the paper's delivery van to drive her back to the Bickers' cottage after she'd indulged herself one too many times at the open bar during the *Chronicle*'s annual Christmas Party. It took twenty-five minutes heading north on Highway 4 followed by ten minutes ploughing through a foot and a half of snow on the private road leading to the Bickers' A-frame, perched atop a granite ridge overlooking Skeleton Lake. After he'd pulled up to the cedar rail stairs ascending to the chalet's wraparound veranda, Rain asked him if he wouldn't mind coming in until she'd checked the place over, laughing as she said, "You never know what might be hiding under one of the beds."

From the outside it looked like a rather modest affair, but standing in its front lobby it was clear that only a Saudi prince could have mistaken it for that, its structure comprised of a million dollars' worth of cedar logs stacked around marble floors and both overseen by a thirty-foot vaulted ceiling, a hundred feet of glass running along the wall facing the water. Rain made an elaborate play of tippy-toeing up the spiral staircase leading to the second floor, turning back to Deacon every few steps and putting her finger over her mouth, warning him to silence. She took her time upstairs and when she came back down her hair was wet and she was wearing a violet bathrobe with the initials MB stitched in gold over one of its pockets.

Deacon found it a little strange, seeing her like that, but didn't give it any undo significance, the first real sign that he'd wandered into uncharted territory being when she'd reached the bottom of the stairs.

"How old are you anyway?" she'd asked.

Deacon had swallowed hard, for no reason except that there was a sudden lump forming in the back of his throat.

"Seventeen," he croaked out.

"Seventeen?" she mused. "I was a hellcat when I was seventeen. You a hellcat, Deacon?"

Deacon had no idea what a hellcat was but, regardless, it was a good bet that he wasn't. He shook his head.

"No, I guess you aren't. You seem more the shy type. That right?"

Deacon shrugged, though he knew it to be true.

"That's okay," she said and set her hand on his shoulder. "When I was seventeen, I had a thing for shy boys."

She'd then taken his hand and led him past the kitchen to the guest bedroom where she slept. She hadn't said another word until she'd got undressed and was slipping under the covers.

"You coming or not?" she said, and Deacon didn't need to be asked twice.

That first time, he'd barely lasted two strokes before he came, but she'd been plenty understanding, laughing, and ruffling her hand through his hair and saying, "You're a hellcat after all."

For the next four months, hardly two days passed that Deacon hadn't driven the van out to the Bickers after George and Adele had gone to sleep. One night after she'd slid off of him, she lay on her side with her head propped on her elbow, staring at Deacon until finally he turned to her and asked, "What?"

She brushed the long drape of his hair up over his ear, trailing her finger along the scar running in a jagged line just above his right eyebrow—the most visible reminder of the crash.

"George says you don't remember what happened," she said. "Is that true?"

Deacon said it was and repeated the line he'd given Dr. Morrell. He looked back to her. The way she was biting her lip made it plain that she didn't believe him either.

"Doctor Morrell said it's to be expected." Sitting up in the bed, he foraged amongst the covers for his underwear, hoping that would be the end of the matter.

It wasn't.

"You can talk to me," Rain said, setting her hand on his arm as Deacon wrestled to get his underwear over his feet, "you know that, right?"

"If I remember anything," he promised, "you'll be the first to know."

They hadn't spoken a word about it since.

The only other person who asked him about the crash was Crystal Cleary, Dylan's younger sister and George's grand-daughter. She was a year older than Deacon and all through high school she'd taken him under her wing. Mostly this entailed saving him a seat in the cafeteria so he wouldn't have to eat alone and letting him tag along to an endless series of house parties thrown by the sons and daughters of Tildon's professional class when their parents were away, those nights invariably ending with him sitting on a couch nursing a bottle of beer, waiting for Crystal to return from whatever dark nook or cranny she'd retreated to with whatever boy had caught her fancy.

And that's what he'd been doing on the night that she'd asked about the crash, except he was sitting on the end of a dock, his shoes beside him, his feet stretching for the water just out of reach. It was Crystal's first weekend back from her freshman year at the University of Toronto, where she had quickly learned that plenty of her classmates had summer residences on the lakes around Tildon. One of them had invited her, along with a couple dozen of her closest friends, to a bash to celebrate the end of the school year at what Crystal had called the parents' "log cabin," a description that called to mind an entirely different picture than the ten-thousand-square-foot monstrosity that had confronted them after the guard at the front gate had waved Crystal's Prius through.

From there the party progressed with the dull familiarity of all the other parties to which she'd invited him. Crystal asked him to see if he could track down the kitchen and find space for her six-pack of vodka coolers in the fridge. When he came back into the living room she was sitting on the lap of a young black man tall enough to be the centre for his school's basketball team and Deacon made a sideline for the nearest exit. It opened onto a wraparound deck and he followed its steps down to a marble walkway. That, in turn, led him to the dock buffering the beach from the boathouse which did, in fact, look almost exactly like the picture that had sprung to mind when Deacon had thought of a log cabin, though it was larger by a factor of three.

He sat at the end of the dock, sipping from the pint of Bacardi he'd brought and lighting cigarettes with the regularity of an egg timer set to soft boil. An hour or so later he heard

Crystal calling out to him, "There you are! I've been looking for you all night."

"Well, I've been right here," he said, fumbling for another cigarette from his pack.

"You're missing all the fun."

She was going through a Rasta phase. As she slumped down beside him, dreadlocks the size of pine cones battered her brow in sharp contrast to the pigtails she'd worn just months earlier, her orange hair and freckled cheeks making it a natural that she would have dressed up as Anne of Green Gables the past two Halloweens while handing out candy at her parents' house.

"I've been having plenty of fun all by myself," he said, holding up the now three-quarters empty bottle of rum to prove his point.

She gave him one of her patented less-than-bemused frowns, and in the sheen glossing her eyes Deacon could see that she was high on something beyond the joint they'd shared on the car ride over.

Lighting the smoke, he felt her hand brushing at a strand of hair that had slipped loose from his ponytail and the pad of her thumb waxing delicately over the scar above his right eyebrow. His body tensed as it always did when she touched him and he distracted himself from the sudden tingle rising in his belly by blowing misshapen rings into the still night air, aiming them for the moon's mottled globe as if he were trying to hang a lasso around it.

"You know," she said, rubbing the scar, lost in the infinite tactile delight of the stoned mind, "I always wondered."

"What's that?"

"If it was true."

"If what was true?"

"That you don't remember what happened after the crash."

Deacon took another drag off the smoke, knowing then what

he'd suspected all along—that even if none of the Clearys had asked him about the accident, they'd all talked about it, and probably the whole damn town had too.

"It's true," he said.

"You don't remember anything?"

"Not much. Until I woke up in the hospital. But mostly that's a blur too."

"What's the first thing you do remember?"

"Clearly?"

"Yeah."

"A parrot."

"A parrot?"

"Sitting in the window beside my bed."

"At the hospital?"

"No, at George and Adele's."

"In my dad's old room?"

Deacon nodded.

"I woke up one morning and there it was, this big old parrot sitting on the window ledge. Prettiest thing you ever saw."

Recalling it then, the image of the bird appeared clear in his mind. And though, really, it wasn't the first thing he'd remembered, he'd told himself it was so many times that it had come to seem that the bright reds and oranges of its plumage might very well have been like the sun melting away the fog that had become his memory.

He'd lain there in bed, watching it ruffling its feathers and peering over at him through its lizard-like eyes.

It must have escaped from someone's house, he thought, and that had led him to thinking that its owner was likely missing it. The idea that there might be someone out there—a child perhaps—crying over their lost pet planted the seed of another idea in his head. If he could catch it, he could draw up a few pictures, put them on the bulletin board at the grocery store like people did when they'd lost a dog or a cat. But first he'd have to catch it. He was just thinking of how he might do that—*You could go around the other side of the window, maybe chase it inside*—when the parrot, all of a sudden, lit out from the sill.

Deacon jumped out of bed and ran to the window just in time to see it disappearing into the branches of a maple tree at the far end of the yard. He was still in his pyjamas, one of the four pairs he'd found folded in the top drawer of his dresser, along with a half-dozen pairs of socks and underwear. The other drawers were filled with clothes too, and the closet hung with an assortment of jeans and jackets. But in the four weeks since he'd got out of the hospital he'd only ever worn the pyjamas, rarely leaving his room except to use the bathroom and to eat at the kitchen table, though he hadn't often felt hungry and rarely did that either—lying in bed most of his days, sleeping. And when he couldn't do that, pulling the covers up over his head as if he could hide from the past, knowing it was a fool's game, that when the dark settled in it would be there like a monster under the bed, waiting to reach out and grab him.

Seeing the bird and making plans to catch it had awoken something in him that he'd have sworn had died along with his parents and his brother all those months ago. Watching it fly off, he was certain that he'd missed his chance, and then getting to the window just in time to catch sight of it seeking refuge in that maple tree, he saw that maybe the future he'd imagined still had a hope of coming true after all.

You'll need some bait if you want to catch it, he thought.

Parrots eat crackers.

They do.

There's a box of saltines in the kitchen cupboard, next to the cereal. Best be quick about it.

Rushing then from the room and down the hall—the plush of the rug feeling as soft as moss under his feet—and coming onto the cool of the kitchen's linoleum, he found Mrs. Cleary sitting at the table, a piece of graph paper and a dictionary in front of her, tapping a pencil against her dentures as she worked out the crossword for that week's paper. In the years to come, he'd take to sitting with her and they'd work it out together, he flipping through the dictionary, offering her words, and she wearing out endless erasers trying to make them fit, sharing something in those moments that no dictionary in the world had enough words to fully account for: a carefree future sitting right there before him, though he hadn't an inkling of it at the time, the possibilities of the one he'd just imagined chasing him past the old woman, the open-mouthed alarm at which she'd greeted his sudden entrance becoming something else entirely as she watched him climb up onto the counter.

She covered her mouth with her hand, tears wetting her eyes though she'd often say afterwards that she'd never felt happier than she was then, watching Deacon grabbing for a box of crackers and dropping back to the floor, him noticing the look on the old woman's face and thinking maybe he owed her an explanation—they were her saltines after all. In his rush towards the back door the words spilled over themselves, bubbling out of his mouth, and Adele without her hearing aid and so all she'd heard was, "parrot . . . crackers . . . hope . . . don't mind."

And then he was gone again, hurrying into the backyard.

The maple tree was perched at the edge of where the ground sloped into the ravine, its canopy providing shade for what appeared to be a small red-brick barn. Halfway across the yard, Deacon checked his pace, slowing to a fast walk, not wanting to startle the parrot. But when he came to the tree's trunk, peering up into its branches, it was nowhere to be seen. He circled the tree twice and then stepped to the gully's edge, scanning over the tops of the trees lining the valley beyond. He couldn't see it there either and walked back into the yard, looking up at the sky and seeing a dark shape drifting against the blue.

It wasn't the parrot though, it was a bird of prey: a falcon or maybe a hawk, he couldn't tell which.

Falcons hunt birds, he told himself.

He'd read it in one of the books on his father's shelf, about how in some cities they used falcons to hunt pigeons to keep them from shitting all over the place. Pigeon shit was like acid. It'd eat through solid stone if you let it, and in cities where there were a lot of buildings and statues made out of stone—old cities, cities in Europe—they used falcons to hunt pigeons. He didn't know if hawks hunted birds too. He knew they hunted mice and rabbits but he couldn't recall if they also hunted birds. It didn't matter anyways because whether it was a falcon or hawk, it was too far away for him to know for sure.

If you had Pa's binoculars . . .

And thinking that recalled to him the image of his father's face, full of wonder and glee, the time he'd led him and Abel out to a spruce in the back of their property where an eagle had made its aerie, pointing up at the nest then peering through his binoculars, passing them over when the eagle's head appeared over its lip so that Deacon could have a look too. Knowing then that he'd never see his pa's face again—nor his ma's nor Abel's—the dread that had been creeping into his belly ever since he'd seen the falcon or the hawk wrapped its tentacles around his chest.

He knew then that all those weeks he'd spent hiding under his covers, he hadn't been hiding from the memory of the crash and the secret of what had come next, he'd been hiding from a thousand memories from the time before. He also saw that he'd been a fool to think he could hide from them when they were inside of him, each conspiring into a grim certainty that he was all alone in the world and that he couldn't possibly get along without his family and that maybe it would have been better if he'd died too.

He was sobbing now, his whole body shaking as if it couldn't contain all that grief. Then hands were wrapping around him, holding him tight, and he buried his head in the soft weave of the old woman's sweater. Her hand stroked the back of his head and she cooed, "There, there. It's alright. Get it out. It's okay."

Deacon knowing it was a lie and wanting to strike out at her, never so angry at another person than he was at this old woman, for telling him it would be alright when nothing could ever be alright again. His hands balled to fists and he pounded at her back though the blows felt feeble, no harder than a baby would have made.

After a while, his anguish relented and his body stilled. Mrs. Cleary kneeled in front of him, smiling up at Deacon as if him sobbing like that had meant something beyond mere grief. She wiped away the tears from his cheeks with the back of her hand. The skin on her knuckles was as soft as silk.

"Now, what was it you were saying about a parrot?" she asked and Deacon looked down at her, suddenly ashamed of crying like that and more so for pounding on her back and wishing her harm.

"It was sit-sit-sitting in the window," he started and the rest came pouring out, the words stuttering and tripping over one another, barely making sense even to himself. The old woman, though, seemed to have caught the general drift and her face brightened.

"Binoculars?" she asked. "You want a pair of binoculars, is that it?"

Deacon nodded.

"George's got a pair in the barn. Or at least he did. Why don't we go see if we can find them?"

"Okay."

Standing, she took him by the hand. As the old woman led him towards the barn's front door, Deacon cast fleeting glimpses at the sky, searching about for the hawk or the falcon. It was gone, which meant the binoculars wouldn't be of much use, but he trailed after her anyway.

The old woman was telling him about how George would sit up by the window on the second floor of the barn for hours sometimes, peering through those binoculars.

"He was looking for blue jays," she continued. "Boy, does he ever have a hate-on for blue jays. Whenever he spied one, he'd shoot at it with this pellet gun he bought himself. Imagine that, an old man buying himself a pellet gun to shoot at blue jays. Me, I always liked them. Such cheerful birds. I don't know how many times I told him to cut it out, but he's like a kid with that pellet gun. How about you, do you like blue jays?"

"I-I do."

"Good," she said, turning towards him with a conspiratorial grin. "Then you and I will get along just fine."

They'd come to the barn and the old woman lifted up a stone that was sitting on the window ledge beside its door. The rock was about the size and shape of a softball, except it had a flat bottom. It was painted green and speckled with colourful dots—red and yellow and orange—and there was a plastic tree glued on top of it: a child's idea of a grassy hill covered with wild flowers. A school project maybe, done in art class for Father's Day, and now just another artefact amongst the thousand that spoke to Deacon of the life George and Adele had shared before he'd come to stay with them.

Underneath the rock there was a bronze key, and while

Adele was inserting it into the door's lock, Deacon got his first inkling that the building wasn't really a barn after all, or at least wasn't anything like the barn his father had built. The bottom half of the door was made of steel and above it there was a window of frosted glass—a regular door like for a house—whilst the door to *their* barn had been made of wood slats nailed against three ten-by-ones. Surrounding the metal door was a patchwork of bricks, a shade lighter than the rest and spanning almost half of the front wall.

He'd later learn that George had done the work himself, first removing the old double-wide wooden doors and bricking up the hole they'd left behind. He'd then installed a regular door, afterwards insulating the interior walls and covering them with barn board to maintain their rustic quality, lining those with shelves. It had taken him less than five years to fill them with books, and now thirty-five years later, the floor, the windowsills, the desk, and the steps leading up to the loft had all taken their share of the overflow. It was like a library had exploded, such was the impression it made anyway when Deacon first stepped through the door.

His amazement must have been written large on his face. Seeing his widening eyes, Mrs. Cleary said, "It's something isn't it?" though the way she pursed her lips suggested she hardly shared the wonder Deacon felt.

"I've been after him for years to clean this place up," she said, flipping the switch beside the door. The dull glow cast from the overhead fixture sparkled off the dust glittering the air and she swat after it as she made her way towards the staircase, muttering more to herself than to Deacon, "Getting so a body can hardly move in here."

By the time she was halfway up to the loft, Deacon had overcome his initial trepidation and taken a step inside.

"Be careful not to touch anything," Mrs. Cleary warned, leaning over the loft's rail. "You'll be buried alive if one of those piles comes down on top of you."

Deacon was pretty sure she was joking but still he nodded and made sure to keep his hands firmly at his sides as he followed the narrow path through the stacks. It split into two at the desk and he followed it to the right, stopping only when he came to the typewriter sitting in front of the chair at its fore. It was old, he could tell because it didn't even have an electrical cord. Remington Rand was etched in gold print along its hood and from the dust layering its keys it was obvious that it hadn't been used in years. As if by its own volition, his hand reached out and his index finger pressed down on the letter J. An arm lashed out, striking with such a loud clack against the spool that he gasped and looked up towards the loft, waiting to be reprimanded.

But Mrs. Cleary seemed to have other things to worry about. He could hear her muttering a litany of grievances against the mess she'd found upstairs, and he turned to the shelf behind the desk, finding at eye level a row of books wedged between two brass elephants.

It struck him as odd, the rest of the shelves crammed as they were, and here on this shelf only a dozen books held together by the two elephants, their heads bent low, their legs straining as if it took every ounce of their strength just to keep them in place. It was only when he took a step closer that he could see the name printed on their spines and realized they were the ones George had written.

Running his finger over the titles, he came to the last in the row and eased *The Stray* out of its place. He held it suspended between his hands, gazing at the cover, the picture of the man carrying the woman who looked to be dead enough to bring tears back to his eyes.

He was still staring at it when Mrs. Cleary came down the stairs, griping, "Well, I don't know where in hell's half acre he put them. Maybe the family of rats that have moved in upstairs could tell you, but I sure in Hades can't."

When she'd come to the open door she glanced about and then craned to look past the stacks of books.

"Deacon, you back there?"

Deacon stepped out from behind the pile on the desk and she squinted as if she couldn't quite make him out through the veil of dusty light.

"I couldn't find them," she said. "We'll ask George when he gets home. Now why don't you come inside, I'll make you some breakfast."

Deacon started towards her and then stopped. He looked down at the book in his hand and turned back to the shelf, thinking he should put it back but not wanting to part with it just yet.

"What's that you got there?" Mrs. Cleary asked.

When he looked back at her she was walking towards him, setting the reading glasses that had been propped on her head down over her eyes and reaching out for the book. Deacon passed it over with grave reluctance. She gave it a quick glance, frowning when she saw what it was and then clamping it against her chest, showing no sign that she was willing to give it back.

"You like to read?" she asked.

Deacon nodded.

"Well, this is hardly a book for children," she said, turning for the door. "There's a box in the attic of the ones I saved from when Edward and Louise were young. Why don't we go and take a look in there?"

"I want to read that one," Deacon said, his voice forceful enough that it stopped her in her tracks.

"It'll give you nightmares. Now come on—"

"But it's about my ma and pa!"

His voice cracked as he said it and when the old woman turned back to him he looked like he was set to start crying again. She frowned as if he was just being unreasonable and then looked down at the book in her hand. Her expression softened, all of a sudden realizing that what he'd said was true. She shook her head and peered sideways at Deacon. Then, frowning again as if she still couldn't reconcile herself to being party to the corruption of a boy as young as he, she set the book down on top of the nearest stack and turned, calling over her shoulder as she strode through the door, "Just be sure to put it back when you're done."

10

Deacon read it sitting under the maple tree beside the barn, not looking up until Mrs. Cleary was setting a plate in front of him. There was a ham and cheese sandwich on it and some potato chips and she was holding the plate in her hand with the two pieces of toast and jam she'd left him for breakfast. He hadn't taken a bite of those and didn't feel hungry now but when she said, "You should eat something," he picked up a sandwich half and took a bite. That satisfied her enough that she left him alone for the rest of the afternoon though he didn't eat so much as a crumb afterwards. The only time he remembered the sandwich at all was when a squirrel startled him from the page by stealing the top piece of bread from one of the halves. It had dragged it a few feet away and was standing on its hinds, mocking him with its cheerful natter, but Deacon paid it no mind, eager as he was to return to the book.

He was on page 107. So far, other than the scene where the dogs had attacked the homesteader's son, which was indeed quite frightful, he hadn't found any indication of why his father and Mrs. Cleary had said it wasn't a book for children. Up until then the story had been rather tame, more so even than *White Fang*, as it alternated between the homesteader's hunt for the pack of stray dogs that had killed his son and the two Chippewa brothers searching for their sister who'd been kidnapped by a trapper working for the Hudson's Bay Company. Like his father, the homesteader was a Dane, whom George described as being *five foot four, he'd joke, on a windy day who in spite of the shortness of his stature, or perhaps because of it, had become renowned in logging settlements stretching from Lake Simcoe to Georgian Bay, for there wasn't a man among them more able with an axe or with a fiddle, nor more generous with a helping hand or a kind word*, a description that Deacon thought fit his father to a T.

There were plenty of other things about the man, named Asger, that reminded him of his dad and George had such a deft facility with words that he seemed to spring to life right off the page. For most of the book so far, he'd been walking from one logging settlement to the next, hearing stories of the dogs' rampage from all he encountered, one old priest going so far as to call them *unholy daemons unleashed by an Indian witchdoctor as a pox upon those who'd stolen his People's land*. Every time one of Asger's chapters ended and one about the two brothers searching for their sister began, Deacon had a powerful urge to skip ahead, to get back to his pa, his restless anticipation tempered only by the knowledge that the girl in question, whom George had named Niimi, was his mother and the hope that his patience would be well-rewarded once she finally made an appearance.

When she did, on page 121, the trapper was leading her through the woods *by means of a manacled chain around her neck such as the slavers used*. The trapper was known only as The White Devil though *he had a face as red and swollen from drink as the ass end of a baboon.* When they reached his shack he looped the chain around the trunk of a tree a dozen paces from its porch and secured it with a padlock, the key to which he wore on a leather cord strung around his neck.

Niimi slumped to her knees within the tree's shade, her head lowered, penitent just like The Crows had commanded her to do when offering prayers to their God. After almost a week of being dragged through the bush, she was in a most sorrowful state. The White Devil hadn't fed her more than a few scraps since he'd taken her and the sharp lines of bones appeared on the point of cutting through the skin of her once ruddy cheeks, now calloused with mud and lined with channels like the tributaries of long-dead rivers. Her hair was clumped with knots and burrs so that it struck out at odd angles from her head remaking her into a half-mad witch. The soles of her bare feet had long been reduced to a bloody pulp, and the scrape from innumerable brambles made her legs look like a dozen games of tic-tac-toe had been played on them by a spastic at a school for the blind. Her back bore the sting of his whip, freely given whenever she'd slowed or stumbled, and her neck was rubbed so raw by the manacle that its edges felt like razor blades whenever she shifted against the weight of it pressing into the flesh of her shoulders.

Encountering his mother thusly, Deacon clamped the book shut, afraid of what might happen to her next. He had the sudden urge to throw the damn thing away, so he'd never have to find out. He'd gone so far as to cock it back in his hand before the thought reared, *But you can't just leave her like that.*

Gritting his teeth, he set the book back on his lap, flipped to his page, and, taking a deep breath, began to read again.

Her every breath was an agony.

With no hope of better days ahead she waited until The White Devil had disappeared through the shack's front door and then fished about with fevered eyes for a sharp stone within reach that she might use to end her suffering. The ground around her had been scoured clean into a circle of hard-packed dirt showing no trace of anything save the odd pebble and the gnarled finger of a root that had broken through its surface, the perimeter of which ran at a distance about the length of the chain tethering her to the tree. She was just on the cusp of gleaning the significance of that when she heard the shack's door thudding open.

When she looked up, The White Devil was walking towards her. He was carrying a body slung over one shoulder. It was naked and its legs were as stiff as logs and teetered against the sanction of his crooked arm. In his free hand he hoisted a spade shovel. When he'd come to the edge of the circle of hard-packed earth he planted that in the ground, pushing down on its blade with his foot to secure it. The body he dropped in front of Niimi with all the care of a sack of potatoes.

It was a girl, she could see that, with long black hair like her own. She couldn't have been much older than her first cycle as a woman, though her exact age was hard to measure due to the ravages inflicted upon her. Her ears had been removed and so had both of her breasts, leaving holes encrusted with black blood in her chest. Her body bore the mark of The White Devil's whip, crisscrossing her skin in a beaver dam's worth of thatched welts. Some of them hadn't yet been old enough to clot when she'd died and within their ragged clefts, maggots swarmed in the ecstasy of their feast. But it was the ones that time had seen fit to heal that spoke most truly to Niimi of her own fate, as did the toothless cavity that had become the girl's mouth. From its yawning chasm, tendrils of dusty white ran down her chin and there was more of the same crusted over the thin mat of her pubis, which Niimi took to mean that even death had provided the girl no relief from The White Devil's lust.

Staring down at the girl, she knew he meant her as a warning and she swore a solemn oath to herself that no matter what he asked of her she would suffer through it without complaint, comforting herself with the knowledge that it would only be a matter of time before her brothers arrived to rescue her, making a further promise that once they did she would make The White Devil pay double: for the horrors he had inflicted upon this young girl as well as the ones she knew were in store for her.

So when, a moment later, he pointed to the shovel, commanding her to dig, she scrambled to her feet, took up the spade, and pitched its blade into the ground with eager obedience. Prying loose a morsel of the hard-packed earth with its tip, she looked up, smiling, seeking The White Devil's favour.

When he said, Well, go on, then, she drove the blade into the ground again.

He watched her dig, standing at the edge of the circle of dirt, stroking his beard, until she'd cleared away the top layer of soil. Then, foraging in his pocket for his tobacco pouch, he returned to the shack and sat in the crude birch bark chair within the shade of its eave, smoking his pipe and watching the girl labour under the noon's oppressive heat.

By the time she'd dug a hole six feet deep and almost as long, the sun had descended amongst the trees. Her hands were blistered and her arms ached as if they meant to spring loose from her shoulders at any moment. She was tired beyond measure and it took every ounce of her being to pull herself up and out of the grave. She lay at its side and such was her exhaustion that it felt like she was drifting out of her body. She was levitating towards the treetops, her suffering all but a bad dream, until the overwhelming stench of the girl's body brought her hurtling back to earth.

Rising to her feet, she looked to the shack. The White Devil had fallen asleep in the chair, or so it seemed. She watched him for any sign that it was a ruse. She saw a fly circling him and then land on his nose. He didn't so much as twitch and she turned once again to the girl. Her docile form, spackled with shovelfuls of dirt, reminded her of something else The Crows had told her, and she took up the shovel in both hands, holding it like a fishing spear and bringing the sharp tip of its blade down onto the girl's chest. The blade penetrated her paled flesh as easily as it would have mud and a stifled crack told her that her aim had been true.

Falling to her knees, she reached into the wound, finding as she had hoped the broken shaft of a rib bone. She yanked it out and with a quick glance at The White Devil, to make sure he was still asleep, she pressed its tip into the earth, pushing down upon its end until it was even with the ground. *She covered it with a handful of dirt and planted a pebble to mark its place. She then bent to the girl, begging her forgiveness for stealing that, the most sacred part of her, and whispering into her ear of how she would use it to visit upon The White Devil a thousand torments: the only words of comfort she could think to offer the girl before rolling her into the grave.*

11

Recounting this to Crystal, those five years later on the dock, she muttered, "That's horrible. How—I mean, how could he have written such a thing?"

"You never read it?" Deacon asked.

"I've never read any of George's books. Dad wouldn't let them in the house. Now I can see why."

"But weren't you curious? Later, I mean."

"I guess I kind of forgot about them. I never was much of a reader."

"But he's your grandfather."

Crystal shook her head as if, like Deacon, she was trying to reconcile the man she knew with the person who could have written that.

"He's a twisted fuck, that's what he is," she said after a moment. "Why, I mean, why would he write that about your mom?"

"Pa must have told him a few stories."

"About her being kidnapped by some psycho?"

"She was never kidnapped, far as I know."

"What then?"

"About her life before they met. She didn't talk much about it but sometimes, when I was in bed, I'd hear them arguing."

"About what?"

"Who she was with before him, mostly. One time I heard her yelling that if my pa was any kind of real man he'd carve that motherfucker's heart out and bring it to her on a stick."

"She said that?"

Deacon nodded.

"He ever tie her to a tree?"

"I don't know. But I've seen the marks on her back enough times to know he used to whip her something fierce."

"Jesus."

They sat there on the dock, both of them staring out at the lake, listening to the gentle lap of the water against the dock. A loon cried out in the distance and Deacon fumbled another smoke from his pack.

"So'd you finish it?" Crystal asked while he was lighting it.

"What?"

"The book."

"Of course."

"I never could have, reading something like that about *my* mom."

"I had to."

"What do you mean?"

"Same reason anyone finishes a book."

"And why's that?"

"To find out what happens next."

"So?"

"Huh?"

"What happened next?"

"I wouldn't want to spoil it for you."

"Go ahead, I don't mind."

"Sorry. You'll have to read it for yourself."

She frowned again, and while he was occupied with the thought that she never looked prettier than when she was frowning at him, she snatched the cigarette from his mouth. She drew heavy on it and held the smoke in until it seemed her chest might burst.

"So is that it?" she asked, finally exhaling.

"What?"

"The end of your story."

"Hardly."

"Well, go on, then."

12

H e finished the book two hours later, tears wet on his cheeks from when he'd finally got to the part where Asger and Niimi met, at the end of the last chapter. It happened just like it had on the cover, and the way George described the waterfall immediately reminded Deacon of the place his father had taken him and Abel every year, camping out there for a week to mark the beginning of summer.

Their mother only joined them on the last night, bringing marshmallows and hot dogs to roast over the fire, treats that seemed like a king's feast since for the previous six days their father had only let them eat whatever they'd killed or caught. And after they'd eaten their fill, their father would take out his fiddle and Deacon and Abel would dance with their mother around the fire, Rose never happier than she was then, laughing and carrying on like a woman possessed, the sound of her joy echoing off the granite forming a horseshoe around the falls so that it seemed that the world itself was laughing right along with her.

Deacon knew that the waterfall was indeed where his parents had met, his father had told him that much.

"The first time I saw her," he'd told Deacon when he was six, pointing to the top of the ridge, some thirty feet high, over which a thin veil of water fell, "was right up there."

But whenever he'd pressed him further, he'd say, "That's more your mother's story than mine. You'll have to ask her."

But whenever he asked her, which he'd invariably do when he and Abel were lying between their parents on the soft bed of grass at the pool's edge—all of them sweaty and tired—she'd make snoring sounds, pretending to be asleep.

Deacon would nudge her, saying, "I know you're not asleep," and she'd answer, "Well, how am I supposed to sleep with someone poking me in the ribs?"

"You said you'd tell us."

"Tell you what?"

"How you and Pa met."

"When did I say that?"

"Last year," Abel would pipe in.

"I did?"

"And the year before that and the year before that too."

"You going to tell us or what?"

Their mother would peer up at the night sky, as if when the time came for her to share the story it would be written in the constellations along with all the rest, the two brothers holding their breath waiting on their mother to speak. After a moment a shudder would run through her. She'd blink and shake her head and say, "Maybe next year."

They'd protest plenty hearing that and she'd silence them by kissing each on his cheek. She'd then roll over onto her side, making snoring sounds again and this time no amount of elbowing would be enough to rouse her.

So when Deacon finally came to the part at the end of the book where Asger and Niimi met, he knew his father must have told George the story and Deacon cried tears of joy, imagining that it must have happened just like he'd written.

He read on to the end and when he got to the last page he turned back to the first, intending to start reading it all over again. But his legs were cramped from sitting cross-legged on the ground and he stood to shake out their stiff before getting back to it. That's when he saw George standing at the back door of the house. He was leaning against its frame and watching him with the same bemused smile he'd once used to greet his mother while his father was inside fetching the rifles. Seeing him like that, Deacon had a sudden impulse to run to him, to hug him tight, to bury his head in his chest, to never let go, such was the gratitude he felt towards the old man, for bringing his parents back to life, if only for a few hours.

He was struck suddenly shy though and lowered his head, summoning his nerve. When he looked up again George was gone and in his place Adele was at the door, calling to tell him that dinner was served. He was just stepping inside when he realized he was still carrying the book. He thought he ought to put it back on the shelf, like Adele had told him to. But he still wasn't ready to part with it just yet and ducked up the stairs to his room and hid it under his pillow.

The three of them ate in silence: Deacon sneaking glances at George between bites of mashed potatoes layered with hamburger hash and creamed corn, trying to think of what he might say to tell him what his book had meant, his words failing him; Adele looking to Deacon as if knowing what was on his mind and wanting to help him along but her words failing too; George, all the while, oblivious to the triangle he was caught up in, lost as he was in the simple pleasure of eating a well-cooked meal.

After he was done, Deacon excused himself and hurried up to his room. He fetched *The Stray* from under his pillow and read it all through the evening. When he'd come to the end, he cried again, though it wasn't joy he was overcome with this time but that familiar feeling of helplessness, knowing that no amount of words on a page could ever really bring his parents back to life and feeling evermore the loss of his brother, who wasn't in the story at all.

He buried his head under his pillow and lay there as the room grew dark.

I n the morning, he awoke feeling the same despair that had trailed him out of his nightmares every other morning he'd awoken in this stranger's bed.

After a while, an errant hair tickled against his nose. He reached to brush it away and his elbow knocked against the book laying in the bed beside him. Its cover was folded in half from rolling onto it while he slept. Alarm swept through him and he grabbed it up, bending the cover back and smoothing the crease. But there was nothing he could do to make it right.

You ought to put it back on the shelf before someone sees what you've done, he told himself and that was enough to get him out of bed.

He dressed in the first pair of shorts he found in his dresser and added to that a plain blue T-shirt. When he came into the backyard, *The Stray* clutched to his breast, Adele was kneeling at her vegetable garden, pulling weeds. She didn't look up and a moment later he was opening the barn's door with the key he'd fished from under the rock on the windowsill.

He slipped the book back into its place on the shelf and pressed the elephant's weight against it to hide the crimp to its cover then stood there for a moment, telling himself he ought to go help Mrs. Cleary in the garden. Instead, he ran his finger along the spines of the other books until he'd come to *A Bad Man's Son*. There was an armchair in the corner, its green leather seat worn smooth so that Deacon knew it had been well used. It was the only space not cluttered with books. Beside it there was a small table with stacks of paperbacks clustered around a reading lamp. He turned on the light, sat in the chair, and began to read.

T he next two months went by in a blur.
  A Bad Man's Son led him to *The Passage*, and that to *My Brother's Keeper*, *The Pines*, *Marble Mountain*, *The Sons of Adam*, *The Road Ahead*, *Into the After*, *A Precious Few*, *Land's End*, until finally *The Unnamed* lead him right back to *The Stray*. Most, as his father had warned, were chock full of violence and sex, often of a most deviant variety, interspersed with moments of such stark terror that they'd make him clamp the book shut. Sometimes it'd be days before he'd summoned the nerve to return to it. But as he read on he also found an equal share of love and joy, and it wasn't long before he began to divine that there was something more at play within them than a mere catalogue of the horrors man could inflict upon his fellow man. He couldn't put into words exactly what that was: a mystery of some sort that always seemed to be fleeing forever beyond his grasp.

  The first ten were written in chronological order, *A Bad Man's Son* set in the 1860s and *Land's End* in some dark and dismal future where dates had little or no meaning. Only the middle three were set in what might be considered George's present—the 1960s and 70s—and all of these ended with a cataclysm, never fully revealed, that brought about the end of civilization. The following three took place in the world that George imagined was to follow—"a burnt-out district of mythic savagery over which the course of empire runs in reverse," in the words of one reviewer blurbed on the back of *Land's End*. The eleventh, the only hardback among them, seemed to take as its aim the unification of all that came before. As such, *The Unnamed* was the longest of all his books, by a factor of three, and it took Deacon better than a week to get through its 694 pages. It was divided into seven sections, the middle five introduced by titles bearing the dates 1600 through 2000, the first and last introduced by a blank page as if the past and the future they imagined were beyond the bounds of time itself.

The story revolved around two Omushkego, which Deacon was to learn was the name of a tribe of Cree who lived on the shores of James Bay in Northern Ontario. One of them was a girl and the other a boy and both were born on the same spring day at the exact moment Old *Chiishaayiyu*, the village's Story Keeper, saw the first wave of *kihchiniska* returning from their migration to the south. Their parents took this to be a sign that good things were in store for the two, but, as Deacon would shortly learn, they couldn't have been more wrong. Such suffering as they'd endure made his own seem trifling by comparison, and all thoughts of his grief seemed to fade away as he followed the many trials and tribulations of the protagonists, who, as the book's title had indicated, were known simply as the boy and the girl, in the first two sections and the man and the woman in the latter five.

The other odd thing about the book was that as one century passed into the next, the two lead characters aged but a decade. As such, they were ten when they spotted the white sails of a *wapiskiwiyas* ship cresting the waters of *Wiinipekw* and seventy when *wapiskiwiyas* civilization fell, restoring the Omushkego to their former prominence within the natural order. Or so it had seemed, for in the last chapter a black fume of smoke—what they called *pikithew*—appeared on the southern horizon, warning of a new threat yet to come. Deacon could only assume that this was the Sons of Adam, the doomsday cult introduced in the book of the same name and then forever hovering on the periphery of the books that came after, stalking the scattered remnants of humankind in their eternal quest to burn the world back to Eden.

As to the man and the woman's ultimate fate, George did not say, but given what they'd lived through thus far, Deacon was left with a lingering hope that, regardless of what happened after George had written *The End*, they'd make out just fine.

After he'd finished with it the first time, he'd set the book back in its place and plucked out *The Stray*. Peering down at his parents on the cover, the despair that had overcome him when last he'd read it threatened to once again swallow him into its fold. Thinking of what he'd just read, he told himself he'd be okay too. He read it through in a single sitting and this time did not cry at all. When he was done he put it back on the shelf. It was an act that had seemed meaningless at the time but, in the years to come, would take on an almost mystical significance: his own past becoming, in that moment, just another one of George's Fictions that he could put back on the shelf along with all the others.

At the time though, he didn't get even an inkling of that, and he ran his fingers along the spines of the others until he came again to *The Bad Man's Son*. He stood staring at it for a moment, shaking his head and muttering to himself, "Maybe it's best if you give your eyes a little rest."

Wending his way back through the stacks he came to the door, squinting against the light and catching sight of a swallow pecking at the grains of seed in the bird feeder hanging from the cherry tree. He could hear other birds too: the playful chatter of chickadees and cardinals warbling to their kind and the ruckus of black birds overlaid with the soothing chirrup of frogs from the creek running along the bottom of the ravine. A dragonfly flit by his face. He watched it hover over the lawn and though he'd seen dozens, maybe hundreds, doing the same, he was struck with a sudden awe at its grace and its beauty. Such a feeling of peace as he'd never known settled over him, lasting, as such feelings do, only the briefest of moments before a frantic fluttering of wings turned him back to the cherry tree.

A blue jay was descending towards it, its wings raised like an avenging angel. It landed on the bird feeder's perch with such force that it sent the seed scattering in all directions. The way it sat there ruffling its feathers and squawking its glee, as if it were king of the world and wanted everyone to know it too, made him all of a sudden understand why George had such a hate-on for them.

I wonder if that pellet gun's still up by the window where he liked to shoot, he asked himself.

Only one way to find out, he answered and hurried off into the barn.

13

By the time he'd reached that point in the story, the moon was lost behind the curtain of evergreens on the far side of the lake and the party had emptied into the water.

The beach was cluttered with a deluge of shirts and pants, underwear and shoes. Their owners were splashing about the shallows, all of them naked and five or six of the girls riding on the shoulders of heavily muscled young men playing at a game of joust, trying to knock the others from their steeds. Their drunken revelry seemed a world away from the dock as Deacon told Crystal how he'd found the pellet gun propped against the chair by the window and spent the afternoon prowling the backyard, shooting a half-dozen blue jays.

"It seemed the least I could do," he explained, "after what George had done for me."

"He brought you back to life," Crystal said.

"I guess he did."

He cast her a sideways glance. The way she was staring

at him recalled at once the mischievous zeal with which Rain had looked at him after she'd led him into the guest room of the Bickers' chalet on the night he'd driven her back from the *Chronicle*'s Christmas party. Seeing *that* look in Crystal's eyes, he was just then thinking how sweet it would be if—

A thought splintered into shards by a booming voice just then yelling over to the dock, "Crystal, I need a partner!"

Turning towards the shallows, he saw the basketball player standing waist deep in the water. Moonlight glistened over his chiselled flesh making him look like some sort of mythical hero risen from the depths.

"Duty calls," Crystal said and then he felt her hand on his shoulder.

She used it to push herself to her feet, squeezing his arm once before she let go as if to provide some consolation. He watched her slip her bra up over her head and drop it onto the dock. Her back was to him. All he could see were her slender curves silhouetted in the dark and as she slipped from her bottoms he searched about his thoughts for anything he could say to get her to turn his way, if only an inch. The basketball player was wading towards her and Deacon turned to him, seeing in his wide-mouthed grin a fair view of the one he was missing out on.

He heard a splash and turned to the shallows where Crystal had just dove in, tracing ahead of the ripples she'd made and seeing her head come up at the basketball player's waist. Lifting her out of the water, he set her backwards on his shoulders, burying his face within her belly. She responded by laughing at what he must have been doing with his tongue and slapping at his back, yelling, "Turn around. I can't see. Turn around!" as he blindly hastened to join the fray.

14

Recalling the scene as he turned off Hiram Street and started up Baker, he was overcome by a familiar sinking feeling. It was the same way he always felt when he was approaching the end of *The Stray*. Walking up the Cleary's driveway with the book weighted in his jacket pocket on the night after he'd discovered George was writing again, he now regretted bringing it, knowing that he'd never be able to reclaim the profound sense of calm he'd felt the night before, sitting with his back propped against the barn's wall, lost in the numinous clatter of the *clackety-clack*.

The driveway's cobblestones led him towards the house. Its windows were dark and the brick path leading into the backyard darker still. On either side of the alcove overhanging the front door were two cement planters painted red and as big as well-heads. They had once been filled with tiger lilies but had gone the way of all of Adele's carefully cultivated flower gardens, filled now with weeds—mostly dandelions and timothy grass—windblown from the neighbours' yards. When he stepped from between them he paused, seeking out the rhythmic pulse of keystrokes from the Remington Rand but could hear nothing beyond the faint strains of a country song leaking through the Quimbys' open garage door.

He started down the walkway into the backyard and when he came to the tufts of grass curling over the bricks at the path's end he paused again, tracing the barn's outline to the lone front-side window and finding that dark too.

George is probably just taking the night off, he thought, *best try again tomorrow.*

And yet still he lingered, his gaze settling on the vague outline of the rock on the barn's windowsill. He told himself he shouldn't even be thinking of doing what he was thinking of doing but started forward nevertheless. It was well after nine and shadows ranged long over the unmowed lawn and overgrown flowerbeds. He kept within the shadowed fringe of the treeline, ducking low and coming at the barn as a burglar would.

He unlocked the door as quietly as he could and eased it open with the caution of a drunk teenager sneaking through his bedroom window just before dawn. He shut it behind him with similar care. From his inside breast pocket, he retrieved his cell phone. He activated its flashlight and kept the beam at his feet, gracing the floor with just enough illume to avoid toppling the stacks of books on either side of the path leading him towards the desk. Light splashed over the two stacks of paper sitting side by side to the left of the typewriter. Moving to the smaller of the two, he pried the bottom page up ever so delicately with a fingernail, so as not to disturb the rectangle that framed the stack amidst the scattering of ash covering the desk.

The sheet was blank except for the title centered on the page: **No Quarter.** He let the sheet drop. On the second there was a quote: **If the soul is left in darkness, sins will be** committed. The guilty one is not he who commits the sin, but he who caused the darkness. V.H. At the top of the next, there was the word **Prologue** and he lifted the page until the first line came into view.

How long it had been following her, she couldn't say.

He'd barely got to the end of that when he was startled by a whimper arising from the other side of the door. The pages slipped from his grip, slumping back to the desk, their sudden descent blowing at the outline of dust, blurring its sharp lines. He froze stock-still, listening. The dog whimpered again and this time it was accompanied by the rake of claws against steel. Alarm hastened him away from the desk. He followed the flashlight's glare back through the stacks of books, seeing Trixie's snout raised up to the door's window, her seeing him too and emitting a sharp whine as he reached for the knob.

As he closed the door behind him, Trixie barked and he bent to the dog, shushing her and letting her lick his cheek.

"You just getting back from a walk?" he asked and glanced towards the house, expecting George to be standing there at the end of the path, wondering why she'd set off into the backyard.

But the brick path was empty and he scanned over the house's windows looking for a light or a shade of movement, anything to tell him that he'd gone inside. It was as still as a tomb. Trixie had turned around and was walking towards the garden. Deacon watched after her, scouring the backyard for any sense of where she might be headed.

Amongst the gloom he couldn't see much except that the door to the garden shed was open. Three summers previous, someone had stolen a jerry can full of gas out of the same shed. They'd used it to paint a pentagram in fire on the field surrounding the helicopter landing pad behind the hospital, and ever since George had been real particular about making sure the shed's doors were locked up tight. Seeing it open now didn't exactly set off any warning bells but it did provide a focal point to the sense of foreboding that had begun to settle in his belly. He took a direct line for it and was just cresting the cherry tree when he caught sight of something jutting from within the nettle of barbed stalks at the edge of the raspberry patch. It took him only a moment to see that it was one of George's workboots. Its sole was crusted with dirt and its toe was pointed skywards.

He set off at a run.

Trixie was laying down beside George when he made it to the edge of the garden. She looked up as Deacon craned forward and peered down at the old man, sprawled on his back amongst the brambles. His eyes were open, vacant and dark, and his right hand was resting on his heart. A blotch of what appeared to be blood soaked his shirt from the collar to his belt. At first glance, it looked to Deacon like he'd been shot. The shock of finding him that way and thinking that the violence so intrinsic to his Fictions had somehow caught up with him didn't relent even when he bent to the old man and set his hand on George's shoulder, seeing, or rather feeling and smelling, that it wasn't blood at all, but motor oil.

He'd learn, a week later, it was from the Rototiller sitting not five feet away. Deacon had started it up so he could cart it off to the dump and had been startled by a geyser of the black fluid spraying from a corroded gasket. He'd seen then an image of George startled too, a sudden shock too much for the old man's heart to bear. Not that it mattered a damn bit whether it was blood or motor oil, for the result was much the same.

George was clearly dead.

RENÉ

❝A funeral?" René asked in answer to his grandfather's question. "Who died?"

"A friend."

"I didn't think you had any friends."

René was standing, travel mug in hand, on the porch leading into his grandfather's clapboard bungalow. He'd awoken in his trailer with a tickle in his throat that might have been the start of a cold. When he sat up, the room seemed to tilt away from him and he shivered like someone was running ice cubes up his back, so he knew he'd be lucky if that was all it was. His grandfather kept a box of what he called lemony citron in his cupboard, and René had skipped making his morning coffee, thinking a couple of packets of that might do him a world of good.

His grandfather had called to him from the garage's door as he'd mounted the porch steps, and when René had turned he was hurrying towards the house, beseeching him with eager eyes, an expression he often wore and which always reminded René of a dog begging for a treat. At René's rebuff his expression turned dour and he scratched at his billy goat scruff, trying to think of a name to prove his grandson wrong. He mustn't have been able to for after a moment he said, "They's gettin' thin on the ground, that's for sure." Then looking up again, "So can I get a ride in with you or not?"

"Saturday, you say?"

"I did."

"You know I see Tawyne on Saturday."

"I also know you meet him at the Tim's in town. Ain't but a ten-minute walk from the church."

"What time's it at?"

"The funeral?"

"That's what we're talking about, ain't it?"

"It's at one."

"I was planning on leaving around ten."

"That's fine too."

"You were just going to hang around?"

"Well, I was hoping to see . . ." he said, sneaking a peak at René out of the corner of his eye, "Tawyne anyhow. Saturday's his birthday, ain't it?"

"No, it's on Sunday."

"But you're going to celebrate it on Saturday."

"You know I am."

"So what do you say? Can I get a lift?"

René thought about it.

"Jean'd have a fit she saw you," he finally said. "It's one of her rules. I toldya that."

"Ain't no harm in wishing him a happy birthday."

"Tell that to Jean."

The old man man's face sunk.

"Didya get him a present?" René asked after a moment.

"I figure I could rustle something up."

"Jean'd just as likely take a hammer to it as let him open it. If she knew it was from you."

It came out sounding mean, and he'd meant it to. He felt bad all the same. It wasn't the old man's fault he was in a pissy mood; it was the thought of starting a ten-hour day feeling like hammered shit.

Clutching at the wolves on his hands and counting to five, René waited for his calm to return. When it did, he let his gaze wander back to the old man.

"Okay," he finally said. "I'll let you come. As long as you stay out of sight."

The old man's expression brightened.

"You can count on it."

René had just filled his travel mug from the electric kettle on his grandfather's kitchen counter when his Samsung rang. It was Roy, telling him that he was running late.

"I'm just passing Rainbow Ridge," he added. "I'll be there in under twenty."

"I'll be here," René said, and Roy hung up without bothering to say goodbye.

He drank his lemony citron sitting in his grandfather's chair at the kitchen table, about the only surface more than two square feet in the entire place that wasn't covered with an odd assortment of engine parts, which leant the house the appearance it was more an extension of the garage than a home, good and proper. On any other day, he would have taken it outside, since his grandfather didn't abide smoking in his house. But he didn't much feel like having a cigarette just yet and besides the latest issue of the *Chronicle* was sitting at his grandfather's spot at the table.

It was the headline on the front page that had caught his attention.

George Cleary, 1942–2015, it read and it didn't take more than a second glance at the name to know that he must have been the friend his grandfather was talking about. Below the headline there was a picture of a man sitting at a typewriter with a cigarette crooked in his mouth. He was clean-shaven and couldn't have been older than twenty-five and hardly resembled the old man who used to drop by three or four times a year to go fishing with his grandfather.

He drove a 1970 Ford Ranger XLT, its make, model, and year permanently etched in René's mind. He'd helped his grandfather repair it a half-dozen times, though he'd only met its owner on three occasions. The first two times René had been there when he'd pulled up into the driveway. His grandfather had come out of the garage where he was working on a car, standing at the door and shaking his head, like it was the devil himself who'd come to pay a visit.

When George stepped out, René's grandfather would call over to him, "You still driving that old piece of shit?" and George would call back to him, "I'll be driving it until I find the son of a bitch who sold it to me. I aim to run him down and then good riddance to the both of them, I say. Hey, wait, there he is now!"

George would then hurry back into the cab of the truck. He'd gun the engine and the truck would lurch forward as if he meant to make good on his threat, and René's grandfather would make a game of scurrying for cover—two damn fool old men playing at being teenagers.

After a moment, George would turn off the truck's ignition

though when he'd get out he'd be cursing, "Goddamned piece of shit, stalled on me again. I guess it's your lucky day."

He'd be grinning when he said it and René's grandfather would be grinning right back as he walked towards him.

"Good to see you, George," he'd say, and George would look over to René, suddenly struck shy by the old man's pointed gaze.

"Good to see one of you anyway," George would say.

George'd then collect his rod and tackle box from the back of the truck, and René's grandfather his own rod from the garage and they'd set off up the path leading through the woods at the back of his grandfather's three-quarter-acre plot, neither in any hurry, it seemed, to get to Lake Koué.

The last time he'd seen him, he was seventeen and George had brought along a boy, whose name René couldn't remember. He was some years younger than himself and a shade lighter skinned, though he was unmistakably Indian. René's grand-father later told him that George and his wife had adopted him after the boy's family had died in a car crash and that he was Chippewa, on his mother's side. Whenever she said grace, René's grandmother was careful to pay tribute to "these honourable People" who had lived in Mesaquakee before *Hunio 'on* and their diseases had chased them north, their own People migrating there from Kanesatake, Quebec, several generations later after a dispute with a Jesuit priest had threatened to turn ugly.

While the old men were shaking hands, the boy had gone to fetch the gear from the truck's bed. With two rods and tackle in hand, he stood staring at René with the same daft expression as the tourists who'd come up to the reserve to see some "real" Indians. René had fled into the garage to get out from under his gaze, and a short while later his grandfather had poked his head in the door to ask him if he'd like to come fishing with them, the first time he'd ever done so. René answered that he ought to be getting home. It wasn't exactly the truth, and after they'd departed he took his time putting the tools away and sweeping the floor, all the while fighting a losing battle to keep his attention from wandering towards the hardcover book wedged amongst his grandfather's collection of owner's manuals, one of every make, model, and year of car or truck he'd ever sold, over one hundred in all.

He kept them on a grey steel utility shelf arranged in chronological order, the oldest dating back to 1972, the year he'd got the job at Bailey's Auto Wreck through Corrections Canada's work-release program. Seeing the endless parade of cars meant for the crusher, he'd been alarmed at such waste. Whenever he found one that he thought worth saving, he'd buy it from Clarence Bailey for its scrap fees, fix it up, and sell it for cheap, mostly to teenagers buying their first car or to single moms who couldn't afford anything better. He'd give them a two-year warranty on labour for when it broke down, which was a damn site better than they'd get at any of the used car dealerships in town. He kept track of the dates of sale by affixing a label to the spine of their particular owner's manual, ordered in, new, from the Auto Parts store in town and stored on the shelf as much as a record of his life's work as it was for reference.

The manual for George's truck was three-quarters of the way through the middle row. It was purchased, according to its label, on October 23, 1983. The truck had been in and out of the garage a couple dozen times since. As such, the manual was dog-eared and stained with innumerable oily fingerprints. René was thirteen years old when the Ranger's alternator had started making a grinding noise. He'd dropped by after school, as he often did on the afternoons his grandmother had her drum circle, or council meetings, and he knew he wouldn't be missed. He'd found his grandfather under the Ford's hood. Engine parts and tools were strewn haphazard on the floor around his feet.

"Do me a favour," his grandfather said by way of a greeting, "fetch me the book."

"For the '70 Ford Ranger?"

The old man grunted in answer, as he often did when he shouldn't have to answer at all.

"What's the date?" René asked as he stepped to the shelf and scanned over the manuals.

"Eighty-three. Should be on the middle shelf."

"I got it."

Reaching for it, he caught sight of the book beside it and his hand had stalled. The book was four fingers wide, George Cleary and *The Unnamed* running lengthwise down its spine. But it wasn't those that made him pause a moment, it was the picture above. It was of two child-sized silhouettes sitting on a tree branch with their legs a-dangle beneath them. Both had long hair and the one—a girl most likely—had her head resting on the other's shoulder, the boy—most likely—pointing at something in the distance. It struck him as oddly familiar, though he couldn't exactly say why. The thought arose in his mind like a question begging for an answer, and he was powerless but to pull the book out to see what the cover might reveal.

The picture there was a painting of a sunset over water. A thin rail of hazy light was mirrored along the surface of a lake, and the sky overhead was overcast and dark, the clouds fading into a starry night above. And at the bottom: a pine tree looming at the water's edge, the silhouettes of the two children sitting on a high branch. The boy he could now see was pointing out at the lake where there was a small square of white where the sky met the horizon—maybe the sail of a ship. The feeling that he'd indeed seen the two of them before furrowed his brow, and while he was pondering on where that might have been, his grandfather gave out a coarse shout: "You writing the damn manual over there yourself?"

Slipping the book back onto the shelf, he pulled out the Ranger's manual and hurried over to his grandfather.

The old man snatched up the manual without looking up. He flipped through it until he found what he was looking for and then lay it down on the engine block, propping his socket wrench over the crease to hold it flat. His reading glasses were propped on his forehead and he lowered them over his eyes, bending a hand's width from the page and tracing over the words. His lips moved in silent recitation for a moment, then he nodded and turned back to the truck.

"You can put it away now," he said, picking up his socket wrench and reaching it deep within the bowels of the engine.

René walked the manual back to the shelf. After he'd slid it into the gap he again paused a moment, staring at the spine of the one next to it.

And that's when it came to him.

It's like the photograph Grams has up on the wall in her kitchen.

It was black and white and the kids were in full light, not in shadow, but they were sitting on the high branch in a pine tree at the edge of the water. The girl was indeed resting her head on the boy's shoulder and he was pointing at something across the lake—maybe a sailboat just out of reach of the camera's focus.

When he was seven and he and his older sister Jean had first come to live with their grandmother, he'd often caught her staring up at the photo whenever she was standing at the stove. She was a large woman who always wore one of a half-dozen brightly coloured dresses imprinted with wild flowers and impregnated with the flavour of the stew that, for as long as René could remember, she kept at a slow boil on the stove, in case someone happened to drop by unannounced. She'd spend hours, it seemed, stirring at that big old char-bottomed pot with a wooden spoon, all the while staring up at the photograph.

Once he'd interrupted her revelry by asking, "Is that you in the picture, Grams?" and she'd startled same as if he'd given her a static shock.

"Huh?" she'd said, looking down at her grandson.

"In the picture. Is that you?"

She'd then turned back to the photograph, appraising it as if she wasn't quite sure what to say. After a moment, she shook her head.

"No," she'd said, "it's not me."

"Then who is it?"

"Just a couple of ghosts, is all."

"Ghosts," he'd gulped, for in those days he'd been a timid boy prone to bad dreams and sometimes wetting his bed.

He'd looked back at the photo. The steam rising from the pot leant it an eerie gloss so it wasn't hard to imagine that they were, indeed, ghosts. Seeing the look of terror spreading over her grandson's face, the old woman bent to him and brushed the hair out of his face with the back of her hand, as she often did to soothe him when he'd awake in the night, crying out for his mom.

"There's nothing to be afraid of," she'd said, running her hand through his hair on the way to easing herself back up to stand. "They won't bother you as long as you don't bother them."

Still, in the days, weeks, months to follow, the mere thought of the picture was enough to send a shudder up his spine, and it would be years before he'd even think of entering the kitchen without turning on the light for fear that the ghosts, freed from the photograph, might be lurking there in the dark.

Scared of a damn picture, he thought, staring at its double on the cover of the book. His cheeks flushed with shame from the memory, and he turned the hardcover over as much to distract himself from thinking about the boy he used to be as to see what it might say on the back.

At the bottom, there was the picture of a white guy sitting in front of a typewriter. He was wearing a button-down white shirt, its sleeves rolled up to his elbows, and had a hand-rolled cigarette crooked in the corner of his mouth. His eyes were wide as if whoever had taken the photograph had snuck up on him. *George Cleary lives in Tildon, ON* was all it said by way of explanation, and René read the first line of the paragraph that took up the remainder of the back cover.

> *In the dying days of the time before, a boy and a girl are*
> *born amongst a small band of Cree living in an isolated*
> *village on the shores of James Bay. They will come to*
> *hold the fate of a nation in their hands.*

That's as far as he got before his grandfather was calling over, asking him to fetch something or other.

"What?" he asked.

"The three-quarter-inch socket!" the old man hollered.

René went to fetch it from the tool cabinet and by the time he'd returned to the truck, his grandfather was wrestling with the bit on the socket wrench. He wiped his hands on his coveralls and tried again but he still couldn't get his fingers to stop from slipping.

"Goddamned arthritis," he complained. "Might as well be wearing oven mitts." Then passing the wrench to René: "You mind?"

René was still holding the book in one hand, the bit in the other. He tucked the former under his arm, set the latter on the truck's bumper, and took the socket wrench from his grandfather.

He popped the bit off with no more effort than twisting the cap
off a near-empty bottle of ketchup.

"What's that you got there?" the old man asked.

"Huh?" he said, handing the wrench back.

"Under your arm."

René drew the book out and held it up.

"I found it on the shelf."

"Shoot, I wondered where I put that. I was looking for it just
the other day."

"Well, it was sitting right there on the shelf."

"Shoot, don't that beat all."

"The picture on the cover . . ." René started then stopped.

"You recognize it, don'tya?"

"It's kinda like the one Grams has hanging over her stove."

"That still there?"

René nodded.

That gave the old man pause, and he rubbed at the greying
scruff under his chin as if trying to divine some deeper meaning
to it.

"She ever tell you about it?" he said after a time.

"All she'd say was it was of a couple of ghosts."

The old man let out a laugh, short and to the point.

"They ain't ghosts. Not yet, anyway."

"Who are they?"

"It's me and her."

"You and Grams?"

"Ya-huh. It was taken by this feller from the university who
was visitin' the reserve one time. We was five, maybe six. He was
a . . . watchamacallit. Someone who studies Indians?"

"An anthropologist?" René said, recollecting the word from
history class and surprising himself that he'd actually found a
use for it.

179

"That's it. He saw us up in this old tree we used to climb down by the lake, snapped a picture. Gave a copy of it to your gram's dad and one to mine."

"Why's it on the cover of this book?"

"I had the same picture hanging on the wall," he said, pointing then at a blank space above his workbench where a screw hole could just be made out, "right over there. Got wrecked the time the snow collapsed the roof, of course, but that was years after George saw it. It was the day he'd bought the truck, point of fact. I was just signing the papers over when he asked me about it. I told him the same as I told you and a few things besides. That's how he come to write the book."

"What do you mean?"

"It's about me and your grams."

"This book here?"

"Yeah."

"It says on the back it's about the Cree. You and Grams is Mohawk."

"Well, George took some liberties, I won't deny that."

René shook his head as if he didn't believe him but when he looked back at the cover there was no denying the picture. His expression must have still relayed doubt, for it wasn't but a moment later his grandfather said, "Look inside, you don't believe me."

René opened the book. Its spine let out a sharp crack as he turned to the first page.

"Keep going," his grandfather urged.

René turned to the next. On the left side there was a bunch of words in small print, the copyright and all that. On the right it read, *For Guy.* And below, in an almost childlike scrawl, it read: *There must be some way out of here.*

"What he wrote there, it's from a song," his grandfather said.

The book was weighing heavy in René's hands. As far as he knew, his grandfather had been a mechanic at Bailey's Auto Wreck ever since he'd got out of jail, pretty much his entire adult life. How anyone could have found enough in that to write a book as heavy as a brick seemed unlikely, verging on the impossible.

"Is this book really about you and Grams?" he asked.

"I don't stake a claim on the whole thing, but parts of it are anyways. And I'll let you in on a secret." Then leaning close enough to whisper in his grandson's ear: "You're in it too."

"I am not."

"Shades of you are, at least."

Now he knew that his grandfather was having him on and he had the proof to call him on it.

"Can't be," he said. "Says here—" pointing at the date on the copyright page, "it was written in 1986. That was before I was even born."

"I know."

"Then how? I mean, how in hell? There's no way."

"I don't know how George managed it, but you're in there as sure as I'm standing here before you. Even got your name right."

Shutting the book, René flipped it over to its back, tracing over the words, not really reading any of them as he searched for mention of his name. It wasn't there. Reaching the end of the paragraph, his eyes again sought out the picture at the bottom. Something about the man's startled grin, like he'd never had a damn worry in his entire life, brought the taste of bile into his mouth.

"How the fuck would he know what it's like being an Indian?" he said before he could stop himself, knowing, as he did, his grandfather's disdain for swears.

He hadn't seemed to notice though, or at least paid it no

mind, and without skipping a beat, he said, "I guess you're going to have to read it, you want to find that out."

"It'd take me a year to read through all that."

"That's okay. I ain't in no hurry to get it back."

René flipped it back over to its front cover and stared at the picture as if he might actually be considering it. Truth was, the two "ghosts" had already filled enough nightmares to last him a lifetime, and he'd as soon have the book sitting on the shelf at the head of his bed as he would a live rattlesnake. But when he looked up, the old man was beseeching him with those eager eyes, and René knew he'd be sorely disappointed if he said no.

"I don't think it's a good idea," he said, suddenly seeing a way out. "Grams'd know I got it from you and she's like to burn it. Hell, she'd throw a fit she kno—"

The words choked in his mouth, realizing the kind of trouble he'd just made for himself. A knot twisted in his belly, thinking of the seven kinds of hell he was about to catch for lying to his grandfather, and to his grandmother too.

"She don't know you've been coming to see me?"

René shook his head with downcast eyes and the old man turned away.

"Best put it back where you got it from, then," he said, his voice like it had been squeezed out through a mouthful of gravel.

"It's probably for the best," he added as René returned it to the shelf. "It's not really a book for children anyhow."

I t would be ten years before he'd hold the book in his hands again.

He'd just been transferred to Fenbrook Medium, where he'd serve out the last six months of his sentence. It was right off the 11, not a fifteen-minute drive south of Tildon. Every week the old man would be there waiting for him in the visitor's lounge. He was the only visitor René ever had during his incarceration, his grandmother having died of a stroke three years before he'd been found guilty of aggravated assault, which at the time had seemed to René about the best thing to be said about the whole sad and sorry affair.

The first time he came, he brought the book, passing it to one of the guards who, in turn, rifled through its pages before setting it on the table in front of René. René hadn't glanced at it longer than to see what it was, and when he looked back up at his grandfather he was beseeching him again with those eager eyes.

"I thought you might like something to read," he said. "Now you got the time."

René nodded, once. It was about all he ever gave by way of an answer as his grandfather filled the half hour they had together by telling him about whatever old junker he'd last saved, who its previous owners were, what was wrong with it, and then a virtual play-by-play of what he had to do to get it safetied, René nodding along to the endless prattle and passing furtive glances at the guards patrolling the aisles between the tables as if he was expecting one of them to jump him at any moment.

When their time was up that day, his grandfather stood, setting his hand on the book and drumming his fingers on its cover like he was having second thoughts about leaving it.

After a moment, he turned towards the door then looked back.

"The part about you," he said, "starts on page three-ninety-seven."

The truth was, René'd just as soon read the dictionary from A to Z, but he'd taken the book anyway. It'd be a month before he'd have cause to open it. He'd finally given in one morning when his cellmate, a Croatian named Dinko who was serving ten for his part in a human trafficking scheme, had fished it out from under the mattress on the top bunk upon which René was reclined.

"What the fuck you think you're doing?" René had growled, sitting up on the bed.

"I read," Dinko answered, sitting on the toilet. "It helps with—" searching for the right word and then only coming up with a sound as if he'd learned to speak English while watching Saturday morning cartoons, "plop!"

"Well, it's mine," René snarled, dropping to the floor. "Give it back!"

Dinko opened it in his bare lap, showing no signs that he meant to do anything of the sort and said, "A book is for read. What good is book sit under bed? No good, that is what. I read."

René reached out and grabbed at it but Dinko was expecting that. He held on tight, gritting his teeth and staring back at René with hate in his eyes. It was the kind of look that could get you killed even in medium security. Dinko was a big man, pushing two-eighty with hands meant for crushing rock, but if it came to a fight René knew Dinko had a compressed vertebra from the car crash that had killed three of his "migrant workers" and had led to his incarceration. He could barely stand on a good day and sitting on the toilet with his pants at his ankles René gave himself better than even odds that he'd be the one walking away. Hell, if he could get the book away from him, he could beat him to death with it, which, if it came to *that*, would have been the only useful thing a book had ever done for him thus far.

Recalling the memory of being locked in a life-and-death struggle with a fat man on the shitter—over a book he didn't even want to read—would give him plenty of hushed chuckles in the days to follow, but at that moment he'd never been more serious.

"Give it back!" he yelled and jerked one last time.

Dinko relinquished his hold at the same moment and René was flung back against the bed, his head knocking against the steel frame. The sharp pain turned his world red. He was on the verge of slapping that fat Croat fuck upside the head with the book gripped now as a bludgeon in both hands. But in the instant he was raising it to the task there arose an unmistakable *plop!* from between Dinko's legs. That and the sudden smile parting the fat man's mouth was enough to stay René's hand.

"Fighting over book is as good for 'plop' as reading book," Dinko said, reaching for the toilet paper and grinning as if things couldn't have worked out better. "I must remember that."

By then René was already settling onto his bed, muttering "Fuckin' jail," as he opened the book on the mattress before him.

He made a go at the first page but his head was aching so bad by the time he flipped to the next it was a good bet it'd feel like a nail had been driven into it if he tried to read the whole thing. He was on the verge of closing it when his curiosity got the better of him and he flipped forward to page 397.

This is what he read:

> The old man was seventy the first time he met one of his grandsons.
>
> He was living in the hunting shack his grandfather had built when he was but a young man. It was on the shores of a lake too small to bear any mention of on a map but which he'd called Koueeeeee, stretching the last syllable so that it sounded like a wolf howling a mournful lament. It was kihcêyihtâkwan—a sacred place—and when he was a boy his grandfather would take him and his brother up there for a month every summer to teach them what he called "The Old Ways."

During the fifteen years and change he'd spent laying on the bunk in one cell or another, his thoughts would often wander back to the shack and the good times he and his brother had had there. After he was released it was only natural that it was the first place he'd want to see again.

He hadn't meant to stay more than a few weeks, long enough, he'd reasoned, to summon the courage to return home to beg his wife's forgiveness for the hurt he'd caused her and the kids. When the summer had passed and he still hadn't, he wrote her a letter telling her where he was and leaving it in her mailbox one night, thinking that was at least something. That was thirty years ago. Every spring he cleared the path leading from the lake to what had once been their backyard and was now only hers—a distance of almost three miles—but she'd never come to visit. Aside from the twice yearly visits from his brother—once in the spring and once in the fall—nobody else had either.

The year that he'd turned seventy, he hadn't seen his brother in five years. He assumed he was dead and he'd all but given up on the hope that he himself was meant for anything short of dying old and alone, his bones like to have turned to dust before anyone stumbled across them. Still, he went out as soon as the snow had melted with his machete and his bow saw, the latter in case a tree too big to move had fallen over the path. There usually was and this year wasn't any different. It was a cedar tree, its trunk two feet thick and its base uprooted from the ground, most likely in that storm in late February that had torn the roof off the shack, shocking him awake under an avalanche of snow.

He'd cut a three-foot section out of the middle of the cedar. He was using a thick branch as a lever to roll it off the path when, from behind him, there arose a snarl. Spinning around, he saw what appeared to be a grey wolf, standing in the middle of the path, not five yards away. Its lips were curled back and the span of drool leaking out from between its exposed teeth left little doubt in the man's mind as to what it meant to do.

He'd lodged the machete in the crux of a tree, five or six strides at a hard run from where he now stood facing off against the wolf. It might as well have been on the moon for all the good it would have done him. The wolf took a step forward and growled again, yet the man did not feel afraid. He'd known all along that the violence that had marked his previous life would catch up with him and, knowing that the time was finally at hand, he closed his eyes and released himself to his fate, conjuring her face so that it would be the last thing he would see before he met his end and finding that he could no longer remember what she looked like.

And in that absence he saw his life for what it was: a gaping black hole as big as the night sky. He cursed himself for his idiot pride and in the sudden up-swelling of rage tightening his chest he knew then and there that if it had been a hundred wolves standing before him he'd kill them all with his bare hands if that's what it took to see his beloved one last time.

Opening his eyes—his fists clenched and the snarl curling over his lips revealing his own intent—he motioned to charge. He was thwarted in this by the sight of a boy now standing beside the beast. He was wearing a pair of black jeans, worn to tatters at both knees, and a black hooded jacket pulled over his head, the drape of his dark brown hair flowing from within, almost to his navel. His hand was set on the ridge of hackled fur raised along the creature's back and in his eyes there was a look of such stark fear that it revealed to the old man who the boy was (for hadn't his own daughter all too often gaped at him in exactly the same way when the darkness had come pouring out, most often through his hands and his feet and washing over the girl's mother with the fury of a springtime flood— an image he'd often called to mind when wrestling with thoughts of the man he'd once been).

Seeing the child thus, the old man was suddenly stilled. His hands loosened at his sides and his eyes averted from the boy, settling on the machete cleaved into the tree, yet another reminder that the violence that had forsaken him was still lying in wait, as much a part of his being as his skin.

For if he'd had it at hand when the wolf had appeared—

A thought that was mercifully interrupted by the boy's first words.

He said: It's okay, mister. He won't hurt you. He just gets a little jumpy around strangers.

The old man turned back to the boy, seeing in the restless fret with which his fingers stroked at the dog's fur that he too had seen where the old man's gaze had settled and was even now worried for the safety of his pet.

There passed then between them an uneasy silence, the old man clearing his throat as if preparing to speak, the young boy biting his lip as if trying to summon the courage to do the same.

When it seemed that neither would, the old man cleared his throat again.

What's his name? he asked.

Fang, the boy said. He's part wolf. Leastways, that's what the man who gave him to me said.

Well, he sure looks it.

He's real friendly. Once he gets to know you. Then looking down at the dog: Go on, Fang, say hi. It's a'right.

The dog stepped away from his master, his snout low to the ground, his ears perked, and his fur still bristling. The old man bent to one knee and held out his hand. The dog approached it as he might have a porcupine. He gave it a sniff and the man ran his fingers along the thick mat of hair behind his ears. At that the dog nuzzled into the man's chest, almost knocking him over.

I told you he's friendly, the boy said, taking a step closer.

I can see that now.

He's just a big old suck, is what he is.

The man stood. He wiped the hair that clung to his hands on his jacket and the dog lay with lolling tongue, panting at his feet.

I— the boy started then bit his lip again.

What's on your mind, son?

My uncle, he started again. He said if I followed this path back to the lake, I might find my gramps there.

That right? And who's you uncle?

The boy told him.

He still alive?

He had the pneumonie most of last winter, but he's out of the hospital now.

That's good to hear.

You know him?

Course I do. He's my brother.

The boy nodded, then snuck a sideways glance at the old man as if he was now unsure more than ever of how to proceed.

What'd you want with your gramps?

My uncle said he might be able to help me with some trouble I've been having.

And what kind of trouble's that?

The kids at school—they've been picking on me on account of my dad's in jail and my ma's—well, they say she's whoring herself down in Timmins.

Hearing such a thing, out of the mouth of a boy as young as him, struck the old man with the sting of a hard slap.

Well, kids'll say all kind of things, he said after he'd recovered. Like they's just feelin' bad about themselves. You ought just to ignore them.

That's what my grams says.

She's a wise woman, your grams.

I know. But it still don't stop me from getting beat on three days out of the week.

He couldn't conjure any words to argue with that.

And your uncle said your gramps might be able to help you?

He said my gramps was the toughest sumbitch he ever met. He said anyone might learn me how to fight, it was him.

The old man scratched at the greyed scruff beneath his chin, pondering on that for a moment.

Then:

*As far as I know, your gramps' fighting days are
long past.*

*The boy's face sunk. His fingers picked at the seam
of his pants and he craned his head ever so slightly back
the way he'd come.*

*But I guess he might could still remember a few
things, the old man said, his only defence against the
boy leaving.*

*The boy turned back to him and in the sudden
brightening within his eyes the old man saw that
he'd been right, that he had been waiting for someone
to come, even if it wasn't exactly the someone he'd
hoped for. And that it would be the violence he'd been
fleeing all these years that would bring his family
back to him hardly diminished the joy he felt as he
wheeled around, motioning for the boy to follow with
a sweep of his hand.*

*Come on, then, he called over his shoulder. Let's go
and see if we can't find where your gramps is at.*

Here René slammed the book shut.

Ever since René'd known him, his grandfather had lived in
the house at the corner of the 118 and Moose Point Road, bought
from Clarence Bailey after Clarence's brother, Earl, had died of a
heart attack while returning from the fridge with a bottle of milk.
The first time they'd met, his grandfather had been in the garage
he'd built beside the house, rotating the tires on a Honda Accord.
And René's dog, which had indeed accompanied him that day,
was a border collie named Richie, and nobody but a blind man
could have mistaken *him* for a wolf. Still, it was close enough to
the truth that it seemed George had somehow stolen this, his
most treasured moment.

What kind of devilry is this, he'd thought, overcome with the sudden urge to tear the book up, light the cursed thing on fire, have at any guard who'd dare try to put it out before anything was left but ash.

Taking a deep breath, he massaged the tail on the wolf on his left hand. When his anger had relented some, he flipped the book over as if the picture on the back might reveal to him how George had managed to divine so clearly his future before he'd even been born. His rage swelled again at the sight of the white man, grinning with his crooked smile as if he hadn't a care in the world, and he punched that arrogant-looking son of a bitch square in the jaw hard enough to peel the skin off one of his knuckles.

He never read another word.

N ow, sitting at his grandfather's kitchen table and looking at the same picture on the front page of the *Chronicle*, he no longer felt anything but a mild irritation for thinking George— through devilry or otherwise—had stolen that moment from his past, as ignorant an idea as those Indians in South America believing a photograph could steal their souls. René's grandfather must have told George a few stories and he'd, what was the word, extrapa-something or other, the rest, a realization that itself didn't provide much comfort, revealing to him only that he was caught up in an endlessly repeating cycle, helpless to do anything but play a part assigned to him before he was even born.

He drank the rest of the lemony citron staring at the picture on the front of the newspaper, not bothering to read what was written below, certain that he already knew everything about the man he'd ever care to know. After he'd finished his cup, he emptied two more packets of the powder into it and was waiting on the kettle to boil again when he heard a honk.

Roy's Silverado was idling in the driveway when René stepped onto the porch. The caustic drone of death metal blared through its window glass and he took that to mean Roy and his wife had been fighting again, which would explain why he was late. Roy wouldn't want to talk about it—he wouldn't want to talk at all on the way to the job site, in fact—and that suited René's mood just fine.

He'd made about two steps away from the stairs before the old man stuck his head out of the garage's door.

"You drink the last of the milk?" he yelled over at him.

"I didn't touch it," he called back.

"There ain't but two drops left in the jug. You'll pick up another on your way home?"

"The job ain't anywhere near town."

"But you're going through Maynard's, ain't ya? You can stop in at the store."

"They charge eight bucks for a jug a milk. And I ain't paying no eight bucks for a jug of milk."

"I'll get you back."

"I heard that before."

The old man stared at him like he didn't know what he meant. In the look of static befuddlement René saw his future spread out in front of him as clear as the strains of sunlight winking between the pine trees on the far side of the road: the old man standing in the parking lot of the Tim Hortons as he drove past with Tawyne. He'd be wearing his moose hide jacket, black cowboy hat, and freshly polished boots, black jeans, loose at the waist from the weight he'd lost since he wore them last and cinched with a bronze belt buckle bearing the image of an eagle, what he called his "Indian getup." He'd be staring after them, lost and forlorn. No doubt, Jean would see him standing there too, and there'd be hell to pay when he brought Tawyne back, four hours later.

"I really don't ask for much, René. Really, I don't," she'd say.

It was enough to have his thumbs twitching at the tails of the wolves on his hands for the entire twenty-minute drive to the job site. To chase away thoughts of the recrimination that would be souring Jean's voice while she said it, he replayed his plans for his son's birthday. When he came to them soaking in the whirl-pool at the base of High Falls, he nodded, again thinking: *It was shaping up to be a helluva day, alright.* But as the truck dipped into Maynard Falls, passing by the tourist shops and cafés lining the village's main street, he couldn't shake the feeling that something was missing.

An ending, he thought, *that's what it is. The perfect end to the day.*

"The way a day ends most often depends on how it began."

It was something his grandmother had once told him. He'd been fourteen and had just been suspended for fighting in the high school's parking lot. She'd been plenty sore and hadn't said a word to him on the drive home from the principal's office. But when they'd pulled up in front of the house and René was reaching for the door, she'd grabbed him by the arm. The pudge of her fingers made them feel like breakfast sausages against the taut of his bicep but her grip was plenty firm as she said, "I know you're feeling pretty good about yourself."

It was true. He couldn't have been happier about the way things had turned out—there having been two of them, both a grade older, and him with only a black eye to show for it.

"But you listen to me and you listen good," she continued. "You can tell a lot about how a day ends by how it begins. And I'm not talking about when you woke up this morning. Most days don't start when you wake up. They start weeks or months or even years before that. I want you to think of this, right now, as the beginning of one of those days and give a long hard thought as to how you think *this* one's going to end."

During his incarceration, he'd had plenty an idle hour to spend pondering on that. What she'd meant, he'd come to understand, was that he had a choice in the matter. It hadn't given him much comfort in jail but now it seemed it might, at least, provide him with some direction and he traced back in his memory, searching out the beginning of the day he hoped would end this Saturday at High Falls.

It's Tawyne's birthday, he told himself, *so it must have been the day he was born.*

But thinking of what had come after was enough to ruin even the best of days, and he discarded the thought, skipping ahead instead to the first time he saw his son after he got out of prison.

That first visit had been supervised and had taken place in the family room of the Children's Aid Society in Tildon. There was a thirty-two-inch flat screen in one corner and a sliding door that led out into a fenced-in play yard. Across from that was a mirrored window that was meant to give the "supervised" visitor the feeling that they were alone though, as René paced the room waiting for his son to arrive, it had produced the opposite effect. During his pre-visit briefing, a social worker he'd never know as anything beyond Amy had suggested, for an "icebreaker," he might want to play a game with his son. So to distract himself from the feeling that he was being watched, he wandered over to a shelf on the far wall that was stacked with enough board games for a lifetime of rainy days.

There were all the old standards—Monopoly, Life, and Chinese Checkers, Snakes & Ladders, and Operation—and a bunch he'd never heard of before—Labyrinth, Carcassonne and

Break the Safe, and a stack of boxes with Munchkin written in colourful script on their spines. None of them piqued the slightest interest and he'd pretty much given up on the hope that he'd find something he might want to play with his son when he spotted a familiar red plastic box tucked in the shelf's bottom-most corner.

Perfection, he thought as he carried it to the child-sized table in the middle of the room. *I haven't played that in years.*

It had once been his favourite. He'd play for god knows how many hours when he was a kid, dialling the clock down every time he'd managed to get all the pieces into place before the board popped. His best time was twenty-five seconds, a full ten seconds quicker than Jean. It was a record he'd taken great pride in since it was about the only board game he'd ever beat her at.

Sitting on the white leather couch in front of the table, he opened the storage compartment in the back and dumped the pieces out. He pushed down the rack in the middle and set the timer at twenty-five, rubbing his fingers together like he always did to get them warmed up before pressing the start button. He'd barely got half the pieces into place before he was startled by the inset popping up, launching the pieces into the air like a toaster in some old cartoon and René shaking his head that he could have been so rattled by a child's play thing.

He cleared the board and reset the time for forty. And he would have made it too, had the door not opened. When he glanced up, Amy was standing there holding his son's hand. He couldn't have been looking away for more than a second, but when he looked back down, trying to find the space for the crescent moon, the board popped, startling him all over again. His hand jerked and the moon dislodged from his fingers, bouncing across the table top and pitching to the floor. He bent to pick it up and when his head crested back over the table top, Amy was smiling in his direction.

She was wearing a white blouse that fit her a little snug as did her black slacks, the tension in both lending the impression that she'd recently gained a few, or twenty, pounds. She had dark circles under her eyes, so René also knew she was having trouble sleeping. Strands of hair stuck out at odd angles from where it was pulled back into a loose braid and her cherry-red lipstick was a little lopsided, which René further took to mean that she and the mirror hadn't been getting along too well of late. But she had a kind smile, if a little nervous, and Tawyne seemed to like her just fine. When René rose from the couch, his son hid behind her leg, peering through his drape of shoulder-length brown hair, shading to black, and casting skittish glances at the man he'd been told was his father.

It had been his hair that had inspired René to call him Tawyne. He'd been born with a slick wash of it and between that and his button nose he'd looked to René just like an otter. And so he'd always called him Tawyne—Iroquoian for the same—though his real name was Kiefer, which his mother had taken off one of the actors in *The Lost Boys*, her all-time favourite movie.

René's own hair was the same shade and longer even than the boy's. He usually kept it loose but that morning, after he'd showered, he'd tied his hair back in a ponytail, wanting to look, as his grandmother might have said, at least halfways respectable. He'd bought a button-down shirt—navy blue—for the occasion. It was extra large so the cuffs hung almost to his fingernails, all the better to hide the ink on his hands. He wore it with the collar pulled up to also hide the two wolves howling up his neck, lest they might frighten the boy. He had on a pair of blue jeans, also new, and in the pocket of those he had the jackknife that his grandfather had given to him for his eleventh birthday, because he hadn't wanted to come empty-handed.

When he'd gone to the Walmart in Tildon to buy the jeans

and shirt, he'd perused the toy aisles, finding nothing but over-priced junk, and that's when he'd remembered the knife. He thought he'd lost it years ago but, later that day, when he'd asked his grandfather about it he'd told him it was in his tool cabinet in the garage.

"I found it lying around, years ago," he said. "I put it in there for safekeeping then I guess I plumb forgot about it. Whadya want it for?"

"I was thinking of giving it to Tawyne."

"That right?"

The old man looked at him through keen eyes, the words coming out in a whisper as if he'd suddenly lost his breath, both telling René that nothing could have pleased him more.

The knife's haft was made of antler and the blade four inches of stainless steel. It had been well used, sharpening sticks into makeshift spears and once a bow he'd carved out of a length of rock maple he'd cut down himself with his grandfather's bow saw. After he'd fetched the knife from the garage, he'd used a stone to mill its edge into a razor and proved that by splitting a piece of grass lengthwise down the middle, all the while recalling the joy he'd felt when his grandfather had given it to him and hoping maybe he could pass a little of that onto his son.

But standing in this brightly coloured room full of plastic toys and cardboard-boxed games—the fingers in his pocket groping for the knife as he watched Amy bending to Tawyne, saying, "Don't you want to say hello to your father?" and seeing in the look of stark fear crimping the boy's face that there wasn't anything he'd rather do less—he thought of how one of the conditions of his parole was that he wasn't allowed to carry. And here he was bringing a knife to his son, not even batting an eye as he walked past the sign on the building's front door that clearly read: You Are Entering a Secure Facility. Absolutely No Firearms, Knives, or Weapons of Any Kind.

Goddamn, what an idiot, he thought, wrenching his hand from his pocket. *You should have just bought him a Lego set or a remote-controlled car. A damned knife. What the hell were you thinking?*

Amy then was turning towards him and smiling.

"He's just shy," she said. "He'll come around."

René nodded and then Tawyne was craning his head up at Amy, whispering something too quiet for René to hear.

"You'll see her in a little while," Amy answered him. "She's waiting for you outside. Just a few more minutes, okay?"

René knew that the *she* in question was his sister, Jean, and also that she wasn't outside, she was behind the mirrored window. No doubt she would be shaking her head and if her husband, Carl, was there, scoffing, "See, he's terrified. I knew this was a bad idea."

It was the same thing René was thinking himself so maybe it was only his imagination running wild. Could be she really *was* outside pacing up and down the sidewalk like he had not a half hour ago, or in the waiting room leafing through one of the parenting magazines, their covers emblazoned with smiling happy faces and laughing children, most of them the colour of a pig's skin so he knew they'd be about as useful to him as the stack of *Swank* magazines Dinko kept secreted under his mattress. Either way, he couldn't stop himself from glancing at his reflection in the mirrored window, seeing in his slumped shoulders and the cowed expression on his face a man he barely recognized as himself.

"Your dad's playing Perfection," Amy was saying. "Have you ever played Perfection?"

René turned back to them in time to see Tawyne shaking his head.

"It's fun," Amy said. "I used to play it all the time. Why don't you go over and let your dad show you how to play."

Tawyne shook his head again but Amy wasn't taking no for answer. Holding him by the hand, she led him to the table. René dropped the moon piece onto the pile and gave the pieces a swish with his fingers, a rule that Jean had always insisted on.

Not wanting to look the fool in front of his son, he set the timer for sixty. He finished the game in just under forty. It was hardly a record and he could see by the mild indifference on Tawyne's face that he wasn't too impressed either.

"See, it's easy," Amy said while René was dumping the pieces back out. "Why don't you give it a try?"

Tawyne looked up at Amy, the look in his eyes spelling out a resolute No.

She prompted, "Go on," and he looked down at the pile of pieces.

René had set the timer again and his finger was hovering over the start button.

Tawyne looked over at Amy. She touched him on the shoulder and he turned back to the table.

"Just tell me when you're ready," René said.

Tawyne scanned over the board, maybe memorizing where all the pieces went, which René took as a good sign.

After a moment, the boy took a deep breath, still stalling for time.

"Go!" René barked, his voice as urgent as a starter's gun.

Tawyne jumped right to it, his hands working in a whirl, his eyes, it seemed, shooting laser beams, they were so focused on the task at hand. As the timer passed thirty, René looked up at Amy. She was backing out of the room, giving him two thumbs up, and René went back to watching his son, knowing he wasn't going to make it and waiting in anxious anticipation of what he knew to come next. And when it did, his son jumped at the pop of the board, startling back and breathing heavy, his hand pressed to his heart as if he was afraid it might have stopped.

"You almost got it," René said. "And your first time too. You're a natural. You want to try again?"

Tawyne stared at the board a few seconds then shook his head.

"Do you mind if I have another go then?"

Tawyne shook his head again and René pressed the board in then dialled the timer down to twenty-five. When he looked back up at Tawyne, there was a dubious look in his eyes.

"What?" René asked. "You don't think I can make it?"

Tawyne's mouth opened like he wanted to say something, but no words came out and he closed it again.

"Well, I guess we're going to find out," René said, wetting the tips of his forefingers and thumbs on his tongue. "You going to press the button for me?"

Tawyne motioned to reach for it.

"Just give me a second, now."

René scrutinized the board and then gave the pile of pieces a good looking over too.

"Okay."

Tawyne paused ever so slightly before hitting the button and barking, "Go!"

He went at it hard, never in his life concentrating on anything more than getting those little plastic pieces home. Still, he had four pieces left when the timer passed into the red. He knew he wasn't going to make it and pressed the stop button with one tick to spare.

"Hey!" Tawyne blurted. "That's cheating."

"I know," René answered, "but it scares the hell out of me when it goes pop."

The boy was looking at him like he couldn't believe anything could scare the man sitting in front of him.

Then, after a moment, he smiled, shy and demure, almost like a girl.

"It scares the hell out of me too."

They'd played Monopoly until the hour was up and afterwards Amy led René back to her office.

She told him that Jean had agreed to let him see Tawyne for two hours on the first and third Saturday of every month and that she'd suggested they meet at the Tim Hortons in town.

René answered that that was fine by him but three days before he was to see his son again they'd got a big dump of snow and the idea had occurred to him that maybe Tawyne would prefer to go sledding. He called Jean's cell phone. She answered with a perfunctory, "Yes," and René asked her if it'd be okay if they met at the field behind the high school, which was at the bottom of the biggest hill in town (and only a block from the Tim Hortons to boot).

"I'll ask Keef," she replied.

She was gone for less than a minute and when she came back on she said, "That's fine by him."

"Great," René said. "Now does he have his own sled or—"

"I'm sure we can find something," she interrupted, her voice impatient and weary.

"Great. See you on—"

The phone clicked before he'd finished and he felt a sudden surge of anger, for being talked to like that and then hung up on. His hands clenched into fists, grabbing those wolves by the tail and searching out the image of his son to lend him its calm.

But it wasn't Tawyne that sprung into his mind, it was the memory of what Amy had said after she'd led René into her office following his first visit.

"Well, that went well," he told himself and was surprised that it seemed to help.

On Saturday, he was just pulling the GT Super Pro Racer he'd bought at the Canadian Tire in Tildon out of the passenger seat in his grandfather's tow truck when he saw a late model RAV 4 pulling up behind. Tawyne stepped out of its passenger seat, looking every bit as shy as he had the last time they'd met.

"Come on and see what I bought," René prompted.

Tawyne took a couple of steps forward, enough for him to get a view of the sled. It was white with a black frame, its imitation gas tank and nose cone lending it the appearance of a snowmobile. When René had first seen it on the shelf he'd thought it was a pretty slick ride, and from the look on Tawyne's face he seemed to think so too.

"Is that for me?" he asked.

"It's Christmas coming up, ain't it?" René answered.

Footsteps crunched on snow and Jean came around the side of the truck.

God, hasn't she gained weight, René thought, staring at a woman he hardly recognized as his sister. He could already feel his lips curling into a sneer and that filled him with shame, knowing all that she'd done for his son.

She had three children of her own before she took in Tawyne, he reminded himself, *so maybe you ought to cut her a little slack*.

She was pulling an old plastic sled. Compared to the Super Pro it wasn't much better than the black garbage bags he'd used as a kid before his grandmother had given him his own GT for Christmas when he was eight. She was frowning, so René could tell she wasn't nearly as impressed as Tawyne. He nodded at her and she shook her head, as if it had meant a world of trouble getting the sled though likely it belonged to one of her own kids and hadn't required more than a trip out to the garage.

René picked up the GT's string and as he turned towards the hill, he called over his shoulder, "You coming or not?"

The hill was empty but there were a dozen or so runs carved into its two feet of snow. The single lane of asphalt that cut at a diagonal up the slope on its way to the high school's parking lot hadn't yet been ploughed and about halfway up someone had fashioned a five-foot-high ramp of hard-packed snow. Giving a quick check back to make sure Tawyne was following him—he was—René cut off the road, taking a direct line up the side of the hill. Tawyne hadn't made it more than five steps behind when he slipped and fell. He stood up, dusting the snow off his wool mitts on his pants and looking up towards the summit, some eighty feet above.

"Get on," René said, motioning towards the sled. "I'll give you a lift."

Tawyne's face flashed doubt that René would be able to manage such a thing but he sat on the seat anyway. He leaned forward and clutched the steering wheel tight to keep himself from sliding off. It took damn near every ounce of René's strength to pull him all the way to the top. When he'd finally got there he was breathing hard and had a strong desire to sit down, rest awhile. But Tawyne was looking at him with something like amaze and that was enough to keep him on his feet.

"You want to try the ramp first?" René asked when he'd finally caught his breath.

Tawyne shook his head and René pulled him to a spot in the

middle of the hill where there was a run of untouched snow all the way to the bottom.

"How about here?"

Tawyne peered down the slope, biting his lip and shaking his head again.

"If you're scared . . ."

"I'm not scared," he said matter of fact, though when he turned back to René his eyes told a different story.

"Go on, then."

"Why don't you go first?"

"Don't mind if I do."

Tawyne slipped off the seat and René pulled the sled to the head of the run leading to the jump. Straddling the seat, he crouched low. He wrapped the cord around the steering wheel so it wouldn't get hung up and then took the wheel in both hands.

"Watch this," he said, kicking off.

He couldn't have been going more than twenty kilometres an hour when he hit the ramp, though the chill wind whipping at his cheeks made it feel double that. The Super Pro bucked when it hit the jump's hard-packed snow. It seemed like he was about to lose control then it caught a line and straightened out. The instant before it was to become airborne, he pushed off with both feet and leapt skyward, jerking his feet up over his head and executing a back flip in midair. He felt his boots touch down and tried to get them moving fast enough to catch up with his speed, but the moment they hit the ground his feet slipped out from under him. He landed on his back hard enough to knock the wind from his chest, the shock of that immediately eclipsed by the icy blast of snow shooting up under his jacket.

He slid to a stop and lay there catching his breath, thinking how if he didn't get up he couldn't possibly do anything else so damn-fool stupid.

He could hear the crunch of footsteps hurrying down the hill. A moment later Tawyne's face appeared beaming at him against the cloud-greyed sky, his expression full of wonder and awe.

Seeing that, René grinned wide, and a moment later, Tawyne was grinning wide right back.

H e spent the next three months chasing that look.

They hit every hill in town and then a few on the outskirts as well. After she'd nearly froze her toes off the first time, Jean opted to keep warm at the Tim Hortons, and if they weren't back in time, she called his cell phone the exact second his two hours were up. They finished the season by hiking the back way into Medley's, a sandpit just off Highway 11. They followed a snowmobile trail along the hydro line that formed its western perimeter and that led them through a hole the skidooers had cut in the fence in open defiance of the No Trespassing signs spaced along it at intervals.

"Auntie Jean would have a fit she knew we were trespassing," Tawyne said, hurrying to keep up with his father, pulling the Super Pro along the path, winding through a forest of perfectly spaced Jack pines.

"Then it's good she ain't here."

The answer seemed to satisfy him, and Tawyne didn't utter another word until the forest broke against the lip of the pit. It was one hundred feet from there to the floor, at a seventy-five-degree pitch, the top five of which went straight down. Ski-Doo tracks wove in and around the bowl, its diameter maybe a quarter of a kilometre at its widest. In the distance, they could hear an engine growing louder in staccato bursts but for the moment they had the place to themselves. Their breaths rose white before them, the only shield they had against the sun glaring down out of a cloudless sky, its rays shimmering in a hundred blinking eyes over the ocean of rippling white.

"Wow," Tawyne said. "I mean—Wow!"

He had that look on his face again—of wonder and awe—and though it wasn't directed at René, it made him feel just about as good as it had the last time.

"It's something, ain't it?"

"It sure is."

"Alright, now," René said, straddling the sled and preparing to kick off. "Give me some room."

"Hey!" Tawyne said. "It's my turn to go first."

"I thought you went first last time."

"The hell I did."

"You say so."

"I do."

"That first five feet's a doozy," René said after Tawyne had taken command of the sled. "You're going to want to push off hard and pull up on the nose, elsewise you're bound to go arse over teakettle."

"I know."

"Well, get to it then."

"Give me some room."

René moved a step back. Tawyne took a deep breath and then kicked off hard. The sled dropped at a steep angle. The boy all but disappeared when it hit the slope's two feet of powder, the drag of it hardly slowing him as he careened down the hill, the billow of crystals unleashed in his wake sparkling against the sun like confetti made out of glass, born aloft and plying their glitter in the chill morning air.

H e wouldn't see the look again for two months.

Over the spring he'd taken Tawyne fishing, choosing a different spot every time they met like he had when they'd gone sledding. It was the third week of May when he caught his first fish. They were at Wilson's Falls, casting off the pier at the base of the hydroelectric station. Tawyne was beaming when he reeled it in and there was that look again as he held up the speckled trout thrashing at the end of the line. René took a picture with his phone and later he'd make it his wallpaper so he could get an eyeful of it anytime he wanted.

The fish barely weighed a pound and by all accounts they should have thrown it back, but when Tawyne asked what they should do with it, René had answered, "We ought to light a fire. Cook it up."

"But the sign said no fires," Tawyne said.

And it was true: the sign bolted to a metal post in the parking lot had said that and a lot of other things besides.

René scratched his head, trying to think his way around it. And then it came to him.

"Hey," he said. "I just remembered something. You're always allowed to start a fire if you're hungry and need it to cook on."

"Really?"

"It's the law. And a sign don't change the law. You hungry?"

"I'm practically starving."

"Alright, then."

They'd gone a ways back into the woods and built a firepit and cooked the trout on a stick like a hot dog. After it was done, René made a big show of prying one of its eyes out with his grandfather's scaling knife, holding the jellied globe on the end of the blade, and licking his lips.

"You really going to eat that?" his son asked.

"Hell, it's the best part. My gramps taught me that."

He slurped it up and pried out the trout's other eye and held it out to Tawyne. He didn't think the boy would eat it, but he did, slurping it right off the knife, and René would never feel closer to his son than he did right then.

T he days turned hot and his thoughts began to drift towards plans for Tawyne's birthday.

You could take him up to your grandfather's old fishing shack, he'd thought on the morning he and Roy were raking algae out of a private beach on the northern shore of Lake Mesaquakee.

By the time Roy was turning onto Hidden Cove Road, two days later, René had got back to imagining himself soaking in the whirlpool with his son when the perfect end to the day came to him with such ease that he'd known it had been waiting for him all along.

He'd ask Tawyne how his birthday was shaping up so far.

"It's been the best," he imagined he'd answer. "Better than the best."

"Glad to hear it."

"I can't wait to tell Jean how I jumped off the twenty-foot ledge."

"You do that, chances are she won't let you come back."

"I hadn't thought about that."

"I'm just saying is all."

"So I won't tell her."

"It'll be our little secret."

"Yeah."

Their eyes would meet and there'd be a twinkle in Tawyne's that'd speak to René of other secrets yet to come: a lifetime full of them.

"I was thinking," he would then proffer, "maybe I could take you up to my gramps's old fishing shack sometime. We could spend the night there."

"Like camp out, you mean?"

"Yeah. Would you like that?"

"I sure would."

"Can you talk to Jean about it then?"

"Can't you?"

"There'd be a better chance of her agreeing to it if she heard it from you. Whadya say?"

"I'll ask her."

"Alright, then. Now we best get going. Jean's like to have called a dozen times by now. She'll be wondering where the hell we're at."

Roy was clicking the music off and signalling left, turning into a driveway barred by a wrought-iron gate bearing the graven image of two gold embossed rams butting heads.

It's going to be a good day, René told himself.

No, better than good. It'll be the best.

"Just so you know," the guard who'd emerged from the gate-house said after he'd written their names down on a clipboard. "Mr. Wane doesn't allow smoking on his property."

"Got it," Roy said, though the guard was looking at René when he said it, the cigarette he'd hoped to smoke the moment he got out of the truck tucked, as it was, behind his left ear.

"Now where do we park?"

"Over by the maintenance shed."

"And where's that?"

"Behind the tennis courts." Then pointing, "Go right at the Y, you'll find it."

The guard returned to the gatehouse, and a moment later the two rams butting heads parted ways.

"You need a puff?" Roy said, turning to René. "You could walk in. I'll meet you there."

"I'm good."

"Suit yourself."

The Y in the driveway wasn't fifty feet inside the gate. To the right, the road switched from cedar chips to gravel and led them away from the lake. Through the forest on the left, they couldn't see more than parcelled fragments of the cottage at its heart: a gable-roofed cedar plank ranch house that looked to have about the same square footage as a football field. The road shortly opened into a parking lot that could have fit twenty Silverados. The so-called shed on its far side could have housed four of the same, two of which could be driven, side by side, through its pair of retractable steel doors. Otherwise, it was built as if out of scraps from the main building. On its right side, the cedar shingled roof extended over several rows of corded firewood.

Roy parked in front of that and while he and René were dousing their arms and the back of their necks with palmfuls of Muskol to ward off the bugs, he kept a watchful eye on the two young women batting a ball back and forth through the mesh of the tennis court's fence. Both were as pretty as models and wearing sport bras trimmed with sweat, one in short shorts that barely crested her hip bones and the other in a skirt not much longer. The latter wasn't much more than a skeleton with skin. Every time she made contact, she let out a feral grunt and, faced with the ferocity of her volleys, the other was having a devil of a time getting her racket on the ball, much less getting it back over the net.

The skeleton woman served an ace that just caught the corner of the box. The other called, "Fault." The skeleton shook her head and yelled back, "The hell it was."

"I just call 'em like I see 'em."

The skeleton shook her head and lobbed another ball into the air. She hit it even harder than the first, and in the next instant it struck her opponent in the thigh, causing her to cry out and drop her racket.

"Now that's a fault!" the skeleton woman yelled over to her.

René was just heaving an old scuba diver's tank onto his shoulder as the injured party limped towards the court's gate, rubbing her leg to relieve the sting.

Then the skeleton was yelling, "What the fuck are you looking at?"

When René glanced her way, he saw she was scowling at Roy, who was blushing under her glare and averting his eyes, looking sheepishly towards René, who was closing the pickup's tailgate and shaking his head, trying not to smile too hard.

T he job for the next few days was trimming trees.

A branch from a hundred-year-old walnut had come down on the driveway during a storm the previous week. The arboriculturist who had been called in had given it a clean bill of health, but a quick survey of the property had told him there were a couple dozen or so other trees that could use some attention. Herb Delroy, the owner of the Delroy Property Management Co., had accompanied him as he walked the grounds and later in the day had called Roy to see if he could fit him in, ASAP.

Roy was his odd-jobs man. *No job too small or too shitty* was his informal motto, and over the five years and change he'd been plying his trade at high-end summer residences on the Mesaquakee and Joseph lakes, he'd proven he was a man of his word such that Herb had rewarded him with enough work to fill thirteen months out of any given year. Finally, it had become too much for Roy on his own, so he'd posted a help wanted ad on the website of the employment agency in town two days before René's parole officer had scheduled an appointment for him with a counsellor at the same. He only met her once and at the end of the ten minutes they'd spent in her cubicle she'd handed him a stack of twenty-some-odd employment listings. René had called every one of them, but Roy was the only person who'd called him back. After they'd arranged to meet at the Tim Hortons in town, he'd asked René how he would know him, and René had replied, "I'll be the Indian sitting in the corner."

Roy had paused only a second before he'd replied, "Gotcha."

"How about yourself?" René had then asked, though he probably needn't have.

"Oh, you'll know me."

"How's that?"

"Just look for The Mountain," Roy answered.

"The Mountain?"

"It's what they called me in school."

René would later find out that it was a play on his last name—Hill—and that the nickname couldn't have suited him better, Roy being so tall he had to bend over to get through the coffee shop's side door.

Their meeting lasted all of two minutes after he'd sat down across from René with his takeout cup.

"You got a car?" Roy asked, taking his first sip.

"No," René answered. "But I can use my grandfather's tow truck pretty much anytime I want."

"That's okay, best I pick you up anyway. Where'd ya live?"

René told him.

"Shoot, most of the jobs are out that way anyhow. There was one other thing—"

He couldn't think of what that was and while he tried to remember it he scratched at the top of his head with the fingernail of his index finger (something René would find out he always did while he was thinking, which maybe explained why he had a dime-sized bald spot there).

"Oh, right," he'd finally said. "Heights. You're not afraid of heights are you?"

"They don't bother me none."

"Perfect."

He was already holding out his hand while he said it, but it was a moment before René extended his.

"You mean I got the job?"

"As long as you can start tomorrow."

"I can."

"Signed and sealed then."

They shook to close the deal and Roy left him to finish his coffee. On the way out he made a big show of stepping clear over a young boy, couldn't have been older than five, waiting with his mom by the pickup counter. The way the boy gaped in awe as the giant's legs arched over his head made René smile, the first time he could recall having done so since he'd got out of jail.

That had been nine months ago.

Until they came to trim the trees surrounding the Wanes' summer residence, René had all but forgotten that Roy had asked him if he was afraid of heights. Now as they walked amongst the ten acres' worth of forest enclosed within a wrought-iron fence, it was foremost on his mind. Maybe a quarter of the trees had been marked with an orange ribbon and half of those had notes tacked to their trunks, further instructions provided by the arboriculturist beyond the general one that Herb Delroy had given Roy the week before: "If a branch is dead, cut it. Easy-peasy right?"

The tallest of the trees was a red oak, a hundred feet tall if it was an inch.

When they came to that, Roy planted his hand on the tree's trunk and stared up at the lowest branch, fifteen feet off the ground.

"You said you weren't afraid of heights?" he said, turning back to René.

"They don't bother me none."

"Then I guess you're up."

Roy bent to his duffel, searching within for the throw ball and line, and René took off his shoes. He was just slipping off his socks when Roy asked, "What the hell are you doing?"

"I can't very well climb a tree with my shoes on."

"That's why I brought the spikes."

"I don't need no spikes to climb a tree."

"You say so."

"I do."

"But you're gonna wear the harness."

René looked at him like he thought he might want to argue the point, and Roy gave him a hard look.

"You're gonna wear the harness."

While he strapped it on, Roy clipped the line to the throw ball, which wasn't really a ball at all, it was a neon orange nylon sack as big as an avocado and filled with lead pellets the size of BBs. To launch it, he'd fashioned a makeshift canon out of a fire extinguisher and a three-foot length of PVC pipe. At ninety psi, it would shoot the throw ball two hundred feet straight up. He filled it to just over fifty with the old scuba tank, then angled its barrel a little off-centre, pointing it towards the tree's highest branch.

René was just securing the last of the harness's clasps when Roy shouted, "Fire in the hole!"

Jerking the lever, Roy turned his head to the side as the canon popped with a whoosh of air. The ball shot out, the line *zzzting* behind as it soared past the high branch and landed with a thud twenty feet from the base of the tree.

"That's how you do it."

They used the throw line to string a length of climbing rope over the branch and to this René attached his harness. Roy looped ten feet of the rope into a coil at his feet and clamped one foot down over the long side of it.

"You're gonna want to give me more slack than that," René warned.

Roy made no sign to say he'd heard him except a slight tightening of the muscles at his jaw and René stepped back until he was ten paces from the oak. His back foot had hardly touched ground when he shot forward again, coming at the tree full bore. He leapt at it with two strides to spare, his left foot finding purchase in a knot some six feet up. He pushed off from it hard, getting a good two feet of thrust and grabbing for a hold around the far side of the trunk. Deep grooves ran in vertical channels throughout the bark. His fingers clamped onto two of these, giving him plenty of support, and he clambered straight up the tree with the ease of a raccoon.

It was how his grandfather had taught him to climb the white oak in his backyard, which the old man made him do a hundred times before he'd even think about teaching him how to make a fist. But René hadn't climbed a tree in ten years by then. When he was within arm's reach of the lowest branch he was damn near out of breath and he'd torn the nail on his right index finger after the bark had given way beneath his grip, halfway up. He'd managed to hold on with his other hand and he wasn't really in any danger, but still Roy called up to him, "You think falling out of a tree is gonna get you the day off, you got another thing comin'."

Pulling himself up onto the perch, René sucked at the droplet of blood squeezing past the cuticle, trying to catch his breath as he unclipped the rope from his harness. He lowered it down to Roy so he could hitch the saw to it and while Roy was doing that his eyes wandered towards the cottage, though they didn't make it any further than the driveway.

There was a young man standing there.

He was blond haired and wearing athletic shorts and a pair of running shoes, wraparound sunglasses and black wireless Beats. His chestnut tan stretched all the way to the platinum glint of his wristwatch, his six-pack and the veins running in rivulets up his arms leaving little doubt he used the timepiece exclusively to mark the hours he spent in the gym. He was arching his shoulders, swirling his arms at his sides and shaking out his hands. Likely, he was just loosening up before getting on with his run. But the way his expression suddenly flattened, settling into a vacant gaze as he bandied his head from side to side, made it seem like something more.

It's like the show a fighter puts on while he's waiting for the bell to ring, that's what it is.

René didn't have long to ponder on what that might have meant, as just then Roy called out, "Heads up!" The chainsaw's blade was swivelling towards him and one of its teeth grazed his forearm. He felt a sharp prick as it drew a fine line over his skin. It was already beading blood by the time he grabbed the saw by its handle.

As he unclipped it from the rope, he glanced down at where the young man had stood. It hadn't been more than a couple of seconds since he'd done so but he was nowhere to be seen.

I t would be an hour before René saw him again.

They'd done two more trees in the meanwhile. Roy had climbed the second, walking up its trunk using the spikes attached to his boots and the belt slung around the tree's trunk to inch his way up, slow and steady. René was rappelling back down the third when the man came walking back up the driveway. His skin was aglow with sweat and there was a black SUV—a Lexus—keeping pace beside him. It had tinted windows and René couldn't see who was driving, but it was plain he'd done something to piss the young man off.

"You want to wipe my ass while you're at it?" he was yelling.

René unhitched the harness and held it out to Roy, who was rubbing at his eye and wincing against whatever grit was in there.

"You catch some sawdust?" René asked.

"A goddamned black fly."

"They sting like a bitch, they get in your eye."

"You don't have to tell me. I'm going down to the water, see if I can't wash it out. I guess we'll call that break."

René's gums were aching like they always did when he hadn't had a smoke for a few hours, much less twelve. Whatever good the lemony citron had done had long worn off. The tickle in his throat was back and his head felt like it was floating two feet above his shoulders. Taking a break would have done him a world of good, but he'd have to hike off property if he wanted a cigarette so there didn't seem much of a point. He busied himself instead, lugging the gear to the nearest marked tree: an elm beside the driveway directly across from the boathouse. It split into three about halfway up and René didn't need the note attached to the trunk to tell him that two of the limbs were rotted clear through.

He was just filling the fire extinguisher from the scuba tank, thinking he'd like to take a shot himself, when he heard a shrill voice calling out, "There you are!"

The skeleton woman was coming down the marble steps leading from the front door of the so-called cottage. She looked to be naked except for a pair of bright red stiletto sandals. As she passed the black SUV, just now pulling to a stop, René could see that it was just a trick of the light, though the two strips of tan fabric covering her delicates—more string than bikini—hardly fit his idea of being dressed. The driver of the SUV must have had the same thought because as he stepped from the vehicle, he was lowering the dark shades from his eyes and peering over top of them to get a better look. He was almost as tall as Roy but had at least eighty pounds on him. His neck was like a tree stump and his arms just as thick, their muscles bulging the sleeves of his hooded black sweatshirt, its tint roughly the same shade as his skin. René followed his gaze to where the young woman was hobbling over the driveway's cobbled stones on a direct line for the young man walking towards the boathouse.

When she reached him, she grabbed him by the arm and the young man startled at her touch, spinning around. His lips were moving so he must have said something, though it was too faint for René to hear.

"Well, I hope you didn't tire yourself out too much," the woman replied, making her meaning plain by running her index finger down his chest, drawing a line through his sweat and then sucking on her finger—her fervency making the act more desperate than seductive. The man seemed to think so too. He responded by spinning around and marching brusquely past.

He must have said something else for as she trailed after him she asked, "You mind if I join you?"

He made no sign that he cared one way or the other. When she caught up to him, she swiped off his headphones. She placed them over her own ears and dodged away from his grasping hand, walking backwards, doing a little dance to the beat of whatever song it was he'd been listening to. All it would have taken was a strobe light and a pole to make it into a striptease and to that the man responded much the same as René—shaking his head and trying not to laugh at the comic luridity of her gyrating hips. She'd come to the dock and hadn't taken more than two steps onto it when one of her heels caught in a space between the boards. She let out a startled shriek as she teetered backwards. She would have fallen too had the young man not darted forward, sweeping her off her feet and into his arms.

"My hero!" she exclaimed and then shrieked again as the man slung her up and onto his shoulder.

He set off at a run and the last thing René saw of them before they'd disappeared behind the boathouse was the sandal jostling from her foot and bouncing off the dock, pitching with a faint splash into the water.

René was already up in the tree when Roy returned. Even from there he could see his eye looked like a burning ember and that he could barely keep its lid from wincing shut.

"You get it?" René called down to him.

"No. It'll be in there all day, I know it. Son of a bitch, if it ain't one goddamned thing it's another."

"Whenever I got something in my eye, my grams'd roll up tissue into a point, use it to fish out whatever it was. Never failed."

"Your grams handy?"

"She's been dead going on seven years."

"Then I can't see how she's going to help me now."

Roy rubbed at his eye again.

"There's a box of tissues in the truck," René said.

"You aim to play nurse now?"

"I'm just saying is all."

"It'll come out by itself."

"You're the boss."

T he day had turned hot.

René's shirt was soaked with sweat before he was even halfway done with the elm. The streams running down his back carried the sawdust lathering his neck into his pants and by the time he was lowering the first branch it felt like there was sandpaper chaffing at the crack of his ass. The back of his arms and neck were itching from mosquito bites, and he would have liked nothing more than to take a break—smoke a couple, maybe have a swim. But it'd be two hours before lunch and even then he'd have to hike off property if he wanted a chance to do either.

Roy seemed to have been reading his mind for René barely had time to brush off the flakes of wood from his arm when he was calling up to him, "If you're jonesing for a smoke, you could take the truck—"

"I'm okay."

"You sure?"

"I'll grab a couple at lunch."

"You mind getting started on that second branch yourself then?"

"What's up?"

"Thought I might try your grandmother's trick with the tissue."

"It still bothering you?"

"It's like a piece of glass is stuck in there."

Roy started up the driveway and then René remembered something.

"You got to wet it first," he called after him.

Roy turned back.

"What?"

"The end of the tissue. After you roll it to a point."

"That the trick?"

"Works every time."

The second branch was bigger than the first and René dropped it in two pieces. Roy wasn't back yet and after he'd scaled down from the tree, he searched out another orange ribbon. The gauge on the scuba tank was reading into the red. He figured it'd be good for at least one more shot before they'd have to fill it with the compressor in the back of the truck. He was just hooking up its hose to the fire extinguisher when he heard the skeleton woman's shrill voice again, rising in a fever pitch from directly behind him.

"There he is!" she was shrieking. "That's the son of a bitch I saw peeping through the window."

René craned towards her. She was pointing straight at him and the young man was striding forward on the same line, no more than five paces away. René hardly had time to open his mouth to say not even he knew what—a denial of some sort—before he caught a blur on his periphery: the man's shoe on a collision course with his head. It struck René in the jaw. His world went suddenly white and the next thing he knew he was on the ground, his cheek pressed into the mat of pine needles nettling its surface. The world had canted sideways and within its tilt he could see the man standing a ways back. He was bouncing on the balls of his feet and his head was bobbling from side to side.

There was a piercing glint in his eyes: a challenge, daring René to get back up.

He could see two other young men, moving on a quick lateral away from the other, circling towards René on a wide perimeter. One was short and stocky and the other tall and lank. Both were wearing tan khaki shorts and garish Hawaiian shirts and staring down at the screens of identical cameras held at their waists, one pointed at René and the other at their friend. Them being there, filming as they were, meant something, René knew that but not what. All he did know was that he was lying on the ground, a static whine ringing in his ears, and the taste of blood in his mouth.

Then the skeletal woman was screaming, "Kick his ass!" and the man was striding towards him again.

René had pushed himself to his knees. He was bent over on all fours, a trail of bloodied spit spanned from his lips to the ground, and the man was bringing his foot up hard into René's chest. There was a voice screaming in his head, "Don't do it! Don't you fucking do it!" By the time he felt the hard sting of shoelaces striking his ribs, he already had, snatching the man's leg in both arms and thrusting himself backwards and up. He caught the man off balance and threw his weight forward, toppling the other to the ground and coming down on top of him.

The back of the man's head hit hard enough that René felt his own teeth rattle, but the other hardly seemed to notice. His leg had sprung loose from René's hold. He scissored that and its mate around René's waist, wrapping them together in a vice grip and twisting him just enough that when he lashed out with his elbow its point drove square into René's ear. An explosion of such pain, it seemed to hurl him backwards off the man so that he'd become just another spectator watching whoever it was who had taken his place bear down on the other with both fists, pummelling at his face as if hell itself had been unleashed through them.

A sharp crack brought René back to himself. One of his hands was clamped on the wrist of the man's right arm and the other on his elbow. In between them, a sharp spear of bone piercing the skin and spewing blood. How he'd done such a thing was a mystery to René but not what it meant. The broken arm and the mash he'd made of the man's face spoke to him of all that he'd just lost, and the image of his son appeared to him as clear as the bubbles frothing red at the man's lips.

Tawyne had that look in his eyes—of wonder and awe—and he knew he'd never see it again.

The man beneath him was begging, "Please, no more. Please." The whimper to his voice made René madder still and his hands were already wrapping around his throat. Someone was screaming, "Motherfucker, motherfucker!" Maybe it was himself, he couldn't tell. The man's legs thrashed feebly at his back and he would have squeezed the life out of that son of a bitch had he not then felt the sharp yank of someone grabbing a fistful of hair at the crown of his head. The hand jerked him backwards with such force that René felt the skin on the young man's neck grating under his fingernails. Reeling, his hands flailing helpless at the air and his feet clambering for solid ground, finding only the whisper of pine needles brushing against his bare toes. And then even that was lost to him as he was swung with all the grace of a wrecking ball.

He slammed into the trunk of the tree at his back, his breath wrenched from his chest to the staccato beat of three fingers' worth of hair snapping at their roots. He barely had time enough to register that it was the man who'd been driving the SUV standing before him now and then the man's hand was lashing out, the point of its thumb driving knuckle-deep into René's eye. It felt like a firecracker going off in his head. Pain such as he'd never felt. Half his world in the dark and the other half almost as black, comprised entirely of the man holding him by the hair at arm's length, his other hand clenched, the nail on its extended thumb as sharp as an arrowhead and René knowing it would be the last thing he ever saw.

René's own hand now working with a will of its own, thrusting into his tool belt and finding his utility knife, slashing it upwards, the blade slicing through the drape of the man's sleeve with such ease that it might have only caught fabric had the man not let out a startled gasp. His grip lost its hold and he stumbled back, clenching at his arm. Strands of hair straggled between the fingers on his one hand and blood burst in a flood through the ones clamped over the gash. Such hate in his eyes that René could see only death on the other side. Waiting on the man to make good on their threat, René's every muscle tensed, the utility knife's sharp quivering before him with singular intent, a lone breath all there was to buffer this moment from the next.

Then:

"What in the hell?"

Roy was standing not ten feet away.

All it would have taken was a quick sideways glance for René to see the alarm spreading over his face. But it would have taken the voice of God himself to distract René just then, seeing nothing beyond the folds of skin oozing from beneath the man's collar, one clear swipe at that maybe his only hope of getting out of this day alive.

Neither did the black man look up, though he did pause mid-stride just long enough for René to see another way out. He dodged sideways, clearing the tree and backing away, the utility knife guarding against the other moving to pursue. René had two steps on him by then, enough of a gap that he did now pass a glance at Roy, seeing no trace of the alarm that had just a moment ago defined his face, his shock absorbed in the interim by something else. If René had to put a name to it, it'd be despair, but the tenor of his voice when he spoke again would have placed it closer to contempt.

"What the fuck did you do?"

Such bitter recrimination in the gentle giant's eyes that René would have had to have been blind in both eyes not to see his fate spelt out within.

He turned and ran.

15

Deacon hadn't been back to the barn for four days. All thoughts of the Fiction George had been writing had fled the moment he'd found him lying dead in the garden, and it would take that long before he'd have cause to think of it again.

In the interim, he hadn't talked to anyone except Grover. Only a few minutes seemed to have passed from the time he'd found George to the point of getting over the shock and dialling his number, but the display on his phone had put it at closer to an hour.

"What's up, Deke?" Grover had answered with after two rings.

"It's George," he said.

"George?"

"He's—" The word couldn't find purchase on his tongue and he discarded it, pressing on. "I—I found him. In the garden. Heart attack. I think."

"Is he okay?"

"No. He is not."

Silence now on the other end.

Then after a moment: "Is he—" Grover's voice choking on the same word that had defied Deacon only moments ago.

"Yes," he answered.

Another silence. Then:

"Have you called anyone?"

"No, I just—"

"You haven't called nine-one-one?"

"No."

"It's okay. I'll call. Are you at the house?"

"Yes."

"I'll be right there."

Not wanting to face George again, Deacon had circled to the front of the house and called Dylan. He wasn't answering his phone and after the beep Deacon had let the time run out without saying a word.

Crystal was the only other person he'd have cared to speak to, the only person who might have known how much George had meant to him, who wouldn't offer him petty condolences as if to say the price of living was dying and that alone should have made him feel better. But Crystal's last Facebook post had shown her lighting a candle—"For Grams"—in the Santa Marie Del Mar Basilica in Barcelona, one of a continent's worth of stops on the all-expenses-paid European tour that her parents had given her as a reward for graduating, with honours, from the U of T.

Over the following days, he bided his grief the best he could, lying in bed from sun-up to sundown and wandering the streets most of the night trying to wear himself out enough to fall asleep.

On Thursday morning there was a knock at his door.

"Deacon," Rain called out. "I know you're in there."

He lay still, holding his breath until he heard the creak of the stairs' rickety wooden frame as her footsteps led her down into the alley. He then rolled over, turning his back on the door. There was a small bookshelf pressed against the wall beside the bed and he found himself tracing over the titles of George's books pressed between the two brass monkeys he'd found at Ye Olde Antique Shoppe in town. There was a gap at the end where he'd taken out *The Stray* and it was on this his gaze settled, recalling how he'd brought it with him to George's on the night he'd died and trying to think of what he'd done with it.

It must still be in the pocket of your jacket.

His jacket was hanging on the hook by the door and sure enough *The Stray* was there. He was just slipping it back onto the shelf when he reconsidered and returned to bed. He read it all through the morning and into the afternoon. When he reached its end, he returned it to its place and ran his finger along the spines of the others until he came to *A Bad Man's Son.*

It was the only book in his collection that wasn't identical to the ones on his father's shelf, it being a reprint after it had been adapted to the screen. On its cover there was a reproduction of the movie's poster. It made it appear to be nothing more than a trashy piece of pulp, with its mean-faced desperado set against a backdrop of a mother, father, and young boy standing huddled on the porch of a one-room shack, watching him walk away. His father's copy, along with George's other eleven novels, had been boxed up while Deacon was in the hospital. Later, Deacon had asked about them and George had sworn he'd stashed the box under the stairs in the barn but when they'd looked it wasn't there. They'd mounted a search but it never turned up, George finally conceding that they must have been shipped off with the rest of his parents' things, sent god-knows-where, the Sally Ann or Goodwill most likely. Deacon had bought his copy on eBay along with its translation into German, which George had once told him had outsold the ones in English by a factor of fifty to one, its appeal there predicated on the success of *Der Wüstling*, what a German producer had renamed *A Bad Man's Son* when he'd made it into a movie.

The way Grover told the story of how this came to be would have made a pretty good book unto itself, bound as it was with coincidences so unlikely that they couldn't help but point to fate, startling reversals of fortune, and finally a simple act of generosity by a kind-hearted producer in a business otherwise known for the ruthless zeal with which the moneymen took delight in screwing anyone foolish enough to call themselves a writer. It was so unbelievable, Deacon had his doubts even half of what Grover told him was true, but there were several unassailable facts.

In 1971, said producer did find a tattered copy of *A Bad Man's Son* on a bench at a train station in Munich, one of only five hundred copies then extant. Something about the picture on its cover must have impressed him enough to pick it up. It was a charcoal sketch of a man with a cowboy hat pulled down over his eyes, sleeping against the trunk of a spindly old tree. A noose was draped from its lone branch as if the man was sitting there waiting for the hangman to arrive. The synopsis on its back described it as a retelling of *Hamlet* set between the American and Canadian Midwests just after the Civil War. It was an era that, for some reason, German readers seemed to have no end of an appetite for, and maybe because of that or simply because the producer had neglected to bring something else to read on the eight-hour train ride ahead, he'd pocketed the book.

The story goes that he was travelling to Berlin to hand a director a cheque for an entirely different film. By the time he'd finished *A Bad Man's Son* he'd changed his mind and a short while later he'd changed the director's mind as well. He'd contacted Leonard Ruby, George's publisher, who'd sold him the rights for five hundred dollars and a 10 percent share of its revenue. Certain that he'd never hear from them again, he hadn't even bothered to tell George who, at the time, was barely making enough at the *Toronto Star*'s city desk to keep his newborn son in diapers and, with another on the way, could have sorely used his cut of the option. So it was a great surprise when, a little under two years later, George had opened a letter postmarked from Germany and found within a plane ticket and an invitation to the world premiere of *Der Wüstling*, to be held on September 19, 1973, at the Zoo Palast Theatre, Hardenstraae 29a, Berlin.

He'd immediately called Leonard to see if he knew anything about it. Leonard wasn't so much a bad guy as someone whose own literary aspirations exceeded his grasp and was ever in the red because of it. He'd answered that he did, apologizing profusely for "the misunderstanding" and blaming his secretary who was supposed to have sent him a cheque last year, but what can you do, good help is so hard to find, and of course he'd send him a cheque right away so he'd have some spending money for his trip. With a new baby at home, George was nervous about leaving his wife alone, but Adele, convinced that it was a once-in-a-lifetime opportunity, packed his bags and even went so far as to call a taxi to drive him to the airport, leaving him no choice but to acquiesce.

He arrived in Berlin five hours before the premiere and was treated to a hearty dinner of schnitzel and sauerkraut at the producer's house. It was, in George's own words, "a wonderful time," and he was in fine spirits when he'd finally settled down to watch what they'd done with his book.

And that's when things got a little strange.

Perhaps it was because he wasn't used to kirsch, which had been flowing freely during the dinner and also on the limo ride to the theatre, or that he didn't understand enough German to follow the dialogue, but as he watched the screen it became increasingly apparent that he and everyone else in the audience were watching two entirely different films. While he was watching what appeared to be a fairly faithful adaptation of his work—though, for sure, it was quite a lot less violent and almost entirely devoid of the sexual depravities that had led his only reviewer to call the book "morally repugnant"—the other audience members seemed to be watching a slapstick comedy.

With every new bout of laughter, George sunk ever more into his seat, embarrassed not so much for himself but for the director and the producer, who he had found to be warm, intelligent, and of a disarmingly gracious nature. He was practically sitting on the floor by the time the credits rolled, the audience bursting to their feet in spontaneous applause as the director's name flashed over the screen. George was the only one left in his seat and growing more and more confused by the moment. He waited until the audience was on its way out before standing and joining the throng in the hope that, hidden within the crowd, he might slip into a taxi without suffering through the uncomfortable moment sure to take place should he run into the producer and/or director.

And he would have made it too, had he not flagged down such an irascible and, possibly, psychotic cab driver. He had been standing in front of the theatre with his arm raised to signal the taxi he could see parked at a red light at the end of the block. The taxi flashed its lights to signal him in return and he lowered his arm, casting a furtive glance at the cinema's doors to make sure he was in the clear. Finding no sign of the producer or director amongst the theatregoers spilling onto the sidewalk, he turned back to the road just as the light was changing.

That's when he heard a squeal of tires.

Another taxi, he saw, was doing a high-velocity U-turn, or,

rather, an r-turn, for it was just then racing on a collision course with the unsuspecting throng on the sidewalk, of which George was standing as its vanguard. At the last possible moment before impact, the driver simultaneously spun the steering wheel and jammed on the brakes, sending the car into a sideways slide that brought its rear door to within an arm's length of the curb.

The other taxi driver, possibly as amazed as George was at the temerity and downright impertinence of his competitor, was a split second too late applying his own brakes and slammed into the back of the cab with a resounding crash. The door to the first cab flung open. The driver was a small man such that he had to stand on his tippy-toes to see over the roof of his car, and even then all George could see of him were two beady eyes beneath a mad frizz of white curls. He held up one finger, advising, "*Einen Moment, bitte.*"

He then stormed off towards the other taxi. Its driver was concealed by the bright lights of the theatre's marquee reflecting *Der Wüstling* off his windshield. All George knew of him was a pudgy hand clenching the top of his door as he stepped from his own cab, an action he reconsidered immediately after catching sight of the tire iron wielded in the right hand of his frizzy-haired competitor. The second taxi spun into reverse. Its driver's side door flapped open and its tail end swerved into traffic on a direct line for a bus just now passing through the intersection. George watched in muted horror as the taxi veered into the oncoming lane. The bus driver was quick enough to avoid a head-on collision but a fraction too slow to avoid catching the taxi's open driver's side door. It wrenched backwards with a horrendous grating of metal. Sparks tore along the side of the bus. The instant it had screeched to a halt its driver charged out of the front door, screaming at the cab, the tone of his voice and the spittle flying from his lips telling George that scant few of the words he was using were likely to have been found in the German phrase book he'd bought, on a whim, at the Toronto International Airport.

For his part, the frizzy-haired driver seemed not to have noticed the calamity he'd caused and was just then opening his car's rear passenger side door.

"*Wohin möchten Sie?*" he asked.

It was one of the phrases that George had memorized on the flight, thinking it might come in handy, and he answered, "The airport." And when that elicited only a confused look from the man standing before him, he corrected himself.

"The uh, *Flughafen*," he said.

"*Gut, Gut. Steigen Sie doch ein, worauf warten Sie? Machen Sie mal los!*"

And though George didn't understand what he'd said, the way the taxi driver was grabbing at his arm made his meaning clear enough. If George had simply given himself over to the man's will, letting himself be ushered into the back seat, he would have indeed accomplished his goal of getting out of Berlin without ever again seeing the director or the producer, both of whom had just spotted George standing at the curb and were fighting their way through the crowd before their writer could slip into a taxi, something he seemed rather reluctant to do.

"Uh, I uh, I think—" George was stammering when he felt a hand slapping onto his shoulder.

Spinning, he came face to face with the producer, the director standing a short ways behind. The both of them were breathing heavily, and the latter, who had patterned his career, and his appetites, after his hero, the Great Alfred Hitchcock, was dabbing at the sweat draining in rivulets down his brow with a handkerchief.

"Zer you are," the producer exclaimed. "Vee haf been looking for you everyvhere."

"I—" George stammered again, glancing back at the street.

It was filling up with passengers pouring from the bus, joining the masses on the crowded sidewalk, their stream dampened to a trickle by those who'd stopped to watch the bus driver dragging the stunned taxi driver out of his car.

The latter, George could now see, bore a striking resemblance to a character in the film he'd just watched. In his book he'd simply called him The Butcher, though in the movie he was known as Herr Metzger. He'd described him as being the son of a pig farmer *who so much resembled his father's prized sow that when he was in school his classmates had often teased him that he'd been birthed by her and not his mother.* He was clean-shaven in the book but the director had taken the liberty of giving him a small square moustache above his top lip that had made him not so much resemble Germany's former dictator as it did Oliver Hardy. In both the book and the adaptation, The Butcher/Herr Metzger's daughter was the prettiest girl in town, *a specimen of such rarefied beauty that more than once Father Rabe, the parish priest, had used her as proof that any theory suggesting it was science, and not God's will, which made a person what he or she was amounted to nothing more than the insane ravings of a diseased mind.*

She'd fallen in love with the titular bad man's son, and her father had chanced upon them while they were consummating their teenage lust in the smokehouse behind his shop.

> *Enraged at the sight of his little lamb rutting with some no account half-breed, he reached for the cleaver he always kept tucked into the strap of his apron. Raising it on high, he charged at the couple with a bestial roar. The young man ducked the slash of the blade and snatched up a meat hook hanging from a chain, driving its sharp point up and into The Butcher's billowing chin. Blood flowed like from a stuck pig, showering him with*

its sticky effluence as he cranked the lever of the hoist to
which the chain was attached, lifting the madly flailing
man off his feet.

In the book, the bad man's son then returned to the horror-struck girl, intending to finish what he'd started. Seeing her father strung up like that had soured her mood though, and she fought him off. Not taking no for an answer, he grabbed her around the throat and forced himself upon her, the chapter ending with *her lifeless body thrashing in wild palsy at mercy to the young man's ecstasy.*

In the film though, he let her live. She ran to the sheriff, bursting through his door and exclaiming, *"Da ist ein Unfall!"* The rough translation of this being, "There's been an accident!" and that was also the only thing George could think to say when he turned back to the director and the producer.

"An accident?" This from the producer. "I hope you ver not hurt."

"No, I, uh— It was—"

Before he could explain further, the director, who had finally caught his breath, interrupted him by blurting out, "But vhat did you sink of za film?"

"I uh," George stuttered again. "I mean, the audience, they thought they were watching a . . . comedy."

"Ja, ja. It is very funny. Just like your book. What is the English? Hilarious. Ja, ja. Zer hilarious. The first time I read it, I could not stop laughing. Tell him, Dieter."

"I thought I vould haff to call a doctor."

"I could not catch my breath, I vas laughing so hard."

The look that flashed over George's face must have alerted the director to the consternation he was feeling just then, and his own expression turned suddenly dour.

"It vas not meant to be funny?" he asked.

Before George could answer, the cab driver was once again grabbing at his arm.

He could hear the distant wail of sirens now and they went a good way to explaining the urgency in the taxi driver's voice as he said, *"Wir müssen los! Schnell!"*

"You are leaving so soon!" the producer exclaimed as George let himself be ushered into the open back seat, his earlier apprehension about getting into the crazy little man's cab evaporating, seeing it now as his only hope of getting out of the conversation.

"I guess I am," he said.

"But—" was all the producer could get out before the taxi driver slammed the door shut.

A police car was screeching around the corner at the end of the block and that hastened him towards the driver's seat.

And that was the last George expected to hear from either the producer or the director.

Two years later though, the former sent him his cut of the film's box office, along with the suitcase that he'd left, tucked under the bed in his guest room so that it had remained hidden there until the producer, flush with profits from *Der Wüstling*, had sold the house, deciding to try his luck in Hollywood. George's share was considerably more than he'd made in the five years he'd spent at the *Toronto Star*'s city desk and, like the producer, he made plans to use the money as a means of pursuing his own dream.

While he'd been raised in the city, George was a country boy at heart and the social upheaval that had marked the previous decade had long since convinced him that Toronto was no place to raise kids. Recalling an advertisement he'd happened upon in the *Star*'s classified section several months previous, he searched the archives until he'd found what he was looking for. "Newspaper for Sale," the ad had read, the copy below promising "a guaranteed circulation and a state-of-the-art printing press." When he called the number included, he'd learned that it was still for sale and three days later he signed the papers, making him the new owner of what was then called *The Tildon Examiner*. There was enough money left over to put a down payment on the house on Baker Street and to give Grover Parks a six-month advance on his salary, which had been his condition on agreeing to become the newly rechristened *Chronicle*'s managing editor.

"I had plenty of doubts that I'd even last that long," Grover would say at this point in the telling. "But I'd been a copy boy for five years by then. In that time, I'd seen a dozen others promoted through the ranks above me, the only thing they had to their advantage being that they were white and I was not, so I figured it was at least worth a shot."

He'd had to work twice as hard as anyone at the *Star* just to keep his job and it was because of Grover's propensity for coming into work early that he had come to know George, who was always in his chair at the city desk by five a.m., three hours before his real job began. Adele was prone to migraines, and the *clackety-clack* of his typewriter at their kitchen table made it seem like each keystroke was driving a nail into her head, so it was the only time he had to work on his Fictions.

It was Grover who had taken the photo that graced the back cover of every one of George's books. One morning, he'd been tinkering with a camera that one of the reporters had dropped in a puddle and needed a test subject to see if he'd managed to fix it. He'd come up behind George at his desk saying, "Smile," so that when he turned around, startled by the harsh glare of a flashbulb, there was a surprised grin on his face to accompany the droop of the hand-rolled cigarette in the corner of his mouth, his fingers still poised on the keys of his typewriter and the ashtray beside it trailing butts over the rim—that is to say, the classic pose of a writer at work, circa 1966. The picture would be the start of a somewhat unlikely friendship, the only real friend either of them had until then. Lubricated with coffee liberally spiced from the flask of Canadian Club George kept in his top drawer, Grover became George's first reader, and, in return, George would offer a sympathetic ear as Grover vented his frustrations about what it was like to be a poor young black man whose dreams seemed to always be fleeing just beyond his grasp.

So when George bought the *Examiner*, he'd asked Grover to join him, acquiescing immediately to his demand for a six-month advance on his pay, in case, as Grover suspected, the paper would be just another dead end in a lifetime of the same.

"Of course," Grover would then add, laughing and shaking his head, "it never occurred to me when I'd accepted his offer that I'd be the only black man in a town where civil rights was a four-letter word and was rarely mentioned without a shotgun being alluded to somewhere in the conversation."

Deacon, himself, had been the only "Indian" for the two years he'd attended Tildon Public School. As such, he'd run into his own fair share of "trouble," and he knew that, regardless of Grover's attempt to make light of his own, there was no doubt he'd had a rough go of it.

"Is a time a'right," was all he'd say about that, his voice taking on a southern drawl and his eyes a certain twinkle as if to suggest he wouldn't have expected to have been treated much different had he relocated somewhere south of the Mason–Dixon.

In the end, what he called his "Respectability Politics" had won over most of his detractors. The only notable exception Deacon knew of was a Mr. Robert Grieves. Mr. Grieves was the principal at the Tildon and Mesaquakee Lakes Secondary School for thirty years. He'd cut his teeth shepherding the youth of yesteryear through the turbulent '60s and had worn them down to the gums by the mid-'80s when the leather strap he so proudly displayed on a hook behind his desk gave the school board reason enough to force him into early retirement.

Grieves was also the father of three daughters. The eldest, Loretta, had earned a degree in Library Sciences from the University of Toronto and had returned to her hometown in 1974 to assume stewardship of the newly constructed Tildon Public Library. Aside from boasting the only elevator in town at the time, it was equipped with a climate-controlled room in the basement to house the town's archives. It was in there that Grover spent most of his free time while researching *They Came Here to Be Free*, a history of black settlers in the area. That had given him the impetus to stick out the six months, but it was Loretta who gave him a reason to stay.

He'd taken a picture of her too, the very one that presided over the checkout counter during her tenure as head librarian. And though it would be decades before Deacon would make her acquaintance, she'd appeared in the photograph much as she did in her later years, which is to say exactly as one would imagine a small-town librarian should look, though perhaps a little less stern. In the picture she was wearing a simple blue dress she'd stitched herself and a smile that, Deacon often mused, was that of a young woman who'd just made love for the first time and wanted nothing more than to shout her joy to the world. It was something her younger variant would have been unwilling to do, fearing that the rancour her relationship with Grover might elicit in her father wouldn't have seemed out of place in *To Kill a Mockingbird*, the book that, incidentally, had topped "Loretta's 25 Best Books of All Time," a full tabulation of which appeared in the first of the monthly columns she began writing for the *Chronicle* shortly after assuming her duties.

A decade later, when she revised the list for the library's

ten-year anniversary, Harper Lee's classic was still number one. But the observant amongst her devoted readers couldn't help but notice that *The Invisible Man*, absent on the previous list, had since assumed the number five position.

"For you see," Grover had added at this point in the telling, "*The Invisible Man* was one of only three books I'd brought with me when I followed George to the *Chronicle*."

His expression had all of a sudden taken on a pensive air, as if he was trying to imagine the man he might have been if things had gone another way. He shortly snapped out of his trance, though there was a most sombre cast to his eyes as he glanced up at the shelf across from the desk in his office where *The Invisible Man* served as a buffer between the other two books he'd brought—Eldridge Cleaver's *Soul on Ice* and Martin Luther King's *Conscience for Change*.

When he spoke again his voice had taken on an uncharacter-istically wistful air so that Deacon knew, for all his struggles, he wouldn't have had it any other way.

"And until the birth of our first son," he said, "the photo-graph and *The Invisible Man*'s inclusion on Loretta's anniversary list would be the only public expressions of the love the two of us had shared, all alone together, into the wee hours after the library had closed for the night."

16

Daylight was fading when Deacon reached *The End* of *A Bad Man's Son*, though it seemed he'd barely read a word, his thoughts having drifted so far from the page.

He returned it to the shelf, taking down his copy of George's second book, *The Passage*. While he read it, he didn't think much about anything, all thoughts, as they were, swept aside by the creeping dread that always descended upon him the moment he'd come upon its opening lines:

> *Black snow, swirling like ashes windswept from a fire.*
>
> *It was the only thing he could remember from the dream when he awoke, the world tilting around him as his body sagged in the saddle atop his old mare, trudging through the drifts remaking the forest into an endless ocean of billowing white.*

The *he* in question was an anthropologist named Edgar Frost who, in 1871, had set out to make an ethnographic survey of the tribes along the eastern fringes of the Rocky Mountains before the civilizing influence of the TransCanada Rail Line would forever mar the perfection of their noble ways. Accompanied by his guide, a member of the Piegan tribe named Chojan, they'd arranged to winter at a Blackfoot village. When they arrived, it was razed to the ground and they were forced to seek shelter from a blizzard in a nearby trading post dubbed Fort Whoop-Up by the whiskey traders who'd built it to exchange their wares for fur. Huddled within its walls, they'd find the survivors of the Blackfoot village, comprised solely of two dozen or so women and children. The only sustenance they'd had for a week had been three of their dogs.

> *The one they'd spared was as emaciated and weak as his masters so that he barely had the energy to lift his head to growl at Edgar and Chojan staggering through the front door, their frosted beards and snow-encrusted leathers lending them the appearance of grim spectres, perhaps come to lead the souls of these soon-to-be departed into the netherworld.*

With only a bit of pemmican and some dried strips of venison left from his own stores, Edgar was forced to slaughter his prized mare. While he roasted the meat, Chojan translated the tale of woe recounted by the eldest of the women. She spoke of how after the men of their tribe had traded in their furs for "firewater," they'd become drunk and enraged. Convinced that they'd been taken advantage of, they'd launched an all-out assault on the fort. In reprisal, the whiskey traders had opened fire on them with the Gatling minigun they'd brought along for protection. They'd killed every last one of their assailants and then sought out their village to satisfy their blood, and other, lusts on those who remained behind. A young woman, who had witnessed the slaughter, ran back home to warn the others and they'd hid in the woods, watching as the whiskey traders burnt their village to the ground. An early winter storm was approaching and the whiskey traders fled south against its advance, leaving the remaining Blackfoot no choice but to seek shelter in the fort that, mere hours before, had spelt their ruin and now provided them their only hope of surviving the winter.

The old woman had just finished speaking when the whiskey traders returned. They'd lost two of their party in an avalanche and the six that remained had barely made it back alive. The moment they barged through the door, the dog, reinvigorated by its share of horse flesh, attacked their leader, an ex-Jesuit priest still garbed in the sacraments of his order. He killed it with his pistol and then shot Chojan a moment *later for the sin of palming the hilt of his knife and staring at Brother Marée with a defiant sheen glossing his eyes.*

Edgar would have met a similar fate had the ex-Priest not found the notebook in his bag. Brother Marée had taken this as proof that God had set him in his path so that he might chronicle his great deeds; a bard, so to speak, to his knight-errant. Manacled and chained to a wall, Edgar was helpless but to watch the whiskey traders have their way with the survivors. What followed was a nightmare of unbridled misery and despair, no child too young nor woman too old for the whiskey traders' savage lusts. There was only one moment of reprieve. Having managed to escape his restraints by chewing off his thumb, Edgar killed the whiskey traders whilst they slept and freed the remaining survivors who, by then, amounted to a teenage girl and her ten-year-old brother, both of whom Brother Marée had claimed for himself.

But the relief was short-lived. No sooner had he released them from their bondage than the older girl had taken up the ex-priest's knife and slit her brother's throat before turning the blade on herself.

The book ended with Edgar setting fire to the fort.

> *Watching it burn, the ashes swirling around him like black snow reminded him not so much of his dream but of how, less than a year ago, he'd stood at the train station in Oxford, his studies behind and the promise of a future filled with adventure perfectly rendered in the fume of coal exhaust bent over the locomotive speeding towards him. Recalling the up-swelling of hope he'd felt as the train screeched to a halt at the platform, its black plume enveloping him the same as the billow from the fire before him was doing now, the thought reared in his mind that maybe the civilizing influence of the TransCanada Rail Line wouldn't be such a bad thing after all.*

This would prove to be wishful thinking, as George's next book was plain to point out. *My Brother's Keeper* started with three young Cree brothers waiting at the station in Long Lac for the train that would take them on the last leg of their journey to a residential school in Kenora, some six hundred miles from home.

> *It was the first time any of them would see an "iron horse," but they'd heard plenty of stories about them from their uncle, who'd earned a Victoria Cross fighting the Germans in WWII. Each were thinking of the same story as they huddled together at the edge of the platform. It was about the time he was scouting behind*

enemy lines and he'd come upon a train pulling an endless stream of cattle cars. It wasn't livestock they were
carrying though, it was people. He could see their fingers poking out from within the air holes and hear their
ghastly cries as they sped past.

"Why were they in cattle cars?" the eldest of the
brothers had asked, hearing him relate this.

"Because they were taking them to the slaughterhouse, I guess."

"But you said they were people. Why would they be
taking people to a slaughterhouse?"

Their uncle had thought on that for a moment.

"There ain't no rhyme nor reason to it," he'd finally
replied. "It's just the way of the White Man. I seen
enough of his doings to know that wherever he goes, the
devil ain't never too far behind."

And here they were, waiting for the White Man's
train to take them to god knows where, maybe hell itself.

Unbeknownst to them, the train that would take them west
was carrying two brothers—William and James—who were
fleeing Toronto, hoping to find work at a logging camp. Their
futures would become intertwined the next winter after the
youngest of the Cree boys dies from tuberculosis and his brothers
retrieve his body from amongst the dozen or so in a common
burial pit, determined to carry him home so that he may find
peace amongst the spirits of his ancestors. Along the way, they
happen upon William, the eldest of the other brothers, who himself was fleeing the logging camp after shooting the man who'd
killed James for cheating him at cards.

Aside from its rather grim beginnings, *My Brother's Keeper* was
the most hopeful of all of George's Fictions, the only one that

didn't end with a world on fire, in one way or another. The bulk of the narrative had the two boys teaching William to survive in the woods during the dead of winter and ended with William recounting the tale to the Cree villagers gathered around their communal hearth, *the flames contained within the ring of stones murmuring in warm contemplation along with the villagers as William told them of how two of their sons had saved him from no uncertain death.*

It was a welcome balm from *The Passage*'s unrelenting despair and also so intrinsically linked to *The Pines*, which came after, that Deacon couldn't possibly imagine reading the others without the one in between. But the only copy of that was on the bookshelf behind George's desk in the barn where Deacon himself had returned it six months previous, unwilling, if what Dylan said was true, to leave the only remaining copy wedged so ignobly between a bathtub and a toilet.

17

Ten minutes later he was walking up Baker Street.

There was an upside-down garbage bin at the end of the Cleary's driveway. Habit had Deacon taking the latter by the handle and dragging it to the garage's side door. It was locked, and he left it there, skirting up the brick walkway and following it into the backyard, coming into sight of the barn and hurrying across the lawn, recalling the last time he'd done so.

He'd been after a sneak peak of what George had been writing.

And even though there was an urgency in the recollection, his pace slackened as he came to the rock on the windowsill, each step, like one taken in fresh cement, weighed down by the fear that George's children, Edward and Louise, had spent the last three days sorting through their father's stuff. The only key to the barn Deacon knew of was under the rock on the window ledge. They must have known about that and, if they did and had .

used it to let themselves into the barn, it was a good bet they'd found the manuscript too.

But the key was still under the rock and when he'd reached the desk there was indeed a stack of pages on the left-hand side of the typewriter, though the shock he felt coming across it was hardly lessened. There couldn't have been more than thirty sheets in the pile, whereas George's rewrite had numbered over a hundred pages before, and beside it there was only a faint square outline in the dust to say that his rough draft had ever been there at all. The pages that did remain were sitting face up and **Prologue** was clearly outlined along the top of the first. As he peered down at it in torpid dismay, he saw that even that was only a photocopy of the original.

What in the hell? he thought, and when an answer wasn't forthcoming, he circled the desk, still thinking it must have been some sort of mistake.

He rifled through all six of the desk's drawers but found nothing but a dozen or so pens, three extra spools of ribbon, two unopened packages of paper, and a half-empty forty of Canadian Club. He only bothered taking out the latter and by the time he was placing it on the desk beside the stack of photocopies, his alarm had faded into a bitter sort of resignation.

Gathering the pages up with little of the care that had afforded him his first glimpse, he sat in the chair, setting on his lap what was left of the manuscript, and scanning down towards the opening line.

PROLOGUE

How long it had been following her she couldn't say.
    It had been a half an hour since she'd walked out
of the Baileys' driveway, casting one last glance
at her father's pickup truck and cursing asshole
under her breath as she set off down the highway.
Her twelfth birthday had been last Tuesday and her
grandmother had given her fifty dollars. She'd been
after her dad all week to drive her to the Walmart in
Tildon where she had in mind to spend her windfall
on a new pair of jeans and a T-shirt, maybe a bag of
Hershey's Kisses if she had any money left. After
five days of pleading with him, he'd finally relented,
telling her at dinner that evening that he'd promised
his sister he'd stop by Bailey's Auto Wreck to see if
they had an alternator for her Tercel, the old one
dying just that afternoon and a new one costing more
than the car was worth.

Won't be but a moment, he'd said as he stepped out
of the truck.

She'd brought a Walmart flyer with her and read
over it for what must have been the hundredth time,
waiting for him to return. When a half hour had
expired and he still hadn't, she got out and walked
past the dozen or so vehicles that were scattered
about the front yard, all of them with For Sale signs
in their windshields. Their owners had sold them for
scrap but Clarence Bailey had seen a little life left
in them yet, so, instead of towing them to the ten-
acre field behind the house where he kept the wrecks,
he had fixed them up, selling them for cheap, mostly
to high school kids buying their first car and single
moms who couldn't afford anything better.

Beyond them: the Baileys' two-storey brick farm-
house. A bare bulb projected from the wall above its
front door, shining over the stack of cinder blocks
they had in place of steps. As she came into the
light, the smell of skunk drifted through the open
window that looked into the kitchen and she heard
a blood-curdling scream shortly given way to an
undulating wail—her father, she knew, imitating an
Indian war cry.

Laughter greeted it and then there was the scrape
of a chair's legs against linoleum.

You want another beer? a voice she recognized as
Clarence's son, Duane, asked.

Her father answered, I'm sitting here, ain't I?

That got another laugh and she turned around and
walked back to the truck. She sat in the passenger seat,
stewing as the sun faded between the trees on the

far side of the barn that had once housed the Baileys'
herd of Jerseys and was now where they kept their
store of auto parts. It had been dark for a good while
when she finally said, Fuck him, not so much angry at
her father as she was at herself for thinking this
time might have been any different.

Bailey's Auto Wreck was not two hundred yards
from Moose Point Road, which everyone called The
Moose Point Expressway. If it had been the daytime
she would have cut down the half-kilometre stretch
of hard-packed gravel that dead-ended just short
of the Moose River separating the reserve on the
north side from the wooded land to the south. From
the road's terminus there was a path leading down to
the water and one of her cousins, Jesse she thought
it was, had had the bright idea to tether a raft
between two maple trees on either side, fashioning
a makeshift ferry. It made so that anyone looking to
hitchhike into Tildon could cut fifteen clicks off
their trip. Being as it was the second week of July,
she probably wouldn't have bothered with the ferry
though. It was god-awful heavy and it would have
taken her twice as long to pull herself across the
river as it would have to swim, something she'd have
preferred to do anyway, the river's cool carrying
with it the promise of a brief respite from the heat
that even now was turning her shirt into a sponge.

If it had been daytime she'd have almost been home
by now but halfway down Moose Point Road the county
had placed a metal Dumpster so the tourists wouldn't
have to drive all the way to the landfill to get rid
of their trash. The smell of garbage attracted the

bears. Unwilling to take the risk of running into a brown or a black in the dark, she stuck to the highway even though that meant a ten-K hike to the bridge spanning Maynard's Falls and another five clicks spent backtracking along the road on the other side of the river.

If she was lucky she might catch a ride at least part of the way, so every time she heard a car coming up behind her she turned around and stuck out her thumb. And that's what she'd been doing when she caught sight of it: a glimpse of grey fur bristling within a car's headlights as it passed by on the road. It might have been a coyote or just as likely some stray. The message board at the Maynard Falls General Store was plastered with missing dog signs posted by cottagers who'd made the mistake of letting their dogs roam free. As far as she knew, most of them never saw their pets again, meaning a few of them must have still been out there, grown wild and hungry.

The car, a black Mercedes, sped past without even slowing down and the dark again swallowed whatever animal was about. She froze stock-still, peering into the shadows, trying to figure out if maybe it had been her imagination.

It didn't take her more than a breath to see that it wasn't.

As another vehicle approached from the opposite direction, two glints of light shone back at her. They couldn't have been anything but eyes and she turned, waving her hands over her head, trying to get the driver's attention. If he saw her he made no sign

beyond, it seemed, pushing his foot a little harder on
the SUV's gas.

Spinning back around, she tracked the vehicle's
progress and there it was again: the bristle of grey
fur crouching in the ditch.

It was a coyote, there was no doubt about that now.

It had frozen within the headlights' glow, but the
moment they'd passed she heard the crackle of leaves
under paw. It was walking towards her. Bending, she
scooped a handful of gravel from the shoulder and
flung it, screaming, "Go on. Shoo. Leave me alone!"

She heard the rat-a-tat-tat of the stones pelting
the ground and even before they'd settled she was
backing away, reaching for the knife in the back
pocket of her jeans. It had been her brother's, what he
called a butterfly knife. She'd been carrying it ever
since she was nine and her neighbour, a man she'd
known as Uncle Pete her whole life, had followed her
one morning when she'd gone down to the river to pick
fiddleheads for her mother. He'd said he'd snap her
neck if she ever told anyone what he'd done to her,
wrapping his hands around her throat and squeezing
just a little so she'd know how easy it'd be. She promised him she wouldn't and he released, patting her
on the head and calling her a good girl, though she'd
felt like anything but.

That night she'd stolen the knife from the
glovebox in her brother's truck, making another
promise, this one to herself, that she'd kill any man
who dared lay his hands on her again. She'd spent
hours practising how to quick draw it as she'd seen
her brother do, snatching it from her pocket and

flipping the blade up with a flick of her wrist, stabbing the point upwards under some imagined chin then flicking it again, snapping its grips back over the blade. When she'd mastered that, she painted the stainless steel handles of the knife with the black and orange nail polish she'd used last Halloween when she'd gone as a witch. Now when she spun it around, the handles blurred into a flutter almost resembling a monarch's wings.

With a brazen clack, the handles scissored together and she thrust the blade out. The sound stilled the coyote and its shadow was lost again into the greater shade. She held her breath, peering into the dark and listening for something to tell her if the coyote was still there. There was no sound save for the mosquitoes buzzing about her head and the crunch of her sneakers shifting against the gravel underfoot.

Just as she was exhaling, two spots of light appeared around a far bend in the road. She watched the bright approaching, watched it scour over the asphalt, watched it touch on the coyote, its head turned, craning towards the vehicle slowing as it approached, close enough now that she could see it was a red minivan. She stuck out her thumb and as it passed her by it was already angling onto the shoulder.

She set off after it at a run.

Before it had come to a complete stop, the driver's side door was opening and a man was craning his head out. The cherub pudge to his cheeks defied his age, in his midfifties she guessed, so that it almost looked like a baby's face had been glued over top of his own. Above, he had a thin stubble of bleach-blond hair, and below, doughy folds of flesh oozed out from under the collar of a brightly coloured Hawaiian shirt.

You need a lift, little miss? he asked.

I sure do, she answered coming to the door, out of breath.

Well, go around the other side then.

She circled around the van's front, running her hand over its bug-splattered grill, her racing heart eased by the bright of its headlights. When she came to its far corner, she looked up at the driver watching after her through the windshield. He smiled, warm and friendly like her grandfather would, and that gave her enough courage to crane forward and peer around the edge of the van.

Beyond the taillight's red glow, she wasn't able to see much beyond the dark, and if the coyote was lying there in wait for her, it made no sign.

Deacon paused here long enough to light a smoke before flipping to the next page.

CHAPTER 1

A two-by-ten bolted to a rock at the river's edge.
Someone's notion of a diving board. Now broken. The
platform projected a mere six inches over the water.
The end frayed into splinters. Needle points that
speak to some long-ago summer's day suddenly turned
foul.

The bear grunts at it. Snorts. Beads of water
glisten over its back, trailing from its coat. The lap
of the current against the shore. The rush of a car on
the highway whooshing against the sway of the cedar
trees creaking above.

The smell of rotting meat.

It turns, padding up the footpath until it comes to
a loop of gravel cut into the forest in the shape of a
figure eight. A picnic table where the two loops meet.
The wood softened by damp and mildewed. One of its
legs rotted away, the bench sagging, almost touching

the ground. A garbage can beside, its lid clamped
tight against scavengers. Not much to recommend our
bear.

Except there is the cage: an eight-foot-long mesh
of reinforced steel, six feet high. Its silhouette,
this night, is as dark as the inside of a cave.

The bear walks towards it, wary. Sniffing at
the bait, rancid from the heat and befouling the
air though it smells as sweet as honey to our weary
traveller. It pauses. Raises its nose to the breeze.
Something else. It snorts again. Shakes its head.
Takes a step backwards.

Come on, you son of a bitch, Del whispers.

He's sighting on it over the steel tip of the arrow
drawn back on the bow he'd fashioned over the winter
out of a length of black ash.

His brother Andre had hawked over him, sneering,
while he used his father's hatchet to hack at the six-
foot log he'd dragged into the garage, later refining
it with a paring knife and using an awl he heated in
the fire to stencil a wolf's head, mid-howl, along the
top half's inside curve. Rubbing it with linseed oil
to keep the wood supple while he bent it into shape,
millimetres at a time, tying it off with kite string,
saving the line he cured out of sinew from a deer his
uncle had shot that spring. Only stringing it proper
when the bow was ready, six months from the morning
he felled the ash.

And when he had shot it that first time—never
more proud of himself than when he saw the arrow
fly true—Andre was there again, standing beside him,
shaking his head. Scoffing.

What you aim to shoot with that thing?

Del answering, We'll see.

You'd be lucky to kill a coon. Forget about a deer.

No, not a deer.

Then what?

We'll see. We'll see.

The bear is walking forward again, each step taken as if on thin ice. It's a black. Three foot to the shoulder. An adolescent. Not much more, really, than an overgrown racoon, and Del smiles at that, thinking of what his brother had said. The cage is nestled in a small recess in the northwest corner of the rest stop. The bear isn't yet halfway to it from the path leading up from the river.

For his blind, Del had chosen the hollow within a grove of cedars some twenty feet behind and downwind of the cage. The only thing about cedars though is that they attract the mosquitoes. Hordes buzz about him, like flies bobbing on the end of fishing lines. To hide his scent, Del has smeared boiled poplar sap mixed with crushed juniper berries over his face and the back of his hands and neck, a recipe he learned from his grandfather. One of the skitters has become stuck in the syrupy goo plastered to his forehead and he can hear its zzzt zzzt as it struggles to pull free.

The bow's line digs into the joints between Del's index and middle fingers, cutting off the circulation. It's been two minutes since he first saw the bear. It feels more like an hour.

He should have waited for the bear to come to the stone he'd stood upright five feet from the cage to mark his range. Shouldn't have drawn back the arrow the moment he saw it lumbering out of the river, sighting on it between the cedar boughs. Del knows this now but still he won't release the tension, won't give his fingers the relief as if feeling them growing numb means something beyond impatience.

Come on, now, he whispers.

Three more steps. Now two. Just one more—

Headlights flare against the screen of trees, a vehicle slowing on the highway, angling into the rest stop. The bear reels around, bolting back towards the river.

Son of a—

The vehicle's headlights wash over his blind.

Ducking low, pressing his face to the ground, Del curses again, Damn it all.

When the crunch of its tires has quieted, he rises to his knees and peers through the cedar boughs. He can see that it's a minivan parked at the far end of the loop, its driver's side fronting towards him, its engine still running, exhaust flaring red in its taillights, its interior dark, not even a shade of movement.

Probably just a couple of teenagers, he thinks. A quick fuck, or a blow job, on the way home. Had to be tonight, didn't it? Right now. When you've been out here for six hours every night this week. Goddamn.

He watches the van for a minute or two. Nothing. He stands, looking through the forest to where he's parked his motorbike, some thirty paces through the scrub. It'd be a five-minute ride along the forest path to the Moose Point Ferry, another ten to get across the river, five more after that to get back home where Andre would be waiting up for him in their room, whispering the moment he pulled himself through the window, So?

Del crawling into bed, not saying a word.

Fuck it.

Setting his bow on the ground, the quiver on top, he removes the bandana he's tied over his head to keep the bugs off the back of his neck. Folds it in a triangle. Ties it over the bridge of his nose. Grinning now with malevolent foresight, thinking of the teenagers' startled shame when he taps on the van's window with the point of his knife, given over to horror when they see the mask over his face.

He draws the knife from the sheath on his belt. It's ten inches, haft to tip. Serrated teeth down the one side. The blade sharp enough to shave ice.

He's just prying apart the cedar boughs when he sees another set of headlights turning into the rest stop.

You got to be kiddin' me.

He freezes, crouches down again. The second vehicle is a sedan, black and sleek. As it pulls past, Del can just make out the shadow of a word spanning its doors: POLICE.

It's one of those ghost cars, the kind cops use to catch speeders.

Del watches it coast to a stop beside the picnic table, so rapt he can hardly breathe.

You need to get the fuck out of here, he tells himself as the cruiser's door opens.

Still he doesn't move an inch, watching the cop

getting out. In the yellow glow from the car's interior light, Del can see that the officer is young and white and also that he's seen him plenty of times before, cruising Highway 118 in the same car and once at the Maynard Falls General Store, pulling into the parking lot while he and his brother sat at a picnic table, licking ice cream cones. He'd even tipped his hat and smiled in their direction on his way towards the port-a-john stationed around back. Hard to forget a face like that, the cop's left cheek, as it is, looking like someone had squeezed his head in a waffle iron.

As the cop approaches the van, his right hand settles on the grip of the gun slung low on his belt and he holds the flashlight in his hand up over his head, angling its beam on the driver's side window. A splash of red smears the glass and he jerks the flashlight downwards. Glances about, shining the light over the forest in a quickening arc.

Del drops to the ground. The beam skirts the cedar boughs above him, then moves on.

Did you see that? he thinks. Smeared on the window of the van. It looked like—

He shakes his head.

Your eyes are just playing tricks on you.

If it was though—

Ain't nothing you can do about that now.

He lifts his head again, wedging two fingers into the cedar boughs, prying its screen apart, not seeing anything but sprouts of grass. Every bit of reason telling him to just forget about it. Get the fuck up. Go.

Instead he stands, taking hold of the branch in

front of him, pressing it down just enough so that he can see through its drape.

The cop is at the van, shining the light in at the driver. His body is blocking Del's view of whatever it was he thought he saw.

A slight hitch then to the light, shining it on the passenger maybe. Del hears a door opening. The cop mutters something, sounds like, Shit! Then he's dodging sideways, his two legs moving with military precision as he darts around the front of the van. A moment later a figure flashes through the lights at its rear, running hard, its feet finding the asphalt and its body hunkering down, pushing for more speed, the cop in frantic pursuit.

Del can see now that it's a girl. She's wearing a skirt anyway, her hair dark and about as long as his, hung halfway down her back. She couldn't be much older than thirteen. As delicate as a fern and running like she was trying to beat the devil. The cop two strides behind, chasing after her, reaching out, clawing at the air a hand's width behind her head. She zags, ducking the cop's grasp and he stumbles, suddenly off balance. That gives her another step.

She's going to make it!

It takes a mountain of will for Del not to call out, cheering her on.

Then, all of a sudden, her feet give out from under her. She reels, flailing madly, trying to keep herself upright. She can't and goes down hard. As her knees and arms scrape over the gravel, Del sees that it's the stone he'd used to mark his range that's tripped her up.

Bad luck, he thinks, knowing that really it's not.
It's something else. His fault.

He watches her scrambling back to her feet, not
more than ten paces from his blind. Her face, suddenly unmasked from the drape of her hair, comes
into clear relief within the moon's glow an instant
before she's jerked backwards by the cop grabbing
at her arm. Just enough time for Del to see that he
knows her.

It's Emma Dupuis, he thinks, dumbstruck by the
notion. They've been in the same class since kinder-
garten.

How—?

Shaking his head, his confuse eclipsed by
thoughts of Emma's older brother, William, who
everyone calls Big Willy, though never to his face.

As mean a son of a bitch as you're likely to find
this side of the pound (Del's father's words). In and
out of juvie until he was old enough to do some real
time. Mostly for drugs but the last time was for
shooting at a surveyor he found on contested land.
That made him a hero amongst some of the younger
men on the reserve, Del included. It was while Big
Willy was serving eighteen months for unlawful dis-
charge of a firearm that Sarah Decaire, Del's second
cousin on his mother's side, had gone missing. She was
fifteen and known to sniff gasoline and fuck anyone
who'd give her a taste of something that packed a
little more punch. When she disappeared it wasn't
much of a surprise. Word on the reserve was that she'd
run away, and the Mountie they sent out to investigate agreed, assuring her parents that, sooner or

later, she was bound to turn up. That was over a year ago and no one'd heard a word from her since.

When Big Willy was released, he went around telling anyone who'd listen that she was dead, killed by a cop no less, he heard it from someone on the inside. Most people thought he was just trying to stir up shit and there was even a motion put to council to have him kicked off the reserve. That had failed, and afterwards Big Willy kept to himself. Rumour was he was back to selling drugs, using the money to buy guns, handing one out to anyone who promised to use it the next time some Hunio 'on would come onto their land.

Del, himself, knocked on his back door one night last fall, offering his pledge. Big Willy laughed at the fierce peel to his scowl, telling him he liked his spirit, but refused to give him a gun.

Come back in a few years, he'd said, ruffling his hand through the boy's hair like he was no more than a child. After you got more than peach fuzz on your pecker, then we'll see.

The young men gathered around the kitchen table beyond the door laughed along with their leader. It was their ridicule that had followed Del over the winter while he cured the strip of black ash, bending the wood's will to his own.

He would bring them the heart of a bear he'd kill with a bow made with his own two hands. And if that wasn't enough, he'd drop his pants right there, show 'em he was plenty enough a man, any way you cared to measure it.

It seems then like divine providence chancing

upon Emma at a rest stop that, this late at night, might as well have been at the end of the world. Watching her fighting off the cop, thoughts of what her brother had said about Sarah had him reaching for his bow. Certain now that he was the same cop who'd killed his cousin and that he was in league with the driver of the van and that Emma had killed the latter for something he'd done, even though she's now screaming, I didn't do anything! Let me go! Stop! Let me go!

Back kicking at the cop's legs, thrashing against his grip, his hands clamped tight to her wrists, crossed over her chest, holding her tight, not saying a word, letting the girl wear herself out.

Del's bow is in his hand again, his fingers drawing back the arrow on its string. Aiming the point now at the space between the cop's eyes. But even as he releases, the cop is dropping to his knees as if the hand of God has willed it so. The arrow misses its mark, instead striking his hat. It sweeps from the top of his head like in one of those old westerns his dad likes to watch. The cop startled, his hand chasing after it as if the wind is to blame. Realizing it's not, his eyes darting about, frantic, now settling on the grove of cedars not ten feet in front of him. His hand drawing his sidearm from its holster.

The sound then of footsteps crackling at a hard run through the underbrush. The brrm brrm of a motorcycle kick-starting followed by the high-pitched whine of its engine roaring to life. Couldn't be more than 50 ccs. A child's bike.

The girl hearing none of this, lost as she is to her

rage and her grief. Sobbing now. The cop turning her around, pulling her tight to his chest. She hammering at him with clenched fists, pleading, Please, let me go. He stroking the back of her head with his hand.

Shhh, he says. It's okay. Shhh. You're safe now.

18

O nly when he'd reached the end of the chapter did Deacon look up from the page again.

What George had written seemed oddly familiar but he couldn't put into words exactly why. Staring up at the crevice of dark swallowing the far corner of the room, he thought back over what he'd read. A man picking up a hitchhiker, driving her off to a secluded rest stop. A red smear of blood over the car's window, all there was to say about what had happened. Except he wasn't driving a car, he was driving a . . . van.

A van, he thought, *yeah. And wasn't Ronald Crane driving a van on the night he'd been murdered at a secluded rest stop just this side of the Moose River?*

Thinking back to the article he'd read in the *Globe and Mail,* how Ronald Crane's throat had been slashed before he'd been set on fire.

Biting his lip, shaking his head.

It couldn't be.

Measuring the passage of time—barely a week since Ronald Crane had been killed—against the memory of the twin stacks of paper, five hundred combined pages at least. It would have been impossible for George to have started after Ronald Crane had died. And hadn't George once told him, on most days writing felt like he was trying to force a sliver out of his thumb with a ball-peen hammer? It was a sentiment starkly at odds with the recollection of the *clackety-clack* of a train hurtling down its tracks, but then that had been him doing a rewrite. He would have to have been working on it for well over a year before Ronald Crane had been killed.

Looking down then at the page in his lap, as if the answer might by lying in wait for him there, and seeing one more page beneath it. Slipping the top sheet under the manuscript, he traced past **Chapter Two**, his gaze trailing down to the first line, halfway towards the bottom.

> The siren reared as a sharp declaration through the open window like an exclamation point on the end of Nina Simone's desperate plea from the stereo that she was feelin' good. Rain was bent over the couch, her black and red, vaguely oriental, robe hiked up over her bare ass and he was behind her, his pants around his ankles. He had forty years on her own thirty-nine but the pill he'd taken made him feel half his age as he thrust into her with the precision of a—

"Knock, knock."

"Jesus!" Deacon gasped, looking up, startled as much by what he'd just read as he was by the sight of Dylan craning his head through the barn's open door.

"Hey, Deke," he said, grinning wide, taking untold delight in the fright he'd just caused. "I thought I might find you here." And when that only resulted in Deacon gaping back at him, he added: "Shoot, boy, you look like you've seen a ghost. I catch you in the middle of something?"

"No, I uh—" Deacon stammered, trying to think of something, anything he might say. He looked down at the pages in his lap as if there might be an answer waiting for him there. The words **bare ass** and **thrust** stood out against all the others, and neither did him a damn bit of good.

"I mean," he said, looking back up, "Loretta, she asked me to go through George's papers. You know, for the, uh, library archives. I've been meaning to ever since."

That much was true anyway.

"Find anything interesting?"

"No, uh, mostly old manuscripts. Rough drafts, you know, that sort of thing. A few letters . . ." His voice trailing off, seeing Dylan smiling and nodding like he didn't believe a word of it.

The grandfather clock in the corner of the room chimed the half hour and that seemed to let him off the hook as Dylan checked the time against his own watch.

"Shoot, it's ten thirty already? I was supposed to be up at Moose Point Road a half hour ago."

"Moose Point Road?" Deacon asked in alarm, having read the same name on the page only moments ago.

"I caught some overtime, on account of the manhunt."

"Manhunt?"

"You haven't heard."

Deacon shook his head.

"No, I guess you wouldn't've. What with Gramps and all."

His gaze then elevated to a dark corner, taking on a distant air. His brow furrowed as if maybe he was trying to figure out something he might say and knew there weren't enough words to express even half of what he felt thinking about his grandfather dying like he had.

Deacon didn't much want to talk about it either.

"You were saying?" he said. "About a manhunt?"

"Yeah, it's a helluva thing. I'd tell you all about it, except I'm late as it is."

He was already turning towards the door.

"Oh shoot," he said, turning back. "Almost forgot what I came for. Dad wants a few words. Whenever you have a moment. Something about the will? You'll get in touch?"

Deacon nodded and Dylan's mouth opened like he was thinking of saying something else. Whatever it was he must have decided it could wait. He was slapping his hand against the door frame and checking his watch again.

"Alright, then," he said. "See you when I do."

TAYLOR

T he drugs had worn off some time ago.

His arm, in a plastic bubble cast and a sling, throbbed like a nail had been driven through it. His two top front teeth were broken off at their roots and he greeted every breath with stilted caution, even the slightest intake of air shooting electric shocks through his gums, same as if he was chewing on tinfoil. His nose was broken too and his throat felt like sandpaper, but the one and only time a nurse had offered him a drink of water, he might as well have been sucking it through a raspberry bramble as a straw, his lips were so swollen and raw.

His hospital bed had been raised to a seventy-five-degree angle to afford him a clear view of the iPad his father's lawyer had propped in its stand on the wheeled table where patients were meant to eat their meals. He'd known Garland Derby most of his life, though he could count on one hand the times they'd spent more than two minutes together off the golf course,

Taylor having become the alternate for his father's weekly round when business got in the way of pleasure for one of its foursome.

Garland was a confounding figure for the young man. He was shaped like a VW Beetle set on end and his sagging jowls had the pallor of someone who'd just choked to death on the last morsel of a thirty-six-ounce T-bone. Still, even on the best of days, there wasn't a man in their group who could come within four strokes of his score approaching the nineteenth hole. As to his proclivity with a wood or an iron, he was real humble. The only words of explanation he'd ever offered Taylor was that golf is like most things: "The trick is to figure out where it is you want to land the ball," he'd gone on to say. "Other than that, try not to swing too hard."

It had been a riddle at the time—Taylor then being eighteen and never feeling better than when he'd hammered the shit out of the ball off the tee. But he most certainly knew what he meant now, watching the screen in front of him and seeing Mike the Bouncer pressing the tip of the bat under the biker's chin.

"Goddamnit, Lester," he is saying. "Take it outside."

The screen fades to black.

Trevor had added three seconds of blank screen to draw out the suspense, and while Lester had been manhandling Taylor up the stairs on their way towards the sidewalk, he and Darren had hurried out the Diplomat's back door. They'd taken up residence on the far side of the park, afraid to move more than a few paces from Trevor's BMW. In the meantime, Trevor had traded the pinhole camera for the handy cam. It was a Sony FRD-AX100/B, a black cylinder about as thick as a roll of one-hundred twenty-dollar bills, which was how much it had cost Trevor's dad on his last birthday, its price a reflection of Sony's promise that its patented Nightshot ® Infrared System would render images taken in near dark as clear as those shot in the full light of day.

So when the players reappear they are in sharp relief. Lester is pushing Taylor roughly up the path leading into the park beside the Diplomat Hotel, and the two Flaming Eagles who'd been sitting at his table are walking slightly ahead, guarding against the chance that Taylor might try to make a run for it. The Girl is hurrying to keep up behind and The Cripple is hobbling after her in his lopsided gait.

Coming to the bench upon which The Junkie appears to have fallen asleep, the stouter of the two men grabs hold of one of Taylor's arms, turning him to face Lester.

"It's all been a misunderstanding," Taylor says, and the desperate whine in his voice makes it seem not altogether a lie.

The shot then pans from Taylor to Lester, who's drawing out the suspense by winnowing two sapphire-studded rings from their respective fingers on each of his hands. Taylor, for his part, is doing his best to play the role of a man begging for his life. "My dad's rich," he's saying. "He'll pay you. I'll call him now. The money'll be here in fifteen minutes, all you have to do is give me the word."

But his pleas are falling on deaf ears. The biker remains as grim-faced as an executioner.

After he's removed both of the rings, he drops them into The Girl's cupped palm. She clamps them tight, then stands on her tippy-toes, giving him a peck on the cheek and whispering something into his ear. Lester nods. The expression on his face is more a scowl than a smile, though there's plenty of joy in it. Crackling his knuckles backwards at the end of his outstretched arms, he motions for his friend to release the prisoner. As the stouter one obliges, the lankier of the two bends to Taylor's ear, whispering loud enough that the microphone has no problem picking up the snarl in his voice as he says, "I told him to save your asshole for me."

The camera zooms out to a medium shot as Lester strides forward. Taylor's hands are raised over his head in the traditional salute of surrender. As he circles away from the larger man, he says, "Can't we talk about this?"

Lester responds by taking a clumsy swipe at him. Taylor easily dodges that and responds with a shot of his own, his right hand as flat as an iron and moving too fast to be anything but a blur in twenty-four frames a second. Its fingertips catch Lester in the throat and stop him dead, stunned by the unseen stab that has rendered him momentarily breathless.

"Suit yourself," Taylor says, cracking his neck once to the left and once to the right.

Lester's mouth opens in an involuntary spasm as if he means to reply, but Taylor's foot is already arching into a roundhouse. It strikes the biker on the side of his head, the camera struggling to keep him in frame as he reels backwards. When the focus again shifts to Taylor, he's fitting his black leather sparring gloves over his hands and moving in on Lester fast, delivering three quick jabs, mostly to feel punching him in the face rather than trying to do any real damage beyond bloodying his nose.

If this were a real movie—of the Hollywood derivation—the ritualistic drawing of first blood would elicit a brief cessation. The stakes are on the table now, and whoever's anteed in will take a moment to wipe at his nose with the back of his hand, maybe give the red smear a lick to taunt the other.

That all you got?

No such pomp here.

The moment Taylor backs off a step, Lester charges at him with his arms raised into a nascent bear hug, meaning, no doubt, to grab that little shit, squeeze him until he hears the crack of his bones, and feels his body go limp. And maybe that's the way it would have played out except Taylor is too fast by a factor of three. Ducking low, he slips from his grapple, popping up beside Lester and bringing the heel of his foot down at forty-five degrees onto the outside of his knee, caving it sideways.

Lester's hands pinwheel and his wounded leg lurches forward, the bottom half dragging along the ground, trying to find purchase in anything but the pain. Then his body is tilting at a precarious angle even as Taylor executes a gravity-defying lotus spin kick. His heel makes contact with the bridge of Lester's nose, snapping him backwards, his unbroken leg seemingly planted in the ground, his body toppling at an ugly angle over it, pinning the broken one beneath his substantial girth. Such a blow might have killed a lesser man, or at least knocked him out. Lester isn't so lucky and the guttural wail he unleashes serves as the perfect soundtrack to the frantic lash of his hands hammering at the ground.

Taylor has by then succumbed to the earth's pull and is standing over the vanquished, striking the same pose as Bruce Lee on the framed poster hanging on the door to his walk-in closet opposite a full-length mirror: his right arm stiff and pointed towards the ground, his left locked in a ninety-degree angle at his chest, his gaze tiger-eyed.

"Behind you!" Darren calls out, his voice faint and altogether unnecessary, as Taylor's right foot has already halved the distance between himself and the lankier Flaming Eagle, charging headlong towards him.

The sole of his foot strikes at six foot two, catching the biker square in the chin, and the action onscreen slows to a quarter of its original speed. It's the only alteration to the footage that Taylor had allowed, conceding that it did look pretty cool when viewed on the 152-inch plasma screen in the Wane's entertainment room later that night, seeing two of the biker's front teeth spraying from his mouth as his feet are flung out from under him.

The camera doesn't linger long enough to witness the man's fate, panning in real time again over to the third biker. Moonlight glints off the silver sheen of the telescopic steel baton he is flicking open in his right hand as he stalks towards Taylor. He swings it down hard but locates only grass, Taylor pivoting out of harm's way with inches to spare and lashing out with a punishing jab. It strikes the biker's temple causing him to reel sideways, his legs turned to rubber and the club lagging, harmless, on the ground after. But his infirmity is only a ruse, for the moment Taylor has come within three paces of him he lashes out with a quick flick of the baton. Taylor jumps backwards, catching only its wind. He then surges forward again, clamping his hands down on either side of the man's elbow and bringing his knee up into the space between, snapping his arm at the joint, the sharp crack of bone now making Taylor wince, it sounding so similar to the way his own arm had sounded not twenty-four hours previous.

Such a howl the biker lets out that the audio crackles under its anguish.

The club has dropped from his hand. Taylor bends and picks it up, brandishing it as he turns back to the biker. But it's clear that the fight has gone out of the man. He turns tail and flees, doing a fair impression of Dr. Frankenstein's hunchback as he lurches away, bent over and coddling his broken arm as Igor might have a brain.

The Cripple is already in flight and the camera zooms after his stiff-legged hobble as he scuttles after his friend. He all but disappears into the shade cast by the walnut tree, and here the scene fades to black though it was hardly the end, The Girl then jumping onto Taylor's back, clawing for his eyes, Taylor grabbing her by the hair and wrenching her loose, spinning and smashing the baton into her jaw, her shriek as she fell enough to rouse The Junkie from his stupor so that it was he who had the last word.

"Hey, buddy," he'd said, looking over at Taylor, oblivious to the spectacle that had just played out before him, "you got a smoke?"

And though Trevor had suggested that it would have been nice to end with a touch of levity, he'd finally agreed with Taylor that him hitting some emaciated teenage girl with a length of reinforced steel was hardly the way he'd want his audience to remember him.

The screen hadn't gone dark for more than a second when Garland Derby was plucking the iPad from the table.

"I understand," he said, skirting a look at Taylor, "the two young men who filmed that were present during the *alleged* assault at the cottage."

The way he'd emphasized alleged gave Taylor every reason to suspect that he'd drawn a fairly conclusive connection between the fight he'd just viewed and the one that had landed his client's son in surgery for four and a half hours. Taylor didn't know what to say in answer to that, so he played it safe and simply nodded.

"What are their names?"

He told him. It was the first time he'd spoken since he'd awoken, a half hour earlier, and the words felt like razor blades slashing at the stitches that were preventing what was left of his lips from dribbling down his chin.

"Phone numbers?"

"I—they're on my phone. I—"

"It's okay, we'll find them. We'll need to get their stories straight anyway."

"Why do we need to get their stories straight? Taylor was the one who was attacked."

This from Celia Wane, sitting quietly until then in a chair under the room's lone window. She'd been thirty-six when she'd had Taylor and hardly seemed to have aged a day since, though when she frowned—as she was doing now—the wrinkles splayed from the corners of her mouth placed her in the early forty range, still a fair clip from her *real* age, as carefully avoided a subject in the Wane household as the prenup Bryson kept in the floor safe secreted beneath the desk in his den.

Garland paid her about as much mind as he would have a fly circling his head during a backswing. He was fishing a black note-book from his pocket. He flipped to a page near the middle and ripped it out, setting that on the table in front of Taylor.

"I've already spoken with—" he started then looked down at his notebook. When he didn't find what he was looking for he flipped a page back. "Monica Fornier." Then looking back up at Taylor. "I understand she's your girlfriend."

"Monica was there?" Celia asked, her scorn doing as good a job of flattening her features as any plastic surgeon. "I should have known that little bi—"

"She's not my girlfriend," Taylor interrupted.

"But I understand you were having, ahem, coital relations prior to the *alleged* assault."

Taylor could feel pins prickling the side of his face, and when he looked at his mother she was staring needles. It was a carbon copy of the expression she'd worn when Taylor was fifteen and she'd walked into his bedroom one night and caught Monica giving him a blow job.

"She's only thirteen!" she'd screamed then.

"I—I—" Taylor stuttered, fumbling with his boxer briefs, trying to hide the still throbbing evidence of his indiscretion. "I was asleep. I—I thought I was dreaming."

It was the only time she'd ever struck her son out of anger, and the way she was looking at him now suggested she was thinking it would have done him a world of good if she'd let her hand slip a few, or a dozen, more times.

"She said we were fucking?" Taylor asked, turning back to Garland.

"I spoke to her not an hour ago. It's all in her statement."

"Well, it's a lie. We weren't—"

"Yes, you were," Garland countered. "And you caught the *alleged* assailant playing peeping Tom. You confronted him and that's when he went ape shit on you. It's all in there." He stabbed his finger at the paper on the table. "You'll need to familiarize yourself with it before you speak to the police." Then, checking his watch: "And you'll want to be quick about it too."

Not more than thirty seconds later he heard his father shouting from down the hall, his vitriol, Taylor supposed, directed at one of the local Roscoes.

"What do you mean you can't find him?" he screamed. "He attacked my son. He almost killed him!"

The Roscoe's response was too faint for Taylor to hear, but he must have been offering his assurances that he had every available man on the hunt. After a brief pause his father was screaming again: "Your men couldn't find a body in a goddamned graveyard!"

A moment later the door opened and Bryson Wane stuck his head through the crack. He himself had been fifty-one when Taylor was born and, like his mother, didn't seem to have aged a day since, though that was hardly a compliment. His hair had blanched white in his early thirties. Between that and the chalky white hue lending his complexion a sickly pallor, he'd always seemed prematurely aged to his son. And he'd never looked older than he did now, the scruff of whiskers over the folds of skin hanging loose at his neck speaking to Taylor of a sleepless night.

He didn't say a word, nor did he look to his son, searching out his lawyer instead. Garland was already tucking the piece of paper into the pocket of his jacket, nodding to his client as he did so.

"He's awake," Bryson said, glancing back into the hall.

Opening the door, he stepped out of the way, letting the officer pass through. The bulge at his waist was of roughly the same girth as Garland Derby's, though the shag of greying bush over his top lip made it appear he'd be more comfortable on an entirely different sort of range than the one behind the fifteenth hole at the Rosedale Golf Club. Meeting the fourth richest man in the country and his (once) famous wife had apparently inspired him to wear his dress blues, the tightness to the jacket's fit making him look like it had been years since he'd done so. He scanned over the room. As was so often the case when a man found himself in the same room as Celia Wane, he seemed not to notice anyone else but her.

Courtesy had him removing his hat, and static in the air stood his comb-over to full attention.

"My apologies, ma'am," he said, smiling apologetically as he smoothed the thin spire of hair over his balding crown. "My name's Sergeant Marchand. I need a few words with your son?"

His voice rose at the last word, as if he was leaving that up to her.

"It's okay," she answered. "I was just leaving anyway."

She was already reaching into her purse as she rose from her chair, drawing from within a pack of Benson & Hedges Slims. She only ever smoked when she was angry at her husband, knowing how he loathed it so, and as she strode through the door offering him nothing but the click of her heels, it was clear that she was feeling the same towards her husband as she felt for the younger variant laying, broken and bloodied, in the bed.

A ny concerns that Garland Derby might have had regarding the law holding Taylor complicit in the alleged assault were put to rest within two minutes of the sergeant's visit. He'd already spoken to Davis Grimes and Monica Fornier and all he needed, given Taylor's current condition, was for him to look over their statements and see if there was anything he'd like to add.

Grimes's was only a few sentences long. He introduced himself as a security guard for Wane Enterprises and explained that he was doing his morning rounds of the property when he'd heard someone screaming. He ran to investigate and that's when he'd found what appeared to be an Indian trying to strangle his boss's son. He'd pulled him off, and the Indian had slashed him in the arm with a utility knife. His training had then kicked in. He thumb-jabbed one of his eyes and would have done the same to his other if that tall fellow hadn't distracted him long enough for the Indian to escape.

Monica's statement he recognized as the one that Garland Derby had given him only moments before. It explained that she and Taylor "were engaged in a rather intimate act" when she'd seen someone standing on a tree branch and peeping through the window. She was, she said, understandably shaken, especially since she recognized the man as the "scary looking Indian dude" she'd seen gawking at her while she was playing tennis with the victim's sister earlier that morning. Taylor had made it to the window in time to see the man hurrying away and had gone out to confront him. "He was plenty pissed off, naturally, but no, he never laid a hand on him." All he'd done was reach for his cell phone, so that he might have that "dirty little pervert" escorted off the property. "That's when the Indian attacked him, and if Mr. Grimes hadn't happened by I have no doubts that Taylor would have been lucky to get off with only a broken arm and a couple of missing teeth."

After Taylor read it over, he agreed that it was exactly what had happened, and the sergeant provided him with a pen so that he could testify as much at the bottom of both sheets.

"Don't you worry, son," Marchand said, taking up the pages again. "We'll get the son of a bitch who did this to you."

Two hours later a pretty young nurse was pushing him in a wheelchair through the emergency room's waiting area towards its exit.

"Is someone coming to pick you up?" she asked as they approached the sliding door.

Through the door's window, Taylor could see his father's Cadillac stretch limo parked over both spots reserved for "Emergency Vehicles Only." He answered her by motioning his good arm in its direction.

Craning her head, she took long enough to scan over every inch of the vehicle before she said, "Then I guess you won't be needing the chair anymore."

The tone of mild indifference in her voice suggested that she wasn't nearly as impressed as Taylor might have assumed. Pushing himself to his feet, he turned back to thank her but she was already whisking the chair away—Taylor just one more inconvenience in a day already filled with its fair share.

His father's driver, Jules, was opening the limo's rear door by the time Taylor had reached the sidewalk.

He was the nephew of Bryson's previous driver, a man Taylor had known since he was a baby and had called Uncle Harley from the time he could speak. He hadn't had any kids of his own due to his wife suffering from Lupus and her not wanting to pass that burden onto her kids. As such, he'd treated his nephew like his own son ever since Jules was eight and his brother Charles—the boy's father and an RCMP constable—had been shot through the front door of a house where he'd been answering a domestic abuse call. Before enrolling in the RCMP academy in Regina, Charles had risen to the rank of lieutenant during the six years he'd spent in the armed services. Jules had made to follow in his footsteps, enlisting in the latter right out of high school and doing two tours in Afghanistan. The same day he'd filled out his application to attend the former, Uncle Harley had taken him out to lunch to celebrate, and while they waited for their sandwiches, Jules's desire to become a "bulwark against the chaos"— his father's words—had evaporated right then and there. The story goes that Harley had placed two slips of paper on the table. There was a number written on each and he explained that the lower of the two was the starting salary for an RCMP constable and the higher what he'd be paid as the driver and personal security guard for the fourth-richest man in the country.

Taylor had been on hand when Harley had related that to his dad, on the day he'd brought Jules in for his interview. He'd finished it off by saying, "I asked him to choose the piece of paper he'd prefer and if he'd have paused more than half a tick I'd have known it wasn't the job for him."

It was a Sunday morning, and he was driving Bryson and Taylor to the golf course, the wife of one of their foursome having called that morning to excuse her husband who had thrown out his back while bending down to retrieve the morning paper. Through the rear-view mirror Taylor could see a twinkle in Uncle Harley's eye to match his sly grin. He'd clapped his twenty-five-year-old nephew, in the passenger seat, on the knee before adding, "Yes, sir, he's the man you're looking for, there's no doubt in my mind about that."

Never one to take another man's opinion for his own, Bryson

was scrutinizing Jules's resumé in his lap with the attention to detail that had branded him, in a recent profile in *Business Weekly*, as "The King Of The Micromanagers."

"It says here," he said after a moment, "you were top of your class in defensive arts."

"Yes, sir," Jules replied with military precision.

"You know, Taylor's not so bad in the defensive arts himself. If you're looking for a sparring partner, I imagine you could find worse."

Jules opened his mouth to give his no doubt equally precise reply, but Harley beat him to the punch.

"With all due respect, Mr. Wane," he said, "I'd as soon put my nephew in a cage with a hungry lion as pit him against Young Master Wane."

"How's that?" Bryson asked, for it had been years since he'd taken the time to attend any of his son's tournaments.

"He's a right beast when he puts those gloves on. No, sir, I wouldn't wish that fate on my worst enemy."

That "Uncle" Harley was only trying to curry favour with his boss—in hopes, perhaps, of padding the retirement bonus he'd been told to expect on his next cheque—was evident to everyone in the car but Jules. The smirk Jules had given Taylor as he'd opened the door for him at the clubhouse steps spoke plenty of how he thought Young Master Wane would have measured up against him. And it was a facsimile of that smirk that he was feeding Taylor now as he watched his boss's son easing into the rear seat, looking very much like he *had* gone a round (or two) with a hungry lion.

But Taylor was too tired and sore to care how he looked.

All he wanted to do was fall into his own bed, go to sleep, maybe never wake up. He'd be sorely disappointed on that count for when the limousine reached Tildon's Main Street, Jules hung a hard right. He wasn't driving Taylor home at all, but back to Hidden Cove. Undoubtedly, he had his orders, and if the twenty-minute drive from the hospital to the Wane's summer retreat was any indication, they also included a firm directive to make the return trip the first lesson in what Taylor had begun to suspect would become a full curriculum on paternal acrimony.

They didn't pass a pothole the entire stretch that the back wheels couldn't locate—the jolt of the car *tha-wunking* over each, radiating electrified shocks up Taylor's arm. And every hairpin turn on the winding road provided Jules with ample excuse to push the gas pedal all the way to the floor, causing the back wheels to slide, careening, off the asphalt, leaving Taylor no recourse but to grit his teeth and hold fast to the leather strap hanging from the ceiling with the zeal of a man clinging to a life preserver as a stretch of rapids led him towards a waterfall.

The rock wall passed him by but he barely registered it.

A short while later, the limo slowed as the highway wound down towards Maynard Falls. The reduced speed offered him some respite as the road dipped into a valley and led them through several blocks of tourist shops and cafés, accelerating again as they neared the general store that marked the village's western perimeter. Two hundred yards past that, Jules turned off the 118 onto Hidden Cove Road. Taylor had since let go of the handhold and the resulting fishtail catapulted him against the far door, the grit to his teeth replaced by a stifled whimper approximating the sound a toddler might have made if it were being smothered by a pillow stuffed with broken glass.

Hidden Cove Road hadn't been graded since the last rain and all four wheels battered over its mottled tarmac with the fury of a baby hammering away at a xylophone. Each note struck at the pins in his arm like a tuning fork, pain cascading in needle points throughout his body, each successive wave pressing further afield so that by the time they reached the gate even his hair—the only part of his body that didn't hurt by then—was bristling with thoughts of revenge.

Their driveway was softened by cedar chips so Taylor, at least, had thirty seconds with which to grapple with his composure before the car was pulling to a stop in front of the cottage's front door. Jules took this—the end of their journey—as an excuse to call that break. The slow deliberation with which he chewed at the first bite of the apple he'd fished from his lunch bag left Taylor little recourse but to reach for the door handle himself.

There were only three other vehicles parked in the circular driveway—his mother's limousine, identical to her husband's but with pink trim, his sister's Prius, and a black Navigator. On the matter of where his own Lexus had ended up after Davis Grimes had driven him to the hospital, he could only speculate. Given the rough ride he'd just experienced it was a good bet his father had had it towed back to the city, The Reaper sanctioned in its passenger seat, the two-hour drive and the corresponding subway ride to follow all that stood between the life of affluence he'd so fleetingly glimpsed and whatever hole Bryson had enticed him out of.

Cold comfort to Taylor now as he stepped out of his father's limousine.

His gaze meandered past his mother's car to the Navigator, at the back of which stood four men Taylor had never seen before. All of them were wearing matching charcoal-grey suits and dark sunglasses, three of them as big as linebackers so that seeing them standing all bunched together put Taylor in mind of a huddle, the fourth man about the size of your average quarterback. He had just reached a plausible conclusion regarding why they might have been there when his mother came sauntering out of the house. She was dressed in her sailing outfit—an oversized collared white blouse with blue trim and matching pants—and was smoking a cigarette with the urgency of a fire alarm.

As his mother passed the four men, she flicked her butt at the smallest, hitting him square between the shoulder blades. The man didn't seem to notice the obvious slight, but when she turned towards the thirty-two-foot Catalina sailing vessel tethered to the end of the dock, the man's head cocked slightly in her direction. So maybe he had or maybe he just wanted to catch a glimpse of the way the high curve of her slacks seemed to be winking at him as she strode towards the dock.

Taylor trailed after her at a distance, letting gravity pull him down the subtle slope of the driveway's cobblestones. When he reached the dock, his mother was storming up the Catalina's gangplank, at the foot of which her "Captain," Mark Spratt, stood saluting after her in caricature of naval protocol. He was wearing the uniform she'd bought him so as to better assume the role, though the tanned ripple of his six-pack displayed prominently within the billow of his unbuttoned shirt made him look more like a male stripper's idea of a captain than a genuine seaman. By the time Captain Spratt was untethering the vessel from the dock's mooring rings, Taylor had made it to the stairs at the backside of the boathouse leading up to what more and more seemed to have again become his personal sanctuary.

The year he was born, his mother had remodelled what had then been a guest room to look like a turn-of-the-century log cabin. Aside from the forty-eight-inch flat screen bolted to the rightside wall, he hadn't changed a thing in the ten years since he'd claimed it as his own. Various animal heads were mounted around it, along with a cluttered assortment of litany proclaiming the simple pleasures of cottage life: framed sepia-tinted photographs capturing lazy days at the beach or dockside, old fishing poles and paddles, and a full-size birch bark canoe suspended from the rafters over a queen-sized mattress supported by a drift-wood frame.

Propped against one of the pillows at its head was an envelope, the size and shape of a gift card, and beneath that a DVD. When Taylor lifted the former he saw that the latter was *Two Minutes to Midnight*, his mother's last film, and that suggested to him that it was she who'd left them. After all, in the introduction to *The Wind at My Back*—her (mostly) ghostwritten memoir—hadn't she related how before she'd met Bryson Wane she'd been reduced to a third-rate actress scrambling after bit parts, her best roles behind her. The only moment in her entire body of work that she'd likely be remembered for, she'd lamented, was a sultry tango she'd danced for the lead actor in her third film—*Primal Heat*. Unbeknownst to him, or the director, she'd performed without the encumbrance of underwear. During the dance's climax, she'd whirled her dress about her uplifted leg and thus afforded the infamously stunned-looking lead, and later the equally delighted audience, an unobstructed view of the Brazilian wax job she'd instructed her aesthetician to provide her with, all the better to make a bold—or in one reviewer's words, "bald"—impression in this, her first starring role in an A-list movie. The scene had guaranteed her a top-ten placement on every Best of Beaver Shots list throughout perpetuity and she'd long-since resigned herself to the dire prospect that this would stand as her legacy.

In her own words, "Meeting Bryson Wane opened up a whole new world to me, and whenever I was feeling low, I'd curl up all alone with a bowl of popcorn and watch *Two Minutes to Midnight*, taking refuge in the knowledge that even on the darkest of days, the sun was still there hiding behind the clouds, waiting to share it's [sic] light."

Her recent actions to the contrary, Taylor took the DVD as

an assurance that she understood what he was going through on this, most surely, his own darkest day. He hurried back to the door, hoping to catch a glimpse of her, maybe give her a wave to say he appreciated the gesture. But Celia's sailboat—the name of which had provided her with the title of her memoir—had already caught a breeze. All he could make out of her, at the helm and with the wind quite literally at her back, was the billow of her hair as she angled it towards open water.

It would only take a moment for him to discover that she hadn't, in fact, been the one who had left him the gift. The accompanying card, replete with an altogether-too-cute picture of a mournful Boxer pup with a cast on one of its paws, read: *This will make you feel better, Sis.* By that, Taylor took to mean the two yellow pills he found in the bottom of the envelope, rather than the movie itself. Having had ample experience with his sister's rather twisted sense of humour, he knew she'd left that for an entirely different reason, *Two Minutes to Midnight* not only serving as their mother's final film but also Taylor's introduction to his old fighting instructor, Master Lo, whose character had been listed in the credits as The Viper.

As he jostled the pills in the bottom of the envelope, the brightness of their neon hue was urging him towards caution but his arm was feeling again like someone had driven a nail through it and his face like it had got in the way of the hammer a couple (or nine) times while they were doing so. The doctor who'd stopped in to check on him before he'd been released from the hospital had told him he'd given his father a prescription, "to help with the pain." The preceding rough ride had provided Taylor a pretty good idea of what his father was likely to do with anything meant to ease his son's suffering. Certain, in the least, that whatever was in the two gel caps his sister had left him couldn't possibly make him feel any worse than he already did, he popped both into his mouth and dry swallowed them on his way to the bathroom.

He hadn't had a chance to look at himself in the mirror at the hospital, the IV on a slow drip into his arm requiring him to pee into a bedpan the one and only time he'd felt the urge to go there. The face that confronted him now was hardly recognizable as his own, and it took only the narrowest of glimpses to know that he'd never want to see it again. Lifting the toilet lid, he was overwhelmed by a sudden dizziness. His legs wobbled and he sat down hard. When he'd done his business, he was unable to summon the strength to push himself back up. A short while later, his head began to feel like it was filling with helium and his belly like there was something living in there. A snake maybe. Coiling around his intestines, cramping his stomach. His tongue was sticking to the roof of his mouth and when he peeled it off, it caught on the jagged fray of one of his front teeth. He flinched with the memory of the all-consuming rage in the Indian's eyes as he'd born down upon him and its rancour was enough to drive Taylor back to his feet.

His face was staring out of the mirror again: a twisted and red-faced devil leering at him, the four fingernail scratches gouged on either side of his throat looking all of a sudden like horns sprouting from his neck.

"What the fuck did she give me?" he gasped, backing away from the mirror.

Fingers touched lightly on his shoulder and he spun, startled.

Sandra was standing behind him.

"Are you alright?" she asked.

Though her tone was one of concern, she was looking at him through bemused eyes, laughing at him, it seemed, for taking those pills when she knew what he thought of her "little indulgences."

The floor was all of a sudden tilting beneath his feet like the deck of a ship in stormy seas, and he stumbled back, knocking his hand on the bathroom door's frame. Pain shot up his broken arm and the Indian's snarl appeared before him again, his teeth bloodied and clenched, one of his hands gripped fast at Taylor's wrist and the other at his elbow, a geyser spewing from the bone shard piercing the skin.

"You need to sit down," Sandra was saying. "Get yourself together."

Her voice was echoing around him as if from the end of a long and cavernous hallway. He opened his mouth to reply but nothing came out but a strained whimper. Then he felt her hand on his good arm, steadying and tugging gently, leading him towards the couch.

He'd been sitting there for a shade over one hour and forty-seven minutes, or so said the digital display on the Blu-ray player beneath the TV. His bubble cast was propped on a pillow beside him though he hardly registered that, his world, in the interim, reduced to what he saw onscreen: an all-consuming present rendered in such vivid and immediate detail that there had arisen within him the creeping sensation that he's not watching a movie at all but has stumbled upon a portal into a world created solely as a backdrop against which the war raging within his *own* embattled heart is cast.

How else to explain what is happening now?

Master Lo is wrenching a burlap sack off the head of a woman whom he knows to be New York City's top-rated news anchor but thinks of only as his mother, even though she'd never be caught dead looking like she does: her hair a mess of frizzy curls and her makeup smeared, remaking her into some kind of demented clown figure. She is standing at the edge of an as-of-yet unfinished top floor of a skyscraper overlooking New

York. The city is a twinkling starscape at her back and the man who'd confined her to a shipping container for all but ninety-six seconds of screen time is standing in front of her, wearing the uniform of a Russian General and shaking his head, *tsk tsk tsk*ing at what he sees.

"Why the frown, Kelly Jones?" he says. "I'm about to make you the most famous voman in America."

At that, she spits in his face.

The thick gob oozing down his chin only serves to bring a smile to The Russian General's lips and he turns to Master Lo, giving him the slightest of nods. The Viper responds by snatching her hand and taking hold of her pinkie, snapping it backwards. The disbelief that Taylor felt the last time he'd watched it, as to why a man trained in the Chângquán long-fist style would be dressed as a ninja and why said ninja would then be working for an embittered Russian General, is suspended by the now-familiar crack of bone and the even more familiar pitch to his mother's scream. The both of them serve to dispel any and all artifice. In that instant, it seems it is not The Russian General who's ordered it so but his own father. It is a feeling of such rare and potent clarity that all memory of the act that spawned it is subsumed by the dreadful certitude that he himself is to blame—that his father is merely using her as a vessel through which to exact revenge on her son, a feeling enhanced by how, at the moment Master Lo snaps her finger back, the shot cuts to an extreme close-up of The Russian General. The crack and the subsequent scream is seen solely through The General's eyes, grey-filmed and as lively as two acorns trapped under a thin sheet of ice, which is to say they are his father's eyes, the sight spurning within Taylor a simmering rage found expression in his hand, scrabbling now beside him, searching for something to throw. His fingers brush over a rectangle of plastic that could only have been the remote though he hurls it with the sober intent of a brick.

The Russian General has since departed, replaced onscreen by the film's two heroes, both now stepping from an elevator. One is a rogue KGB agent dressed in a charcoal-grey suit with the perfectly coifed hair of a department store mannequin, the other a disgraced and possibly psychotic New York City cop who also happens to be Kelly Jones's ex-husband, defined "Everyman" by the thin stubble outlining his cheeks and his ripped Yankees jersey. The remote strikes the latter between the N and the Y so that it seems it is Taylor himself, and not the assembled horde of heavily armed mercenaries now confronting them, who causes the heroes' eyes to widen in sudden alarm.

Cracks splay outward from the cop's chest, momentarily quartering him before the screen erupts in an explosion of brightly coloured pixels and then goes black.

"Kill zem!" Taylor hears The Russian General scream.

This is followed by an almost pathological barrage of machine-gun fire, out of which shortly arises his mother's voice.

"Five years ago today," she says, reading off a cue card at gun point, "the U.S. Military Industrial Complex launched a cruise missile at a wedding taking place at a secluded villa in Chechen's Caucasus Mountains . . ."

The footage is being fed, via satellite link, to the TV station where her character works which explains why a man, whom Taylor remembers as being a rather pudgy and bearded studio tech, shortly exclaims: "I'm getting a live feed. It's from Kelly!"

"Kelly?" This from the news director who further responds with an exclamation of his own: "Well, what are you waiting for? Patch it through!"

More machine-gun fire and then the cop's voice: "That's your plan? It's suicide."

"Being shot," the KGB agent responds with his characteristic nonchalance, "is better than dying from radiation. Trust me."

"I told you, if you said, 'Trust me,' one more time—"

"Yes, yes, you shoot me. But you are out of bullets, no? How you do this without bullets?"

"I'll kill you with my goddamned hands," the cop screams back. "That's how I'll do it!"

(There is a slight pause here: the KGB agent checking his watch, as he's inclined to do every thirty seconds or so to remind himself, and the audience, that time is rapidly running out.)

"Better make it quick then," he quips.

Now Taylor's mother's voice again: "Fifty-six people died that day, twenty-three of them women and children. The American government denied all responsibility for the attack, but on this day, a day that will forever live in infamy, they will remember what they did. You will all remember."

"What's that?" This from the bearded tech, so the scene must have shifted back to the TV control room. "You see that? What he's wearing?"

"It looks like," the news director responds, "a . . . parachute."

A parachute plainly visible to all but Taylor is strapped to The Russian General's back as he stands at the edge of the precipice readying himself to jump. He takes a moment before he does to gaze down upon the photograph of his son in his hand. A singular tear drop trails down his cheek and spatters onto the young man's chin. Confronted now with the black TV screen in front of him, the recent events of his past and the movie bend seamlessly into a fiction of Taylor's own devise. In this moment he does not envision The Russian General crying over his dead son but instead spitting in the young man's face before releasing the photograph. The camera in his mind's eye follows its descent, drifting downwards at mercy to unseen currents, settling at last on the sidewalk where it's trampled underfoot by passers-by and then kicked mindlessly into the street, fodder for the sweeper just now approaching, its whirling brushes forever consigning the photo, and by extension The Russian General's son, to oblivion.

And though spawned from the vain certainty that his father has doomed Taylor to a similar fate, the scene itself is hardly of his own imagining. It's the scene, in fact, which closes the film. The photograph becomes dislodged from the Russian General's harness after the cop commandeers the construction crane poised above the unfinished building, using the hook at the end of its cable to snag the parachute's billow and swing The Russian General like some child's plaything, the fabric tearing at the limit of its arc and hurling him into the Hudson River an instant before the timer on the nuclear bomb strapped to his chest reaches 23:58. Cue then the requisite kiss between the ex-cop and his ex-wife and the equally requisite moment of levity, this one involving a playfully winking Mickey Mouse taking a bent over Minnie from behind, which the now-shirtless KGB agent is revealed to have tattooed between his shoulder blades—"Don't ask!"

With the two heroes' jocular exclamation still hanging in the air, the scene shifts to the photo floating downwards with the lassitude of a feather, its subsequent ignoble end meant, or so says the director in the DVD's commentary, "to signify that the true tragedy of war, or really any act of violence, is how easily the *real* victims are consigned to the dustbin of history."

A sentiment starkly at odds with the dramatic up-swelling of music, vaguely militaristic in its ode to triumph, which now blares from the TV to accompany the credits. This shortly gives way to an overly sentimental, though slightly less anomalous, pop ballad blithely proclaiming, "Love Is a Battlefield." But by then Taylor has stopped listening, his world since reduced to the persistent throb in his arm and the equally pervasive vision of an endlessly repeating cycle of feet trampling a photo bearing *his* likeness under heel on a sidewalk that might as well be at the very epicentre of a cruel and merciless world.

He awakes sometime later in the dark.

At first he thinks that the movie must be replaying itself for he hears what is unmistakably an explosion: a rumbling boom that bears no small similarity to the sound the cruise missile made when it obliterated the wedding party in the film's opening scene.

At the time, The Russian General was watching, horror-struck, from the elevated vantage point of a mountainside. Seeing the fireball consuming the villa where his son had just been married, he screamed, *"Nyet!"* and rushed forward. His second-in-command grasped him by the arm, telling him, "There's nothing you can do. We must go!" Shrugging from his censure, The Russian General ignored him and hurried down the slope, even as the camera swooped skywards, zeroing in on a Blackbird spy plane flying miles above. The explosion below was defined in infrared as a receding blot on the monitor in front of which sat a reconnaissance systems officer already speaking into his headset, "Target eliminated at twenty-three hundred hours and fifty-eight minutes. I repeat, target eliminated."

That none of the preceding follows the explosion Taylor unmistakably hears and that the glass in the window on the boat-house's northern wall rattles from the resulting shock wave still isn't enough to arouse him to the suspicion that the blast did not emanate from the TV but from outside, less than a hundred feet from where he sits. The rumbling boom shortly gives way to a faint whining noise, no louder than a mosquito battering against the ceiling would have made, yet escalating with the dire intent of a runaway boat racing towards the dock, except its pitch is too high for it to be that.

It sounds like . . . someone screaming.

The thought has barely penetrated his consciousness when a sudden illumination flares on his periphery, as bright and orange as a nuclear blast. Its intrusion upon the quieting dark spins Taylor's head on an abrupt pivot towards the door.

All he can see are flames within the frame of its window so that it appears the very air beyond has ignited.

This sight, at last, is enough to rouse him from his stupor. His good hand clutches at the couch's cushion, prying his body from within its seam, up and onto unsteady legs turning now towards the door. He approaches it with stuttered step, feeling not so much alarm at the sight of the raging inferno beyond its double-glassed pane as the same incredulity he'd felt when he was ten and, entreated by his father, had peered over the rail of the boathouse's deck and found on the dock below him a man he'd known, until then, only as The Viper.

He and his father had also just watched *Two Minutes to Midnight*, sitting on the very couch receding behind him now, two weeks to the day since his cousin had beaten him up and forced him to eat dog shit. Whenever they'd crossed paths in the interval, his father had greeted him with a stilted silence. It had spoken to Taylor of his disappointment and so, when his father had finally broken the silence, asking him if he'd like to watch a movie and holding up a DVD of *Two Minutes to Midnight*, which his mother had staunchly refused to let him see due to its R rating, he'd taken that as a sign that he was making an effort towards reconciliation. It had been a great comfort to Taylor at the time. Peering down from the boathouse's deck, a moment after the credits had rolled, and seeing a familiar Asian man with two cobras lashing out along his forearms, his incredulity then was tempered by a sinking feeling, knowing that he'd been wrong about why his father had shown him *that* particular film and also that the real reason wasn't likely to provide him with any comfort after all.

Coming now to the door and peering through its window, Taylor sees that it's not the air that is on fire but his mother's boat and his own sense of incredulity is only tempered by a slight confusion as to how such a thing has come to be. The flames have engulfed the sail, and a piece of the fabric has torn free. Born aloft in a swirl of wind, it rises at a frantic pitch as if striving to make its place amongst the stars, its betters unblinking in their contemplation of such earthly pride, Taylor watching its ascent much the same. Its moment of glory is measured by no more than a single inhale before its light is vanquished by its own ambition, reduced now to a ribbon of ash, an ember filament razing its surface and making it seem to wink at Taylor before its grey is absorbed into the sky's speckled black.

Taylor is just exhaling when a slighter incandescence prods at his periphery. He turns towards the beach, finding at once the source of the illume: what appears to be a bonfire, except that it's oddly misshapen—not like a bundle of sticks at all but like a log, a foot thick and six feet long. A branch juts from the log's end, almost like a . . . an arm stretching for the water just out of reach of its fingertips. Then he notices other specks too: a trail of smaller fires running on a direct line away from the main blaze and leading his gaze towards the grassy expanse at the beach's perimeter.

There: a fringe of light pushing against the dark with the simmer of the rising sun.

The memory of the rumbling boom, the flicker of the bonfire, the trail of flames, and the impossibly approaching dawn aligning now in perfect symmetry with the escalating scream he'd heard only a moment ago, the cusp of understanding provided perfect exclamation by a jolt of glass smashing at his back. The bottle that made it explodes against the wall above his bed, not more than ten feet from where he stands gaping in mute terror as the bottle's lit wick unleashes a torrent of flames washing over the wood panels and dousing the bed. Droplets of it splatter the carpet like motes of burning tar. The smell of gasoline is ripe in the air, and he can hear the crackle of hairs along his forearm singeing from the heat of the rapidly keening flames.

Now clawing at the door's knob, flinging the door inwards, never more awake than he is throwing himself through the gap and onto the landing. He pitches hard against the balustrade and flips around, afraid to turn his back on the fire as if it might contain some sort of malevolence hitherto unrevealed. Flame then lashing out through the door, and his good hand finding direction in the rail's downward slope. His feet stumble clumsily, his heels careening over toe, neither able to find sanction on the steps as if their sole function is to trip him up, finding at last the dock's even plane, though the wobble in his legs makes it feel like anything but.

Above him, the boathouse's cedar panels crackle, hissing smoke in thin streams, and the open door emits a monstrous bellow like a just-sprung-to-life creature of hell's creation venting the agony of its birth. But Taylor barely registers it, such is his alarm at what he sees on the far side of the driveway.

Flames lap in fevered spires from the house's gabled roof against a funnel of black smoke whipped into a frenzy by the inferno below. The stained-glass window at its fore has been reduced to a gaping maw of sharply fractured shards providing a clear view of the furnace within. Directly beneath it, his father's limousine is a smouldering husk of cratered-out windows, its back doors askew, hanging off their hinges, its rear-end splayed open like it had been packed with dynamite. His mother's car is littered with flaming debris from the fallout, and the tops of the trees enclosing the building are also ablaze, crimson embers flitting about the canopy of the trees yet unafflicted with the wilful petulance of fireflies. The sinister totality of this panorama is so perfectly aligned with the devastation wrought by the cruise missile he thought he'd heard blaring from the TV only moments ago that his earlier confusion about how such a thing could have come to be is swept aside, knowing that his *own* father must be to blame for the apocalyptic vision confronting him now.

The notion that such a dastardly act of revenge—perhaps over a business deal gone wrong or simply one bad guy sending a message to another—would only seem plausible to some coked-up Hollywood screenwriter who, never in his wildest imaginings, would conceive of such a thing happening on *our* home and native land, carries about as much weight in Taylor's no less drug-addled mind as the haze of smoke swirling about him.

Flame gusts whoosh from tree to tree on either side of the house. The only things within his spectrum not on fire are the sand and the water and, beyond those, a narrow strip of forest on the far side of the beach. The spaces between the palisade of trees are filling with smoke, but it'd be a few minutes before the flames caught up, plenty of time for him to reach the fence separating their property from their neighbour's, and from there only thirty seconds at a hard run to their front door. No matter that the fence is eight feet tall, designed with the expressed intention of deterring unwanted visitors, and him with a broken arm on top.

That's a mountain he'll have to climb when he gets there.

He's just taken a deep breath in anticipation of the sprint ahead when a lumberous crash turns him back to the house. Its roof is caving in and its facade toppling too. The combined force unleashes a cloud bank of seething grey spilling over the driveway, approaching the beach like an avalanche in slow motion, consuming all within its reach. Taylor treats that as good as any starter's gun, lunging off the dock and keeping low, moving fast. The beach's sand is cool against his bare feet, though the air there is just as hot, the breeze wafting in from the lake miasmic with the heat spurned by the boat burning at his back. The sting of its smoke blurs his vision so that as he approaches the slightest of the fires, not more than ten paces hence, he can't divine much about it except that it's a body.

Its fire's fervour has lessened some but flames still roil over the subtle curve of its spine, its skin peeling in crisp curls. Its face is buried in the sand and the back of its head is scorched bald, not an inch of it left unscathed except for one of its feet, curiously intact at the end of a charcoaled and still-smouldering leg. As he approaches, he can see there's a chain draped over its ankle and from that a glint of gold dangles in the shape of two masks—one laughing and the other frowning.

It's his sister lying there.

His legs slow to a plod, coming at the body with the same measured determination The Russian General had come upon his son buried under a pile of rubble, dropping to his knees, tilting his head towards the heavens, venting his rage. No time for Taylor to release himself to a similar act of grief. At that very moment a hand clutches at his arm, spinning him towards the lake and he finds Jules standing there. He's naked save for a pair of Speedos which tells Taylor that he'd just returned from one of his midnight swims. In his right hand he clutches an axe. It's the one that his uncle Harley had dubbed Axcaliber and for as long as Taylor could recall had remained cleaved into a block of hardwood beside the firepit his grandfather had built on the far side of the beach. When Taylor was fourteen he'd finally wrenched it loose after years of trying and had held it aloft like he'd imagined King Arthur had done with its namesake. Uncle Harley had fallen to his knees, bowing in mock reverence, and Taylor had never been so proud of himself as when he'd proclaimed, "Long live the King!"

The sight of Axcaliber and the frantic pitch of Jules's voice as he pulls at his arm, yelling, "Move it!" leaves no doubt that they really are under attack. But neither are able to wrest Taylor from his shock and his eyes track back to the charred corpse as the vaporous deluge unleashed from the house washes onto the beach.

Coughing against the smoke, unable to breathe, yet knowing he has to do something. He can't just leave her there.

It's his sister!

"Goddamned it, move!"

Jules pulling hard at his arm again, giving Taylor no choice. Dragging him backwards, Jules's hand suddenly loosens its grip. A strangled gasp. Enough to turn Taylor away from Sandra.

Inexplicably, Jules is stumbling towards him.

Axcaliber is lagging in one hand, its blade dragging along the sand, and his other is clenched around his throat, a geyser spraying red between his fingers as he teeters sideways, lost at once into the swirl of smoke. And beyond that: an endless murky dark, empty of all reason except that a blotch of it appears to be moving closer.

Taylor startles back as the blotch merges into the shape of a man. He is wearing black jeans and a black hooded sweatshirt. Curls of long dark brown hair hang in loose garlands over his face and within its drape, Taylor can't see much beyond the angry grit to the teeth glowering out from beneath.

It's the Indian!

A thought that's barely reared in his mind before his left heel bumps against his sister's arm. The heat of her flames singes the hairs on the back of his leg but he can barely feel that, his world now reduced to the hunting knife clenched in the man's upraised hand. It lashes out with the whip of a snake's bite, and he stiffens under the sudden pinch of its blade piercing his gut and the grate of it nicking his spine on its way to skewering out his back.

His good arm flails out, feebled and weak. The man bats it away as if it were no more nuisance than a fly, then draws himself close, cinching the blade deeper. Pain now like he'd been bathed in it, the sum total of all he is and ever would be compressed into the beads of black hate that have become the man's eyes: pinpricks as sharp as any knife. And though there is a truth in them unmasked by any movie, Taylor feels only a tremor of doubt.

Something . . . the man's face . . . his left cheek . . . a scar . . . like . . . like his head had been squeezed in a . . . a waffle iron.

19

He'd slept like the dead and awoke feeling not much better. The grandfather clock was striking the hour and each successive chime tolled like a sledge driving a spike deeper and splintering the back of his head. The empty bottle of Canadian Club that had done the damage resided within easy reach on the table in front of George's reading chair, and so it wasn't much of a mystery to him why he was feeling the way he was. The clock, though, was another thing entirely. Its incessant clang was rising in stark defiance of time itself, for it couldn't possibly have been that late, the greyed light parsing the window's dusted pane telling Deacon that the night had passed but the sun was still a long ways from ordaining the day.

But still the bell kept on tolling, Deacon counting along with each stroke thinking they'd never stop. The twelfth hovered for a moment and then faded, and then nothing but the lash of branches raking against the roof and a bluster of wind rattling at the barn's eaves.

Must be a storm brewing, he thought, rubbing the sleep from his eyes, which would explain the hour's gloom.

He had to pee something fierce but couldn't yet summon the verve to raise himself out of the chair. Habit had him reaching for the cigarette pack inside his jacket pocket. He knew it was empty before he'd pried open its lid, and his eyes sought out the ashtray beside the bottle, one filling up as the other emptied, the both together forming a clear record of the hours he'd spent in restless deliberation; the mystery of how George had come to write what he had was steadily losing ground to the more beguiling question of why someone would have taken it, leaving only a few photocopied pages in its stead.

Before he had fallen asleep the night before, he'd read them over a half-dozen times, looking for some sort of answer and finding nothing to satisfy the question of why someone would take them, but one line giving him a clue, at least, concerning the matter of who.

Hard to forget a face like that, the cop's left cheek, as it was, looking like someone had squeezed his head in a waffle iron.

Reading that had given him a line on filling in a few of the other blanks as well.

What was it George had said the morning he'd come to tell him about Ronald Crane?

"Helluva thing, him dying like that."

Could have been, he conjectured, when Dylan was pulling traffic detail up on the 118, he'd spotted Ronald Crane's Caravan cruising the highway with a frequency that had struck him as too regular to be anything but part of a larger pattern. Maybe he'd mentioned something about it to George. With the reserve so close, it would have been natural for him to make a connection to the recent investigations into missing and murdered Indigenous women, George had spoken of it often enough.

A seed of an idea then planted in George's head: Dylan tailing Ronald Crane as the real estate tycoon patrolled the 118 looking for young hitchhikers to abduct, knowing that any missing girls from the reserve would most likely be treated as runaways, their cases closed without more than a cursory investigation, one of them a girl who'd swore she'd kill the next man who laid a hand on her. The story progressing from there, filling four hundred pages and when he'd finished with those, making his corrections and typing it out all over again.

Dylan must have come into the barn and found what George had written and taken the originals.

But why leave these? Why go through the trouble of photocopying the first two chapters and the first page of the third?

Recalling then what Dylan had said after he'd startled him the night before.

"I catch you in the middle of something?" he'd asked, Deacon tracking the shit-eating grin he'd worn while he said it back to the night Ronald Crane had died.

"Hope I didn't catch you in the middle of something," he'd said then too, fronting him the self-same expression.

He'd been talking about Rain that night and her name had been right there on the page in front of him when Dylan had knocked at the barn's door. Too strange a coincidence in a night already filled with more than its fair share. Deacon flipped to the last page in his lap, reading it over again. It was obvious that Dylan had included it as a wink and nod, as if he'd wanted to make sure Deacon knew he'd left them for *him* to find.

But as he read the last line, he couldn't shake the feeling that he'd meant to tell him something else as well.

He had forty years on her own thirty-nine, but
the pill he'd taken made him feel half his age
as he thrust into her with the precision of a
see saw, she gasping, "Oh! Oh! Oh!" which he took
to mean that she was about to climax!

There were several inches of space at the bottom of the page,
which got him to thinking that maybe Dylan had blanked out a
few (or five) of the lines that had come after.

But why would he do that?

The obvious answer was that he didn't want him to read what
came next.

*Maybe he really was working with Ronald Crane, as the boy—Del—
had thought, and that only came out later.*

But that didn't ring quite true either, a thought spawned
from how his gaze had settled on the final word. The exclamation mark seemed starkly out of place and between the c and
the l there was slight gap and limax! was a little darker and
also a trifle askew. Deacon ran the pad of his index finger over
the word, feeling the subtle indent of the characters and in this
way came to know that Dylan had typed the last five letters after
he'd made the copy. There were faint threads above and below
them: traces of the white-out he'd used to blot out the word he'd
replaced, the curiously anomalous c making it a good bet that it
had originally been come.

"Climax," he said aloud as if speaking it might provide some
clue as to why he'd do such a thing. And when it didn't, he studied
the word, certain now that it held the key to unlocking the secret
of what Dylan was trying to tell him, and that only giving rise to
the vague impression that he'd just missed something.

He thought back to the night Ronald Crane had died, not so
much recalling the conversation he'd had with Dylan at the rest

stop as what George had written. He'd clearly meant for Ronald Crane's death to be the beginning of something and he saw now that Dylan, for reasons he couldn't fathom, had wanted him to see that too, but not what came after.

His eyes drifted back to the page.

climax!

The culmination of events leading towards the end, an end that George had already written and that Dylan must have read, seeing something there that he'd wanted to keep hidden, revealing to Deacon only how it started, but not how it ended, an end that George had written and that Dylan must have read . . .

His thoughts circling from there like they were caught in a loop or a, a— There was a term for it. Now what was that called? It was on the tip of his tongue and he searched his recollection, trying to locate where he'd come across it.

It was in . . . *A Precious Few*.

Propelling himself to his feet, he hurried to the shelf behind the desk, tracing his finger along the spines of George's books until he came to the ninth in the row. Taking it out he flipped to Chapter 1, the first line of which read:

> *He'd been walking in circles for hours, skirting the perimeter of the lake and crossing over the loose wash of gravel strewn beneath the ridge atop which resided his grandfather's cabin, following the base of the cliff towards where the granite sloped downwards into the forest, stalking along the perimeter of its rise. And when that, in turn, led him back to the steps, skirting again the perimeter of the lake, this time in reverse, as if his feet were striving to give expression to the torment cycling*

through his mind: an infinitely spiralling Möbius Strip
of his own devise.

That was the term. Möbius Strip.

It had stuck in his mind, because he'd had to look it up. And this is what he'd found in the dictionary George always kept on the table beside his reading chair:

> *Möbius Strip. A topological figure, named after the German astronomer, A.F. Möbius, made by putting a 180-degree twist in a long, rectangular strip then pasting the ends together. Also Möbius Surface.*
>
> *Möbius Surface. A surface both sides of which may be completely traversed without crossing either edge: made by joining the half-twisted ends of a rectangular strip of paper or other flexible material. Also Möbius Strip.*

The definitions themselves, by default or design, providing perfect illustration of their meaning even without benefit of the sketch of a twisted figure eight that had accompanied them. Following one back to the other had called to mind the memory of his father reading George's Fictions over and over, an hour after dinner each night in an endlessly repeating cycle as if he was compelled to do so by forces beyond his control. Or so it had seemed to Deacon when he was a child, before he himself was driven by the same impulse, finding then that George had planted the seed of that compulsion into the very fabric of his Fictions, the last line of *The Stray*—*It would be a long walk home*—and the first line of *A Bad Man's Son*—*He was a long way from home*—themselves forming a Möbius Strip of *George's* devise; a recognition that Deacon, perhaps, had only stumbled upon because, driven by circumstances beyond his control, he always started with *The Stray* and ended with it too.

Having chanced upon this, in his subsequent readings he'd taken care to look for any hint as to why George would have aligned his books in such a fashion. He'd found the most promising clue, albeit a slight one, in a scene in *The Unnamed* when The Old Man, having just found out from his nephew that his grandson René has been killed, puts his favourite record on the ancient hand-crank Victrola his brother had bought for him years earlier. As he's frying up the trout he'd caught that afternoon, the record begins skipping on the first line of the fourth song, repeating, *There must be some way out of here*, over and over again as if the Creator herself had chosen it as a conduit to impress upon him the need to finally, and perhaps terminally, lift himself from the gloom of his own endlessly repeating days.

And so whenever *Into the After* led him back to *A Precious Few*, he'd pause there, reminded of his pa and feeling then an up-swelling of grief beyond even that which he felt while reading *The Stray*, coming upon its opening line without having first steeled his resolve as he did before reading the other so that it always came at him by surprise. Möbius Strip would recall the memory of his father sitting in his easy chair, a chair not so different from the one he himself sat in while reading George's Fictions over and over so that he began to see himself as but one half of the twisted figure eight, joined forever with his father beyond the bounds of death itself as long as he kept reading, that thought sufficient incentive for him to wipe at the tears redolent upon his cheeks before returning to the open page before him. A teardrop would be splattered there too and over the years they'd accumulated in a patchwork of blotches on the page. He counted five now residing as a counterpoint to the opening line, those speaking to him now only of the futility that defined any human endeavour aspiring towards the infinite.

Yes, everything must end, he thought, closing the book and, perhaps, paradoxically thinking that only served to lead him back to where he'd begun, which in itself was just another terminus, punctuated as it was by the word `climax!`

It was enough to make his head ache.

Returning to the chair, he forsook all efforts to make sense of it, distracting himself with the bottle, the last sip from which he'd taken in tandem with the last drag from his only remaining cigarette. He was well drunk by then. As he mashed the stub into the overflowing ashtray his hand slipped, knocking it to the floor and upending its contents onto the photocopied pages he'd discarded there. Cursing his folly, he leaned over, picked up the ashtray, and set it back on the table, gathering then the scattering of butts onto the top sheet. His head swooned as he sat up holding the piece of paper folded over in the middle. It took every ounce of his concentration to funnel the pick-up sticks game worth of butts into the ashtray. Finally, he'd achieved this and in the so doing spotted a half-smoked Cameo: one of George's.

Dusting off the grit smudging the cigarette's filter, he lit the butt, blowing the first exhale at the page still in his hand to dislodge the ash clung there. When the smoke cleared, `bare ass` and `thrust` once again stood out against all the other words.

"You old dog," he slurred, the reproach he felt the last few times he'd read the same washed away by the conviviality of his drunk.

His eyes then settling on the last word on the page.

"Well, you know how George'd end it," he said, stealing another drag. "A world on fire, no doubt."

Fire, then, was the last thought on his mind before he'd fallen asleep. It was also pretty near the first as the twelfth chime faded, Deacon peering at the window, trying to account for what appeared to be flecks of greyish snow powdering the glass. He could smell the faint tang of woodsmoke, probably just someone—the Quimbys perhaps—lighting a woodstove to chase away the morning chill, a thought cleaved in two by the trailing wisp of a siren that couldn't have been anything but a fire truck moving at a fair clip along Main Street.

Hearing that, he heaved himself to his feet. His legs hadn't quite recovered from last night's indulgence and their first uncertain steps towards the door had his toes catching the edge of a stack of books, toppling it into his path.

The siren had reached its crescendo, a slight hitch in its fervour telling Deacon the fire truck must have been turning down into the valley, descending towards the strip malls on either side of the 118. Clambering over the books, he fought his way to the door. When he opened it he was met with a stiff gust. The wind blew back the hair from his cheeks and he braced himself against its bluster, his eyes wincing at the sting of what he could now see were ashes swirling like dirty snowflakes in whirls about the yard. The sky overhead was overcome with the billow of clouds: a turbulent seam of utter black coursing against the grey, frothing at the tops of the trees enclosing the yard. Not a bird in sight nor a remark of their cheerful natter. The only sign of life at all was a squirrel standing on its haunches in the middle of the lawn, its head raised heavenwards as if it too, was trying to make sense of the strange turn in the weather.

The pressure in his bladder hastened Deacon towards the maple tree beside the barn. As he relieved himself, another siren alighted from behind: a fire truck coming down Entrance Drive, heading westward from the 11, an odd enough occurrence given that Tildon's fire station was on Dominion, a block south of the downtown core. He was still zipping his pants as he hurried across the yard, the siren growing louder with every footfall, urging his legs towards a run undiminished until he'd reached the traffic lights at the corner of McDonald and Main streets just in time to see the fire truck dipping down the hill into the valley. North Bay FD was decaled in shiny gold letters over its rear bumper, and Deacon hardly had a moment to ponder the significance of that before the truck carried on down the steep slope, providing him with an unobstructed view all the way to the horizon. At its fringe, a charcoaled mass was billowing smoke *as if the ground had opened up and was venting its bile at the sky's eternal mockery of its earthbound ways.*

It was how The Old Man had described the black smoke plume that had appeared on the horizon nearing the end of *The Unnamed*, gaping at it from the platform atop the lookout tower at the edge of his village with the same creeping dread that Deacon felt standing at the top of the hill, seeing its perfect twin fissuring the sky. In the book, two of The Old Man's grandsons had accompanied him, young warriors who felt none of the apprehension he did seeing the sky sullied so. The blight to them was no more than a mild curiosity, the likely result of a lightning strike, a natural enough occurrence and certainly not a portent of dire things yet to come—only a foolish old man could conceive in it of that. Harkened back to their day by the idle pursuits of youth, they'd left their grandfather alone to ponder its significance, Deacon knowing just then the oppressive weight of the isolation he felt, the passers-by in cars and on foot all taking in the spectacle with mild diffidence, none allowing time for more than a fleeting glance or a selfie as they carried on through the intersection—too many things to do in the day already without fretting over something as trivial as a little smoke on the horizon—the only thing that separated Deacon from them being that they hadn't just read what he had. Most likely, they hadn't read any of George's books at all and even if a few of them had, again most likely, they'd sought in their pages only a harmless diversion, an escape from the rigours of modern life. His Fictions couldn't possibly have become for them, as they now had for Deacon, a lens through which he viewed the black plume confronting him as the end of a story he'd thought had only just begun.

The past night's restless musings swirling again with the gale force of a hurricane, and Dylan at its eye.

Is this what he meant to tell you?

Searching his addled mind then, looking for clues in his recollections of the man who'd been his only real friend and who'd treated him more like a brother, trying to reconcile the person he knew with the person who could have done this.

It couldn't have been him, it just couldn't have.

A thought that did little to dispel that familiar feeling of dread, lumped in his belly like a stone. He heard another far-off siren drawing nigh and it turned him back to the ever-present **climax!** imprinted in the sky, its malevolent billow consuming all thoughts now but one:

Whose world had just been set on fire?

20

The quickest route to answering that question was as close as the *Chronicle*'s office at the far end of town, a mere ten-minute walk away. But that would have meant talking to Grover, something he was reticent to do, looking the way he did and probably smelling a whole lot worse.

Passing the library, he turned off Main Street at Dominion, following that to the alleyway that cut behind the storefronts. He mounted the wooden stairs leading upwards from the *Chronicle*'s rear entrance with cautioned steps, thinking of all the times he'd smoked a joint at lunch and had tried to slip unnoticed into his apartment so that he could brush his teeth and splash a little water on his face before returning to work. The creak of the rickety wood slats beneath his feet would hardly be audible even to himself, yet there Grover would be, sticking his head out of the back door and calling up to him, "You just getting back now?" Deacon would mumble some excuse, telling him that he just had to use the bathroom, he'd only be a moment, the elderly black man shaking his head in silent reproach. And then, as Deacon slipped the key into the lock, calling up to him again: "Mind you don't get lost on your way back down."

This day though, the journey up the stairs and into his apartment went uncontested. Casting his jacket atop the sheets twisted over his unmade bed, he took a direct line for the TV on the stand against the far wall. He hit the remote's On button and when the screen flared to life, he turned the channel to 26, his preferred national news network, hedging his bets by backing towards the desk beside the bookshelf, which was where he kept his laptop. The latter would prove to be unnecessary for onscreen there appeared a petite twenty-something brunette standing on the deck of a barge and holding a microphone.

"—o'clock this morning," she was saying, "the province officially declared a state of emergency."

She was wearing a bright red jacket opening onto a white blouse, and as she spoke, her free hand waged a losing battle to keep the gusts of wind from lashing the drape of her hair about her face.

"Municipalities as far away as Brandon, Manitoba, and Gatineau, Quebec, have pledged their assistance," she continued, "and fire trucks have been arriving all through the morning. The high winds you can see swirling around me have greatly hampered efforts to contain the fire. Thus far, crews have concentrated their efforts on keeping Highway 118 open as it is the only overland evacuation route available to the estimated five thousand people who have been forced to flee the fire's advance. But there are also many smaller, mostly dirt roads that connect with the highway and many of these have been rendered impassable. Ultimately, it may be the area's vast network of lakes and rivers that provide many evacuees with the best hope for safe passage. You can see behind me—" the camera then panning right to reveal dozens of watercraft, from canoes to cabin cruisers, trailing after the barge—"a caravan of boats filled with fleeing residents. Barges like the one I am standing on now, which would normally be used to transport construction materials along these waterways, have been enlisted to transport firefighters to otherwise inaccessible locations and to assist in the evacuation. Officials are urging anyone who does not have a boat and is trapped behind the fire line to get to the nearest body of water and make yourself visible to rescuers."

"But where did it start?" Deacon implored as the scene shifted back to the studio. A middle-aged news anchor with the plasticized hair of a Ken doll was sitting at the desk wearing a charcoal suit and a red tie. He thanked "Melissa" and assured viewers they'd be following the story all day long. Dramatic music flared to accompany the montage leading towards a commercial break: a graphic reading *Fire in Paradise* set against the backdrop of footage of a water bomber dumping its load on an inferno engulfing the southern shore of Lake Mesaquakee given way to oxygen-masked firefighters advancing on a burning cottage, their hoses drawn with the resolve of soldiers marching off to war, and finally ending with a scene shot through the window of a pickup truck, the forest a seething mass of flames on either side and a fire-soaked tree crashing onto the road just ahead.

Turning, Deacon made to reach for his laptop. There was a notebook where it would normally be and he was helpless but to scan over the four lines he'd written at the top of the open page.

> *Because you escape nothing, you flee nothing, the pursuer is what is doing the running and tomorrow night is nothing but one long sleepless wrestle with yesterday's omissions and regrets.*

It was from the last book that George had recommended he read, written by none other than "Bill" of the barn's framed quote: a thought sprung from the sleep-deprived mind of a teenage boy trying to make sense of an act of violence that had lifted the veil off his innocence, forcing him to confront the world as it truly was.

When Deacon had come upon the line, it had spoken to him of the sleepless nights he himself had endured when he'd first come to live with George and Adele, and he'd known that it wasn't a coincidence George had suggested he read that particular book. He'd jotted down the quote in the notepad he'd reserved for when he'd found a line or a paragraph in one of the books George had lent him from his library and which suggested the start of a conversation they might have the next time they met.

He'd forgotten all about it until, sometime towards dawn on one of the restless wanderings that had punctuated his past few nights, he'd got it in mind that he should say a few words at George's funeral. He'd sat at his desk and opened the notebook, flipping towards a fresh page and finding the quote. Coming upon it after yet another sleepless wrestle and trying to think of a few words to express all that George had come to mean to him, it had seemed like as good a place to start as any.

He'd fled from his own omissions and regrets using George's Fictions as the equivalent of a getaway car, there was no denying that. But as he'd sat there tapping his pen against the page, he knew there was more to it. What that was he'd never figured out, and he'd finally given up, telling himself that it'd be best to get a fresh start after he'd caught some sleep.

And here those words again, staring at him off the page, never more in need of a refuge than he was now, the full measure of what he suspected Dylan had done playing out on the TV behind him, with worse likely yet to come, his only proof of either suspicion being a dozen photocopies, which didn't really prove a damn thing and, the more he thought about them now, the less likely it seemed that Dylan could have possibly left them to mark the conclusion of some diabolical scheme. The mere suggestion seemed preposterous in the extreme, easily dismissed as the lunatic ramblings of a mind drunk on rye and more so on grief such that it contrived to keep George alive by projecting his fictional world onto the real when Dylan had probably just left the pages because he'd read that bit about Rain and he'd thought it'd be funny to see the look on Deacon's face when he stumbled across what George had written.

But why then `climax!`?

His gums were aching, which they always did when he hadn't had a smoke for a few hours. At least that was a problem he could solve. As he reached for the desk's top drawer, where he kept his spare packs, a familiar voice cut through the TV's blather. He turned to the screen and there was none other than the *Chronicle*'s intern, Suzie Chalmers, standing at the sharply pointed prow of a speedboat. She was dressed in a dark blazer opening onto a white blouse, the short bob of her hair unmolested by the gusts of migrant smoke blowing in from the fire engulfing the densely wooded shore behind her.

"The fire is spreading rapidly," she is yelling above the bluster of wind. "It appears to have begun somewhere in Hidden Cove. You can see behind me that it has already claimed several cottages nestled along this inlet on the eastern shore of Lake Mesaquakee."

The camera pans past her to reveal what appears to be a medieval castle perched atop a granite ridge, its windows belching fire as if it were under siege. Just then there is a rumbling boom accompanied by a bright flare to the left of the screen. The picture goes all wonky and off-screen Suzie exclaims, "Jesus!" When the camera locates her again she is clutching onto the boat's rail and gaping in alarm at a fireball just dissipating above the fringe of trees demarcating the cove's perimeter.

"Did you see that?" she gasps at whoever's holding the camera.

Cut to a shot taken over the bow of the speedboat, the picture bucking against the waves as it races towards a harbour full of boats set ablaze.

Then: a battered and charred sign floating in the water amongst sprouts of fire bobbing like tea lights.

elcome T

idden Cove Ma in

eed Lim   Km/

The camera lingers barely long enough for Deacon to fill in the missing blanks before it's panning upwards, centring itself again on Suzie at the speedboat's bow.

"Moments ago," she is saying, "the fire ignited the gas tanks in the marina behind me."

The camera then zooming in on a large grey cylinder beyond the harbour, the picture focusing on the word imprinted in red over its shell: Propane.

"Suzie, I think—" the cameraman says, only to be interrupted by Suzie pointing off-camera and yelling, "A fireboat!"

Cut to:

A close-up of the fireboat, its water canon dousing the harbour as a commanding voice booms: "Vacate the area immediately." The shot pans left and zooms towards its source: a fireman holding a megaphone pointed directly at the camera. "I repeat," he booms again, "vacate the area immed—" his voice now drowned out by another explosion, the camera backtracking to the harbour, all but consumed by the bright white flash unleashed by the exploding propane tank. Flaming debris rains down, sputtering in the water around the speedboat and Suzie is screaming, "Go. Go!"

Cut to:

A tracking shot of the unbroken wall of flames that has become the shoreline, settling on a boathouse similarly engulfed, the crackle of its wood not quite enough to drown out a faint *yap yap yap*: a dog barking.

"Over there!" Suzie shouts and the camera tracks left, blurring momentarily as it zooms in on a swim raft, floating fifty feet from shore. A drift of smoke renders the figures huddled on top as vague outlines. One of them is that of a man standing, his hands waving, frantic, trying to get their attention.

Cut to:

The screaming face of a toddler. Suzie must be holding the camera now because it's the guy—*What was his name again?*—she'd picked up at the Harcourts' anniversary party who's taking the jumper-clad child from his mother's arms. He's lifting him into the boat. The woman clambering after is a vision of finely rendered beauty wearing a skimpy nightdress so that it looks like she might have just stepped out of a Victoria's Secret catalogue. The man behind her, in boxers and plain grey T-shirt, is slightly older and a trifle dowdy faced. He's coughing against the smoke and clutching a chihuahua to the paunch at his belly.

"Boy, are we glad to see you," he says as he climbs aboard. "I thought we were goners."

A terrific splintering of wood then jerks him, and the camera, towards the boathouse. Its roof is caving in and the camera holds it in frame as the boat circles away from the carnage, angling towards open water. The shot pulls back then to reveal the family sitting in the boat's rear seats, the child squirming in her mother's lap, the dog in the man's licking at the child's face, momentarily stemming the girl's ire. The woman's head is propped on her husband's shoulder and tears carve thin lines down her cheeks. The man squeezes her leg, offering her the only words of comfort he can as a flourish of fire erupts through the windows spanning the cedar plank cottage now receding in the distance.

"We're okay," he says. "That's all that matters. We're all okay. We're going to be okay."

Now the camera is pulling back again, revealing the screen behind the news anchor's desk upon which the scene has been cast.

"This remarkable footage," the anchor is saying, "was captured by a second-year journalism student and her boyfriend earlier this morning." Then turning to the screen where the petite reporter from earlier can be seen standing at the end of a dock.

"Melissa," the anchor continues, "I understand you caught up with the couple at the young man's cottage on Lake Joseph."

"It's where I am now. I'm joined by Suzanne Chalmers and Rance Harcourt."

As she speaks, the frame widens to include the happily beaming young couple.

"Harrowing stuff," Melissa says, turning to Suzie. "Tell me, how is it that you happened to be out on the lake at seven o'clock this morning?"

The remote was in Deacon's hand and he clicked the TV off before Suzie could respond. He was pretty sure he knew the answer anyway.

Reaching then for the phone charging beside his laptop, swiping his hand across its face and seeing he had forty-three unread messages. The majority were from Rain and he thumbed through those until he reached the last five, all from Grover. The first time he'd called was at 4:43 a.m. that morning and the last at 6:23, the contents of the text he'd then sent giving Deacon every excuse to disregard the previous four.

Don't worry about it, it read. *I've sent Suzie. See you tomorrow at the funeral.*

Fumbling a smoke from the pack in his hand, gritting his teeth.

On top of everything else, he'd missed the biggest damn story ever to hit Tildon.

The realization was accompanied by a flash of heat simmering at his collar, knowing that even if Grover had been able to reach him, he wouldn't have made it past the blockade on the 118 where he'd be lucky to get a few quotes from Gerald Billings, Tildon's fire chief, maybe a couple of snaps off the dock at Meeford Bay. He certainly wouldn't have been cruising the lake at the prow of some speedboat, in the thick of things, rescuing supermodels off rafts, getting himself on the national news, grinning like it was the best damn thing that had ever happened to him.

He lit the smoke cursing his bad luck, though he knew it wasn't really that, it was something else: his own damn fault. And feeling that, he again recalled what George had written, for hadn't Del thought the same thing after the girl—Emma—had tripped over the chunk of asphalt he'd used to mark his range. Del had made amends by shooting an arrow at the cop and when that had failed, he'd fled. It was the same thing Deacon himself had a strong urge to do now.

With George dead, there's nothing left for you here, he told himself. *You ought to just get in your Jeep, head north on the 11, leave all this shit behind.*

Nodding like it was a done deal even as his eyes again sought out Grover's text, zeroing in on the last word with terminal abandon.

You can't leave, not until tomorrow anyway. You owe George at least that.

And that thought offering him nothing except a tremble to his hand as he took a drag off his cigarette.

What in the hell was he going to say at George's funeral?

21

The following day, he left his apartment just after noon.

He'd dressed in the same outfit he'd bought for Adele's funeral—a black pair of jeans and a black button-down shirt. He cautioned himself that it was too warm a day to wear George's corduroy jacket but grabbed it off the hook beside the door on his way out nevertheless.

The service was set to begin at one.

From the end of the alleyway behind Main Street it was only a half block to the United Church on Dominion, but he wanted to get there before the pews were filled with prying eyes, like they had when he'd arrived at Adele's. Those and the whispers from the congregation of (mostly) elderly mourners had followed him down the aisle, the urgency in their hush speaking volumes to Deacon about what they were saying: ten years and change not yet enough for them to see in him anything but a twelve-year-old boy wedged between the seats in his father's Jeep, his family dead in the front and his face doused by a trickle of blood from the gash over his left eye so that when a man on his way to buy cord wood from Bergin had come across the accident he'd thought Deacon was dead too.

The wind had shifted in the night, blowing the inferno back upon itself and sparing Tildon the order that had evacuated Meeford Bay and Maynard Falls. The sky was a thin wedge of blue parting the alleyway's ragged box tops and the only evidence of the fire was a thin film of grey powdering the slats of wood leading downwards from his door and the balustrade's rail. The street's asphalt was dulled by the same and a single set of footfalls imprinted in the ash led up the four cement steps towards the red-brick church's front door. It was made of oak and arched at the top and had two black cast-iron rings bolted at shoulder height, all of which lent it a medieval quality at odds with the cheap plywood panels encasing the lobby.

Deacon eased the door shut behind him and crept up the stairs leading to the chapel, trying not to make a sound. The plastic slip guard covering the dusty grey carpeting crackled underfoot and checked his pace, stopping him altogether just before his head would have breached the top. He listened for any sign of movement. When he heard nothing, he abandoned all thoughts of stealth, taking the last six steps two at a time and striding past the coat area, even reaching out and knocking at the empty metal hangers on the rack, making them jingle and clang.

He paused again at the chapel's open doors, absorbing the heady odour of old wood tainted by mildew. Dust motes flitted about the strained light filtering through the stained-glass windows. He rubbed at his nose as if he was about to sneeze, though it wasn't that; it was an involuntary twitch giving expression to the sudden tightening he felt in his chest upon catching sight of the two silver urns on the sanctuary's altar. There was a picture of George in front of the left and a picture of Adele in front of the right and one of them both in between.

In his, George's mad flop of hair was wetted down and his beard trimmed and he was wearing a brown suit and a peach-coloured tie, what he called his "old fart getup." In hers, Adele was wearing the white blouse with a Rorschach squiggle of purple and red lines on either breast that Louise had bought her one Christmas because, she said, they made her think of but-terflies—her mother's favourite motif—but which always put Deacon in mind of two eviscerated lungs.

He'd seen the pictures plenty of times before.

For the past five years they'd resided on the mantel over the fireplace in the Cleary's living room, arranged the same as they were now. They'd been Louise's idea. Adele had just been diag-nosed with Parkinson's and she wanted, she'd told her father, to preserve her mother the way she was. George had balked at the idea, countering that they had plenty of photos of Adele and himself and also of them together—"enough to wallpaper the damned kitchen," is what he'd said. But Louise had already made an appointment at Pond's Photo Shop a mere two doors down from the *Chronicle* and wouldn't take no for an answer.

"Goddamned ugliest pictures I ever saw," was George's opinion on the matter.

In the weeks after he'd come home from work to find them adorning the mantel, he'd made a game of turning the photos to face the wall, Adele *tsk*ing every time she turned them back and Deacon trying to keep a straight face as she muttered under her breath, "It's like living with a damn child!"

This, now, just one more memory amongst thousands to remind him of the life they'd shared together.

He sat down in the far end of the front left-side pew, one of the two Reserved For Family.

He was reading over what he'd written in his notebook last night, his ragged scrawl leading him from, *I was twelve the first time I read one of George Cleary's novels* to *From that day forward, I'd always eat my share of liquorice allsorts staring up at* The Stray *in the far-right corner of the bookshelf's top row, thinking about how it'd be a shame if Ma burnt it up in the yard before I had a chance to find out what happened next.*

He'd written through the night as a balm against thoughts of Dylan and the fire, filling the notebook to the last page, the pen's ragged scrawl, by then, reduced to a series of fractured squiggles hardly decipherable even to himself. He'd stopped where he had because his hand was cramped and also because he wasn't quite sure of how to tackle what came next. It was over thirty pages in all and when, finally, he'd crawled into bed it was with the grim certitude that he wasn't any closer to figuring out what he might want to say than when he'd begun.

Sometime along the way, the mourners began to arrive.

He could hear Edward greeting each at the chapel's door, his voice suitably hushed and reverent. That gave over to the no less venerable shuffling of their feet as they made their way down the aisle and the almost apologetic creak of wood as they settled into the pews. Shortly then, the organ. Its first breath huffed like a bear's after a long winter's sleep and this was channelled into a morose succession of notes: a funeral dirge ubiquitous in its solemnity and having absolutely nothing useful to say about the man it was meant to honour but, in the very least, providing perfect accompaniment to the ceaseless drone of those who'd come to offer their respects.

On and on they came until it seemed that half of Tildon must have been filing into the church. Closing his notebook,

Deacon returned it to his jacket pocket and took *The Stray* from the pocket on the other side, setting it in his lap and looking down at the picture of his parents on the cover. And though it hadn't been his intention in bringing the book, he mused that it was right they should be there too, having, as they did, given *an old man new hope*. The measure of satisfaction he derived from that was short-lived, for just then he felt someone bumping up against his side. Turning and seeing it was Dylan, wearing his dress blues. He was leaning in close so he could whisper something in Deacon's ear, a gesture that for the people in the pews behind couldn't have appeared to be anything but that of one family member offering another a few words to ease his grief. But that was the exact opposite of Dylan's intent, hidden from all but Deacon because of what he alone knew and by the hush in the other's voice.

"You look a little pale there, Deke," he whispered.

Now, draping his arm around his shoulders in a firm embrace and lowering his voice quieter still.

"Buck up, son," he said, "we ain't hardly yet just begun."

The reproachful alacrity in his voice was exactly as Deacon would have imagined had he been offering the same to a new recruit shaken by his first taste of war; Deacon feeling shell-shocked as Dylan withdrew his arm, patting him on the knee, and then scooching back towards his mother sitting in the aisle seat.

Eleanor Cleary had gained some weight since he'd seen her last, when she'd almost been a skeleton, the result of the chemo treatments she'd undergone for breast cancer the year before. Her cheeks were still gaunt though and she was wearing a black bandana to hide her thinned-out hair. There was a hand reaching out to tug at the back of it. Eleanor and Deacon looked up in unison and found Crystal standing in the aisle. She'd let her hair grow out and a frizz of curly red struck out from beneath the flop of a felt bowler hat, the same charcoal grey as her blazer and slacks, her outfit completed by a man's dress shirt, its top three buttons undone and its tails hanging loose beneath the jacket: Anne of Green Gables playing at being Annie Hall.

The sight propelled Eleanor to unsteady feet, and she wrapped her daughter in a deep embrace.

"You made it!"

She kissed her on the cheek and Crystal kissed her back and then withdrew, holding her mom at arm's length.

"Look at you," she said. "We're going to have to put you on a diet soon."

Eleanor frowned and waved her off with a dismissive flutter of her hand, though she couldn't have looked happier. The organ was then fading. Crystal helped her mother back to the pew. She sat beside her and craned forward, offering Deacon a sprightly smile and a finger wave, Deacon forcing a strained smile of his own as a hush fell over the church.

Reverend Stephens was standing at the pulpit, clad in a white frock and purple sash. Beads of sweat were already glistening over his brow and a straggle from his thinning hair was plastered to his forehead. His eyes were closed and he was raising his hands, signalling for quiet.

The service was about to begin.

22

Henry Mueller, Mesaquakee Lakes' MPP, spoke first.

The Muellers were one of the oldest and wealthiest families in town. Because they were Catholic and their boys tended to be, as Henry was, blond-haired and blue-eyed, they were often referred to—only half in jest—as the Mesaquakee Kennedys. He set a whimsical tone as he spoke of George as one of the last of a dying breed: a man who always put the good of the community before his own needs; whose accomplishments were modest and who wouldn't have had it any other way; a man who would be fondly remembered not so much for what he'd done but for what he'd stood for; a beacon for the people of Tildon, "may his light shine forevermore."

Grover spoke next.

He recounted the story of how George had enticed him to Tildon, giving him six months' pay, in a cash advance, and sweetening the pot by offering him the use of the apartment above the *Chronicle*'s office rent free, further promising him that there'd always be a plate for him at his dinner table. And how on the morning his six months were up he'd been packing his bags and had heard a knock at the door.

"It was George," he said, "as I knew it would be.

"'Getting an early start?' he'd asked. 'Train doesn't leave until ten.'

"I told him I knew, grinning at him with the insolence of a young man with six months' pay in my pocket and not a thing in the world to keep me from the promise of a whole new life, anywhere—and I mean anywhere—but here.

"He asked if he could walk me to the station and I told him it didn't matter to me, weren't nothin' goin stop me from gettin' on that train, I tellya that."

Telling then of how after he joined the queue at the station's ticket window he heard George's voice alight from behind.

"'It is a deep personal privilege to address a nation-wide Canadian audience,' he was saying. He'd produced a milk crate from somewhere. He was standing on it and his eyes were roving over the half-dozen other people waiting for the train, all of them staring at him with the same startled unease as I, myself, felt, though there was no doubt in my mind that their discomfort and mine stemmed from an entirely different source."

For, unlike the others, Grover had immediately recognized what George had said as the opening line in the Massey Lecture Dr. Martin Luther King Jr. had delivered four years previously on the CBC and that he himself had heard along with his whole family and most of their neighbours, the lot of them cramped in the Parks' living room listening in rapt amaze over four nights as if the voice of God himself was being transmitted through his father's RCA console. Later, the speeches were published as *Conscience for Change*, one of only three books that Grover had brought with him to Tildon and which, at that very moment, was pressed inside his suitcase along with *Soul on Ice* and *The Invisible Man.*

"'What the hell are you doing?' I asked hurrying over to George, my anger mounting for I knew exactly what he was trying to do. And how dare he use *His* words towards his own selfish end!"

George ignored Grover's desperate plea and the simmering rage hardly contained within his glaring eyes, answering him only, "Over and above any kinship of U.S. citizens and Canadians as North Americans there is a singular historical relationship between American Negroes and Canadians," which was the speech's second line.

He continued from there, delivering the third and fourth lines from memory and those leading him on and on with the same measured determination as a train chugging down its tracks. By the time he'd been speaking for ten minutes he'd attracted quite a crowd, accumulated in dribs and drabs as ten o'clock drew nigh. Grover was standing as its vanguard, his own anger deflating as the full weight of what George had done sunk in, and even more so by the force of the words flowing from between his lips. His voice had risen to the sonorous boom of their creator and, to Grover, it seemed he had become but a conduit through which the Reverend King was speaking directly to him.

He'd just got to the part—"You know the bit," Grover had said as an aside, as if he'd taken it for granted that everyone should have known it as well as he did—where "negroes have endured insults and humiliation for decades and centuries but in the past ten years a growing sensitivity in the white community was a gratifying indication of progress, and the depravity of the white backlash shattered the hope that new attitudes were in the making." Hearing this again, his younger variant couldn't help but measure his own humiliations over the past six months

337

against the ones endured by his brothers and sisters south of the border. Those were often accompanied by savage acts of brutality and the worst thing that had happened to him was the time someone had thrown a rock through his kitchen window late one night, "no small matter at the time," Grover added, "alluding, as it did, to a violence yet to come.

"When the train's whistle finally sounded from the far end of town, George was down to the last paragraph. The rest of the crowd was wandering off to wait in line or to say goodbye to their loved ones and I was the only person still standing before George as he stepped off the milk crate. He was grinning at me when he did and though I was trying not to, I couldn't stop myself from grinning right back."

Deacon had never heard the story told quite like that. On any other day he would have rejoiced in its telling, but sitting not five feet from Dylan he'd barely registered a word, fighting a losing battle to keep his glances towards him fleeting and when he'd failed at that, trying to find some crack in his calm and failing there too.

"George must have spent the last six months memorizing the speech," Grover was saying from the pulpit, "and when I commented as much, he said, 'Shoot, I started the moment you agreed to come with me.'

"'Now why in the hell would you do that?' I asked, and he answered, 'Because I figured it might buy me another two months?'"

Grover then clenching his teeth, fighting back the tears. Loretta was too, as were the three children they'd raised, all of them a perfect blend of their parents and sitting alongside their mother in the pew behind Deacon amongst their husbands and wives and five children—the youngest still a baby and sitting in her mother's lap, chewing on the braided tassels of her hair.

"It did," Grover choked out.

Laughing then through tears.

"And don't you know it, Loretta took the job at the library not three days later. And I don't have the words in me to ever thank George enough for what he did."

Grover shuffled back to his seat wiping his eyes and then Reverend Stephens was at the pulpit again.

"Uh, thank you Grover," he said, pausing there, perhaps trying to think of something he might add and not finding the words, a strange enough feeling for a man who'd made his life out of always knowing exactly what to say. Looking down then at the piece of paper clipped to the pulpit's stand, searching out the name that would show him a way forward and saying, "Deacon Riis, I understand, would also like to say a few words."

Hearing his name came as a surprise. He'd since realized that he hadn't told anyone he'd wanted to speak and had resigned himself to thinking maybe that was for the best. Grover, he now saw, must have spoken to someone on his behalf and with all eyes then beating into the back of his head, it left him little choice but to stand and step into the aisle. He locked his gaze on the pulpit's microphone, telling himself that if only he could make it there without a sideways glance at Dylan, the next few minutes, at least, would take care of themselves.

The moment he reached the centre aisle he heard a familiar bark. He turned to the front leftside pew where Louise sat in the aisle seat, her husband, Ted, beside and their three teenage sons stretched at intervals towards the end. Trixie was lumbering up from the aisle, wagging her tail and straining against the leash held fast in Louise's hand. Traces of the acrimony she felt towards Deacon lingered in her pursed lips as she jerked on Trixie's lead, making the dog whimper and lie back down.

It seemed an unnecessarily harsh rebuke, and Deacon spun

quickly on his heel, mounting the pulpit's stairs and setting *The Stray* on its stand. He opened it to the page near the back he'd marked with an ace of spade's playing card and, taking a deep breath, leaned into the microphone.

"I'd, uh, just like to read something George wrote," he said. "It's about my ma and pa."

Clearing his throat, he began to read.

> *"He'd been walking for he didn't know how long.*
>
> *His feet were plodding with a will of their own, treading through the creek's shallow, the water cold and numbing all sense of himself below his knees, fleeing along this ragged vein, towards what end he couldn't fathom nor did he care, only that it was leading him away from the bodies of the two young men he'd left on its bank—their blood on his hands and spattered over the wild fray of his beard and on his lips—knowing that it was a fool's game, that he could flee to the ends of the earth and still never be free of them, for they had become a part of him, who he was and ever shall be: a taste of blood on his lips and the younger's dying breath, a desperate plea: Niimi! Niimi!"*

Carrying on from there his voice brokered a deathly still within the congregation, unmoored until he'd come to this:

> *"Scanning over the wall of flame remaking the clifftop into an inferno, he saw a figure perched at the edge of the precipice, her feet straddled in the thin veil of water cascading over the falls. Within the drench of smoke he couldn't see much beyond that it was a young woman and that she wasn't wearing any clothes. The dark*

triangle of her pubis and the two small mounds parting the hair draped to her waist left little doubt of that. The current's flow was lapping at her ankles and she was raising her right hand. She was holding something in it, a sharpened stick or perhaps a bone. Opening her fingers, she let it drop, her body then leaning forward after it, Asger gasping as she fell into the breach, watching her plummet, her arms limp, adrift like two lengths of loose cord."

Deacon then hearing a corresponding gasp from near the front and looking up and finding Crystal with her hand over her mouth, aghast, so that he knew she'd never found the time to read it herself.

Turning back to the page then and finding his spot, pushing onwards.

"She struck the water headfirst, the splash in her wake consumed at once by the turbulent froth. Nothing then to remark on her passing but Asger's footsteps imprinted in the sand, spaced at a run, leading to the edge of the beach, and the ripples spreading over the reflection of the madly keening flames infecting the pool's veneer from where he'd dived in.

"He was down for a good while.

"When he came back up, he was clutching the young woman by the hair and dragging her onto shore. He set her on her back and kneeled at her side, wiping the water from her eyes. Her body convulsed and she vomited a thin gruel. She coughed twice after that but died nevertheless."

The whole congregation now sniffling and dabbing at tears with neatly folded handkerchiefs or wadded-up tissues, crying like Deacon had so many times when he'd come to the same, not so much because of what George had written, which had always seemed like an ode to hopefulness imagining how the scene must have really played out, but because it spoke so clearly of an even greater tragedy yet to come.

Deacon's thoughts in perfect alignment with theirs as he carried on through to the end.

> *"You ought to bury her, Asger thought, gazing down upon the girl. It's the least you can do.*
>
> *"But he was so tired he could barely stand. He'd have to carry her downstream, find a patch of ground where he could dig a hole with his bare hands, and hadn't he heard, anyway, that her People laid their dead to rest in trees, so as to let the birds pick their bones clean.*
>
> *"They'll get her easy enough down here, he told himself, nodding with the same resolve he'd done when he'd first set out, a lifetime ago.*
>
> *"Best get a move on, then.*
>
> *"It would be a long walk home."*

23

"I'll see you downstairs?"

Crystal was leaning over the rail in front of the pew, beseeching him with a warm smile as the organ piped the congregants out the door behind her: solemn pilgrims making their way to the reception in the basement's auditorium.

Deacon didn't yet have the strength for words and shook his head.

A hand touched Crystal on the shoulder. She turned to her father, her mother beside, finding support with one hand in the crook of his arm. In honour of George perhaps, Edward looked like he hadn't shaved in going on a week. The first curls of white were poking through his beard's chestnut and his eyes were red from crying through his own eulogy, though that hardly softened his expression. He cast a stern glance at Deacon on his way to saying to Crystal, "We'll be downstairs."

"Be there in a moment," Crystal replied, turning back to

Deacon as her parents joined the slow shuffle filing through the door.

Reaching over, she swept a loose strand of hair from his face, tucking it behind his ear and tracing the pad of her thumb along the scar above his left eye.

"I better make an appearance," she said, straightening up. "See you after?"

Deacon gave her a noncommittal smile and then Dylan was pushing her along.

"Come on, then," he said. "You're blocking traffic and I've got a hankering for some of them canned ham and egg-salad sandwiches."

His voice was cavalier and nothing in its tenor suggested it was anything but a harmless comment from someone who hadn't yet eaten lunch, and here it was after two. But the sideways wink he gave Deacon made his meaning plenty clear, as did what he said next.

"We know what George'd have to say about those, eh, Deke, but I kinda like 'em."

For hadn't George, in the opening chapter of *Marble Mountain*, made his own feelings clear about the trays of canned ham and egg-salad sandwiches the women's auxiliary would undoubtedly spend all morning preparing in the kitchen on occasions such as this?

There, the ghost of the deceased, an old man, wandered through a crowd of mourners gathered in the basement auditorium of a small-town church, eavesdropping on their conversations and trying to find anyone among them deserving to reap the harvest he'd sown over a lifetime of toil. Finding only bitterness and acrimony amongst his family and so-called friends, he took no small measure of delight in having had the foresight to empty his bank account the week before he'd died, stuffing the piles of hundreds into his old army rucksack and burying it six feet beneath the plot where he grew his prized tomatoes.

He laughed then, like he'd never laughed before, like he'd never thought he was even capable of laughing. He had always, in fact, been wary of people who laughed like this, believing laughter to be a sign of moral turpitude or, worse, simple-mindedness. He now saw that he'd been wrong about that. The thought that he'd wasted much of his life in flight from the unbridled joy that had suddenly overcome him, when it was about as useful to him now as the withered corpse laying in the chapel above, only made him laugh harder still.

And perhaps he would be laughing yet and this would be an entirely different tale had he not then felt something nudging at his arm.

He looked down at a young girl. She couldn't have been older than four. She had a pink bow in her hair and was wearing a matching dress that was all too frilly for his taste. The front of it was drizzled with the blood-red punch from the plastic jug beside the coffee urn on the food table. In her right hand she held two triangles of white bread, their crusts cut off, the egg salad between them overflowing onto her dainty little fingers. And in her left, another sandwich leaking a mush of canned ham, mayonnaise, and diced pickles.

The expression on her face was so solemn and stern that the moment he set his eyes upon it the laughter that had threatened to consume him had suddenly withered.

Why are you laughing? the little girl asked when he'd gone quiet.

He hadn't been dead long enough to realize how

remarkable a moment this was. It would be years before another of what he would come to call "fleshbags" would have the kind of sense needed to see him. Had he known that then, he might have been a little less impatient to get back to his eavesdropping but as it was, he'd only been dead for two days and so can be forgiven if a little girl nudging his arm produced in him the same scorn he'd have felt when he was still amongst the living.

None of your damn business, he growled at her.

The girl scrunched her face, as if she couldn't imagine that anyone could be so mean.

My mom says you should never laugh at a funeral, she said after she'd recovered. *She says it's disrespectin' to the person who died.*

I'll try to remember that. Now, go on, get.

The girl's face scrunched again and the old man looked away but the little girl would not be deterred.

Do you want a sandwich? she asked. *I have egg salad and ham.*

The old man looked back down at her. She was holding them both up and the look of innocent benevolence in her expression had the old man searching about for something to say to teach her the error of her ways. It took only a moment before something occurred to him and he bent to the girl so he could whisper into her ear.

Do you want to know a secret? he asked.

What?

The best thing about being dead so far is that I'll never feel inclined to eat another one of those.

It was Dylan's way of telling him that he'd been lying about not reading George's Fictions, as if the matter was still up for debate, the subtlety of its inference suggesting he knew them as well as Deacon himself, and perhaps even more so. It was a challenge then, of some sort, Dylan providing him another piece of the puzzle as if he were playing at being the villain in a Hollywood action movie, feeding the hero clues along the way. It had always seemed to Deacon a cheap device to drive the narrative, but now, in the despair he felt watching the congregants filing through the door, Deacon understood it served a more diabolical end: to isolate the hero, drive him crazy, knowing the villain had something nefarious planned and he couldn't do a damn thing to stop it.

But how could Dylan have conceived of such a thing and why would he have chosen me?

In movies it was always personal. Usually it was just a simple matter of revenge, a motif that George himself had often used in his own books.

But what could I have possibly done to Dylan?

A thought punctuated by the emphatic thud of the door in front of him banging shut, making him look up and finding a familiar face staring down at him.

It was Guy Descartes.

He was the old man George had bought his prized Ford Ranger from. Ever since he'd stopped by his garage three or four times a year for an oil change when it was needed and to go fishing with Guy when it was not. George had often brought Deacon along with him too, and so he'd learned that it had been a picture on the wall of Guy's garage that'd given him the idea for *The Unnamed* and that years later Guy had met his own grandson the same way the Old Man had in the book. Both of them were named René and George had always made a big deal out of that.

Guy was wearing a brown leather jacket that Deacon knew he'd made himself from moose hide and hung on a hook in his garage. Guy had even let him try it on one time just to show him how heavy it was. He was holding a black cowboy hat to his chest and seemed, at that moment, to have materialized right off the page to offer Deacon a few words of comfort when surely he needed them most, the same as his character had so often in the book, reading all that he'd gone through and taking strength from his resilience as he set *The Unnamed* back on the shelf, reaching then for *The Stray*.

But when the old man spoke, it wasn't to provide him comfort after all.

"He didn't do it," he said, getting right to the point.

The scrunch to Deacon's brow must have revealed his confusion because then Guy added, "René. He didn't kill those people. I know it."

His alarm at hearing that finally gave Deacon the will to speak, though he hardly had the composure to form a proper sentence.

"René? Killed? Who? What?"

"You haven't heard?"

Deacon shaking his head and Guy biting his lip, squinting like he'd gravely misjudged the man sitting before him.

"Thought you were supposed to be a reporter. Where the hell have you been the past two days?"

His glare carried now a bitter reproach, making Deacon stammer, "I—"

Then shaking his head, trying to find a way out of his befuddle, blurting out at last: "Who are they saying René killed?"

"That family burnt up in the fire."

"The fire!"

Sitting bolt upright now.

"They're saying he set that too," the old man said. "They even got surveillance video they say proves it."

"And you've seen it?"

The old man nodded.

"Didn't prove nothing, you ask me. All you could see was a dark blotch with long hair about the same as René's. Could have been anyone."

Deacon then nodding to himself.

"You know something about that?" Guy asked.

"I— No. Just, I mean—what family?"

"The Wanes they're called. The dad's some bigwig real estate developer, the mom a movie star. It's been all over the news. You really haven't heard?"

"No. I—"

Deacon shaking his head, glancing to the old man looking back at him like he wouldn't believe a word he might say.

"I mean, I know about the fire, of course. But I didn't know anyone had died . . ."

His voice trailing off, for it seemed to him a lie.

"Well, I know you heard about Ronald Crane."

"Ronald Crane?"

"The guy you wrote a story about in last week's paper. Killed in his van. He was burnt up too."

"I know who Ronald Crane is. But what—"

Again stopping himself short, gathering his thoughts.

"They think René killed Ronald Crane?" he finally said.

"That's what they're saying. But he couldn't have. He was helping me that night, in the garage. We weren't done until well after midnight. The van had already been set on fire by then, you said so in the article. I tried to tell them—"

"But why—? Why would they think he killed Ronald Crane?"

"I guess because they found Crane's wallet under his bed."

"What?"

"When they searched his trailer. After he beat up that Wane boy. They were looking for him. Asked me if I'd seen him. I told

349

them not since he left for work that morning. They asked if they could look in his trailer. What was I going to say? I let them. That's when they found the wallet."

"Ronald Crane's?"

"So they said."

"And you haven't seen him since? René, I mean."

"Next I heard, he'd been shot."

The old man then looking to him, such hate in his eyes that it felt to Deacon like a slap in the face.

"He's—"

"Dead, yeah. Made it to the hospital and that was about it."

The old man clenching his teeth, fighting back the tears. One breaking his eyelid's seal anyway and streaking down his cheek. It was a moment stolen right out of *The Unnamed*, after the Old Man's nephew had paid him a visit to tell him that his grandson had been killed. It hadn't come as much of a surprise to the reader, the last fifty-odd pages having recounted the events leading up to how René had become the only suspect in the murder of a man with whom he'd recently been seen arguing in the parking lot of a local bar.

The police had tracked him to his ex-girlfriend's house. She was also the mother of his child, a boy of three, and René had just got back from teaching him how to fish. He was in her backyard showing the boy how to clean the trout they'd caught, so his son watched his own father get shot down. The police claimed self-defence, since when they'd told him "freeze" he'd spun around holding a knife, which he shouldn't have had anyway since he'd recently served time for aggravated assault and one of the conditions of his parole was that he wasn't allowed to carry.

Word on the reserve was that he'd been framed, that it was well-known that one of the cops who'd shot him had recently found out that his wife was cheating with none other than the man René had been seen arguing with several days earlier. It was simply a matter of bad luck, or maybe just convenience, that René'd got into a fight with the victim a short while later, providing the cop with the perfect foil for his own murderous intent.

Deacon trying to process all that he'd heard and measure it against what George had written there and also in *No Quarter*, a clear pattern forming between the two.

"Was it Dylan who shot him?" he asked, though it came out sounding more like an exclamation.

"Dylan?"

"Cleary."

"George's grandson? No. It was another officer. He had a French name, I can't—"

"Marchand?"

"Could have been. Why would you think George's grandson'd be mixed up in it?"

The old man was again squinting at Deacon, like he knew he was withholding something.

"I didn't— I mean." Then: "Marchand, you say?"

"That mean something to you?"

"No. I mean—Marchand doesn't seem like the type who'd just up and shoot a man."

"He said it was self-defence. That René was carrying a rifle."

"Was he?"

"It was a fishing rod. It was wrapped up in brown paper, so I guess it might've looked like one. It was for his son. A birthday present. Way I figure, René was on his way to turn himself in, or maybe he was heading for the hills, I don't know. Either way, he must have come by the house and picked it up so he could give it to Tawyne before he did. That's why he'd gone to the reserve."

"Where he was shot?"

The old man nodding.

"In Jean's backyard. That's his sister. She's been looking after Tawyne ever since he got taken away from the boy's mother."

"Was his son there?"

"Huh?"

"At his sister's."

"No, thank god. The reserve had already been cleared by then, on account of the fire."

Deacon took some solace in that, the old man less so.

"They're calling him a mass murderer," he was saying. "René might be a lot of things, but he ain't no killer. You got to tell them that."

"Me?"

"They wouldn't believe me. But if you print the truth in the paper . . ."

Deacon lowered his eyes, unable to meet the old man's gaze.

"I'm not sure I can do that," he said.

When he looked back up, the old man was nodding like he knew it would come to this and that only firming his resolve.

"I understand," he said, "your mother was Chippewa. They's an honourable People, ones I've known anyway. Terrible thing happened to her, and your father and your brother. I can't even pretend to imagine what that'd do to a boy, you being there and seeing that."

Then shaking his head, clicking his tongue against his teeth.

"What was the name of the fella, you know, the one who found you afterwards?"

Deacon cast him a sideways glance.

"Jon Robinson," he said. It came out barely a squeak.

"It true he chased away a pack of coyotes before he could get to you? There was five or six I understand. That sound about right?"

Deacon shook his head, clenching his lips. The old man

studied him with keen eyes. Clicking his tongue against his teeth again, he nodded as if he'd made his final judgement on the man standing before him and found him lacking.

"Sorry for your loss," he said, setting his hat on his head. "You have a good day now."

Guy was already turning towards the door. He'd just put his hand on the latch when he turned back. There was none of the ire in his expression any more, just a tired sort of look, old and worn out.

"George, you know," he said, "he called you the bravest soul he ever met."

Reaching again for the door, pausing ever so slightly before throwing his weight against it. As it opened, Deacon could hear the muffled babble from the reception downstairs and another voice raised against it.

"You get me a butter tart?" an old man was saying. He must have been sitting in a chair on the landing, unable, or unwilling, to navigate the stairs into the basement. After a breath an old woman's high-pitched fret answered, "No, they only had the jam."

"I hate the jam."

"That's why I got you a piece of lemon cake."

"I'd rather have a butter tart."

The old woman apparently having nothing to say to that as Guy stepped through the door, slow and steady, his left foot treading gingerly like he had a pebble in his boot.

Deacon watched him leave, the full weight of what the old man had come to ask him adding to the pressure in his chest he'd felt ever since Dylan had whispered in his ear. Maybe George had also told Dylan what he'd told Guy about him being the bravest soul he'd ever met and that had seemed to Dylan cause enough to embroil him in some half-baked plot he'd torn from the pages of one of his grandfather's Fictions.

And here was Guy Descartes thinking he would help him for the same reason, neither knowing what Deacon did—what George had said was a damn lie, he knew that as surely as it felt again like the weight of the world was pressing down upon him.

Searching out Adele's picture on the altar, he found a measure of comfort in her smile's warm shining bright, as he so often had after he'd come to live with the Clearys. Fumbling a cigarette from his case, he put it in his mouth and lit it as he turned back to the old man.

"I only ever saw the one," he said through his first exhale.

Guy had stuttered to a halt, holding the door open, his hand shaking on the knob, the same as Adele's had after she'd got Parkinson's.

"It was standing on the hood, a big old grey, as big as a wolf." As he spoke his voice was calm and measured, less emotive even than it would have been reading aloud from a recipe book. "That's what I thought it was. It was only later that I learned there aren't any wolves around here anymore, so it must have been a coyote, like you say. I'd woken up on the floor in the back of the Jeep. I heard something, sounded like an elastic band snapping. I sat up enough so I could look through the seats. My pa had gone through the windshield, you know. He was stuck halfway in and halfway out. That's when I saw the coyote. It was chewing on his face."

The old man's head flinched as if he meant to turn, yet he did not.

"Bravest soul he ever met. George really say that?"

A subtle hitch then to his head, the old man nodding.

"Well, he weren't fucking there!"

24

❝Talk to me!"

Rain was yelling after him as he stormed through the church's front doors. She'd been skulking at the back of the chapel when he'd turned and fled, the look of horror on her face telling Deacon she'd heard everything, and that making him angrier still.

His cigarette was down to the filter when he'd reached the sidewalk. He flicked it into the street and turned towards the alley, starting off at a run.

"Stop!" Rain yelled and that only urging his legs faster.

Fuck her, and fuck Dylan, fuck Guy, and fuck George too!

A *bang!* then, as loud as a firecracker.

Its sharp impertinence stopped him in his tracks, spinning him around. Rain was holding a revolver, no bigger than a starter's pistol, upraised in her hand, pointing it at the sky, a curl of smoke coiling from its barrel-end. She was cringing against the sound, and as soon as she saw Deacon hurrying back towards her she tucked it into her handbag.

"Are you fucking crazy?" he spat at her, scanning the street for any witnesses and spying a young boy, couldn't have been older than three.

He was holding the hand of a woman dressed for a day at the beach, standing in the middle of the street where Dominion intersected with Main and staring straight at Rain. His mother was occupied on her cell phone, oblivious to her son's agape, the shock of hearing the *bang!* given way to the shock of having just let go of the balloon in his hand. His head then tilting back, finding a red dot winnowing skywards, and his eyes squeezing shut even as his mouth opened into a scream. He unleashed a despairing wail and that was at last enough to get his mother's attention, though hardly her sympathy.

"Well, I told you to hold onto it," she scolded, jerking her son roughly across the street.

They'd just reached the far sidewalk when Deacon heard the side door of the church slamming open. Dylan was striding out, his hand on his sidearm so that Deacon knew he'd heard the shot too. Once he'd made the landing though he held up, his hand relaxing and that familiar grin spreading over his lips with the slow resolve of the dawning sun.

In the days to come, Deacon would have plenty of reason to recall how his face had looked. It was a facsimile of the satisfaction Adele's would wear after she'd completed one of the crosswords she'd made for the *Chronicle,* as if hearing the shot and seeing it was Rain who'd fired the gun had completed some sort of puzzle he'd been wrestling with. But as Deacon grabbed at Rain's arm, dragging her on stumbling steps towards the alley's entrance, it only lent him further evidence of Dylan's malevolence, the maniacal grin combined with the scar on his face recalling to him any number of comic book villains.

He'd get his first inkling of what the gun might have meant

to Dylan thirty seconds after he'd slammed the door to his apartment. He locked it with the deadbolt and also the chain, and leaned with heaving breath against its grey steel, his own agitation at perfect odds with Rain's composure.

It was the first time she'd been in Deacon's apartment and was taking the opportunity to give it a good looking over. She was wrinkling her brow at the web of dirty laundry remaking the floor into a labyrinth and more so at the pungent odour, equal parts dirty socks, rotting food, and B.O.

"Jesus, Deacon," she said, turning back to him. "It's a wonder the rats haven't moved in."

Point of fact, they had, at least one he'd seen anyway, scurrying under the stove the last time he'd returned from one of his nightly jaunts. But it was the least of his worries right then, the foremost being the gun stowed in Rain's handbag, its patchwork of brightly hued embroidered chrysanthemums a perfect complement to the psychedelia of her hippie dress, the both starkly out of place though on someone who'd just come from a funeral.

Of course, this was Rain Meadows he was talking about.

Just two minutes ago, he'd have sworn there was nothing she could have done to surprise him and then there she was firing off a gun in the middle of the afternoon not a half a block from downtown, just to get his attention.

"What the hell, Rain?" he stammered.

"Well, you didn't leave me much choice now, did you?"

She'd retrieved a cigarette from her bag and was just then lighting it, blowing the first exhale at the ceiling and waving at the smoke, spreading its drift about the air as if to buffer herself against the room's stench.

"Why—" Deacon sputtered. "Why in the hell do you have a gun?"

"Well, don't blame me. I've been trying to give it to you all week. It's not my fault you weren't answering your phone."

"Give it to— What? What are you talking about?"

She was already reaching into her bag and taking out the revolver, holding it out to Deacon butt-end first. Deacon stared at it as if she'd produced an adder, coiled and ready to strike.

"Go on," she said. "Take it. It's yours."

"Mine?"

"George gave it to me before he died."

"It was George's?"

"He told me to give it to you. Said you might need it before this was over."

Her voice was upraised at the end as if it was begging for an answer.

"He said that?"

"He also said you'd understand. Well, go on, then, take it, my arm's getting tired."

Deacon finally reached for it, taking it by the grip, Rain letting go and Deacon's hand sagging from its weight. He turned it over in his open palm, taking his first good look at the pistol. It was old, he could see that. Most of its nickel plate had worn off, exposing grey steel beneath. It had a piece of copper wire bent and soldered around the trigger guard and along the top on either side of the sight groove was inscribed: *U.S. Revolver Co.* and *Made in the USA*. Likewise on the black plastic grip: *U.S.*

> *It felt heavy in his hand, too heavy for such a small*
> *revolver, but when he took it by the grip and laid his*
> *finger against the trigger, the feeling of weight lifted as*
> *if the gun itself knew how it should be held.*

It was a line from *My Brother's Keeper* and it rang true when

Deacon did the same, pointing the gun at the floor and counting off the bores in its cylinder. There were seven in all.

Again from *My Brother's Keeper*:

It looked like it should shoot six but it shot seven.

To make sense of why that might have been, William had only to recall one of the westerns he'd watched at the Odeon Theatre with his younger brother James. It had ended with a gunfight, as they most often did. The bad guy had got the drop on the hero, cornering him in an alley between the livery and the saloon and pointing his gun between his enemy's eyes. The hero had held up his arms as if he meant to surrender and the bad guy had looked from one hand to the other, seeing four fingers and a thumb outstretched on the right but only his pinkie on the left. It was wiggling at him and he knew what the gesture meant but he pulled the trigger anyway.

The two men heard the click as the hammer struck an empty chamber at the same moment but this time the hero got the drop on the bad guy. He delivered a hard right to his chin and followed that up by reaching for the knife in his boot, flinging it and burying the blade in the other's chest.

William took comfort in the recollection as he closed the top drawer of his father's dresser, thinking he'd never much considered himself the hero-type and if it came to all that, the good guy'd be in for one helluva surprise.

Walking then to his father, passed-out dead-drunk in his bed, snoring in voluminous waves. His head was resting on his arm and the knuckles of his hand were sheared of skin from where they'd caught William's

front teeth the night before. Blood from the next blow,
which had broken his nose, was spattered on his wrist.
Placing the muzzle of the gun into the middle of that
son-of-a-bitch's forehead, he pushed at it hard enough
to open his eyes.

His father awoke blinking against his drowse.
Seeing what his eldest boy was holding in his hand, his
eyes opened wider still.

Good mornin', Pa, William said and pulled the
trigger.

"You didn't know?" Rain asked, snapping Deacon from the
daze of staring down at the gun that William had killed his father
with and then had also used to shoot the man who'd murdered
his brother, emptying every last one of the remaining five rounds
into the posse who'd come seeking vengeance.

Deacon shook his head, though he'd always suspected as
much. George's middle name was, after all, William and he'd
found further evidence in what Dylan had told him about Louise
and Edward burning the copies their father had given them.

Rain was then reaching out and straightening the collar of his
jacket, the one he'd taken from George's closet so he knew she
must have been thinking of him.

"George was a hard man, there's no doubt about that."

Her voice had taken on the wistful tone of a middle-aged
woman recalling her first love. She trailed her fingers down his
chest and Deacon looked up from the gun in his hand. A glisten
wetted her eyes.

"But with me," she said, "he was always quite . . . gentle."

25

They ended up back at Rain's house because she had weed and that calmed Deacon some.

After they'd smoked, they lit cigarettes and she asked, "So what's going on, Deke?"

He told her.

It started out as a trickle of words and ended up a flood, Rain listening without saying anything, until he came to the part where Dylan had said, "Buck up, son, we ain't hardly yet just begun."

"It's just like in George's Fictions," she said then.

"One story always pointing to the next . . ." Deacon offered.

". . . and that always worse than what came before."

Her lips scrunched into a question mark, her brow furrowed as if trying to divine some deeper meaning to it, and he was looking at her with surprise, for she'd never given him a hint that she'd read any of George's Fictions, much less enough of them to have known that. He wasn't sure yet what to make of the idea that she had, and also that she'd been keeping it from him all these years, just like Dylan.

He hid his unease by taking a long slow draw from his cigarette, and then Rain was talking again.

"You didn't know Dylan before he joined the army," she asked, "is that right?"

"Only met him a couple of times. He was six years older than me when I came to live with George and Adele. He was already on his way—"

"He was a real sullen child," Rain interrupted, lost in her own train of thought. "One might even say morose."

That gave Deacon pause for it didn't sound at all like the Dylan he'd come to know.

"So he changed?" he finally said.

"Most people'd say for the better. But not—"

"George."

"Dylan told him one time, he'd seen the truth of what George had written when he was overseas."

"A world on fire."

"Said he couldn't get it out of his mind. Said it was following after him."

"And what did George think of that?"

"Well, you know George. Always hoping for the best—"

"and expecting the worst."

"I know it made him nervous the way Dylan talked. The way he'd become obsessed with his Fictions. And—"

She was shaking her head and biting her lip.

"What?"

"How jealous he'd become of . . ."

"Of who?"

She cast him a sideways glance.

"Of you."

"Me?"

"The way George treated you. Like the son he'd always wanted."

George had never said as much but Deacon had always wished it were true. Hearing her say it now, he felt a sudden shame for cursing his name such a short while ago. The feeling was short-lived for there then arose in his mind the memory of Dylan calling his grandfather "a fucking monster." At the time, it had been just another clue to solving the mystery surrounding the dual and often conflicting natures of George, The Man, and George, The Writer.

But now he saw it as a clue to something else entirely.

If what Rain said was true, he mused, *and I became the son he'd always wanted, then maybe Dylan became the son he'd always deserved.*

A multitude of scenes from George's Fictions cascaded him then: a rapid cycling through several centuries worth of depravity and despair.

Such horrors and yet . . .

Had George really written anything outside of our own history?

Nothing, except . . .

The future.

And thinking that, the two things all of a sudden became one.

Maybe then, he thought, *we shouldn't expect our future to be any different from the one he'd imagined.*

A fleeting enough thought, no doubt abetted by the current state of his high.

And then he felt Rain's hand on his own.

It seemed for a moment that she must have read his mind and meant to offer him some sort of reassurance that it was just his imagination running wild. But it was his cigarette she was bound for. Half of it had been reduced to a thin column of ash leaning precariously over the rug. She scissored it between two fingers and, with a cupped hand beneath, brought it to the ashtray on the green steamer trunk.

"You okay?" she asked as she passed it back. "You had a strange look on your face there for a moment. Like you'd seen a ghost."

He gave her a curt smile.

"Just stoned, is all."

He took a drag from his smoke, trying to recall what they'd been talking about.

"Did he say anything else?" he asked, exhaling.

"Lots," Rain answered. "You couldn't shut George up, he gets a couple of ryes in him."

"I mean, about Dylan."

Rain's expression scrunched and her tongue prodded at her top lip, which is how she always looked when she was wrestling with something.

"There was one thing George was always going on about . . . Something about the darkness . . ." Shaking her head, trying to remember what it was. "He who caused the darkness . . ."

Reaching over then to tap her own ash as if that might have helped recall it to mind.

"If the soul is left in darkness, sins will be committed," Deacon said. "The guilty one is not he who commits the sin, but he who caused the darkness."

"That's it."

"It's the quote George put at the beginning of *No Quarter*."

She thought on that for a moment.

"So it was to be a morality tale," she said at last.

"No surprise there."

She took another drag off her cigarette and Deacon did the same.

"The guilty one . . ." Rain said as she exhaled. "You think George meant Ronald Crane?"

364

"He was guilty, no doubt about that. But Ronald Crane—"

"He died too early."

"Yeah. George would have—"

"Saved the truly guilty one—"

"For last."

"So he must have meant—"

"Someone else."

"Likely someone—"

"He hadn't introduced yet."

Tilting her head back, Rain blew a long train of smoke towards the ceiling. And when she spoke it was to give Deacon pause again, thinking maybe she had been reading his mind after all.

"Well, whoever it was," she said, "knowing George, we'll all end up paying for it, in one way or another."

26

They spent the rest of the daylight filling in some of the other blanks, huddled in front of Rain's laptop like two cave dwellers seeking refuge before a fire.

They started with the article Deacon himself had written when René had been charged with aggravated assault for beating up his girlfriend four years before. When that didn't tell them much, Deacon told Rain what René had told his grandfather and then Guy had told George. That Dahlia Fields, René's ex-girlfriend, had run off with his son, he didn't know where, and then had shown up six months later at his apartment. She was drunk and angry and demanded that René pay her two thousand dollars in back child support before she'd let him see the boy again. René had told her to go fuck herself and had slammed the door in her face. And that was the last, he'd said, he'd seen of her until he was facing her in the courtroom, where she was telling the judge that he'd punched her in the face and thrown her down the flight of stairs leading from the second floor of the house that they'd once rented together. Photos taken at the hospital that night suggested that she'd hit every one of the twelve steps with her face, losing two front teeth in the process and breaking her nose and one of her cheekbones. She'd also suffered a severe concussion which, she said, made it almost impossible for her to provide adequate care for her son, then three years old. She had an eyewitness to corroborate, and Dylan himself had testified that when he'd arrested René, the skin on two of the knuckles on his right hand was peeled back and he had the photos to prove it. René would account for the injury by explaining that he'd punched the door after he'd slammed it shut but no one, save his grandfather, had really believed that.

They'd then trolled for the name Wane amongst the news coverage of the fire, using what they'd found to google Bryson, Celia, Taylor, and Sandra. They formed a pretty clear picture of the former two from their Wikipedia pages and a good idea of who Sandra was from Facebook and an even better idea about Taylor from affluenza.com.

They watched the footage shot at the Diplomat Hotel twice and then watched the latest post. It already had 1,234,067 hits and purported to be from a live stream by three twenty-somethings—two young men and a woman—who seemed to have taken their inspiration from Young Master Wane.

They'd driven a grey Mercedes convertible to some ramshackle bar in the Florida Everglades, filming themselves consuming thirty-two shots between them and taking turns dancing with the bar's equally drunk clientele. There was a fight and they fled the scene as the chairs started to fly, whooping and hollering their delight as the Mercedes tore along a lonely stretch of road cutting through the swamp. And that's what they were doing when the car suddenly, and for no apparent reason, swerved off the road, its occupants screaming like they were on a rollercoaster as the picture caterwauled, turning a full three hundred and sixty degrees.

Then:

A splash of water. The picture onscreen is reduced to a blur out of which there arises a muffled exclamation: "Jesus!"

The camera fumbling and finally locating the driver, slumped over the wheel. They've landed in the swamp and water is pouring in through his door's open window.

"Are you okay?" the woman asks.

The driver groans and sits up straight. There's a gash over his left brow bleeding into his eye, but he says, "I think so."

The camera then shifts to a shot of the empty back seat.

"Where's Devon?"

A frantic scream. The camera tracks back to the driver but finds only his flailing legs as he's jerked backwards out of the car.

A distant splash and then utter quiet.

"Aston?" the woman implores, scouring the swamp with the camera's light and settling on a pair of eyes bobbing menacingly above the surface. Not even a second to ponder them before there's a carnivorous bellow from the back seat. The camera jerks rearwards. The snap of an alligator's jaws fills the frame for an instant and then only black.

"God," Rain said, "it's like they ain't got any sense south of the forty-five, eh, Deke?"

Deacon laughed, the first time since George had died, and Rain rolled another joint to celebrate that. They smoked it upstairs, sitting on her bed. Afterwards, Deacon took her from behind, in honour of George.

They were at it all night.

H e awoke sometime around noon.

Rain had opened the drapes and the window too. There was a band of sunlight warming his bare chest and he could hear a myriad of noises rising from the street below: the steady thump of tires slapping against a pothole and the insistent throb of a bassline from some rap song growing louder as the car approached, the grate of a motorcycle's engine trailing after it, a teenage girl shrieking with the tenacity of someone who'd just had ice water poured down her back—little sprouts of life as if to remind Deacon the town was still carrying on around him though, right then, it seemed miles away, too far removed yet to draw him back into its fold.

There was an odour of burnt bacon fat flavouring the air. He wasn't yet ready to get up to see where *that* future might lead and as he lay on his back plucking idly at the chest hair sprouting into the morning sun, his mind wandered back to something Rain had said while they'd shared a cigarette the night before.

"You ought to write it."

She'd just asked him what he was going say in the *Chronicle* about what Guy had told him.

"Grover'd never let me print any of that in the paper," Deacon had answered, though it sounded like a poor excuse.

"It's not up to Grover," Rain had said.

"What do you mean?"

"George left the paper to you." Smiling coyly and covering her mouth with her hand, speaking through her fingers, "I wasn't supposed to say anything."

Deacon reaching over then to tap his cigarette in the ashtray on the bed stand, seeing the pistol and asking himself:

What would George do in your place?

Rain had all twelve of his books lined up between two crystal balls on her dresser. It was the first time he'd been in her bedroom so he'd never seen them there before. He found himself scanning over them now.

"You ought to write it," Rain said. "That's what you should do."

"Write what?"

"*No Quarter*, silly."

"George already did."

"Your own version, I mean."

"I couldn't—"

"Why not? You already know how it ends. And didn't George always say that as long as you know how it ends, the rest'll practically write itself?"

As far as Deacon knew, he'd said the exact opposite but he wasn't in the mood to argue. He'd picked up the gun, spinning the chamber, and sighting it on one of the crystal balls.

It had ended with a world on fire, the same as in all of George's Fictions, except, of course, *My Brother's Keeper*, which wasn't really a "Fiction" after all.

The revolver in his hand now gave Deacon a pretty clear idea of why that one might have ended so well and, like in so many of his books, the solution to that mystery only served to point to a deeper one, hitherto unrevealed.

And thinking of that now with the band of sunlight so pleasantly upon his chest and the smell of bacon speaking to him of a future he'd always dreaded and maybe wasn't looking so bad after all, he thought again of Rain misquoting George.

"Once you know how its *begins*, then the rest'll practically take care of itself," is what he'd always told him.

Tracking then backwards in time, trying to recall how it had all begun.

A siren, he thought.

He heard the first siren just after midnight.

In Memory Of

George Jackson & Wayland Drew